Brushfire Plague

by

R.P. Ruggiero

Dystopian Fiction & Survival Nonfiction

www.PrepperPress.com

Book One in the Brushfire Plague Trilogy

Brushfire Plague

ISBN 978-0615645643

Printed in the United States of America.

Prepper Press Trade Paperback Edition: July 2012

Prepper Press is a division of Northern House Media, LLC

- To my mom, who taught me to love life <u>and</u> to be prepared for whatever might come my way.

Acknowledgements:

I wish to thank Robert Shepard and Josh Hendryx who provided feedback on the early versions of this novel. Their support and comments improved this work and helped bring it to fruition.

I also want to express my appreciation to Sarah Cairns who provided professional editing that strengthened the story in numerous ways. Her patience was much appreciated. Mike Dostie also deserves recognition for providing copyediting in the later stage.

Finally, and most importantly, is the support and inspiration I received from my family. I thank my wife Cindy, who provided immeasurable support while this was being written. Of course, that's no surprise. She's been doing that since I was 17 years old. She also provided suggestions and edits during the early drafts. My two boys, Justus and Zade, are my inspiration in all things. I thank them for bearing with the numerous times I needed solitude while writing.

About the Author:

R.P. Ruggiero lives in the Pacific Northwest with his wife and two sons. He spends as much time as possible in the outdoors and strives to live by Robert Heinlein's credo that, "Specialization is for insects." When he is not outdoors, writing, or learning a new skill, he helps people achieve common goals. He brings two decades of experience in group dynamics — particularly for people under stress — to good use in writing the *Brushfire Plague*, a novel grounded in neighbors defending themselves during a devastating plague. He is currently writing the sequel to the *Brushfire Plague.*

Visit www.brushfireplague.com for more information.

Chapter 1

Cooper Adams bumped along the road in his old GMC pickup. Patches of white paint fought on bravely, clinging to life amidst the rust that covered most of its body. Jake, his son, sat next to him, staring blankly ahead. When his friend, Paul Dranko, had come to relieve him, Cooper had decided to take Jake with him. He wanted to get him out of the house. His son had been watching his sick mother, likely dying, for far too long.

Before leaving, Cooper had grabbed his Smith and Wesson semi-automatic pistol and it lay holstered on his belt. He stood just over six feet, clear brown eyes and black hair. The cold steel pressed into the small of his back. It was barely concealed and he lacked a permit to carry it, but he decided he had more pressing priorities. He guessed that the police did as well. An extra magazine lay stashed in his jacket pocket. He made a sharp right turn, cranking the wheel hard, onto the main boulevard that led to the local supermarket. What he saw made him pull his gun out and place it on his lap, at the ready.

A Subaru lay ablaze, about two hundred yards ahead, flames spitting from the interior through the shattered windows. Black smoke curled furiously skyward as oil, plastic and metal burned. He slowed down and moved into the opposite lane, to give it the widest possible berth. Already, he could smell the acrid stench. Thankfully, he didn't smell the foulness of flesh burning. He had had his fill of that in Iraq. It was something you never forgot. He saw a few broken cartons and a torn brown paper bag scattered next to the car and he guessed the rest. At least the passengers appeared to have escaped harm. *Probably just a robbery with some Molotov-wielding firebug thrown in for good measure.* As people passed by, they would gawk for a moment and press a shirt or a scarf around their nose and mouth, but they kept moving. What struck Cooper was how few appeared shocked at what they were seeing. *What else have they seen burning? Or worse?*

The station wagon had been burning for a while. The windshield and windows had melted out and the rest of the car almost burned down to bare metal. Yet, there was no sign of a fire engine or even the distant wail of a siren. Absentmindedly, he dialed 911 on his cell phone, "All circuits are busy. Please, try your call again later."

He replaced the cell phone back into his pocket as they rolled past the burning wreck. With it firmly in his rearview mirror, Cooper turned to Jake, "OK, son. From now on, we might see some things that aren't normal. There might be some ugly things. There might be some dangerous things. But, I promise you this, I'm here to protect you. But, I need one thing from you, OK?"

Jake nodded in rapt attention. "I need you to do *whatever* I say. When I say it. I need you to do it, no matter what you might think. You might think what I'm saying is crazy or what I'm saying doesn't make any sense. But, I need you to *do it* without question, without hesitation. Can I count on you for that?"

"Yes, I'll do it." Jake said in his best impression of a full-grown man. Cooper saw the fear that lay behind his eleven-year-old son's eyes.

Cooper smiled to comfort him, "OK. Good. Just remember that. It is the most important thing you can do to stay safe and sound. I *will* do my best to keep you safe and I know *how* to keep you safe, so things should be alright. But, I *need* your help to do it." Jake nodded seriously in response.

Cooper continued down the boulevard. He could smell the fear all around him. He had known streets like this in Iraq. There, the fear had been suicide bombers, improvised explosive devices, and vicious ambushes. Here, it was simply some virus that was tearing through the city's population like a chainsaw through soft pine. Of course, it was worse than that. A chainsaw you could see coming. Its effect was predictable. This virus was unseen. Its cause and path unknown. Cooper knew such things stoked fear and dread in people. *That* was what he could smell in his nostrils and taste on his tongue. He knew panic didn't lie far beyond.

A few people moved along the sidewalks. A woman dressed all in black and carrying a paper grocery bag, clutched to her chest like a newborn, ambled down the street looking furtively about. She had a dirty surgical mask covering her nose and mouth. When a man moving in the opposite direction—he lacked a mask but had a red handkerchief pushed up against his face—approached her, she swung to her left to create a wide arc between them. He swung to his left as well, out into the street, to increase the distance between them. His sudden movement made his jacket ride up his hip a bit and revealed the briefest glint of a concealed pistol stuffed into his belt.

For just a moment, his mind drifted to that fateful call a few days ago, when the nightmare had started for him.

******

When Cooper Adams' cell phone jolted him awake at 2:16 in the morning, he saw her number and his throat tightened. Her call meant only one thing. His worst fears had come true since he'd talked to her earlier that evening. Only once had she ever called him this early. On that night, her mother had died. Tonight, he wasn't worried about an in-law. This night, he knew death stalked his wife like a coyote does the lamb. His heart thundered in his chest. As he answered the phone, he flung his legs off the bed and began tugging his pants on.

"You need to come home," ragged words beckoned from the other end. Absent the caller ID on his cell phone, he would have had no idea that the prostrated voice belonged to his wife.

He stifled the choking emotions that welled up, "I'm on my way." He managed an "I love you," his throat constricting.

She mustered a feeble "OK, me too. See you." It was as if those scant words sapped her. The phone went dead as she hung up.

A man possessed, he yanked a hodgepodge of clothing on — jeans, a black t-shirt, an unbuttoned dress shirt, a brown and a black sock, his sneakers, all wrapped up by a suit coat and ran out the door. He got halfway to his car and then had to run back to his room for his car keys and his wallet.

Seconds later, Cooper's car was squealing out of the motel parking lot. His sedan spat gravel as he careened onto the town's main road and headed towards the highway. He'd left everything else behind. He planned on calling the motel operator in the morning to make arrangements. It was just one of many plans he had that would never happen.

******

The room lay swathed in the last, dying rays of sunlight as day slowly succumbed to night. Like the faltering sun, his wife was fading away. Gone was the vibrant and warm face he had fallen in love with from the moment he met her. It had been replaced by an ashen mockery. His wife's face lost what little color the sun's warmth had provided and wilted to gray. Her breath reminded him of his first car's engine, complete with rattles, fits, and the fear that it might quit on you at any time. He sat a few feet away in an old, rickety wooden chair that Elena's grandmother was rumored to have brought over from the old country, Romania. Knowing her family, it was just as likely something bought at a flea market on the cheap, with a good story added to give it some style.

The chair groaned with relief when he rose. His bones grinded out their protest at being forced to move after hours of immobility. Cooper hadn't yet reached forty, but the last forty-eight hours had aged him dearly. He recalled a friend's favorite saying, "It ain't the years, it's the mileage that matters," she'd said. Now, he understood the meaning of it. The last two days felt like a round-the-world trip in a busted up Model T.

His feet shifted over a few feet to bring himself to the edge of the bed where his wife lay in a fitful rest. The worn, faded carpet underneath grated his feet like sandpaper. He looked down upon his wife, fearing what he might see. Over the past day, every hour had brought a seismic shift. It was if she was aging decades in hours. Faint lines had turned into deep crags in her face. Her hair had faded from a rich, beautiful black mane to a scraggly, matted tangle. The color had washed out. Her skin, which had been a fine shade of amber, now lay mottled. Her once full and firm breasts were now limp and sagging. Worst of all was her breathing. Gone was any semblance of the deep rise and fall of his wife's chest when she slept.

Her chest rose and fell in fits and starts. She had been coughing so often that he scarcely heard it any longer. When he did, he shuddered. The coughs shouted out in desperation. As they frantically tried to clear her lungs and empty them of their life-stealing phlegm, they must have known that they were failing and cried out in wretched protest. Just a few hours ago, in a moment of consciousness, she had croaked feebly to him, "I need air, more air." His eyes filled with tears at the thought, both of his impending loss and of his bitter helplessness: hospitals overrun, no doctors available, and only his bedraggled nurse neighbor doing what little she could for those fallen ill. It was the same across the city, at every hospital and clinic. Some veterinarian offices were even rumored to be swamped with the sick, clamoring for aid.

There was no doubt now. His wife was dying. It was cold comfort that everyone else seemed to be dying as well. Was it really only three days ago, he had risen from this same bed, kissed his wife goodbye, before going off to another week of work?

******

Fresh from the shower, Cooper ambled downstairs, stepping lightly on the stairs to avoid waking his son. Nevertheless, one of the steps squeaked loudly and he grimaced in apprehension. He paused

8

for a few moments, heard the contented breathing of Jake continue unabated and then descended. It was not the first time he smiled about his love-hate relationship with his old house, built in the early 1940s. He loved its style and character, but some of its quirks drove him crazy, too. He often joked, "This house was born during a war and it's been a fighter every year since. I just wish I wasn't its enemy these days!"

He stepped onto the landing and scanned the living room to his right. Sure enough, the black, cast iron woodstove held a few dying embers that threw a shallow orange glow. He debated rekindling the fire, but decided against it. Two hours from now, the house would be empty with Elena off to work and Jake at school. Woodstoves were good for long-term heat, but not so efficient for the short. Instead, he turned the corner into the dining room. The solid oak table that occupied most of the room intimidated the rest of the house. It lay like a hulking battleship docked impressively in some nameless Third World nation's capital harbor. The thing must have weighed over two hundred pounds. Cooper admired how it imparted solidity to their home.

He paused here, as he usually did, and closed his eyes. He inhaled the coffee brewing in the automatic coffeemaker on the kitchen counter and the faint whiff of wood smoke from last night's fire. He felt the wood flooring under his feet and reached out to touch the strong oak table. *This is the way to wake up. I am a lucky man.* He opened his eyes and smiled as a ray of sunlight caught his brown eyes.

He continued to the kitchen, his bare feet shifting from amber-colored oak wood flooring to the green-speckled, and chilly, linoleum. A few minutes later, toast and coffee in hand he returned to the dining room table and put his cup and plate onto the table. He continued to his front door and opened it to retrieve his newspaper. He breathed the chilled morning air deep into his lungs. Cooper loved the fresh, *yes; I am alive* feeling that it gave him.

He gazed out to his front yard. The trio of white birch trees stood as silent sentries watching over his yard. The blueberry bushes still lay leafless, as the season was stuck between the end of winter and the beginning of spring. Between the birches, a jogger was heading down Lincoln Street, twoard the forested park that was two blocks to the east of his home. Dressed in warm running clothes this season demanded in the Pacific Northwest, the jogger's shoes made a distinct *clip-clop, clip-clop* on the sidewalk. A city bus chugged down the hill, heading west, the soft whine of its engine was a quiet contrast to the noise they made coming the opposite direction; when climbing the hill. He closed the door and made his way back to his waiting breakfast and newspaper.

"Let's see what we have today," Cooper mumbled to himself as he opened the newspaper. He munched on his warm, wheat toast. Sipping the hot, black coffee, he relished the feeling of the warm liquid curling its way down his throat and into his stomach. Already, he could feel the caffeine coursing into his veins.

The headlines covered the familiar topics these days. Unemployment. Tensions in the Middle East. Global Warming. Cooper read voraciously and quickly moved into the middle pages of the newspaper. His friend, Paul Dranko, who was a cynic and distrusted every institution ever made by man—be it government, religion, the military or the local PTA—always told him that's where you could decipher some *real news*. Cooper had laughed him off when he'd told him that, but he couldn't help but look at those pages a little more closely ever since. Over time, he'd seen the wisdom in his friend's remarks.

Today, nothing struck him as notable. There were about a dozen church members from Seattle returning from a retreat that were all hospitalized with flu-like symptoms. A brief article appeared about a huge military contract signed with Taiwan for US weapons—mostly aircraft and missile defense systems. Expectedly, Chinese officials were expressing their "deep disappointment" with the weapons sale. Another story showcased a local manufacturing company that was relocating its operations *from* Asia back to the United States due to the need for higher quality controls and stronger connection to its engineering and design team. "Wow, that should have been on the front page," Cooper exclaimed to himself. Finishing his breakfast, he ended by reading the uplifting story of James Michaels, a former high school football star who'd been paralyzed while playing and now was competing in the upcoming Para-Olympics. *Some guys you just can't keep down.* He circled that story with a red marker and left it open on the table for Jake to read later. He was sure his son hated him for it, but Cooper never passed up an opportunity to impart an important life lesson to him.

Twenty minutes later, he was dressed and heading out the door. Before doing so, he stopped in the doorway to his son's room and gazed in. Swaddled up in several blankets, a fresh face with eyes closed, he breathed in effortless slumber. A lock of black hair hung down between his eyes. He caught a glimpse of red pajamas from under the bundle of blankets that held his boy. For years, Cooper had kissed him lightly on the cheek before leaving on his trips, but about six months ago, Jake had started waking up when he did so. So, Cooper now only peered in, welcoming the sight of his boy so calm and peaceful. Cooper smiled and pivoted to head out the door.

He quickly deposited a Samsonite suitcase in the trunk of the diesel-powered VW sedan. Opening the door and getting in, he pitched the black leather soft briefcase onto the passenger seat. As he usually did, he looked back at his home before driving off. He loved his home and the people in it. He hated to leave it behind. He'd done much work on it over the last several years. He had certainly left sweat, tears, and even a little blood in her joints and boards. The green English Cottage style home seemed to agree and peered back at him with an accusatory glare. The dim morning light glinted off the phalanx of windows that faced him, each one looking like an eye with a cocked eyebrow — bent in reproach. *"Yeah, yeah, I know lady. I'm a damned bum for leaving you, Elena, and my boy. But, someone's gotta make that mortgage or we all leave you for good — so cut me some slack will ya?"* He laughed at his own joke, as much to brace himself for the coming day of a long drive punctuated by service calls on his customers.

******

Later that night, he shut the door wearily in a budget motel room. This one looked like every other; a King-sized bed covered in a low-quality beige bedspread and darker brown blankets. The faded smell of stale cigarette smoke belied the fact that this was a "non-smoking" room. *I wonder what they did with the $200 cleaning fee.* Cooper knew they had not received their money's worth. *Or, maybe the manager just pocketed it.* Down the hall, he could hear the harsh racket of the ice machine and the playful banter of children as a family checked in a few doors down.

He kicked his black leather shoes off, put the suitcase onto the stand, and the briefcase onto the particle board desk. The hastily consumed dinner of fried chicken and mashed potatoes sat heavily on his stomach.

He picked up the remote and turned on the TV. Absentmindedly he flipped through the channels. Sporting events. Infomercials. Crime dramas. Nothing caught his eye. It made him think of a line from a Springsteen song, "Fifty-seven channels and nothing on." But, now he probably had over a hundred. Then, something did catch his eye.

A beautiful woman was alive with passion debating a very well-dressed man on some talk show. The host sat between them. What drew his attention was the intense look on the woman's face, the electricity in her voice, and the sweeping gesticulations she made with her hands. She looked like a restless animal and the seat was her cage that she wanted to be free of. This all caught his attention before he heard anything she was saying. The host interrupted her.

"So, Ms. Wheeler, tell us what the biggest threat of global warming is?"

She tossed her head in disdain, deep black hair cascading over her shoulders, "What *isn't* at threat is the true question. Agriculture, water supplies, increasing spread of disease vectors..."

A loud "harrumph" from the other guest broke her flow, "Come now. Here we go again, more liberal hysteria. Next, Ms. Wheeler will tell us that Santa Claus will be killed off because some warming of the polar ice caps!" The small audience roared with laughter at that.

The woman, Ms. Wheeler, fumed, "I can assure you, Mister Lupacs, that your grandchildren won't be laughing when they are sent off to fight a war over water or food supplies!" She infused the word "Mister" with an ample helping of mockery.

The alarm on his cell phone went off just then. *Time to call home.* He turned off the TV and grabbed his cell phone.

He speed-dialed home. When he was on the road, this was his favorite part of the day. The soft voice of his wife on the other end, telling him all the mundane details of her day. The rapid-fire, excited voice of Jake recounting the stories from the latest book he was reading or exhibitions of athletic prowess at school. Cooper soaked it all in. Given his own turbulent childhood, Cooper knew he had it good on the home front. This was something he was thankful for. He would relay a few episodes from his day to keep the conversation going. His real interest lay in keeping them both talking. After thirty minutes and a round of "I love you", Cooper hung up the phone and turned back to the empty motel room. He grabbed a book on wilderness medicine that he was reading for their summer's upcoming backpacking trips and settled in for the night.

******

The next morning, he was out the door and at the local diner by six-thirty. The waitress, Louisa, was a portly woman with long dark hair, deep complexion, and one of those friendly faces that just made you smile every time you saw it. Cooper knew her from previous trips out to Redmond. Her father had been a migrant worker from Mexico and her mother hailed from the nearby Warm Springs Reservation. She brought him coffee without asking how he liked it. She knew; black and hot. She slid a copy of the morning newspaper over to him with her other hand.

"Good morning, hombre," she smiled.

"Morning, Lou," he said easing into a barstool at the counter. "How are the chickens doing this morning?"

"Well enough to keep us fat and our veins filled with cholesterol."

"Excellent," he smiled back, "I'll take the Sicilian Omelet with a double helping of wheat toast then," he said as he completed a variation of a constant theme of banter they had going for the past five years. He laughed to himself at the pretense of the "Sicilian Omelet" which was simply a Denver omelet dressed up in mozzarella instead of cheddar. But, he'd be damned if it didn't taste just right. Cooper made it out to Redmond about every month or two, so he could make sure the hardware store here and in the four surrounding towns were stocked up and serviced well. By tonight, he would have finished those calls and made his way north, up toward Baker City.

The blaring newspaper headline quickly wiped the smile from his face.

Seattle Churchgoers Under Quarantine, 5 Dead

With furrowed eyebrow, Cooper read the article intently. The dozen hospitalized yesterday had swelled to a hundred. Five were dead with a score more reported as seriously ill. The medical authorities were running a suite of tests and had no firm answer as to what it was. "It is clearly a fast-moving, contagious pathogen with a very short incubation period and a very high lethality rate," Dr. David Zhao was quoted. "That could be helpful as it may help us prevent further infection," as he tried to inject a note of optimism. The rest of the members of the congregation had been quarantined by Monday evening.

Louisa saw him intently reading, "Probably just another swine flu or bird flu, or maybe a lizard flu scare this time," she laughed heartily at her own joke.

Cooper could only muster a lame smile, "I hope you're right. Five out of twelve dead is pretty bad, though," Cooper said as he shook his head slowly. He took a long pull of the reassuringly hot coffee.

She smirked, "I think it's all about selling newspapers and TV time. Dios mio! This morning the TV was talking about Seattle and a group of disembarked cruise goers' in Florida who were coming down sick too," she turned to put an order on the turnstile for the grill cook. Turning back toward him, "Of course, no one knows if it's related or just another case of food poisoning on a cruise ship, but I could tell the anchorman was just hoping that they were related somehow. He was nearly salivating. Ratings pigs, that's all they are."

Cooper put his coffee cup down, "Florida, huh? Well, it was probably some bad shrimp or some cook who didn't wash his hands."

"Hey now, watch that buddy! Us cooks mind our hygiene," bellowed Buck Floy, the line cook from behind the sizzling grill. "Except when we don't like the customer's attitude," he smirked. Cooper couldn't help but laugh when he proceeded to mock spitting into Cooper's cooking omelet. Buck was physically an impressive man, over six feet tall and two hundred pounds of solid muscle. He had been a professional boxer for a short time and unlike most aging athletes, he maintained his conditioning. Blonde wisps of hair dangled down from underneath the mandatory chef's hat and his dark green eyes shined with alertness.

"No offense meant, Buck, none at all. You know me; I always save my offending for *after* I've been served my food."

Buck gave him a false glare, shoveled the omelet and hash browns onto a plate, and rang the bell, "Order up!"

Cooper ate quickly. He had a forty-five minute drive to his next stop and liked to call on David Kirby at eight, when he opened. The three egg omelet was delicious. Cooper remembered the first time he'd ordered the Sicilian, about three years ago. He remembered marveling at how good it was and castigating himself for never having thrown some mozzarella on an omelet before. Cooper devoured the two slices of bacon, fat dripping hot off the side. Farm fresh and local. He never understood fellow business travelers on the road who would go to some chain restaurant when a local diner was available. Nothing beat the quality of local food that hadn't been shipped halfway across the country. The hash browns, like usual, were just so-so, Buck's method a little too mushy for Cooper's taste. The sign over the grill proclaiming, "The Best Hash This Side of Idaho" kept Cooper from ever asking for a crispier helping. Cooper downed a second cup of coffee and got up to pay his bill, leaving the newspaper behind for the next customer. He glanced at Buck, who was frantically preparing a slew of orders that had just come in, and stepped over to the register.

"Well, Lou, time for me to run," as he put his money on the counter.

"OK, darling. We'll see you the next time through. I promise to buy lots of hardware and tools I don't need next payday just so we can get you out here sooner." Her warm smile made the food taste even better.

He waved goodbye to Buck, who dipped his head in recognition, but quickly returned to the busy grill in front of him.

"Thanks. You do that! Jake keeps telling me he needs a new bike," he retorted.

It was the last time he would ever see her.

******

A half hour into his drive, he was lost in thought. The sedan glided down the highway, too smoothly for his taste. He knew the car was the right one for his work and the amount of miles he put on. But, he missed his 1973 GMC pickup badly. He preferred the way its bumping and bucking forced you to pay attention to the task of driving and staying on the road. *Yet, more fun off the road!* The radio hummed in the background. Earlier, he had heard the local news and farm reports. Then, he'd switched over to a national news channel. Cooper was a man who liked to stay abreast of the news. From his father, he had ingrained the duty of citizenship like few Americans did nowadays. He couldn't have counted for you the number of times his father had told him of the "blood spilled by our forefathers" so that we could have the freedom to read what we chose. He had considered it a betrayal of their sacrifice to *not read* and stay involved in the political lifeblood of the country. *Yeah, the old man was one who belonged to an earlier era. I guess I do too.*

A light rain started to fall and Cooper flipped the wipers on; the steady click-snick-click rhythm adding to the monotony. Within minutes, the smell of fresh rain and slick asphalt filled the car and Cooper breathed it in, welcoming the change. He loved the smell of rain, which was reason enough for him to tolerate the long Northwest winters and the omnipresent dull gray.

The news announcer's voice from the radio slapped him across the face and brought him abruptly back to attention.

"And, in a story we have been following closely since yesterday, there are more alarming reports coming out about the illness first reported in Seattle, Washington. As the toll rises, authorities remain unable to identify the pathogen responsible. Most likely, they say, it is a new virus, but they cannot substantiate that as of yet. So far, there are twenty-three dead in Seattle with another hundred hospitalized and over four hundred members of St. Andrews under quarantine. There are additional reports that several dozen others in Seattle have fallen ill with similar symptoms and are seeking medical attention. In Florida, Royal Caribbean has issued an emphatic statement that the vacationers were not infected by anything related to the ship's operation. As you may recall, there are reports of hundreds of cruise goers from cities across the country falling ill from that trip. In New York City, we have received initial reports of hospitalizations, but no deaths, that appear related. The Centers for Disease Control has dispatched staff to all of the affected cities to directly assess the situation and assist in the investigation. In some good news related to this breaking story, many of those initially hospitalized in Seattle have recovered fully and are returning to their homes.*

In other news, China has demanded a high level meeting with US officials to discuss, 'the future of relations between the two nations'..."

Cooper's mind drifted back toward the road. *I hope this turns out to be just another flu-pandemic scare. We've had a spate of them the last few years. If it is one, it's moving fast. That should mean it will end faster, right? Poor families. Maybe the kids have all recovered at least. They usually mention it when any children die.* Since the day Jake was born, any news of others' dying — especially children — affected him deeply.

He shook his head to shed the morose thoughts and his fingers punched a button to bring him some music instead. AC/DC's "Highway to Hell" came screaming through the car's speakers. He smiled, needing the distraction, turned up the volume, and allowed the screeching guitar to drown out the news' alarms.

"Living easy, lovin' free. A seasoned drinker on a one way ride..."

Chapter 2

Later that night, Cooper's world was thrown into disarray.

"Hello?" Elena answered the phone, her voice deeper than normal.

"Hi, honey. What's the matter, you don't sound so good?"

"I just have a little sniffle. Just a sore throat and my nose is stuffed up a bit," she replied.

Cooper's eyes sharpened their focus on the wall facing west toward home, despite the fact that he was in a dimly lit motel room a few hundred miles away. "How are you feeling?"

"I'm OK. I'm sure I will be better by morning. Crazy Eddie was taken to the hospital this morning though. Maryann called an ambulance and everything. Said he went from being normal to having a fever of a hundred and six within six hours." Crazy Eddie lived across the street from them, in a red barn-styled home. He'd earned the nickname in his youth for how he rode on the motor cross circuit, but everyone still called him that. Truth be told, he enjoyed the nickname, especially now that it contrasted sharply with his comfortable job as an insurance salesman.

"Really? Are you sure you're OK? Do you have a temperature?"

"No. Not the slightest. Don't worry, I'll be fine."

Cooper breathed a shallow sigh of relief, but his brow remained tight. "How's Jake doing?"

"He's OK, nothing going on with him. I'm sure it's just a late flu bug hitting. How was your day? Did that floozy Lou try to get you to sleep with her again," she asked, reviving a long-running joke between the two of them that started when Cooper had returned from his first trip to Redmond five years ago telling her about this wonderful waitress he had met and how friendly she'd been.

Cooper smiled, "Nah, we just did our business in the stockroom a few times. She doesn't have to ask anymore, you know that."

"I see. Well, I'll have to punish you for that when you get home, baby," she cooed. *Damn, my wife has the sexiest voice around.*

He turned his voice down an octave, "You do that. I dare you."

At that, she laughed. Then, she began coughing.

Later that night, she called again. Sicker. And Cooper had raced for home.

******

Minutes after he had fled the motel, the night bore down oppressively upon Cooper as he sped down the lonely highway. Scant moonlight pierced the heavy cloud cover. Save for the two-halogen headlights, Cooper felt like the dark would have swallowed him up — two tons of steel, glass, and plastic — without a hiccup or a moment's warning. He kept the window cracked and welcomed the sharp sting of the cold night air whipping past his left cheek. He smelled wet juniper from the scattered trees littering the eastern Oregon semi-arid flatlands. His hands gripped the steering wheel with anxious tension. His eyes glared down the distant road as if they could grab the road like grappling hooks and pull the car faster down the asphalt.

His mind raced through a jumble of thoughts and emotions. Despite the frequent denials, he could not shake the apprehension that Elena had this flu that seemed to be erupting across the nation. When he had first jumped into the car, he had quickly turned the radio on, seeking distraction from his troubled mind. That had been a colossal mistake.

First, like a sledgehammer blow to the stomach, the announcer was recounting in detail a flurry of flu-like hospitalizations throughout Oregon, including his hometown of Portland. Thankfully, no deaths had been reported yet in Oregon, but the death count in Seattle had surpassed a hundred. Already, this flu was moving faster than any Cooper had ever heard of.

Next, he called Dranko, a good friend who lived a few doors down.

After just one ring, an alert voice answered, "Yeah?"

"Dranko, it's me, Cooper. You up?" he asked in surprise.

"Of course, brother. Haven't you heard the news? I've been on the Net and the Ham for the past eighteen hours. You wouldn't believe the stuff I'm seeing and hearing. Worse than the news. Didjya here they are calling it the Brushfire Plague?"

"The Brushfire Plague? No, I hadn't heard that yet. So, it's moving fast?"

"Fast would be an understatement. This thing is moving quicker than anything anyone has ever seen. Faster and deadlier. I told you something was coming and I think this is it." Cooper heard the excitement in his voice. For years, Dranko had lived on the outskirts of the 'tinfoil hat' crowd, always alert for the next conspiracy to bring down civilization—or sometimes just America. The heady tone grated on him.

"Damnit Dranko, let's hold the 'I told you so' celebrations for next week. Elena's sick, I need you to go check on her. I'm stuck two-three hours out at least, coming back from north of Redmond."

There was a short pause and a deep sigh on the other line, "I'm sorry. I hadn't heard. A few other neighbors got it yesterday, but Elena seemed fine when I saw her. I'm on my way. I'll check in and call you back in a few."

"If she doesn't come to the door, there's a key in a fake rock just to the left of our stairs. As he finished, the nagging voice of responsibility pulled at him, "Wait!" he shouted.

"What?" Dranko responded.

"I can't ask you to check on her. You might expose yourself to this thing that is going around."

Dranko chuckled, "No worries, brother. First, you're a good friend, so it's a risk I'd take. Second, I'll take precautions. And, third, I saw Elena already today. If she has it, then I've *already* been exposed to this bugger."

Relieved, Cooper exhaled, "OK, thank you. I had to call it out."

"Yeah, brother. That's why you're a good man, Charlie Brown."

"Thanks. Let me know what you find out."

"Got it, I'll call you in ten."

Cooper inhaled and blew out a long, low whistle. He felt better now that someone was in motion to help Elena. He felt helpless being over two hours away. Dranko was a good man. Dranko was stocky, worried brown eyes and shoulder-length hair the color of walnut. Despite his semi-paranoid leanings, he was one of the most solid, reliable men that Cooper had ever met. He also knew that the report he would get from him about Elena would be straight. He wouldn't sugarcoat nor exaggerate the situation. It wasn't in his DNA.

The reprieve was short-lived.

Within ten minutes, and three different AM stations, he had heard a litany of cities that sounded like a heavy metal band's summer concert tour list where reports of the new, strange, flu-like illness were popping up: Boston, New York City, Providence, Atlanta, Miami, New Orleans, Cleveland, Detroit, Chicago, Wichita, Kansas City, Houston, St. Louis, Dallas, Denver, San Diego, San Francisco, Omaha, and on and on. The list included scores of cities, both large and small. The only major city that hadn't appeared on the list was Washington, DC. Then, as if he needed another blow, there were some reports coming in of the flu hitting foreign cities throughout Europe and Asia as well. So far, Africa and Australia were untouched.

Almost to the second, ten minutes after he had hung up with Dranko, his cell phone was ringing.

"How is she," he asked.

"She's got it. No question. Fever is 104. Lungs are filling up pretty good. She's very weak. Lisa just came over to take a look. Jake is OK though. He's been around her all day, so I don't see any reason to separate them." Lisa Moore was another friend who lived in the neighborhood, just across the street. She was a registered nurse, and a good one at that.

A stifled, "No!" was all Cooper could manage. His grip tightened further on the steering wheel.

"Brother, how fast are you going right now?"

Cooper glanced down at the red-illuminated gauge. "Ninety."

"Get it to a hundred."

******

The white markers that lined the side of the highway stood as silent sentinels, whipping past at a hundred miles per hour, telling anyone who would listen not to drift off into the barren landscape that lay beyond. Cooper kept the car's engine pressed hard, alternating between one-twenty and eighty, depending on the curves in the road and the slickness of the wet asphalt. He drove expertly, a man possessed with a single-minded purpose. His mind raced, but he did not panic. He felt like he did the few times he had been in combat in Iraq when his unit had come under fire or had been hit with an improvised explosive. His heart raced, breath deep and rapid, eyes alert and darting from the front and then to the side, and every muscle stood taut and at the ready.

An hour later, he was at the foot of Mt. Hood. In the dim moonlight, he could see the majestic mountain towering above him. The snow-capped mountain glowed in the eerie moonshine. Cooper loved this mountain. He admired its strong, yet elegant, beauty. He couldn't look at it without recalling the winter trips to the snow where he and Elena—and now Jake—would trek across her meadows and wind along her trails. He would always smile to think of their summer journeys; backpacking or simply day hiking. When he gazed her visage from the streets of Portland, he could almost smell the sharp tang of the pine in summer or taste the clean fallen snow in winter. To him, Mt. Hood personified all that was good about the Pacific Northwest.

Tonight, he cursed her like a no good flea-bitten bitch.

Tonight, the winding roads of the mountain were a hated adversary, forcing him to slow down to navigate her curves. Tonight, she was delaying him from being with his deeper love, Elena, in her desperate time of need.

Letting off the accelerator, he let loose with a fierce invective, "Damn you and your godforsaken crooked roads!" The few times his right foot touched the brake pedal, he screamed hell's wrath into the night air. He knew his oaths made no difference and would do nothing to straighten the roads, nor give the tires better grip. But he knew no other way to combat the weary helplessness that threatened to engulf him if he didn't keep it at bay with righteous anger.

He used the barely suppressed rage to keep the other thoughts at arm's length as well. Part of his mind coaxed him to comfort with platitudes about Elena not being sick with this new flu. This voice urged him onward to denial with questions about the real odds of Elena in Portland, Oregon having some deadly bug that had just broken out. She hadn't been on a plane recently, had she? The questions came further and faster the more he let them be asked. Elena was in superb health, wasn't she? This was probably just some run-of-mill cold she had picked up. Your friend Dranko always jumps to the worst-case scenario, right? No, the voice told him, don't you worry, everything will be all right. You've had enough ill fortune in your life already, dear Cooper.

Yet, another part of him knew, was one hundred and twenty percent sure, that Elena not only had this new illness sweeping the land, but that she would die. Whereas the one voice reassured and dripped sugar from its lips, this other voice tormented him and its tongue stabbed him in the heart with each word. Yes, she had it and you better get your ass home in time to see her last breath. Tears welled up before he consciously pushed them away. He refocused on his driving as a distraction.

These two voices battled it out for the entire drive home. Cooper cursed again. *I need to get home. There, I can do something and can get out of this steel box where I'm trapped and can't do a damn thing to help her.*

When he emerged onto the west slope of Mt. Hood, he regained his breakneck speed to a hundred miles an hour, or more. He was well onto I-84 and nearing Portland, when it struck him.

Accounting for it being a little after four in the morning, the highway was still far too empty. Nary a car or truck were moving in either direction. Except for his car and a handful of other vehicles, nothing was moving. Cooper had been on these roads in the early hours many times before, usually heading out for one of his trips. It had never been this empty.

What he did see were a dozen emergency vehicles, both police and ambulances racing to and fro. Moreover, the police cars — despite his excessive speed — didn't give him a second look.

When this all sunk in, his stomach shriveled up inside him. This was something different. This was like nothing he'd ever seen before.

******

A short time later, he pulled into his driveway, cranked his emergency brake and brought the sedan to an abrupt, lurching stop. The first shreds of sunlight were just beginning to light the eastern horizon and only a thin and cold light made its way to his home. The windows reflected darker than the rest of the home, like gaunt, open wounds. His eyes locked onto the upstairs window, into the loft area that adjoined their bedroom. He did so with some meager hope that, somehow, Elena would have recovered and would be at the window, looking down and awaiting his arrival. The window only stared back at him, harshly vacant.

He sprung from the car and raced inside. He wrenched open the door, barely hitting a step on the way up. He sped into his kitchen, his sneakers sliding on the green linoleum floor. When he arrived at the landing, he whirled around the corner, ready to fly up the stairs. Dranko stood at the top of the stairs and beckoned him to halt with his hand upturned in the universal sign for "Stop". Surprised, Cooper involuntarily did so for a moment.

Dranko kept his hand up and talked to him in a strong hushed voice, "This thing is bad, brother. I don't think you can help Elena much. Both Sally and Walt are already dead from it and another dozen, just on our block, have come down with this thing. You might not have been exposed…"

Cooper, hearing Dranko's words, became furious and began again to mount the stairs in rapid leaps, "You've got to be kidding me. Nothing…*nothing* could keep me from her and my boy." The last words came as his face came parallel to Dranko's and he nearly spat the words at him. He brushed Dranko to the side with his left arm and finished making his way up and into the bedroom. Dranko moved aside without resistance, lowered his head for a moment in understanding, and then turned back up the stairs to follow his friend at a respectful distance.

Chapter 3

Cooper cleared the doorway and stopped dead in his tracks. Elena lay sprawled on the bed, groaning in restless motion. The moaning sounded like a wounded cat curled up in some dark corner of a dead-end street desperately tending its wounds after a losing fight with the alley cat and calling to the world for sympathy. Her eyes were closed, but he could see them moving frantically to and fro behind her eyelids. Her black hair was damp and matted, her face flushed. The sheets clung to her body, soaked in sweat. Cooper almost imagined seeing steam rise from her body; she was so clearly burning up.

To the right of the bed, focused so intently on his mother that he was unaware Cooper had come in the room, sat Jake. A surgical mask, too large for his face, sloppily covering the nose and mouth. But, his eyes told Cooper everything he needed to know. They were sunken in and ringed by sorrowful lines. They were thick with worry, narrowed down to slit-like focus, twitching with every movement or noise of his mother. He hadn't slept all night. His head lay propped by his hand at his chin, with the arm on his knee.

Cooper took a step toward the bed and for the first time saw Lisa. She rose from her sentry post to the left of the bed and stopped Cooper with a wave of her hand. The scene had so unsettled Cooper that he offered no resistance. Lisa had a mask on as well and her hands were covered by blue latex gloves, the kind so ubiquitous in hospitals and medical offices. She reached to Elena's dresser and produced a mask and gloves. However, her eyes too were clouded with worry, her brow furrowed so deep that her eyebrows almost touched.

"Here, put these on. I honestly don't know if they're helping, but they are worth a try. Put them on, say hello to Elena and Jake. When you're done, we should talk in the next room," she said as she handed him the materials, and then exited the room.

Cooper's gaze followed her as she left. Her tired steps spoke volumes. At the doorway, Dranko met his eyes, returning a deep reservoir of sympathy. His look shook Cooper to his core. *She isn't dead!* "Don't look at me like that!" he hissed. Dranko didn't display his surprise at his friend's harsh words, but instead turned, and left the room.

Cooper stood there, pondering for several seconds. Then, he set the mask and the gloves down on the dresser. He took Elena's hand into his own. Her hand felt light. Withered. The skin was so dry he worried it might flake off in sheaves if he touched her too firmly.

Cooper shifted and looked toward his son. Cooper's outburst had roused Jake from his intense watch. His round, young face had turned toward his father. His gaze still rested on Cooper, but the faint brown eyes and tense face flew wide in disbelief at seeing him here. Cooper looked at his son and their eyes locked. Cooper moved quickly to his side. He knelt down and caressed his boy's head into his chest, kissing him on his mash of curly black hair. Jake's chest heaved deeply once and then he began weeping uncontrollably, the pent up emotion of the last day finally unleashed in a furious torrent. Cooper gathered him in, wrapping both arms around him in a comforting bear hug. Already, he could feel the warm tears on his chest, quickly soaking through his shirt. His own eyes filled with tears, and they remained in their soothing embrace for some time.

Finally, Cooper pulled his son's face from his chest and cradled his face in both hands. Jake's eyes glistened and his face was flushed beet red. Instinctively, he knew his son wanted him to tell him things would turn out alright and not to worry. Cooper desperately wanted to comfort his son. But, he was not the kind of man to say 'everything will be OK' when those words might well be proven to be untrue. To Cooper, honesty was a sacred trust, never broken. As a young teen, he had seen deceit destroy his father's life. It had cost him much of his own as well.

******

The teenager shifted uncomfortably in the front row of the courtroom. Knees on gangly legs kept bumping into the wooden wall in front of him. The fluorescent lights bore down on him, the light made harsher by the circumstances that had brought him here. The room was abuzz with the murmurs of an excited crowd; punctuated by the occasional gibe shot across the aisle.

The room was divided by a phalanx of bailiffs down the middle aisle. Cooper was young, but he knew the rift in the room was miles wider than that. On the left were those who supported his father, incensed by what they all knew were false accusations levied by a political opponent. On the right were those who backed Denny Smith; said rival.

Today, the jury was coming back to render its verdict.

The stiff oak doors to his right opened and his father was led into the room by two Sheriff's officers. The room fell deathly silent as all heads riveted in that direction.

"Thief!" shouted a voice from somewhere behind, off to the right.

Cooper was instantly on his feet with balled fists; his eyes scanning the crowd for the culprit. A strong hand landed on his shoulder, pushing him back into his seat, "Sit down, son. We ain't having none of that here today." He looked up at a steely-eyed bailiff who outweighed him by a hundred pounds, most of which was muscle. He sat back down, bitter tears of futility burning his eyes.

Landing back in his seat, he did something he hadn't done in years: he reached out and curled his mother's fingers into his own. Their eyes embraced. His mother's despondency clashing with his own fury.

He looked up as his father came to the seat just feet away from him. His father's eyes gripped him, as if to hug him. The connection felt more sincere and warm than most men's actual embraces would have been. He raised his hands to chest level and clenched them into fists of encouragement. Cooper stared deeply into his father's eyes, drawing frantically from the wellspring of strength that he so desperately needed. Doing so calmed the room from spinning out of control, but the black pit in Cooper's gut refused to budge.

The remainder of the proceedings had always been a blur of disjointed images and scenes. He remembered rising to the bailiff's call and sitting once again at the judge's permission.

Like graffiti blighting an ancient redwood, the jury foreman was forever carved into his memory. He could recall every crag in the old man's face. The man's black bolo tie insulted him. The man looked like a caricature of a hanging judge from a cheap Western. Seared deeper into his mind were the man's chapped lips moving in slow motion and exaggerated form as they condemned his father and pronounced a single word: "Guilty."

His father's knees buckled in shock and he abruptly collapsed into his seat. His father was given a scant second of relief, before the judge rapped his gavel and a bailiff manhandled him back onto his feet. He would never forget how his father gave one firm shake of his head back and forth in disbelief. Then, he regained his composure and stood steadfast once more.

His mother let out a stifled wail of despair, her body wracked as she refused to let any sound reach her husband's enemies, who sat mere feet away. Cooper did his best to help bear the tension, gripping her hand more firmly. When that proved inadequate, he pulled her in close, clenching her shoulders under his arm. He felt burning tears on his neck as she mashed her face against him. He bit down on his lips to padlock his own tears inside.

He looked to his right and saw Denny Smith in the front row opposite him, smiling widely at his victory. With the jury's verdict, he knew he had accomplished something he could never have done in an election: taken his father's leadership position away from him. Denny's eyes caught Cooper's. Seeing the boy's misery, he softened none of his rapacious smile. His eyes became more wolf-like and his mouth worked itself into a snarl. Wanting to strike back, Cooper struggled to mimic a hard man's stare. To his regret, Denny didn't seem to notice or care. Dismissively, he'd turned away to accept the congratulations of one of his cronies.

Thankfully, he could evoke bits and pieces of his father's speech. He would never forget the day the verdict came down, and certain words were burned into his mind. He liked to call upon them for solace.

"This travesty comes as no surprise. Many other men, much greater men than I, have been bushwhacked by a legal system written by and for those who own things rather than those who make them. I will confess my surprise that my long-time dear friend Denny Smith is the man who concocted these lies to smear my name and bring me down. This was a man I would have entrusted not only my own life, but the lives of my wife and child as well. That is how deep our bond went. Now, I stand on the other side of a wide river, a river filled with lies, deceit, and false accusations. But, my entire life has been about trust and I will not abandon it now. My entire life I've been a part of people trusting one another and it's been a beautiful thing to see. The men and women I've worked with have stood up together, bonded in trust, to protect their communities, and promote a better life for all Americans. So, I tell you today, Denny Smith, I will not allow the craven act of one cowardly worm of a man diminish my trust in others, proven right and true a thousand times over by better men, and women, than you!"

When his father had finished, Cooper's eyes were red and swollen. Whenever Cooper would think of the proud upright man who stood in the courtroom that day, he could never stop himself from also remembering the same man a few months later: broken, bent, and ragged. His father had been a man of action. Losing his freedom behind the constricting prison's walls had been his version of hell.

******

Watching his father be overwhelmed and swept under by the lies of others, he had vowed never to allow dishonesty any stake or place in his own life, no matter how tempting. Ever since, he'd never uttered a single falsehood. Right now, he frantically wanted to tell the small lie to his son—and to himself—because it would make things easier to face. But, he could not, "I'm here now, son. I'm not going anywhere. We will deal with this together, no matter what." It was the best he could manage.

Jake drank his words in, deeply inhaling once he'd finished speaking. Jake knew his father's words were true, they always were. He nodded his head slowly, never breaking from his father's eyes. He wiped away his tears with a brush of his hand, "I'm happy you're here. I don't want to see Mom like this. It's scaring me." With that, fresh tears washed down his face. Cooper hugged him again, Jake feeling the beat of his father's heart. "Look, it's alright to be scared. I'm scared too. But, we need to focus on your mother now. Let's make her comfortable, let's do everything we can for her, and let's make sure she can feel our love." He waited a few moments and a notion from one of his numerous first aid classes came back to him. *Always put people into motion when in crisis. Just give them* something *to do.* "Can you go get me a glass of water? The drive made me thirsty." Jake nodded yes and slowly ambled out of the room. Cooper took a deep breath and turned to his wife, lying prostrate on the bed.

Cooper took one look at his wife and pressed his latex-covered hand firmly against his face, just above his upper lip to help himself maintain control. Watching her, so clearly in distress, pushed his heart into his throat and made him want to beat the walls in helpless frustration. He hated that he knew so little about what was happening. He took the last few steps to the bedside, slowly, like a man walking to the gallows. Dread gripped him around the throat and pressed the air from his lungs. Each step closer to the bed made the throttling grow tighter. He countered by taking his wife's hand and breathing deeply in a measured, controlled breath.

Elena's hand was hot to the touch, but she squeezed back firmly, filling his heart with hope. "I'm here, baby, I'm here." He pressed his other hand to her forehead. It was burning and covered in sweat. *Damn it, she's cooking inside there.* He took a washcloth that had become dislodged from her forehead, soaked it in the ice water he found on the nightstand and wiped her forehead, cheeks, and chest with it. She moved restlessly and opened her eyes when he did so.

Briefly, the spark returned to her eyes and a corner of her mouth upturned in a half-smile, "Cooper. Oh, Cooper. It's you. It's so good to see you. I was worried you wouldn't make it here." A single, long, oval tear fell from her left eye and glided down her cheek.

He squeezed her hand more tightly and caressed her cheek with his other hand, "You too, honey. I was in the car before we hung up the phone. I'm here now. I'll take care of everything. You need to rest and put everything into getting better." He leaned his head in, pulled his mask down, and kissed her on her blazing cheek, "I love you." She whispered back, "I love you, too." He pulled his head back, looking into her eyes, which belied her next words, "I'll lick this thing. Hasn't been a bug yet that liked my Romanian-Mexican blood, has there?" Her health *had* always been legendary and a source of light mockery between them whenever *he* had been sick and she hadn't.

"Knowing you'll be here, to take care of Jake, will just make it that much faster." Her false words of optimism contrasted sharply with the truth in her eyes. Cooper and Elena could never lie to one another, not even the white ones. The few times Elena had attempted innocent ones when they were first dating, her eyes had betrayed her — as they did now. Cooper had never even tried.

Cooper allowed her the charade. "Don't you worry about a thing. I will take care of everything and I *will*," he choked on the word because he knew she'd know the deeper, barely hidden, import of the word now, "I will take care of our boy." Her eyes and a short nod revealed their understanding and she squeezed his hand firmly. "I have to rest now. I love you, remember that," and her eyes closed slowly.

Within seconds, she had drifted back into restless slumber. He leaned over and hugged her tightly for several minutes, not wanting to leave her. He could not shake the dreadful feeling that she was slipping away from him. Vivid memories welled up. The emerald green dress she wore on their first date. The way her face glistened, drenched in sweat, the day Jake was born. Elena standing, bathed in the early morning light, looking down at him with love-soaked eyes after the first time they'd made love. The sweet taste of her lips whenever they kissed. The timbre of her laughter, which he could not resist. The furrow of brow when Jake was injured or ill that revealed the depth of a mother's concern. When he left the room to go and talk to Lisa, he did so in a daze.

******

He took care to close their door quietly as he exited, vainly hoping it would help. He turned to find Lisa, Dranko, and his son clustered in the upstairs open loft area that adjoined their bedroom. Dranko took one look at Cooper's tired eyes and hunched shoulders and quickly ushered Jake downstairs with a thinly veiled excuse of needing his help to get something for his mother. Even in his debilitated state, Cooper saw the ruse and wondered for a moment just how Dranko would distract his son. But, he knew that Dranko would figure out a way to do so; he was a resourceful man.

Lisa met him halfway across the room, he with tired, ambling steps and her with a few quick, purposeful movements. Lisa was a tall woman, so she inclined her head slightly to gaze into his eyes with a tender expression. Her left hand touched his right shoulder, gave him a comforting squeeze, and asked in a soft voice, "How are you doing?" The faintest hint of her Minnesota background made her words kinder still.

Her tender actions broke him out of his despair and he returned to his usual, calm, matter-of-fact demeanor. His back straightened, his face stiffened, and he took a deep, cleansing breath, "OK. Just tell me how it is. Dranko will tell you, I don't like sugarcoating. I can handle it and I need to know what the score is."

Lisa was momentarily taken aback by Cooper's sudden transformation from the tired, dejected man that had stood in front of her just a moment ago to this firm-backed man, straight-faced, ordering her to give her report. The effect was so startling that she almost barked a "Yes, sir!"

"Well, Cooper, the truth is I don't know too much. This illness that is breaking out all over in the last few days has far too many unknowns. If this were normal times, I would tell you to watch her, make sure she is getting plenty of fluids, give her ibuprofen for keeping the fever down, and get her to a hospital if she develops difficulty breathing."

He clasped his hands together, "But, this isn't normal times."

"No, it isn't," she nodded gravely. "Whatever this virus is — and we do know it's a virus of some kind — appears to have both a very high morbidity or kill rate and high contagion rate. It also moves very quickly. Patients who come down with it are either recovered in 48-72 hours or they…" she paused, her typical self-assuredness in briefing a patient's family member shaken by the fact that it was happening with a friend and in his home.

Cooper made it easy for her, "Or they die, right?"

"Or they die." She paused, debating her next words, "And, I'm sorry to say, most die."

Reflexively, Cooper made a quick circle of the room, pacing quickly, and returning to the same spot. "OK. Can't we do something? What about getting her to the hospital?"

She looked at her toes and shook her head dejectedly, "The hospitals are overrun." She drew the courage to raise her gaze to meet his, "The first thing I did when everyone began falling ill was to call old friends and former co-workers at all the area hospitals. Cooper, every single one told the same story. One, they said don't bring them here; nothing we are doing is making any difference. Two, every bed is full, the hallways are full, as are the tents they hastily erected in the parking lots! Three, the little we can offer is comfort and you can do more of that at their homes."

"This can't be happening! This is like out of some damned movie," he exploded. He pivoted on his left foot and made a rapid circle around the room. He came to a stop back in front of her, "You're telling me we can't do a damned thing for her! That's my wife in there! It's Elena, your friend…not some faceless patient who walked off the damned street! Can't you do something?"

Lisa was unfazed by his loud outburst; she knew it was a normal reaction. She grabbed his arms to stop their waving about and looked him straight in the eye, "Cooper, I know this is tough. But, this is real. It is happening. And while there isn't much we can do for Elena other than keep her comfortable, your son needs you now like nothing else. He's watched his mother fall seriously ill in the last few hours and he needs your strength right now."

Her last sentence had a tonic effect on him and Cooper staggered a half-step backwards. His rage left him like a tire leaking air. After a few seconds he looked back at her, "OK. Got it. Thank you. Sorry for that. I know it's not your fault. Just tell me what I *can* do for her."

"Unfortunately, you already know. From this side of it, it's just like any other flu. Keep her comfortable, make sure she gets plenty of fluids, and…"

Cooper knew the rest and had already tuned her out. He began thinking of Jake and how to help him in this terrible crisis. He also knew he had to talk to Dranko to get the full skinny on what was happening with this illness. He knew he would have the best information around.

Cooper turned away before she'd finished speaking and Lisa stopped in mid-sentence. She was surprised, but not shocked, because she had known for many years that Cooper Adams was a man of incredible focus and action once a course had been chosen. As he began to head downstairs, she returned to the bedroom to look over Elena.

Cooper would typically descend the stairs at a bound, barely touching most of the stairs on his way down. Today, he descended slowly, methodically, the weight on his shoulders showing clearly. His mind raced to catch up to the events unfolding all around him. Already, he was calculating possibilities, probabilities, and options. His mother, after watching his early athletic success and how he reacted to the difficult circumstances of his childhood, used to tell him that he was, "a man born for crisis." It was true. Cooper was rarely debilitated or overwhelmed by circumstances, but would quickly formulate a response based upon whatever situation he was confronted with. Of course, he never had the heart to tell his mother that it was the very shattering experiences from early in his life that had forged him so. He further withheld that he had sacrificed much of the innocence that every child deserved into that crucible.

He entered the kitchen, the early morning light casting a doubtful glow across the green paint that adorned the walls. A myriad of cracks in the plaster loomed larger than before, transformed into gaping schisms in the walls and ceiling. He had promised Elena a hundred times that he would fix them since they had moved in, but something more pressing always kept him away from that job.

Dranko and Jake sat, huddled, in the corner at the small, wrought iron bistro table that lay in the breakfast nook. They had been in earnest, whispered, conversation. Dranko had his arm around Jake and a look of deep sympathy. Dranko's face shined in the light from the nearby window while, in contrast, Jake's lay in shadow. Next to Jake sat a full glass of water. They both turned to face him as he entered the room.

Cooper mustered one of the feeblest smiles of his life, "How are you guys doin'?"

Dranko merely nodded in response. "Fine," Jake answered.

"Jake, will you take that water up to the bedroom. I'd like one of us to be in with your mom. I will be up in just a few."

Jake got up and ambled past Cooper. He tussled his son's hair as he did so. He poured himself a glass of water and then faced Dranko, who stood up and faced his friend.

Cooper caught his eyes, "OK, Dranko, what's the story? What do you know?" Cooper's father had often told him that his definition of a friend was one where you could dispense with the cumbersome politeness of society and just get down to business without so much 'varnish.' At a time like this, Cooper finally understood the wisdom behind those words.

"Well, it's a mess, brother. The worst part is whatever this is, Brushfire is moving so fast..."

"How fast?" Cooper quizzed.

"So fast that no one knows what's really going on. First, let me tell you what I do know. Right now, I know about a dozen neighbors just within the block that have this thing. But, the number grows by the hour. Lisa is on a set of rounds in the neighborhood. She's making the circuit about every four hours and she always comes back with more names."

"How many dead? How many recovered?"

"So far, five dead. In addition to Sally and Walt—Mrs. Collins, Miguel Garcia, and the Garfield's newborn," Dranko saw Cooper's expression and added, "Yes, you got it. This thing doesn't seem to have a preference for age or race. So far, the only recovery is Lily Stott, that old biddie. I swear nothing will kill her. She's too ornery. But, she was also one of the first to come down with it, so Lisa says there is hope for others."

"Have you, or her, heard anything that gives you a guess on how many this is killing?"

"My online contacts, including one in Seattle, give me a guess that we're looking at a 50-75% infection rate with a 25-50% death rate. Lisa thinks it will be less than that."

Cooper's fist crashed into the counter with a loud thud, "Damnit, Dranko, that's a pretty big range. Don't you have any better details?!"

Dranko paused to let his friend gather himself. "I know, brother. I'm working on it." He then put his hand on Cooper's shoulder and looked him straight into his eyes, "Prepare for the worst. From what Lisa has told me, Elena has taken it hard."

Cooper blinked back tears. He didn't care about crying in front of Elena or his son, but he hated to do so in front of another man. "Yeah, yeah. I hear you." Almost automatically, he switched gears as easily as most men turned on a light, "What else is going on? Where are things with the hospitals? The police?"

"Just shot, brother. Overwhelmed. They can't cope with what is going on. Nothing anyone has ever planned for—or hell, even discussed—had something with this level of contagion and morbidity—whatever it ends up being. Add on top of that is just how *fast* this thing is moving. They simply can't handle it. They don't even know where patient zero is for the love of God! From what I'm hearing, this thing sprung up in dozens of places—worldwide—all at once."

"What?" Cooper exclaimed.

"It gets worse, I'm afraid. None of this has been on the news, but the Internet and my ham radio contacts have told me about the first breakdowns in order. It's happening in both the big cities and even in some small towns, too.

"Violence? Already?" Cooper shook his head in disbelief.

"Nobody has ever seen something like this. People are panicked, brother. Everywhere."

"Anything around here?"

"Not that I've heard yet. Maybe our Northwest friendliness is saving us," his laugh ringing hollowly.

Cooper returned a half-smile. Dranko continued, "That being said. You should get to the store as quickly as you can and pick up every non-perishable food you can. I haven't heard that the stores are getting picked clean yet, but it's bound to happen very soon. No matter what the numbers end up being, the supply chains will be severely disrupted. I can watch Jake if you want."

Cooper nodded, "What about you? Do you need to go to?"

Dranko smiled self-assuredly, "Nah. I'm pretty well set. You remember, I've always tried to be prepared..."

Cooper interrupted him, "Yeah, I know. For everything. Just like a Boy Scout."

Dranko nodded, holding up three fingers in a mock Eagle Scout salute.

Cooper thought for a moment, "OK, I will check with Lisa and go as soon as they're open."

"Alright. I'll get back to my place and I'll be back in an hour. Oh, and do you have ammunition for your pistol?"

Cooper cocked an eyebrow, "Yeah, a little. Why?"

"Well, bring it with you. I think the threads are going to fray pretty quickly. I'd buy some more for it today, if you can."

After Dranko left, Cooper and Jake spent an hour in silent vigil with Elena. Lisa left to make her rounds in the neighborhood. Before long, Jake had fallen asleep, head in his father's lap.

Chapter 4

When they arrived at the supermarket, after their drive down Hawthorne, Cooper was surprised to see open spots in the parking lot. *For some, fear of the disease is bigger than any thought of running out of food right now. That will change very soon.* He exited his pickup and Jake scrambled out behind him. He pulled him tightly against him and whispered, "Stay close." People moved quickly to and from their cars. Most looked around furtively while loading their groceries.

Cooper grabbed a cart and entered the store. The relative calm outside was replaced by a flurry of chaos inside. People were rushing through the store, looking for what they'd come for, or anything else they could find. He heard a clang of metal carts crashing into one another and an exchange of obscenities. He heard a man shout at an elderly woman, "Stay away, keep your distance, you're too close," as he poked his hand back and forth at her, motioning her away.

Cooper moved through the store, methodically and with solid purpose. He kept his distance from others — merely to keep them from becoming agitated — and kept Jake locked to his hip. He made short work of the bulk foods, which most people were ignoring. Flour. Rice. Pasta. Oats. He grabbed the heaviest bags of each that he could find. He quickly loaded up at the aisle for spices and salt. He grabbed an armload of boxes of matches and dumped them into the cart. Next, he found some candles and a half dozen cans of camping fuel. The batteries were already mostly gone, but he scavenged what he could. He had saved the canned foods aisle for last. He was just about to turn the corner when he heard shouting from the back of the store.

"Damn you! I know you have some canned stew hidden in the back! Go get it right now! Don't you see this? It's called a gun," a loud, but nervous voice yelled. "Now, go get it!"

The bellowing voice rang throughout the store. Scattered screams of panic responded. Around him, many fled to the front of the store. The quickly clearing canned foods aisle beckoned to Cooper, ready for the picking. Instead, he turned his body towards the angry voice, and looked at Jake, "Get on the floor and stay here. If I'm not back in two minutes, go to the truck, lock yourself in, and call Dranko on my phone." He handed Jake his cell phone. It was not the last time that Cooper would see rank fear in his son's eyes, but he complied. Jake slowly collapsed to the floor and cradled his head in his arms.

With that, Cooper moved in a half-crouch toward the disturbance. He pulled his pistol from his belt, pulled the steel slide back to ensure a round was chambered, and welcomed the odd comfort of the familiar polymer grip and the solid weight of a loaded pistol in hand.

He heard the quiet protest of the store employee, her voice throttled by fear. Around the end cap filled with Doritos, he could see the pair. The employee was a woman, mid-forties, overweight, and just a smidge over five feet tall. She wore a dark blue uniform and light blue apron. Her brown hair, streaked solidly with gray, was pulled up into a haphazard ponytail. She wore latex gloves and a surgical mask. *Must be the new addition to the dress code.* She cowered with her hands upraised and her head tilted toward the ground.

The man stood opposite her, the pistol a few scant inches from her head. Cooper was afraid he was thinking about pistol whipping her. He stood over six feet, well-built, with thick, strapping arms, and a healthy beer belly. *Construction worker, heavy machinery.* He wore a red flannel shirt, blue jeans, and tan work boots speckled with mud. The pistol looked to be a .45 semi-auto, 1911-style. Stainless steel and shining brightly from a high sheen polish finish. *I hope that means he hasn't used this thing much and it was just a showpiece until today.*

"Don't lie to me, bitch! I know you have it back there. I heard you guys talking about keeping some there for yourselves. Now, go get it! I'm going to give you just five seconds! One..."

Cooper readied himself to move like a cougar, first shifting his weight backward, preparing to pounce. His finger slid into the trigger guard and found perch on the trigger.

"Two!" Cooper leapt forward. He was acutely aware of a myriad of smells around him: fear mixed with the man's heavy cologne, fresh fish from a refrigerated case down the aisle, and the sharp sting of urine, most likely from the store clerk.

"Three!" The clerk's face reacted to Cooper's movement by shifting her gaze to him, her eyes flew wide open, and the slack look of surprise blanketed her face. *Damn it!*

Silence greeted the space where "four" should have been shouted. The woman's movement had betrayed Cooper. The man spun to his left, just as Cooper barreled in. The man's eyes widened as he saw Cooper coming at him and he frantically tried to bring his gun to bear. Cooper was only a few feet away. He could see *and smell* the sweat dripping down the man's face. The man's pistol loomed large, the bore swinging around.

Cooper didn't hesitate. He fired twice, the pistol spitting flame from its barrel, both rounds hitting the man in the chest. True to his training, Cooper saw nothing except the front sight of his pistol. The sound was deafening. The man was knocked backward and fell to the ground in slow motion. Blood back-splattered onto Cooper, speckling his face, hands, and chest. Cooper loathed the coppery-taste of blood and reflexively spat. Cooper maneuvered the pistol to keep aim at the man as he fell.

He heard a sharp *chink* of metal hitting metal. From the corner of his eye, just at the edge of his recognition, he saw the large bore of the .45 aimed directly at him. Somehow, after being shot, the man had held onto his pistol and aimed it directly at Cooper's head. The man's face widened in surprise at the pistol's failure. A half second later, Cooper pulled the trigger and the man's face disappeared and gore splattered the floor behind his head. *Most likely he failed to chamber a round or maybe he'd never had the expensive Colt look-alike worked on. Some 1911's were notorious for their need of good gunsmith work before they were reliable.* The man's body collapsed back onto itself and lay sprawled on the ground. A quickly-spreading pool of blood engulfed the body where it lay.

He breathed deeply to calm his adrenaline-pumping body and right his rapid, shallow breath. The pungent smell of blood mixed with the trailing smoke of cordite from his pistol assaulted Cooper's nose.

The woman, who had been threatened with death a moment ago, sank slowly to the ground, her knees buckling, now that death had indeed come, but not to her. A hand clutched her mouth and she let loose a long simper of painful relief, like a long lost puppy who finally finds its home. Sobbing, her body shook back and forth, while her hand covered her mouth.

Despite the impulse, Cooper wasted no time in comforting the shaking woman; he knew he had to leave, and now. The police might be ignoring speeding on the highway; he had no inclination to find out how they'd respond to a shooting in a grocery store. With Elena at home ill, he could not allow himself to be questioned or detained by the police. Without a moment's hesitation, he merely nodded gravely at the woman, pivoted firmly on his right foot and went to retrieve his son.

******

He found Jake curled up on the floor underneath one of their two shopping carts. Nervous eyes peered over his arm that he was using to cover his head. Jake's eyes flung open wide when he saw his father, blood-spattered, come wheeling around the corner. Cooper saw his son's eyes fixate immediately on the pistol that he still clutched in his right hand. He re-holstered it in response. Cooper glided swiftly to his son's side, kneeling next to him when he arrived.

By then, Jake was sobbing the deep tears of relief that his father had returned unhurt and unharmed after two shots of gunfire. Cooper rubbed his shoulder furiously, "It's alright, boy. I'm OK. Everything's OK." Cooper pulled his son's chin up so they could look each other in the eye, "See, look at me. I'm OK." Cooper smiled and did his best to put a twinkle into his eye. Jake looked back, surprised, and unsure. Cooper pulled into a brisk hug and Jake's sobbing abated. Cooper seized the opening.

"OK, son. We need to move now. We need to get out of here and fast. I need you to push the second cart and stay right behind me. OK?" Cooper pulled Jake to his feet.

Jake wiped away the tears with the sleeve of his blue flannel shirt and tried, in vain, to plant his feet firmly on the ground. His knees wobbled a bit as he said and voice was balky, "Yes...OK...Dad."

Cooper planted his son's hands firmly on the handlebar of the cart and then grabbed the other cart. He raced to the front of the store, moving at the breakneck speed that an eleven year old could keep up with. He looked back several times to make sure Jake was keeping up. His son's visage was a vision of child-turning-man determination. His face was screwed up tight, every muscle taut, as he navigated the cart through the store. Cooper knew where his son had picked up such focus.

They spirited past the other customers, having to move around some that still lay scattered in heaps on the floors, frozen in fear. Others were more difficult, the ones that had come back into action and either paused to stare at them in confused amazement, or those already intent on scouring the shelves for the items they were looking for. No one said a word to them, nor did anyone try to stop them.

Cooper would not risk waiting in line to check out, as the rows of those in line pivoted in near perfect tandem to look at him as he raced the cart up. He pulled up next to one of the checkers from an empty lane. Taking all the cash he had in his wallet out and leaned in to hand it to her, "Your co-worker is safe at the back of the store. But, someone should go help her. This should cover my groceries and then some." She stared back in dull shock and absently took his money.

As he and Jake left the store, Cooper could not believe what had just happened in a store he had shopped at for years. A store where the most tension he'd ever witnessed was the occasional embarrassed customers' reaction when their credit card was declined. *Dranko was right; the threads are fraying very quickly. And, so much for the famous friendliness of the Northwest offering us much protection from that.*

Chapter 5

Gray, dimpled sunlight reflected off the windshield of the truck as Jake and Cooper drove home in muted silence. Cooper kept looking at his son, but he only stared ahead, blankly, unblinking. Cooper thanked small miracles that his son had not seen the shooting, but he knew enough from his time in Iraq that mere proximity to an event like that was traumatic; especially to a child.

When they pulled up to their house, Cooper brought the truck to an abrupt stop, followed by a jerk on the emergency brake. Instinctively, he pulled his son close to him and hugged him. Jake welcomed his father's embrace. He could feel his father's muscular arms through his black fleece pullover. This reassured him. The potent mix of shock, relief, fear, and adrenaline overwhelmed him and he let loose with uncontrolled sobbing. Cooper rubbed his son's shoulders and whispered the best words of comfort he could offer.

The ring of his cell phone shattered their relative peace. He dug it out of his pocket, "Yeah?"

It was Dranko, "You here? I thought I heard the truck pull up?"

"Yeah, just outside. What's up?"

"You better come up, right now."

"On my way", he said, jamming the cell phone back into his pocket.

He turned back towards Jake, "I'm needed upstairs. We'll talk later. Let's go."

He pulled Jake along with him out the driver's side door. Cooper swept his hand over the truck bed full of food and other supplies as he moved to his front door. "Jake, I want you to stay at our front door and keep an eye on the truck. If anyone approaches it, I want you to shout to me upstairs and then come inside the house quickly. OK?" Jake muttered his agreement and took up his post, a child sentry with tear-stained cheeks but a set of serious eyes and firmly set mouth.

Once inside, Cooper bounded up the stairs, taking them two at a time. When he reached the top, he turned into the bedroom on his left to find both Lisa and Dranko gathered in conference, talking rapidly. He looked quickly at Elena, who still breathed fitfully, prostrate on the bed.

"What's going on?"

"We thought you should know the latest," Lisa answered for them, turning toward Cooper. "My God, what happened to you," she asked excitedly after seeing the blood spattered on his clothes.

Cooper looked surprised, having forgotten his appearance in his rush to get inside. "There was a situation at the store. I had to put a man down who was threatening to kill a clerk over the groceries."

"People *are* snapping," Dranko exhaled. Lisa shook her head in disbelief.

"I will tell you more later, but what's going on here?"

Lisa recovered, "OK. First, Elena's condition is roughly the same as when you left. Her fever is up a few tenths of a degree, which is worrisome because it's only been an hour plus."

Dranko continued, "Second, we have several more illnesses in the neighborhood and another death."

"Who?"

"Mrs. Ellingsworth, the widower on 58th. But, there's more. Just twenty minutes ago, a pickup full of rowdy teenagers roared through shouting about the end of the world and to get what you could, while you could. They threw an empty bottle against a street sign, but nothing more."

"On Hawthorne, there was a burned out Subaru. It looked like some stick-up robbery, but no one was around anymore. No bodies either."

"Damn," Dranko responded. "Everything's happening faster than even I would have guessed. We better…"

"Help!" a high-pitched yell came from Jake down below. Cooper was charging downstairs before the sound had faded. He cursed himself for failing to reload his pistol since the store. Dranko followed close on his heels. When he saw Cooper drawing his pistol on the way down the stairs, Dranko reached to the holster at the small of his back and drew his .45. "I'm on your six and I'm armed," he yelled as much as reported to Cooper as they hurried down.

Cooper reached the landing and saw his son crouched off to the side of the door. "What do we have?" he asked.

Jake's voice was firm as he pointed out the door, "Pickup, full of guys. Swarmed around ours."

Cooper leaned so that he could see outside the open door. Sure enough, they were clustered around the old, rusty GMC, he counted about six, ranging from a young blonde boy with moppy hair that couldn't have been fourteen to the presumed leader, a tall, muscular, twenty-something with long, dark hair, hanging onto his shoulder. He

44

would have passed for a Samoan if he had more bulk to him. They were hooting and hollering and starting to pass the supplies from the truck back and forth. One of the boys shouted, "Go long!" as he threw a can of peaches to his sprinting friend. The boy missed the catch, and the can splintered as it hit the ground, pouring syrup and peach halves onto the asphalt.

Cooper grimaced. He tilted his head backward towards Dranko, "Let's take it slow. I think they will leave OK. But, be ready, just in case."

With that, Cooper straightened himself up. He knew a little of dealing with a group of rowdy young men. He conjured up every inch of height and lowered his voice another octave, reflexively slipping into what his Drill Instructor had called 'your command voice.' He kept his right hand on his holstered pistol, just behind his right hip. He strode out the front door, with long, firm steps.

"Good morning, gentlemen!"

As one, a half dozen heads swiveled in his direction. Cooper noted that two of them, the ersatz Samoan and another on the older side, a blonde that stood barely five and a half feet with a red flannel shirt draped over faded blue jeans, reached their hands instinctively to the small of their back. *Armed, most likely.* Movement in the cab caught Cooper's eye as well. For the first time, he noticed someone moving on the driver's side. There was no mistaking the long, thin silhouette of a rifle barrel being raised just over the door's window. *Damn.* He knew Dranko had taken this in too as he heard him flank out to his left as Cooper continued walking forward. *Dranko's moving out to give our opponents the widest possible gap between them and to split their angles of fire.*

"I said, good morning."

Their leader moved forward. His apparent lieutenant, the other armed teen, moved lockstep with him, staying a half step behind the leader, but clustered almost on top of his right hip.

The leader responded, cocksure, "It *is* a good morning, isn't it? If you ain't coughing yourself to death, that is." His minions chortled a variety of ragged laughter, from high pitched yelps to low, deep throated, growls.

"You have it right there. We're all very lucky to be healthy today. I do have to ask you to move along to find your fun somewhere else. You are messing with the supplies I have to cook my wife her last supper." Cooper was hoping an appeal to their sympathy might defuse the flush of testosterone he knew was running most of their show right now.

The black-haired leader didn't miss a beat, "Last supper, eh? She must be one fat bitch with all *this* food." This elicited another round of laughter from his minions.

Cooper snarled inside, but retained a comforting smile on the outside. *OK, you want to dig me to impress your new-found followers?*

Cooper forced himself to smile even wider, "Well, she does like to eat, I can't deny that." Now, his smile disappeared, he hardened his face and took another, deliberate step forward, "But, be that as it may, you need to move along. You don't want *our* trouble this morning."

Cooper saw the leader's eyes cloud up with fear. He recalled one of his father's sage words of negotiation advice, gained from years steeped in the harsh conflict between workers and management that was his father's life: *always allow the other guy a way to give you what you want, while saving face in front of his team.* After a pregnant pause, to allow his words to sink in deep, and spread the fear in their bowels, he continued, "I *know* you boys want to enjoy the rest of the fun this day has to offer without the trouble of having to beat down an old man like me."

Unsure, the leader stumbled, "We do. We do." Then, his face turned from slack fear to hardened anger, "And, we will. But, we are going to enjoy it even more with your pickup and what's in it." His right arm tensed up and moved rearward another half inch.

"I wouldn't do that," Cooper barked and deliberately smeared the blood on his shirt with his left hand, "I had to kill one man already this morning, I don't want to have to kill another!"

The man's hand stopped momentarily in indecision, caught between fear and anger. Anger won, "Well, the hell with you," he shouted as he began to draw his weapon.

Cooper moved lightning quick. His left arm pointed sharply across the street, motioning behind the boys, "Frank, shoot him!" His words had the desired effect, his opponent's head swung to his rear, looking for the made-up Frank.

That second was all that Cooper needed. In near unison, Cooper and Dranko drew their pistols and trained them on their opponents. By the time the leader's head turned back toward Cooper, he was staring down the barrel of a pistol.
"Drop it, now!"

Caught flat-footed, he complied, somewhat in shock.

"Now, tell Blondie to slowly put his on the ground. And, tell the one in the pickup to slowly pitch the rifle out the passenger side window. Or, your friends will get to see what a round of .357 will do to a young man's head."

The teen leader grimaced, "Rick, do as he says." Raising his voice, "Smartie, do as he says. Do it slow!"

The blonde lifted a snub-nose revolver out from behind his waist-band, slowly, with two tentative fingers holding the grip. He pitched it a few feet in front of Cooper and it landed in a pile of damp, brown leaves. From the side of his vision, he saw the rifle emerge from the pickup's cab. The walnut stocked, lever action was then flung into the hydrangea bush that bordered Cooper's yard.

"OK, good. We are going to keep these because you owe me for a can of peaches. My wife *really* likes peaches. But, because I'm a nice guy, we are going to let you keep your pickup and drive off. You can go enjoy the rest of the day."

Dismissed, the leader began to turn around and the teens began to move back toward the pickup.

Cooper's words brought them to a dead halt, "Oh, and one more thing. If we see any of you on this street again, you will not receive a 'good morning' as a greeting. You will receive a bullet. Right between the eyes. No warning, no second chances. Got it?"

The leader nodded and gave him a half, angry upturned smile in response. Cooper saw something dark and angry behind those eyes. *This guy likes angry.* He clambered into the cab through the passenger door, slammed it with loud *clunk*, and barked at the driver, "Move it, dumbass!" Their white pickup roared all eight cylinders, squealed rubber, as they raced down the hill.

Dranko came to his side, "Good work, brother. I thought we were gonna have to let the lead fly. How'd you think that old 'man behind you' trick would work, anyway?"

"Simple. Three things. They were young. Afraid. And, on our turf. With all that, the power of suggestion can be very, ah, *persuasive.*" Cooper smiled sardonically.

Dranko smiled, "And how, pray tell, did you come up with Frank?"

As Cooper turned to humor to unload the stress they had just gone through, forced mirth filled his voice, "Easy. Guys this young, the name 'Frank' makes them think of their uncle or their grandfather. That adds a bit more fear and a dollop of credibility to the ruse."

Dranko let loose a loud bellow of laughter, "Cooper, damn you're good. It's no wonder I can never win a dollar from you in our poker games!"

"I'm glad you agree with my mother that I'm wonderful. Now, let's police these weapons and get these supplies inside. As he turned his attention back toward the pickup, he noticed a dozen or so neighbors emerging from their doorways, having watched the confrontation play out, and coming out now that danger had passed. He noticed that Hank Hutchison did indeed have an ancient, half-rusty double-barreled shotgun clutched in his hands.

Cooper raised his voice so everyone could hear him, "Everything's OK. Everything's alright. Take care of yourselves, but keep a sharp eye out. If you have a gun, keep it handy. We don't know what else might come down our road here."

Not eager to come together, the neighbors nodded various agreements and turned back to their homes.

Cooper picked the revolver, a .38 special, the kind that police detectives routinely carried thirty years ago before the compact automatics made by Glock and others came to dominate. It was in good condition, with only some surface rust in a few spots. Cooper guessed that the boy had fished it out of his father's closet or dresser drawer. Dranko picked up the rifle and gave it a cursory examination, "Cooper, this is a nice 30-30 Marlin lever action." The rifle's steel looked brand new and its deep brown walnut stock bore only a few nicks. Cooper bent down and brushed a few leaves off of the pistol. It was a 9mm Glock, also in very good condition.

Cooper turned to go back inside, and saw Jake clustered in the doorway, one knee bent, and holding onto the door. Cooper gave him a wide smile, "Things are OK now, son. You did well by warning us. Next time, though, I need you to tell me as soon as you see anything fishy, OK?"

Jake looked up, eyes full of concern, "Yeah, I know I waited a few seconds too long."

Cooper nodded, patted his son on the head, and got to work.

******

Less than twenty minutes later, they had unloaded the supplies into Cooper's kitchen and basement. They enlisted Hank Hutchison from across the street to stand post with his shotgun, while they hustled the provisions inside. Cooper grimaced each time a car or pedestrian passed by. He knew it wasn't good to have others know that he had some stockpiled food and supplies in his home. However, the alternative — to wait until nightfall — did not strike him as a better option. Fortunately, only a handful of cars passed by and only two pedestrians. On a normal day, the traffic would have been five times as heavy.

When they were finished, Cooper tossed Hutchison the recently acquired .38 revolver. His eyes lit up with surprise, but he adeptly caught it in his right hand.

"Thanks neighbor. I saw how you were eyeing the thing. You used to be on the force, right?"

"Retired, after forty-two years. I used to carry one just like it. Some street punk lifted it about twenty years ago. Hell, I probably have a few boxes of shells for it some where's."

"Well, it's yours. Thanks for your help."

"Anytime, neighbor." Inspecting the revolver, he ambled back across the street, shuffling his feet the way old men do when the thought of a fall and broken bones scares them as bad as a Friday night without a woman did when they were younger.

Good man. Solid. Seen action, too. Maybe long ago, but your body never forgets.

Turning back towards Dranko, "We need to remember, he's been on the business end of bad guys in the past." Dranko merely grunted in affirmation.

******

The night passed in fits. Cooper stood watch over both Elena, still feverish and restless in her bed, and Jake, who was sprawled at the foot of his mother's bed, collapsed in exhaustion. Cooper watched, tormented, as his son's sleep became fitful, limbs thrashing, and his voice whimpering. Cooper could only guess at the nightmares gripping his son. He reached out to comfort him, but bit down sharply on his lip to prevent himself from waking him. He knew from his own hard won experience that sleep, even when punctuated by terror, was better than no sleep at all.

He patted his wife's brow with a damp rag, a fool's errand to quench the sticky hot fire burning within. He helped her sip water whenever he could rouse her to do so. Her lips were now dry, raw and chapped, sure signs of dehydration. Her face looked like a desert, barren. Almost lifeless. She hadn't eaten and it was impossible to get enough water into her. Lisa had promised to return in the morning and get her onto an IV.

Cooper slept off and on, in ten or twenty minute snatches. Casting a long, dark sinister shadow, his black synthetic-stocked Remington 12-gauge shotgun lay propped against the wall, within arm's length. He had gathered it, and a box of shells, from his gun safe. After today's events, Cooper was taking no chances. *I'm glad I have the home defense model with the extra two-shell capacity.* He had loaded it with 00 Buckshot; each shell holding nine large pellets that would devastate anyone they hit. He remembered reading how getting hit with a shell of Buckshot was like getting shot with nine rounds from a submachine gun. His pistol remained on his hip, holstered.

******

In the early morning, while it was still dark out, after inserting the IV attached to a bag of saline solution, Lisa pulled him aside. She looked like death warmed over, hair ragged and oily, face streaked with worry lines, and dark shadows firmly set beneath her eyes. He knew she'd barely rested since this had all started. Even so, she had enough compassion left to remember to put her hand on his shoulder as she whispered.

"Prepare yourself." Her words hit him like a two by four across the temple. In disbelief, he craned his neck to look her in the eye. "Get ready, Cooper. I've seen enough of this thing by now. People either recover quickly, within no more than forty-eight hours, or..." She paused, the fatigue and emotion getting the best of her and tears welling up.

"Or, what?" he demanded, his face tightening.

"They don't." She wiped her eyes, each in turn, with her left hand. "I'm sorry," she muttered as she escaped the room.

Anger flashed hard across his face. He crashed his balled up fists into his legs with a furious and stifled "No!" He did not want to wake Jake, who still slept soundly just a few feet away. *Damn this! This isn't supposed to be happening! She can't die. She's the best one at raising our boy. I can't do it alone.* For the next half hour Cooper paced the room in frantic circles. Praying for God's help and cursing Him for allowing this to be happening in the first place.

He kept a sharp watch on his wife and his son. The contrast could not have been more startling. On the bed lay his wife, barely moving now. Her breath came in labored, shallow heaves that required far more effort than they seemed to yield in benefit. Her color was

50

draining away fast. Elena had always had such a firm, warm glow to her skin. Now, it seemed to waver before his eyes, emitting a weak sallow cast. This morning was the first time he *smelled* it too. The odor was a mix of three day old sweat, phlegm, and bits of stale food. It did not assault or offend Cooper; it merely was a dull reminder that something was very wrong in his world. And, it was something he could do *nothing* about. As he sat watching, his mind drifted to another time when his efforts had been useless in staying the hand of Fate.

******

Cooper ambled into the prison visitation room, like he had done so many times before. The cold from the concrete floor seeped into his body, despite the double layer of wool socks he had donned that morning. His body shook for a moment from the chill. As he slumped into the plastic chair, he looked up to see his father on the opposite side of the glass partition. The visage that greeted him was shocking.

It had only been three months since he last visited his father. From the way he looked, it may well have been a decade. He had watched in grim worry over the last three years how his father had aged since being sent to prison. What he saw today was vastly different. It was decay.

His father's eyes wore puffed, dark circles underneath. The sparkle had left them. Worse, they drooped. Stark white stubble had overtaken what had been an ongoing war between salt and pepper on his face. His face was stretched thin, gaunt. His shoulders humped forward, a demoralizing contrast to his always-proud posture of confidence.

Trance-like his father's arm loped to the phone on the side of the dim gray wall and wrenched the receiver from its cradle. He lazily brought it to his ear. Cooper retrieved the phone that lay on his side of the glass and cement cubicle.

"Morning, son," his father mumbled. The voice didn't belong to his father. It was weak, gruff, and hard to understand. His father's had been a booming baritone that was clear and resounding. His father's voice was one that people would sit up and listen to when he spoke; even those who disagreed with his words.

"Good morning, Papa. How are you?" As soon as the words left his mouth, Cooper regretted them. He felt as if he'd just asked a man who lay sick in a hospital bed how his health was doing.

A corner of his father's mouth cocked upward and bloodshot eyes rose from looking down and stared deep into his son's eyes, "I'm beat, son. Pure and simple. They got me." Tears piled down his father's face.

Hearing his father say words that confirmed his appearance was too much. The emotion he had held back since seeing his battered father sprung forth. His eyes overflowed and he tried to wipe them away with the sleeve of his cotton twill shirt. He couldn't look at his father.

"Look up at me, boy," his father commanded. Cooper wiped his sleeve furtively across his brow and meekly looked up.

"You're gonna have to be a man now, you hear me? I won't last in this forsaken place until I can see you again."

"No, Papa! It can't be!" Cooper shouted shrilly into the phone, his eyes pleading with his father.

His father looked down for a moment and then back up, "I wish it wasn't true, but I won't lie to you, son. My spirit is broken and my body nearly so."

Cooper moaned miserably as his father continued, "I hope I taught you a bit about what it means to be a man. Did I?" Cooper nodded slowly, straightening up.

"Good, that makes me feel a little better. You're going to have to be strong for your mother, OK? I won't worry about her knowing you'll take care of her, alright?"

Cooper never could recall the rest of the conversation. His father died a week later and the grief overwhelmed the memory. The doctor said his father's 'heart gave out.' Cooper knew that wasn't true. It'd been smashed to bits by deceit that had led to the suffocating prison's walls.

That day had always been the most helpless of Cooper's life. Today was the first time he'd ever felt more so.

Chapter 6

Jake lay soundly asleep in a pile of brown and red wool blankets at the foot of his mother's bed. His face was peaceful. His breath was measured and assured. His skin glowed golden. He had inherited the stronger hue of his mother's Mexican and Gypsy ancestors. He lay curled up into a ball, his small arms cradling his head. Black curls framed his face, red lips puffing slightly as he breathed in and out.

Elena offered a picture of a devastating illness, while he gave a portrait of vitality and health. The contradiction overwhelmed Cooper. He needed refuge from the stark reminder of his wife fading away.

He stepped lightly downstairs and turned on the television.

"...fourteen dead in the small town of Independence. Doctors there report similar symptoms and outcomes as we have heard from other locations. After these messages, we will have reports for the Portland Metro region and give you the latest updates on the Brushfire Plague."

He tuned out the commercials, except to find one so morbid it was impossible to ignore, an ad running for a cruise line vacation to the Mexican Riviera. His thoughts ran bitter, *even in the midst of a national crisis, Madison Avenue is still trying to separate us from our wallets? I wonder what pharmaceutical company will buy the naming rights to 'Brushfire Plague'?*

"Thank you for turning to KGW for all of your information needs at this critical time. Despite our own staffing shortages due to the illness, we remain Portland's Number One News Source. Now, I would like to welcome, Dr. Martin Long, Chief Public Health Officer with the Multnomah County Health Department. Welcome, Dr. Long."

"Yes, thank you. I should correct you, though. I'm the Deputy Assistant Public Health Officer. Both the Chief and the Deputy Chief are currently unavailable." Dr. Martin Long looked like a no nonsense type. He wore his hair close cropped. It was black with substantial streaks of gray. His thin lips were set into a firm face that looked like it had been carved from granite with a sharp chisel.

"Pardon me, Doctor. My notes had not been updated. My assistant is, ah, out of work." *You mean sick or dead, don't you, Mr. Newscaster*, Cooper opined darkly.

Dr. Long nodded sympathetically toward the newscaster, who

continued, "But, let's get right to it. Our viewers, I am sure, want the latest update on the Brushfire Plague. What do we know and what can people do to protect themselves?"

"Sure. The truth is that we do not know enough. The illness is moving with such speed that we have simply lacked ample time to conduct the rigorous tests and evaluations that we normally conduct…"

"Yes, yes, Doctor," the newscaster interrupted, "We understand all *that*. Just tell us what we do know or at least give us your best guess."

"Yes, sure thing. Here are the facts that we are aware of. So far, there have been just over twenty thousand deaths in the Portland Metr…."

"Twenty thousand?" the newscaster gasped. *There goes journalistic calm.* "Just last night the report was of only a few thousand!"

Dr. Long barely could hide his irritation at the newsman's lack of composure. Dr. Long was on the air to put oil on the waters and calm things. "Yes, twenty thousand. While that is indeed a tragically high number, I want to remind your viewers that we have over two million people living in this region so, the numbers are less than one percent of the population."

The newscaster slumped in his chair. "Yes, go on please Doctor."

"We also know that there are at least tens of thousands, perhaps more than a few hundred thousand, additional people infected by this virus in the Portland area. The virus still appears to be spreading very quickly and the morbidity rate is alarming indeed." Cooper read between the lines. *They either don't know or aren't sharing the number of infected and the likelihood of death if you get it.*

With each word, the anchorman's face fell further. *He must be sleep deprived like everyone else. Or, maybe he's just feeling the weight of the entire city's crisis since he has to report it all.* "In sum, the situation is grim and likely getting worse. I get it. Why don't we turn to what people can do to protect themselves," he responded tersely.

"Of course. First, we are fortunate here in Oregon. We have one of the nation's leading biotech companies, Admonitus, right here in Portland. CEO Ethan Mitchell has been working closely with our department in getting to the bottom of this plague and a possible cure. Second, we are recommending that people avoid contact with anyone who has the illness. We recommend that all public places be avoided.

Who hasn't been exposed by now? Such nonsensical advice. Normal masks are mostly useless against viruses anyway. "In fact, the Mayor has signed a Special City Ordinance outlawing all public gatherings. This is especially important to those who have, thus far, avoided exposure to anyone who is ill. The National Guard has already been mobilized, so food and water distribution will be done in a manner consistent with the order to avoid public gatherings. As always, good hygiene is our best defense against spreading the disease. So, please continue washing your hands with warm soapy water."

Cooper clicked the TV off. He could guess the rest. *The Government is already working on a vaccine. Stay calm. Take care of those who are ill, but protect yourself.*

The spate of viruses over the last ten years had already told him everything he needed to know about this one. Except this one was worse. Much worse.

He returned upstairs to resume his vigil, growing restless and impatient at his own impotence.

******

He awoke with a start; surprised he'd fallen asleep. The sharp *click* of the front door's old metal hardware sounded again as someone fumbled with the lock. The room was awash in the growing light of morning. *Must be just after sunrise.* The rush of adrenaline sent a surge throughout his body as he came to instant alertness. *Better than coffee.* He was up, across the room, and standing hard against the door frame, shotgun at the ready, and with a clear view of the landing downstairs. A few feet beyond his view, lay the front door. The door creaked open, allowing a wave of morning light to wash into his home and push the shadows further back.

"It's me, Dranko. You guys up," he called into the house, before entering.

Cooper relaxed, the gruff voice of his friend was unmistakable and remembering he'd given him a key. He replaced the shotgun against the wall, exhaled, and called down, his voice muted, "Yeah, up here. Jake's still asleep.

Moments later, Dranko came into view, holding two cups of steaming coffee. The aroma now hit Cooper and already he could feel the rush of caffeine in his veins.

"I've got coffee and news. What do you want first?"

After a quick look to make sure Elena's IV was still in place and that Jake still slept, Cooper began descending the stairs. "You know me, business first. I'll take the news."

They sat down at the dark-stained oak table, Cooper at the head and Dranko to his right. Cooper looked blankly down at the table, absently tracing a uniquely shaped grain with his forefinger, "Lisa says it doesn't look good for Elena. That if she hasn't recovered by now, that she won't."

Dranko looked gravely at his friend, his eyebrows knotted up in sympathy, "Damn. I'm sorry brother." He slid the mug of coffee across the table, into his friend's hand.

"You hear anything different? You hear about anyone recovering after being down more than forty-eight hours?" His voice was tentative and expectant, like a boy asking for a favor a father couldn't grant. His eyes remained transfixed on the table.

Dranko shook his head, "I wish I had. But, no. This thing burns out quick, one way or the other." He hesitated and then continued, searching Cooper's eyes, "Most times, it is the other," he said gingerly.

"Yeah, I know," Cooper said heavily.

Silence lingered for a moment. Cooper took a deep breath, brought himself erect, brushed a tear from his left eye, and met Dranko's gaze. "Alright. I got things I have to do. I've got to keep Elena comfortable and I've got to protect my boy, Jake."

Dranko nodded in return, "You're right about that. I got you. Anything you need, just say the word."

"Thanks. So, what news do you have?"

"Not much you don't know if you've turned on the TV for even a minute. This thing is bad and getting worse by the hour. What you won't get off the tube is *how* bad it is. The entire healthcare system is overwhelmed, everywhere. Not just here, in America. Everywhere. This thing went global, almost overnight. Now, the funeral homes are overflowing, almost nonfunctional."

"The funeral homes? Already? Are you kidding me?"

"No, I'm not. The TV news is actually grossly understating the numbers of dead."

"Really?" Cooper asked incredulously.

"Yes. Really. But, the worst is that the chaos is growing. What happened yesterday with those teenagers, even what you dealt with at the grocery store were small potatoes. There are full blown riots happening in some cities, usually sparked anyplace there is food or medical care."

"So quick?"

"This is a potent mix. We've never seen something like this. It's moving so fast and killing so many, people are ripe for panic. I don't think the cities are safe."

"What cities are rioting? Are they big or small?"

"So far, it's just been the big boys. New York. Chicago. LA. Oh, LA is bad. Yesterday, a crowd dragged a doctor from his car and beat him to death. The word is the doctor had been working forty-seven hours straight, but was trying to get home when word came in his wife was getting sick. Unfortunately, he didn't take his white coat and tie off before going to the hospital parking lot. You can guess the rest."

"Where else?" Cooper commanded.

"Miami. Dallas. Detroit. And, the Bay Area. Yeah, that's all of the ones I've heard about."

"Well, the good news is that it's only the bigger cities."

Dranko rolled his eyes in exasperation and grabbed his friend's arm, "Yeah, for now. For *now,* brother. I'm telling you, the cities aren't safe. This is why I came to see you. I think we should get out of here. I've got a place up near Mt. Hood. A small cabin, but I could fit you guys. It's well stocked. Could hold us for months."

"Leave? When?"

"I could be ready to go in an hour."

"Elena can't travel."

"Elena is…"

Cooper pushed his friend's hand away, held up his finger, his voice clipped and his eyes burning sharp, "Don't you say it. Don't you dare."

Dranko bowed his head and shook it, "Yeah, OK. I got it. Just think about it is all I'm saying." He brought his head back up, "We should do one thing this morning. We should go together to gas up our cars. I think the stations will be empty soon. That's already happened in the cities where panic has set in. Whether you come with me or not, a full tank of gas will serve you well."

Cooper nodded, "Yeah, OK. That makes sense. But, we'll need to be quick. I don't want to be gone for long. He checked his watch, "Lisa should be back in a few minutes, to check the IV. I can see if she can look after Jake for a few."

Dranko straightened up to leave, "Alright. I'll be ready to go. Just honk when you're out front. We can go to the Union Station on 39th."

******

He pulled up alongside the curb, the hundred-year-old cement chipped off in numerous places along the curb in front of Dranko's house. His house was just a few doors down from his own, on the same side of 58th. He pumped the deep-throated GMC horn a few times and then waited for Dranko. To reassure himself, he fingered his holstered pistol and confirmed that he had the two magazine holder clipped to the opposite side of his body on his belt. His shotgun lay on the seat next to him, still fully loaded with 00 Buckshot. Movement caught his eye and he looked up.

Instead of Dranko coming to join him from several houses further up the street, he saw old Mrs. Ferguson exit her front door and begin walking about her yard. She wore a loosely buttoned housecoat, its flap catching the breeze. Her thin, stork-like legs were bare. Only her left foot was ensconced in a fuzzy yellow slipper. Her right foot tramped about in the wet grass of her finely manicured lawn. Transfixed, Cooper kept watching her. She ambled about, going from one clump of flowers to another, bending down, and then walking to the next. Cooper noticed she was moving in a wide-arced circle about her yard, aimless.

Watching her, his face revealed a deep furrow of concern by the time Dranko's house door banged wood on wood and he emerged. He'd always hated Dranko's screen door. It would often disturb a peaceful summer night or a deep thought with its loud clanging and clatter. Dranko clambered down his driveway, and leaned his head into the cab.

"You ready?"

"Sure thing. But take a look down the way. I think Mrs. Ferguson is in trouble. Something ain't right." Dranko pivoted his head and gave her a quick once over for a few seconds.

"Yeah, you're right. Why don't you pull up, I'll be right behind you in the Jeep." He turned back toward his driveway and the parked brown, battered, Jeep Wagoneer that Dranko somehow kept running. It's formerly metallic paint was now chipped, almost beyond recognition. Oxidization had further taken its toll. Instead of a shiny metallic hue, the Jeep was coated in a mottled splotch of varying shades of brown. Watching Dranko clamber in, Cooper remembered that the Jeep still had an *operable* 8-track player. Dranko had only one tape left, a well-worn copy of KC and the Sunshine Band. Whenever they went somewhere in it, Dranko would lament the age of the tape and how he had to take care of it, allowing himself only one song per trip.

Cooper put his truck back into gear and moved up the street toward Mrs. Ferguson. She did not look up nor break her stride as he pulled up. He got out of his truck and walked in front of his truck towards her.

"Good morning, Mrs. Ferguson," he called out.

Startled, she stopped suddenly in her tracks, and almost fell over. He quickly stepped in to catch her and stabilized her. "You alright? It's a little chilly to be out dressed like you are."

"I'm fine. I'm fine. Harry. Harry just needs some flowers right now." Cooper caught how her voice caught on her husband's name.

"Is Harry alright?"

"He's fine. He's fine. He just needs some flowers. That's all." She resumed her haphazard stumbling around the yard.

Dranko had pulled up and was leaning out his window. Cooper continued, "Mrs. Ferguson, is it alright if Paul goes and checks on Harry for you?"

"Sure, sure. But, I told you, he just needs some flowers."

Cooper nodded to Dranko, who exited the Jeep and entered the Ferguson's home. It was an English cottage style home, much like Cooper's, except it had a little more Tudor thrown in for good measure. The dark gray paint was accented with white trim. The Ferguson's home was compact and sat squarely on its finely landscaped yard. A scattering of white, blue, and red tulips lay in various clumps. The other flower beds were dormant, waiting for the planting of an annual or the sprouting of a perennial. Cooper watched Mrs. Ferguson ramble about in silence, waiting for Dranko to come and tell him what he already knew.

Moments later, Dranko came out. He shook his head quickly at Cooper and then raised his voice for Mrs. Ferguson's benefit, "You were right, Harry's fine. Just waiting for some flowers. Why don't you bring him the red ones?" He motioned with his left hand to a clutch of red tulips.

She snapped out of her frantic trance, "Ah, that's a nice boy, Paul. Always full of good ideas." She bent over and pulled the tulips from the ground, using her bare foot to provide leverage. Muttering under her breath, but smiling widely, she went back inside her door.

Cooper and Dranko moved toward the truck. Cooper said what was on both their minds, "I suspect we'll see more of this. Shock. On a mass scale. Anyone with the faintest hint of a feeble or weak mind may just well slide over into shock, or worse."

"Yeah. Harry looks like he's been dead through the night. The sunrise must have put her on this mission of finding flowers for him."

"We'll need to come back later and check on her, and hopefully be able to take care of the body. But, first, she will have to accept that he's passed on."

Chapter 7

Cooper jostled as he drove down the road in the pickup. *Those shocks needed to be replaced 50,000 miles ago.* He could make out Dranko in his rearview mirror. Deep furrows around his eyebrows, firm, thin-set lips, and a tight grip on the steering wheel, both hands. *He's nervous about this run to the gas station.* Of course, Dranko was nervous and careful about most things. *He did tell me to come 'strapped, heavy'.* From someone like Dranko, that spoke volumes.

Cooper saw a light blue Honda Civic approaching from the opposite direction. The Civic lurched suddenly to the right, to the far lane and further away from Cooper's GMC. As the two cars passed one another, Cooper could see the driver and into the front seat of the Civic. The driver was a woman, likely in her twenties, a blonde with her hair yanked back into a hasty ponytail. She wore a tight-fitting black athletic top. Her window was down and the cold air blowing in likely made her regret not wearing a coat. Her face was hard, lips curled up into a snarl, and eyes squinted nearly shut. As she passed, he saw the barrel of a shotgun poke just above the rolled down window, covering him as she passed. From the receiving end, the barrel looked enormous, like the bore of a twelve pounder he'd seen as a child on the *USS Constitution* in Boston. *Well, ain't that the shit.* The incongruity of an otherwise attractive blonde in a Honda Civic rolling down Division Street with a shotgun trained on him was startling. It wasn't until several seconds later that he realized he had reflexively grabbed his pistol with his right hand, where it still stood, ready for action. He smiled to himself, chuckled, and re-holstered it.

Up ahead, he saw the line. At least fifteen cars were queued up in front of the Union 76 station. Immediately in front of him was a convertible, black Porsche, top down. *In this weather? Are you still showing off with everything that is going on?* A middle-aged man with salt and pepper hair, and wearing a high-tech North Face jacket was behind the wheel. Immediately, Cooper saw the large, shiny Heckler and Koch stainless steel pistol lying boldly in the passenger seat. *Guy likes German, I guess.* Beyond the Porsche was an orange van, full size, paint peeling, and rust getting the better half of the wheel wells. He could only see one arm of the van's driver, perched firmly on the door sill, meaty and hairy. Cooper glanced up, into the rearview.

Having parked and run up, Dranko was already at his side.

"Did you see the girl's scattergun in the Civic?"

"Course. Porsche-guy has a pistol in the passenger seat. I guess Sunday drive has taken on a whole new meaning, huh?"

"Yeah, I'll say," Dranko responded.

"Makes sense. With this plague running around, no one wants anyone getting too close."

"Except for those of us who don't believe in the tooth fairy and understand we've probably *already* been exposed," Dranko responded.

Cooper nodded in response, lips pursed in agreement.

"Well, let's get ready to wait. Give me a honk if you need anything." Dranko ran back to his Jeep. Two cars had finished at the pumps and pulled away. Slowly, like a continuously dissected snake, the cars moved forward, separated, and then rejoined.

As time passed, Cooper noticed the man in the Porsche continuously glancing at his watch and growing increasingly agitated. Thirty minutes into their wait, they'd only made it halfway to the pumps. The man in the Porsche began beating furiously on his steering wheel and shouting obscenities into the wind. *I'll need to keep an eye on him.* After he spent his rage, he settled back into a pensive wait, tapping his fingers and looking about anxiously. He also closed the convertible top, so Cooper lost sight of him. *Maybe he'll warm up and get his brain working again.*

Finally, after another half-hour, they approached the pumps. The van pulled up, with the Porsche close behind. The station was down to one pump, the other having already run dry.

An overweight young man wearing faded blue jeans and a green University of Oregon sweatshirt, a pimply face and greasy black hair, emerged from the van and began filling it. He was unshaven and absently munched on a half-full bag of Cheetos. He shuffled his red Converse-clad feet to the time of a song playing on his iPod.

Moments later, the gas pump emitted a loud *shnick* as the pump automatically shut off. The man must have heard it too, despite the iPod, and raised his eyebrows in surprise. He walked over to the pump and tried re-engaging the handle to no avail. He tried it again. He began looking more confused and then replaced the handle onto the pump and then tried swiping his credit card again. He had barely taken the handle back in hand when the door on the Porsche flew open wildly, banging loudly against its hinges. The driver sprang out of his car, his face contorted.

"Hold on, just a minute. What the hell do you think you're doing," he shouted at the man at the pump.

He moved back toward his van and reinserted the nozzle back into the gas tank, "Just trying it out again. It stopped way too early. I'm not full."

The Porsche man gesticulated in wide arcs, which is when Cooper noticed the pistol imprinting on his shirt, near the small of his back. *Uh-oh.* "No, you don't. No you don't. Today, my friend, you get one turn at the pump. One turn. Don't you see this long line? One turn!"

The overweight man continued fiddling with the pump's handle as he considered the man's words, staring back.

"Didn't you hear me, you fat fuck? Move on, right now! I've got a sick wife at home I have to get to." Mr. Porsche was screaming now, veins bulging red on his neck and spittle flying from his mouth.

Cooper silently opened the door of his pickup and slid off the seat. His feet ghosted silently onto the pavement. He kept the door between him and the other men. His right hand held his pistol, low and at the ready, but out of sight. With his left, he motioned Dranko to the opposite side of the pickup.

The overweight man took a step back and put his hands up in a calming, open-palmed gesture. "Alright dude, just calm down. Calm down. I'll move along. I think this pump is dry anyway."

Mr. Porsche exploded, "Empty? Dry? Are you kidding me? You goddamned bastard! You used all the gas. I need some gas. You hogged it all with your huge van just like you hog food with your huge fat ass! People like you don't deserve to walk around hogging everything for yourself." He took another step towards the overweight man and reached for his pistol.

The overweight man's mouth went wide, gaping in surprise. His hands flew up into the universal sign of surrender. The empty bag of Cheeto's fluttered downward in a lazy spiral. In a flash, Cooper braced his pistol onto the door frame of his pickup and shouted, "Freeze, don't!" He trained his pistol onto the center of the man's back. From his periphery, he saw Dranko on the opposite side of the pickup, his own weapon deployed into action.

Mr. Porsche kept moving without a flinch of hesitation. His own pistol was drawn and was rapidly being brought to bear on his intended victim. The other man's jean's suddenly turned dark near his groin, his bladder having let go in reaction to the shock of fear hitting his body.

Just as the man's pistol came around, Cooper fired twice in

rapid succession. Dranko must have as well because Mr. Porsche was simultaneously flung forward and then pushed to his left from the impact of multiple rounds. The overweight man was splattered in blood, an impromptu Rorschach of crimson covering the Oregon Duck's yellow logo on his sweatshirt. Mr. Porsche's shiny steel pistol clattered to the ground and he fell forward, grabbing the overweight man by the shoulders. The two men looked at one another in a shocked gaze. Then, Mr. Porsche slid to the ground into a deflated heap.

The man's sweatshirt was quickly soaked in blood. He began trembling and shaking. Cooper yelled, "Cover me," to Dranko and moved around the truck's door, his weapon still pointed at the apparently dead man. The impact of the bullets had lifted him out of his leather penny loafers and Cooper inadvertently stepped on one as he advanced. He used his foot to pitch the would-be attacker's body over. The overweight man bent over and vomited, spewing bits of bright orange Cheetos all over the ground.

The body let out one long raspy breath. Mr. Porsche's eyes gazed blankly skyward. His chest and right side were a red ruin. Dranko's shots had caught him just in front of the shoulder blade.

Cooper lowered his pistol and Dranko stepped out from behind the hood of the pickup. The overweight man collapsed into a haphazard seated position on the ground.

Cooper put a hand on his shoulder, "Breathe easy. Take a deep breath. You're gonna be OK."

As the tension drained away, Dranko leaned over, resting his hands on his knees and forced a laugh, "Man, can't I catch a break?"

"Whad'ya mean?"

"Why couldn't the punk have snapped *before* we had wasted an hour in line," Dranko responded.

"You are an incurable pessimist with a capital P."

"I stand accused, but it's just the reality-based way to look at things."

"Really? I see that we saved someone's life. You see that we wasted an hour of our day."

Dranko smiled back, "You knew before you married me that I was a half-empty kind of guy."

In their banter, they barely noticed the squealing of tires as the other cars in line made a swift escape from the area. The overweight man sat immobilized, staring stupidly at them, moving his eyes from one to the other as they spoke.

"True, I did know that. But, you promised me you'd *change*,"

Cooper emphasized the last word with falsetto.

Dranko laughed deeply, from his belly, out of breath, "OK, you win. This time."

An older man with an uncombed raft of white hair came running out of the gas station's mini-store. He wore a dark blue smock and stained khakis, "I called 9-1-1. All I get is biz-zee. Five times, I call. Nah-ting." He spoke in a thick Russian accent.

"Don't worry about it. The cops' hands are full today. Go back and keep calling, eventually you'll get through." Without another word, the old man turned back sharply, almost clicking his heels in obedience, and then ran inside.

Looking down at his bloody sweatshirt and wiping the blood and vomit from his face, the overweight man finally spoke, "I just wanted some gas. I didn't want anyone to *die*."

Cooper kept his hand firmly planted on his shoulder. "What's your name, son?"

"Curt."

"Curt, this wasn't your fault. This guy just lost it. Don't twist your mind out of joint over it."

Curt nodded his head, eyes downcast, "Yeah, I guess you're right," although he didn't sound convinced. He raised his head to look at Cooper and Dranko, "Thank you by the way. You guys saved my ass, for sure."

"No problem. Just do me one favor, will you?"

"Sure, anything."

"Go get yourself some water from inside. Drink it down and don't drive anywhere until you've settled down. Here's my address if the cops show up and you need a witness to what happened." He'd pulled a pen from his pocket and scribbled it onto a paper towel.

Curt tipped his fingers from his forehead, "Got it. Thanks again. I know where you live. When things settle down, I'll bring you something to show my appreciation."

"Don't worry about it. If the situation was reversed, you would have done the same." He didn't tell him what was so abundantly clear. *It's going to be a long while before things settle down.*

******

The next gas station they drove to had a shorter line, and they were both able to top off their tanks without incident and get home forty minutes later.

As soon as Cooper stepped into his house, he smelled it. Things had become much worse since he'd left. He leapt up the stairs, taking three at a time. He spilled into the room to find Lisa asleep in the chair next to the bed and Jake perched at the foot of the bed peering intently at his mother. Cooper leaned the shotgun against the wall. Despite his loud entrance, Lisa remained asleep, snoring lightly. *She must be dead on her feet with what she's been doing the last few days.*

Cooper stood next to his son and patted him on the head lightly. He raised his eyes to look at his wife, afraid of what he might see. The bed was soaked in her sweat. She seemed much smaller than before. In the large bed, she thrashed about in delirium, like a boat tossed around by a furious storm at sea. Occasionally, she would say a few words and then devolve into unintelligible mumbling. Each time, Jake would give a start, hopeful of some word from his mother. Cooper moved his hands to son's shoulders and offered a firm grip as comfort. They watched her like this as the hours of the day passed by.

At some point, Lisa awoke and attempted to give Cooper a medical diagnosis. He didn't listen. He already knew. Lisa wandered off to attend to others in the neighborhood. *Hopefully, she can help some of them,* Cooper thought bitterly.

Around mid-day, he force marched Jake downstairs to eat something. They ate their tuna fish sandwiches in silence. Neither tasted the food they ate. In between bites, they would look at one another squarely in the eye, vacant, with shocked looks on their faces. Jake looked at his father and gave a simple nod, as a tear ran down his face. Cooper could think of nothing else, but to offer a similar nod in return.

They left the dirty plates and half-eaten sandwiches on the table and numbly walked back upstairs to resume their watch. With each step, he knew he was learning what walking your last mile felt like. He walked slowly, zombie-like, barely feeling his feet touch the ground. His body felt heavy, each step an effort to make. Everything sounded muffled, as if his ears were full of cotton. His vision was slightly blurred with the sharp sting of pending tears.

Once upstairs, Cooper returned to offering what comfort he could to Elena. A fluffed pillow. A wet cloth. A kiss on her forehead. The day passed like this until the late afternoon.

Without warning, her fever broke and the frantic thrashing ceased. The immobility, wracked now by bouts of coarse coughing fits, was much worse to watch. Each new outburst was worse than the one before. Her body was tortured by each round, which grew longer and louder. Still, she remained unconscious.

As the light gave way to dark, Elena fell silent. Mercifully the coughing abated. Their room remained lit by the glow of the orange streetlight. Neither father nor the son bothered to turn on a light. Cooper moved so he could sit on the edge of the bed and grasped Elena's hand. He motioned Jake to her other side. Jake laid in the bed, next to his mother, and grasped her hand tightly with both hands. He looked at his father with glistening eyes, wide open in grief and fear.

"Tell her whatever you want, son. I think it is time."

"Mama, you can't die. You just can't. Not yet. Please, mama, no!" Jake's voice shifted from soft whimpering, to a high pitched whine, to a plea laced with anger. His plaintive wail cut Cooper's heart to ribbons. Tears filled his eyes. He leaned across Elena and embraced Jake.

"OK, son. OK. I don't want her to go either."

Jake pushed his father away and stared back at him, eyes alive with rage, "No. She *can't* die! I won't let her."

Elena let loose with a rattling cough that sounded like her lungs had come adrift and were hurtling around, loose, inside of her chest. They both looked at her with a mix of shock and fear.

Cooper lowered his voice, "I know, son. I know. If there was *anything* we could do, we would be doing it. But there just isn't."

"Why haven't you taken her to a hospital? You haven't even tried!" Jake hissed sharply in a half whisper and punched his balled fists into his father's chest.

Cooper pushed him back, grasping his fists, "The hospitals are full up, and you can't get there. Besides…"

"You didn't even *try*," Jake interrupted.

Cooper held up his hand, palm out, "Now, listen. The doctors don't have anything, *anything* that works on this bug. I wasn't going to have your mother die in some overflowing hallway or *parking lot* in some hospital gown!"

Cooper's crescendo surprised Jake and he remained silent as Cooper continued, lowering his voice again, "I love your mother as much as any man can love a woman. But, I love you more. I don't want you to do something you'll regret later…not saying to her while you have the chance." The bitter sting of his own last words with his father bubbled up. "The one thing we control, right now, is how we say goodbye."

Jake began to utter a protest, but Cooper's sharp look belayed him, "It *is* time to say goodbye, son. Say goodbye to her now and you can protest to the heavens later. I know she *wants* to hear you tell her just how much you love her and..." His throat tightened, eyes filled with tears, and he could not continue.

"And how much I'll miss her," Jake finished for him. He looked his father, his eyes soft in sympathy.

"Yes, and how much we'll miss her."

Cooper and his son spent the next hour telling Elena goodbye. They alternated between tearful goodbyes and happy reminisces. She drew her last breath with her husband and her only son holding her tight and kissing her on the forehead and cheek.

Elena died at 8:07 in the evening. Cooper's heart was rent asunder and he cried unabashedly. His deep sobs contrasted sharply with his son's high pitched weeping.

Cooper didn't know that his troubles were only just beginning.

Chapter 8

A few hours later, just before midnight, Dranko found them asleep. Elena's corpse lay on the bed. Cooper and his son were in the bed next to her, collapsed in exhaustion from grief. Jake lay curled up to against his father in the fetal position.

Dranko stepped quietly to them and then nudged Cooper awake.

"What's up?" he asked groggily.

"Nothing. Just wanted to check on you. I'm sorry brother," Dranko said, his eyes drifting to Elena's body.

Cooper looked confused, momentarily, and then remembered. He gazed longingly at his wife. His lower lip firmed, "Thank you. I've grieved as much as I can now. More will come, I know that. But, right now, I've got to put it all aside." He paused and took a deep breath, reaching down and grabbing her cold, stiff, hand, "I promised her I'd protect our boy. And, that is what I have to do. It starts now," he said as he placed her hand on her chest and looked determinedly at Dranko.

Dranko squeezed Cooper's shoulder hard, "Right. He does need you now, more than he has his entire life."

Cooper rose from the bed, stretched his arms out wide, yawned and then asked, "In the morning, will you help me take her to the funeral home?"

"Sure thing. If it's all the same to you, I'd like to stay here tonight and keep an eye on things. Your house is better positioned to survey the neighborhood than mine. From what I've been hearing, I think it'd be a good idea."

Cooper suspected that his friend also wanted to keep an eye on him, so he smiled and nodded in return. *They just don't make friends like Paul Dranko anymore.* "Sounds good, but you wake me for second watch. You need to sleep, too. "

"Deal."

"Goodnight."

"Goodnight, brother."

Dranko made his way downstairs. Cooper heard every squeak and groan from the wooden steps. He made a makeshift bed on the ground with pillows and blankets and then gently laid Jake down on the floor to sleep. He didn't want his son to wake up next to his dead mother. He lay down next to him. Within minutes, he was fast asleep as well.

As first light rose, Cooper went into the living room and turned on the TV, looking for news. He kept the volume low to prevent waking Jake. He quickly found CNN. He noticed immediately the absence of graphics and bottom-screen scrolling news updates that had been omnipresent for years on newscasts. The sound was off-kilter. The announcer's makeup and clothing were makeshift, as well. *I guess everything is a bit ragged now.* He was quickly fixated by the deluge of new developments.

"...stated Doctor Jake S. Simpson, Deputy Chief at the Center for Disease Control here in Atlanta. The reports of deaths from the plague continue to come in to our news center from the CDC. The latest report, now six hours old, is of over five million people in the United States who have succumbed to this disease."

Involuntarily, Cooper took a step backward and gasped. *Five million!* He couldn't believe it. He began walking automaton-like backward until his legs brushed the sofa. Then, he softly collapsed into it.

"We have only scattered reports from around the world. The best estimates are that between one hundred and two hundred million dead. The Chinese government has not released any firm numbers of their casualties, but reporters on the ground indicate that they have been only mildly affected by the Brushfire Plague thus far. They have taken aggressive quarantine efforts, including reports of blanket arrests of anyone who recently travelled outside their borders. In addition, much of Africa has been spared the worst from this onslaught. While the Plague appears to have simultaneously broken out across the world on every continent, Africa has appeared to only have had limited secondary exposure from travelers. However, we have received the first reports out of Australia of the plague's outbreak there."

Cooper stopped listening for a few moments, trying to digest what he'd heard. The numbers were staggering. This was already worse than the Spanish Flu Pandemic, with no end in sight. Worse still, that pandemic had taken over a year to run its course. This swath of death had occurred in just a few days.

"Widespread rioting and acts of violence have been reported in most major cities across America. Many small communities have been so afflicted, as well. Authorities are urging people to remain calm, to stay in their homes, and call emergency personnel if there are any problems. Leading medical experts have issued statements to remind people that, while this illness is extremely deadly to those who come down with it, that many people appear to have immunity to it. All research medical resources around the globe are

frantically working on a cure and a vaccine for this new virus."

Cooper could only shake his head in disbelief.

"In business news, all of the world's stock exchanges remain closed during this emergency. In fact, most commercial and industrial activities have ceased altogether given the rampant closure of borders around the world and the massive absenteeism at workplaces and factories worldwide..."

Cooper staggered from the living room to the kitchen. He was famished after the tumultuous day before. He could smell the sausage and eggs before he started cooking. He added toast, orange juice, and a pot of black coffee to round out the breakfast. Midway into the cooking, Dranko and Jake stumbled into the kitchen. Jake's eyes were bleary and blood-shot. He dragged a red blanket lazily behind him that had caught up on his leg. Dranko was shirtless, but was struggling to find the sleeves of a ratty black t-shirt, which advertised some cheap brand of whiskey.

Cooper looked intently at Jake, "Good morning, son."

Jake looked up and offered a tepid smile, "Good morning, Dad." Cooper pulled him close, hugged him tightly and whispered in his ear, "Come what may, we'll be together through this thing." Jake pulled away, looked at him hopefully, his eyes laced with doubt, and began buttering the toast in dull silence.

"Take your seats, gentlemen. Dranko, will you grab some plates and silverware? Everything is almost ready."

They ate in silence, but ravenously. Jake tore his toast to pieces, ripping them into his mouth. Dranko bit a pork sausage link in half, fat spurting out and stinging him in the eye. Cooper devoured his eggs in single bites and yellow yolk dribbled down his chin. He wiped it off with a slice of toast and ate half of it in a single bite. A half-gallon of orange juice disappeared between them amid loud slurping noises as they gulped it down. All told, a dozen eggs, almost a pound of pork sausage links, and a half a loaf of bread were consumed.

Five minutes later, sated, they all sat back almost simultaneously.

Cooper surveyed the scene. Not a speck of food remained, plates were picked clean. Jake had butter smeared across both cheeks and his fingertips were wrapped in grease from the pork. He was furiously licking them clean now. Dranko had bits of pork grease, yolk, and crumbs from the toast coating the better half of his goatee. Cooper could only imagine what he looked like.

"My, we must look like a trio of starving men who've just emerged from prison and had their first meal!"

He burst out laughing. Loud, side-splitting chortles filled the room. Tears streamed down his face and he gasped for breath. Dranko and Jake first looked at him, astonished. Then, looking from Cooper to one another, they too fell into uncontrollable laughter. That caused a new spasm of guffawing. Soon, they were all doubled over, clutching frantically at their sides, and waving at each other to stop.

After what seemed like an eternity, the laughter subsided, defeated by tired lungs and aching abdominal muscles.

"Damn, we needed that," Cooper said, still panting to catch his breath, and wiping his chin and face with a napkin. He used it to dry the tears of laughter from his eyes. Smiling, Dranko and Jake both nodded in understanding.

Cooper went into the kitchen, grabbed the pot of coffee and two mugs. "Why don't you get some milk," he said to Jake. He waited for him to return with a mug filled to the brim with milk.

When he came back, the levity had quickly drained from the room, "We need to take your mother to the funeral home today."

Jake looked at him over the top of the ceramic mug emblazoned with "Keep Portland Weird," eyes focused and unflinching.

"Dranko, can you help?"

"Of course."

"Son, it's your decision if you want to come with us or not. I know it very well may be dangerous. Things have changed. A lot."

"You mean, like the grocery store?"

"Yes, like that, but getting worse. It would be safer for you to…"

Jake interrupted him, "I want to go, Dad." His gaze was firm. Cooper was taken aback by the adult eyes he saw across the table. The wide, creamy white milk mustache above his son's lip made them stand out in stark relief.

"Alright. Why don't you change your clothes and be ready in five?"

******

Ten minutes later they were headed toward Fuhrmann's funeral home in Dranko's Jeep. He had helped Cooper wrap Elena's body in the blankets she had died on and move her to the cargo area of the Wagoneer. Cooper had muttered a few more words of goodbye and kissed her forehead gently. He would never forget how cold she was on his lips. A chill ran down his spine and his shoulders harshly shivered at the discord to how she'd felt in life.

Cooper was in the backseat, one arm stretched over it, and holding onto her body. He was mortified at the thought of hitting a bump and her body bouncing into the air. His shotgun lay on the seat next to him and his pistol was holstered on his hip. Jake was in the passenger seat, back ramrod as he stared down the road. Cooper had noticed how he had assiduously avoided ever laying eyes upon his mother wrapped up in the cloth. Dranko was at the wheel, both hands gripping it tightly. Cooper knew he had his rifle on the seat between them and a sidearm on him as well. The crisp morning air billowed in from the half open windows.

Cooper noticed the distinct smell of things burning. It was not the welcome, nostalgic-inducing smell of wood smoke from a fireplace that greeted their nostrils. Fortunately, he only strongly smelled the stink of rubber and plastic burning. *Cars.* More faintly, he smelled the earthiness of wood smoke, but it was mixed with the tang of plastic and other things that should be not burned. *A house, but not close by.*

"You guys smell that," Dranko asked, breaking his concentration.

Jake nodded silently up front. Cooper responded, "Sure do. Let's keep our eyes open. Jake, give a yell if you see anything." Jake nodded and began actively scanning outside the Jeep.

Traffic was light on the boulevard. The Subaru from the other day was still there, but the fire had gone out, leaving it charred and black. The liquor store had been ransacked. A layer of shattered, glittering glass coated the sidewalk in front. A dozen or so broken bottles lay scattered about the parking lot. Inside, the store was a chaos of tipped over shelves, broken bottles, and scattered newspapers.

A few doors down, the wine store lay unharmed, without a scratch on its large picture window or its door.

"Just goes to show that wine drinkers *are* more civilized," Dranko quipped with a poorly done mock English accent.

"Nah. I think it shows that Monsieur Shotgun enjoys his vino and is willing to protect it," Cooper said motioning Dranko's attention back to the store. A frenzied shop owner, brandishing a Remington 870 police-style shotgun, had emerged from the shadows as they drove past. When his eyes locked with Cooper's, for just a second, Cooper was stunned.

The man looked haunted. His tired eyes were set deep, dark circles under them. He had a scruffy gray beard, just a few days old.

The gray beard blended with the white paper surgical mask he wore. The mask was dirty and looked tattered. His hair was disheveled and unkempt. Cooper had noticed that when he came to the storefront, his feet were unsteady and his legs wobbling.

"He's either sick or dead-on-his-feet tired. I hope he has someone else to watch the store with…"

"Else, he's just a tired wildebeest and the lions are waiting for him to nap," Dranko interjected.

They continued down the street. As a handful of cars passed them they saw a motley collection of firearms and other weapons in several cars. Mostly, they were pistols and shotguns. However, as an old, yellow, beat up and rusted VW bus drove by, Dranko let out a low whistle.

"Will you look at that!"

The passenger was a man in his thirties, long flowing blonde hair, striking features. He was dressed in a green plaid kilt, without a shirt, and the kilt gathered at his shoulder with a dull gray metal broach. In his hands was clutched the biggest sword Cooper had ever seen. The tip reached outside the rolled down window.

"What is *that?*"

"I think it's what our good friends the Scots called a Claymore, a traditional fighting sword," Dranko responded.

"It must be three feet long!" Cooper exclaimed.

As the two vehicles passed, the occupants all turned to look at one another. The driver was a beautiful woman, also in her thirties. Her brown hair was well done, with bits of ribbon and small brass bells woven in. She wore a tight fitting, brown, English woolen peasant-style dress. Her face was rocked with worry and she was holding onto the steering wheel so tightly, her knuckles were white. The passenger raised his sword just a bit and glared at them with wide open eyes and barred teeth.

Cooper almost burst out laughing, but restricted himself to a curt smile, "Do you think he's trying to *menace* us?"

"Me dothinks!" Dranko retorted.

"Ren Faire run amok," Cooper said, referring to the oft-staged Renaissance Faires where people re-enacted various scenes and events from the Middle Ages.

They drove in silence the rest of the way to the funeral home. When it came into view, Cooper immediately wished that he had left Jake at home.

Fuhrmann's funeral home loomed large in front of them several hundred yards further down the road. The parlor had been converted from a large, two story early Victorian. The dark, blue-gray paint was highlighted with the scallops painted copper and the trim in a deep silver. The house sat on an acre of pristine emerald grass, finely groomed. A massive oak tree was perfectly positioned in the middle of the lawn, its limbs thick as a man, reaching skyward.

There were several cars lined up in front of the home and a man in a white lab coat stood out front with a clip board. As they pulled in, Cooper could see that he had a pencil thin mustache and his hair was slicked back. He wore blue latex gloves and had an industrial grade mask with filters on either side attached firmly to his face. He was shaking his head vigorously back and forth to a woman standing in front of him. She had inclined her head towards him in a half bow, and clasped her hands in front of her, fingers locked together.

He waved his hand firmly and appeared to shout at her, but they could not hear anything due to the distance and his mask.

Sobbing deeply, the woman turned back towards her car, got in and drove away. Cooper saw the unmistaken shape of a body wrapped up in a flower bedecked drapery lying in her backseat.

"I wonder what the hell is going on here," Dranko asked himself.

"I'm going to find out. Jake, you stay here with Dranko."

Cooper's feet hit the pavement, even before the Jeep had completely stopped. Cooper strode up just as another man was getting in his car to drive away.

The clipboard wielding man had a smug look on his face as he scribbled some notes down. He didn't see Cooper's fast approach.

"What's going on here?" Cooper demanded.

"I beg your pardon, sir?" He looked up in surprise from the clipboard.

"You heard me. What is going on here? Are you turning these people away?"

Recovering from his momentary surprise, a wry smile reappeared on his face as deliberately shifted the clipboard in his hands, "That depends."

"Depends on what?"

"On who is coming to seek our services."

Cooper was already weary of this man's coy attitude. His fists clenched, "Just what does that mean?"

"Well, you may have noticed that there is an overwhelming need for our services at the current time. Our ability to process remains in a safe and efficient manner, while meeting the quality standards that Fuhrmann's has maintained for generations, is quite limited. So, under these circumstances, we are only able to meet the needs of our pre-paid customers at this time."

Cooper's head swam amidst the prepackaged sales pitch, "Pre-paid what?"

"Our pre-paid customers, sir. Those foresighted individuals who have made pre-arranged funeral plans for their loved ones in the event of someone becoming deceased. Are you one of those customers?" The man's self-assured smile said he knew the question was only rhetorical.

Rage flashed and Cooper slammed the man up against a pearly white column, his forearm across the man's throat. The clipboard hit the ground with a loud clatter, the papers rustling in a sudden breeze.

"No, I'm not. But, what I do have are the *remains* of my wife who died this morning and *you're* going to give her a proper burial. I'll pay whatever the charges are, but it's going to be *done!*"

"I'm afraid I c-c-can-not do that. We need to keep our spaces open for our P-P-Pre-Paid customers only," the man stuttered in fear.

Cooper pressed firmly with his forearm and the man began choking, "How about I pull your gas mask off? Will that change your mind you pompous ass!"

"I ca-nnnn-not do anything...p-p-o-li-cy." He choked out between shallow breaths.

Cooper flushed with rage. He moved in closer to bring his eyes just a scant inch from the other man's. Losing control, he drew his pistol and buried the muzzle against the man's temple. "Damn you! Don't you understand anything? My wife just died. I loved her since I laid eyes on her. My son is here. She needs a proper burial, you bastard!" The man cried out in pain and began whimpering.

From behind, an iron grip tore Cooper's pistol away from the man's head. Another hand gripped him around the belt, restricting his movement. "Ease up, brother." Dranko's quiet, calm voice rang louder than a gunshot in his ear.

Cooper regained himself. He now caught sight of two black-clad men standing outside the funeral parlor's main entrance, one with a shotgun and the other with a military-style AR-15. Both guns were leveled at Cooper. Both wore mirror finish aviator sunglasses that video games and soldier of fortune magazine made popular with the wannabe soldier crowd. Cooper had little doubt they were ill trained with their weapons. But, at this range, it wouldn't matter.

"You'd be wise to heed your friend's words," the one on the left, slightly taller than the other, said.

Cooper eased up on the other man's throat and slowly raised his hands above his head. "Alright, I get it."

The man leaned down, picked up his clipboard from the ground. He made a grand gesture of straightening his clothes and brushing himself off.

"You," his voice was shaky. He cleared his throat, "You need to leave right now or we'll call the police."

"You know damn well you wouldn't see the police for five days," Cooper shot back.

"Well, Brian and Gary can handle things just fine. You just move along now."

The man's patronizing attitude angered Cooper again, "Brian and Gary? Are you kidding me? Were you guys guarding the mall last week? And, today you are full blown mercenaries? Is that it?"

Brian, the shorter one, took a step forward, but Gary's arm restrained him as he spoke. "Just move along, sir. We can't take care of your wife. We're sorry, we really are. But, the morgue's already full up. Trust me, you wouldn't want to leave her here, even if we'd take her. There's no telling how long she'd sit here. Hell, we have some bodies in the hallways. Unrefriger..."

The clipboard-wielding man shot the evil eye at Gary and shouted to interrupt him, "*Mr.* Jenkins is mistaken. Our services have not declined in the least during this difficult time. We merely have been forced to restrict access to our services to our customers with a pre-existing *relationship* with our company."

Cooper turned back toward the Jeep, waving his hand in disgust, "Yeah. Whatever." He turned his head towards Dranko, who had moved back towards the driver's side door. "Let's go."

Wordless, Dranko climbed back into the car. The sound of their doors slamming shut was muted, matching their defeated state of mind.

They drove back to Cooper's house in silence; the only sound was Cooper's fingers rapping on the door frame. His head swam with bitter emotion and confused thoughts. *My father always said the well-off took the best of everything first. That we were left second or third-best. He would turn over in his grave to know they've now taken the right to be buried first, too!*

Suddenly, he punched the window with a loud *thwap* and Jake jumped in his seat and Dranko jerked the wheel to the left, before correcting.

"Damn you, I thought we'd been shot at!"

"Sorry. I just had to direct my brain back to problem solving," and Cooper sank back into ruminating for the rest of the drive home. He didn't tell Dranko he was trying to push away the shame he felt for losing control and threatening the other man's life moments before.

The rest of the drive home was silent and uneventful. As they pulled alongside their home, Jake broke the quiet.

"We should bury her in our backyard. She liked to sit out there and watch the birds. *Any* birds. Do you remember? Even the stupid crows." Jake's voice had surprised him. More so, the words that came out shocked him with their newfound maturity.

"You're right, son. We'll do just that. This way, she'll always be close by," he said in response.

Jake gazed back at him with a look of self-satisfaction stained with grief.

After a moment's contemplation, Jake nodded, exited the Jeep and ran off to get a shovel.

He turned toward Dranko, "Can you get word to any of the neighbors that knew Elena well about the funeral? The ones who are able should be here in an hour." Dranko was off without another word.

Chapter 9

Cooper was bathed in sweat, despite the chilly temperature. He had shed his jacket and shirt, his soaked-through white t-shirt and pants were all that remained. *Cotton kills when wet*, he thought as he shivered. The dark earth lay piled next to the trench he had dug over the past hour. The rich black earth contrasted sharply with the bright emerald grass and clover all around. The deep chasm and the splattered dirt made it look like a gaping, open wound in the Earth. *Like the wound in my heart.* The hole felt much, much deeper than it was. The grave looked like it could swallow him whole and his grief tried to pull him in. He consciously steadied his feet and firmed his legs.

Almost done with digging the grave, he looked toward the sky and wiped his brow. Above, the sky was an oppressively blank gray, not a discernible cloud in view. A black crow had alighted on a nearby telephone wire, just beyond the reach of the rocks Cooper had thrown at it. It had stood vigil over him as he dug, emitting an incessant *caw-caw-caw* that went on and on, scarcely interrupted. Now, as he stood, leaning against his shovel, gazing upward, the crow grew silent.

"Why thank you, my good man," Cooper said feigning to doff a hat. "A moment's peace is appreciated."

Jake giggled from where he sat atop the pile of freshly broken earth. The soil was a farmer's delight—moist, black, solid but without too much clay. Jake had made a good effort at helping his father dig the grave, but a few minutes ago he had collapsed onto the pile of earth. They exchanged a smile and Cooper began digging, scooping out the last bit.

The crow rewarded his work with renewed cawing.

A moment later, Cooper heard the creak of someone stepping onto the deck. His right hand immediately swept back towards where his pistol was holstered, he used the left to lean the shovel against the fence. He stepped forward half a pace, to put his body between the deck and Jake.

He relaxed when Dranko's head of unkempt brown hair came into view. Dranko saw how Cooper was positioned.

"OK. I guess I need to start announcing myself, don't I?"

"Probably a good idea," Cooper said as he returned to shoveling.

"People will be here in about fifteen minutes. Most are either sick or too afraid of getting sick. But Lily, Mark, Lisa, Peter, and Calvin will all be here."

"Just Peter? What about his parents?"

"Dead," Dranko said soberly.

Cooper asked robotically, still digging, "Which one?"

"Both."

The shovel rammed the earth as he looked up in surprise, "My God. Poor kid." Cooper saw the growing look of alarm on Jake's face. "Don't worry. I would be sick already if I was going to get this thing."

"Why don't you and Jake go get cleaned up. I can finish this last bit up."

Cooper stood up and handed the shovel to him, "Good idea. Let's go kiddo, time for a quick shower."

The hot shower was welcome. He inhaled the steam gratefully, letting it cleanse him. He vigorously scrubbed the dirt from his body and from under his fingernails. He was in the middle of washing his hair when he realized he'd grabbed his wife's shampoo by mistake. The distinct smell of it overwhelmed him. He steadied himself with one hand against the wall and the other came to his face as he wept deeply. The sobbing wracked his body as the day's events hit him like a bulldozer. He struggled to stay quiet, he didn't want Jake to hear him like this. He slowly sank to his knees and sat down in the shower, unable to stop. Slowly, the hot water turned warm, and then cold. Still, he sat there, lost in grief, the water washing over him.

He remembered the promise he'd made to his wife. He tightened his jaw and rubbed his face firmly with his hand from chin to forehead. He rose resolutely, turned off the shower, and went to get dressed.

******

He stood silently, Jake leaning into him and clutching his pant leg, as Calvin and Dranko lowered Elena's body into the ground. He wore a black suit, a black tie, and a wrinkled white shirt underneath. He hadn't had time to iron it.

Clustered around him were their friends who either had already been sick and recovered, like Lily, or those who knew they had already been exposed, like himself and Jake. Lily Stott stood directly across from him, her translucent white hair picking up what little light there was. Her eyes often shifted color between brown and green. Today, they shone like light emeralds. Lily was the "Grand Kentucky

Dame" of their neighborhood, in her eighties, feisty, sarcastic, and with a wit still so sharp it could score diamonds.

Next to her stood Peter Garcia, barely seventeen, and just orphaned by the loss of both parents. Cooper was impressed with his strength to be here, attending a funeral. He was of medium height and had chestnut colored hair on the longish side, covering his ears and dropping below his eyes on most days. Today, he had slicked it all back and tucked it behind his ears. He stood stoop shouldered, looking firmly at the ground. Lily had one arm around him, rubbing his back in comfort.

To his immediate right, Calvin was as immobile as a block of granite. He was heavyset, just an inch or two shorter than Cooper, but his shaved head accentuated the difference. It was a perfect, rounded shape and he fondly referred to it "as the black pearl" when he wanted a cheap laugh. Calvin Little was a gregarious man, well known throughout the neighborhood, and enjoyed gaining the attention of those around him. He stared blankly forward, green eyes unique to a black man.

Mark Moretti was next to Calvin; he managed a local appliance store. He was shifting his weight back and forth on the balls of his feet. He was square-faced, with a prominent Roman nose, and was biting the lower part of his lip. His thin, brown hair was in full retreat and what remained he had gathered meticulously and parted to the left.

To Cooper's immediate left was Lisa, the nurse. Her open, round face was full of compassion and her eyes reached out to him in sympathy. She wore a solid black cotton dress and had already deployed a black handkerchief to her glistening, dark eyes. Next to Lisa was Dranko, dressed in an awkward fitting brown suit. *Probably the only one he owns and likely fitted over a decade ago.*

Cooper gave a look skyward and noticed the crow on the wire, a black spot framed starkly against the gray sky. It gazed down at them. Silent.

He cleared his throat, "I want to thank you all for being here."

All eyes turned towards him. "With what's going on, it means a lot that you're here. I know Elena appreciates it, too." He glanced upwards again and nodded.

"Today we put the remains of Elena, my wife, Jake's mother, to rest. She was a good woman. A kind woman. I loved her from the moment I saw her. She had a spirit that was alive with life. Sometimes that spirit would get angry and then, well then you wanted to be across the county line." At that, everyone laughed together.

His voice turned serious again, "But mostly, that spirit filled my life up, and then made it overflow. She always used to say," he choked up and paused, "that she was the pepper to my sauce. She always laughed when she said that. I think it meant more in either Romanian or Spanish, I never asked her. I would just laugh, too." Those around him joined him in soft laughter and smiles. He paused to refocus.

"She was also a good mother. Jake is a fine boy." He turned his head downward to Jake, who looked back up at him, his eyes wet and his nose running. "Elena made that happen. She loved you so much, son." Tears ran down Cooper's face. Jake buried his face into Cooper's side, sobbing.

Cooper turned back toward his friends, "So, in her memory, I make two promises. One, I will do everything I can to protect my son so that she can live onward in him. I will raise him the best I can without her. Two, our home will become a living testament to her spirit, filled with her spirit and her generosity." He took a step back.

After a moment's silence, others stepped forward to say a few words about Elena. They were all kind words, the kind most people reserved until someone was no longer able to hear them. But, Cooper's mind had drifted off. When he looked up at the sky again, the crow was gone. He hadn't cawed once during the funeral. Cooper nodded once to the empty space in appreciation.

When everyone had finished, Cooper dumped a shovel of dirt on his wife's covered body. The soil, as dark as midnight, looked incongruous lying on the floral-patterned blanket that covered her. He was about to hand the shovel to Dranko, when Jake's hand shot out and stopped him, his grip surprisingly strong. His face was set firmly, tight-lipped and dry-eyed. He took the shovel from him, scooped up the cold, dark earth, and threw it across his mother's body. He then gave it to Dranko and turned to go back inside their house. Cooper walked with him, following in astonishment.

******

Cooper and Jake sat in contemplative silence at their kitchen table, Cooper drinking coffee and Jake a glass of water. When Dranko came in almost an hour later, he found them in the same state of torpor.

The sound of him closing the door was a catalyst. Cooper shook his head back and forth, rousting the cobwebs from it.

"OK, it is time to get organized. This thing might go on awhile and we've already seen far too much chaos for my taste."

Jake nodded in agreement. Cooper continued, "First, let's get changed. Then, you can help me inventory all of our useful supplies — food, water, tools, sources of light, ways to cook if the electricity dies, weapons, heck, I'll just make a list while you're changing. After that, we can see what we might need to try and go find."

Jake left to go to his room and change. Cooper rose to do the same, but Dranko put his hand on his shoulder to stop him.

"It is all getting worse. Much worse."

"What do you mean?"

"You've seen it with your own eyes, brother. But, what I've heard will chill you to the bone. Some estimates are that half of our population has, or will come down with this thing. Most of those will die. I've heard about the full weight of our medical resources being deployed to try and research a cure. But, I know it's moving too fast for that to matter much.

Cooper interrupted out of frustration, "So, yes. This is all depressing, what's your point?"

Dranko resumed, "My point is, it's not just the plague we have to worry about. We probably are immune or we'd have it by now. It's the *violence* all over the place that matters. Think about it, you've been involved in two shootings the last two times you've left your home. You almost had another on your front lawn. It's breaking down. You saw the funeral home too. You've *not* seen the police or other emergency services, have you? It's coming apart at the seams."

Cooper met him with a steely gaze, "Where are you going with this?"

"We need to leave the city." Seeing Cooper's quick reaction, he added, "At least for a little while. We can come back when things settle down."

"How dare you!" he hissed. "Her body is barely in the ground and you want me to leave her? Leave my home? No way."

"But, brother, it's quickly becoming unsafe here."

"You always assume the worst is going to happen. Hell, we can organize burial crews to help bury anyone who isn't. We can get organized and take care of what needs to be taken care of. We don't need to run."

Dranko threw up his hands, "I'm not talking about running. I'm talking about relocating, just temporarily."

"No, I won't do it. Jake's been through enough already. I don't want to take him from the only home he's ever known. With your plan, we could come back and find this place burned down or ransacked. Besides, I can't leave Elena behind."

Dranko caught him squarely in the eye and gripped his shoulders, "Elena's *dead*, brother. Dead."

Cooper shoved him so hard that Dranko banged into the wall with a loud thud, and a picture frame crashed to the ground breaking. "You think I don't know that? You think I'm denying reality? Damn you. It's not that at all. I meant what I said out there. Her spirit resides here. I can see her all around me. There is a memory in every corner of this home." He turned to the bookshelf behind him and grabbed the nearest object.

"Here, you see this?" He held up an old-fashioned pepper grinder made of wood and adorned with a coat of arms made of metal, "We bought this at an antique store. I told her it was silly. Of course we never used the damn thing. Not once! But, she wanted it. Since that day, I've made a hundred jokes about her stupid pepper grinder she just *had* to have." He turned to grab something else off the shelf, setting the grinder back on the shelf.

Dranko stopped him, "I get it. I get it."

"No, you don't. You *can't*. It's the same for my *son*. Her body might be dead, but we can stay connected to her by staying *here*. I won't take him away from that. Life ain't just about sucking air, *this* is what makes it all worth living for," he waved his hands indicating the house about them.

Dranko was silent for a moment, then upraised his hands, "OK, brother. I hear you. But, I have to warn you. I'm leaving. Tomorrow. I want you to come with me, but I can't force you. I won't wait any longer, either." He turned and walked out. Cooper could hear his steady footfalls pounding the walkway all the way to the street. He listened to them fading away while rubbing his forehead with both hands in frustration.

He turned to go upstairs to change and decided he needed a shower as well.

Chapter 10

By mid-afternoon, he and Jake had completed their inventory of the house and what they had on hand. He estimated that they had enough food to last almost three months, half that if the electricity went out and the freezer failed. *Just one more advantage to being frugal and buying in bulk.* His first calculations were off because he figured things based upon a three person household. It pained him to erase those numbers and recalculate them based upon only two people.

His weapons included his Smith and Wesson pistol, an old revolver his father had given him, a Remington pump-action shotgun, a .22 caliber rifle, and a heavy caliber bolt action hunting rifle. He had some extra ammunition for all the weapons, except for the revolver. Given what he'd seen so far, Cooper kicked himself for not buying a military-style rifle with a higher capacity magazine that Dranko had recommended to him so many times. He had been shooting with Dranko many times using a couple of his. He'd always enjoyed shooting them, as they reminded him of his days in the Army. However, he had never bought one as some bill or another had always come up.

They had a good supply of toiletries, first aid supplies, flashlights, and over the counter medicines.

"What we're short on," he told Jake as they sat at the table surveying their list, "is water and more medical supplies in case one of us gets hurt."

"Water?" asked Jake.

"Yes, water. With so many people sick, it's possible the water supply could get interrupted. We need to store some here at the house, just in case."

"We could fill up the bathtub?" he suggested helpfully.

"Great idea son. I also think we will buy some large garbage cans and fill those up with water too. Oh, and I just remembered something else!" he remarked in surprise.

"What's that?"

"We need some good, solid hand tools. Most of what I have are all power tools. We need a good saw, hammer, and some other tools, if the electricity goes out. Let's just do one trip to the hardware store. If we grab a couple more deluxe first aid kits, that would give us the additional medical supplies we need and everything else is there, too."

Twenty minutes later, they were in the GMC pickup heading towards the hardware store on Division Street. Cooper had not wanted to bring Jake along; it had become very dangerous on the streets. But, the look of terror that lit up his face when he'd suggested leaving him behind with Lisa convinced Cooper it was too soon after his mother's death.

Dranko had refused to answer his door when Cooper had knocked. *Must still be irate with me.* As a compromise, Mark Moretti was riding shotgun. Cooper did not want to venture anywhere without someone to back him up. Mark had been unarmed when he'd shown up at their house, so Cooper had given him the .38 special revolver. It only had six cartridges in the cylinder and no ammunition to reload. Cooper also knew the rounds were so old there was some question of whether they'd even fire. Mark had been shooting a few times in his life and Cooper reacquainted him quickly with the basics. Mark sat silently in the passenger seat, gazing out the window, and cradling the revolver in his lap. Cooper had a bad feeling about this trip. *I'm taking Jake when I know I shouldn't and my wingman is inexperienced and carrying an old, unsure weapon.* But, he knew he hadn't had any other options. As a compromise, he had forced Jake to ride along curled up on the floor.

The streets were less deserted than yesterday. However, he soon wished they were. What he saw were frantic people, on the verge of panic. A crashed red Pontiac Grand Am lay where it had slammed into a telephone pole. Cooper reflexively reached down to cover Jake's eyes when he saw the young driver slumped over the steering wheel, dried blood covering his face, dead. *What the hell is going on with emergency services? Are any of them functioning?* Cars were driving recklessly, barely obeying the lanes and flow of traffic.

"Mark, keep a good eye out. I don't like the looks of this." Mark nodded.

They drove on, slowly and carefully. Further down Division, they encountered a pile-up blocking the entire left lane of traffic. A silver Honda Civic had rear-ended a black Hummer H2 and was wedge halfway underneath it, lifting the Hummer off of its back two wheels. Cooper had no doubt that whoever was in that Civic lay crushed, dead. A brown Dodge minivan had then rear-ended the Civic collapsing most of the trunk into the backseat. He didn't see anyone in the H2 or the minivan, but several doors lay flung open, either by the passengers or those who had passed by.

Cooper slowed down to negotiate his way around the

wreckage. Suddenly, a contorted, feverish face appeared in his window, grabbing a hold of his side view mirror.

"They got medicine. They got a cure. Down near the waterfront! Please take me there!"

He looked at the woman, only inches from his face, luckily shielded by the window. Her red hair was matted to her head, covered in sweat and filth. Her face glistened with tiny beads of sweat. Her mouth was a chasm of dirty, misaligned, and broken teeth. Her eyes were a faded blue but had the faraway look that always takes hold of the crazy or the delirious. Cooper didn't have time to find out which, although he suspected the latter.

With his right hand, he flashed the pistol out of its holster and stuck it against the window, pointing right at the woman's face and shouted through the glass, "We're *not* headed that way. Get off my pickup!"

Through her mental fog, the woman slowly took in what had just happened. Suddenly, she let go of his car and stood in the middle of the road, giving him the double bird with both hands. He gunned the motor in response to quickly create some separation.

Mark was breathing hard in the passenger seat, while Jake stared ahead. "Do you think it's true? What she said," Mark asked.

Cooper burst out laughing. "Mark, I should put you and Dranko in a room together. You, the Optimist. Him, the Cynic. Put you two in a room and see what emerges! No, I don't believe a word of it. She was a lunatic or she was delirious with fever."

Jake stirred, "I know."

"Know what?"

"What would emerge from that room."

Cooper cocked an eyebrow, "Oh yeah, what then?"

"You would, Dad."

Cooper and Mark laughed heartily at that.

"I hope you're right about that one, son."

When they pulled up next to the curb, in front of the hardware store, what they saw made their hearts sink into their stomachs.

******

A handful of random tools lay scattered about the lawn, with an overturned red wheelbarrow squarely blocking the walkway to the front door.

Cooper exhaled, "Oh my God!"

Larry Nevins, the owner of the store was on the ground, partially concealed by the wheelbarrow and a hydrangea bush. His foppish white hair was streaked with red, with blood covering his face, and running downward and staining his white and blue-striped Western-style long sleeved shirt. He wasn't moving.

Cooper barked orders without thinking, "Mark, cover me. Larry is down, by the wheelbarrow. Jake, lie down on the floor and don't get up until we tell you to."

With that, he was out of the pickup, pistol in hand, moving sideways so he could survey the store and get a better view of Larry before closing in. Through the hardware store bank of windows, he didn't detect any movement. A fluorescent light was flickering on and off toward the far left side of the store. All of the windows were intact, and the entrance door was shut.

"Keep an eye on those windows and the door. If you see anything move, anything at all, give a shout, but don't fire," he called out to Mark. He realized that from this range, with a revolver he wasn't used to, Mark was more likely to hit him than any adversary. He just needed him to be the proverbial eyes in the back of his head.

Cooper closed the gap to where Larry lay prostrate quickly, at a half crouch, keeping his eyes trained on the store. He still saw nothing.

Larry had been shot, twice. The left side of his head, just above the ear had a gruesome crevice that had been carved by a bullet creasing across his head. A streak of congealed blood covered the path where his hair and skin had been shot away. A second round had hit him in the belly and it made a sickening sucking sound as he breathed in shallow breaths. Larry lay spread-eagled, both legs and arms akimbo. He had fallen, and fallen hard when he'd been shot. He had lost a lot of blood, with a puddle almost two feet in diameter from underneath his back. The other bullet had gone through and exited his back.

"Larry, can you hear me?"

A listless moan emitted from his lips, dry and hoarse. His left eye cracked open a millimeter. The brown iris looked at him with a sharply dilated pupil.

"Larry, it's me, Cooper Adams. What happened?" He had already torn off part of his t-shirt and was applying direct pressure to the stomach wound.

"Don't bother," Larry croaked.

"What?"

"It hurts too much and it won't matter. Been here too long," he rasped. "Bleeding."

Cooper eased up on the pressure, but kept his hand in place. He had to do something. "What happened?"

"Punks," Larry coughed and blood spilled from his lips.

"Stealing. I chased them. Stupid." He wheezed and sprayed a mist of blood. Cooper ducked his head to avoid it.

"Young guys, in a van." Cooper felt his blood rush to his face and his right hand clenched.

"Can I do anything for you?"

"Tell Barb I love her and that it was a great life," blood and emotion choked the last few words.

"You're a good man, Larry. One of the best I've ever known," Cooper whispered to him, grabbing his hand.

Larry's eyes shut. He lay quietly for what seemed like an eternity, but lasted only a few more shallow breathes. Then, he was gone, and the feeble grip that had responded to Cooper's went loose.

Cooper bowed his head in silent reflection for a moment.

Then, he turned his head toward the sky, raised his hands, open-palmed, and vented his wrath, "No need! There was no need for this man to die! Larry limped like a three legged dog, you could have just outrun him, you stupid bastards!"

He stood up impatiently. He motioned for Mark to join him and he trotted over. Mark took one look at Larry, grew unsteady on his feet, and then vomited all over the hydrangea bush that lay next to him. He looked back toward Cooper, meekly.

"It's alright. Don't feel bad, it's what happens the first time you see a body that was killed violently."

"What happened?"

"Some punks rousted his store and he chased them. One of them must have turned back and shot at him. They were either lucky or a very good shot. From the shell casings over there, they were over ten yards away when they fired. Not an easy shot when people are moving." Cooper motioned toward the curb, about five feet from where the pickup was parked.

Mark looked toward where he'd indicated and then wiped his mouth clean with the cuff of his sleeve, dirtying his blue cotton twill shirt.

"OK. Let's do what we came for. First, you'll find a blanket for Larry. Then, I'll load up the tools and things we came for in a wheelbarrow."

"Shouldn't we call the police about Larry?"

"I'm not seeing too much of the police today, I'm going to try and find Barbara's number in the store and call her. I have a message to deliver to her."

Cooper quickly explained what he wanted Mark to do while they cleared the store. Cooper would take point with Mark providing another set of eyes and cover.

They found no one in the store, just a few overturned shelves, a broken display case that held knives with some obviously missing, and a smashed cash register with coins of silver and copper scattered across the counter and onto the floor.

"Looks like they took the big Rambo types," Mark commented.

Mark found a blanket and went outside. Cooper quickly found Barb's number on a slip of paper taped to the wall near the register labeled "Personal" that was smudged and dirty from years of use. *I'll call her from the house because we need to move quickly.* He pulled out the list of what they needed and moved through the store methodically. He knew the store's layout well from his years of shopping at Larry's. Larry had also been a customer of Cooper's. He pulled a wheelbarrow inside to load it up.

He was halfway done when Mark came back inside, with Jake in tow. "I figured it was safe to bring him in."

"Yeah, sure. Thanks. I'm loading up the supplies. Why don't you get what you need?"

Ten minutes later they had transferred their loads to the pickup.

"We need one more run back inside," Cooper said.

"Why's that?"

"Two things. We need to leave a list of what we've taken. And, I think we should get some lumber, the kind suitable for covering windows and doors.

"Larry's dead, what's the point of leaving a list?" Mark asked.

"Because Barbara isn't."

Mark nodded gravely, "OK. Got it." His mouth turned upward in a wry smile, "You are one honest bastard, Cooper." Cooper simply shrugged his shoulders in reply.

They took two wheelbarrows full of plywood and two by fours and left behind two signed notes detailing what they had taken from the store. They also left a brief note detailing how they had found Larry and what he had told them. Cooper didn't think it would do much good, but he decided to call the police after all when he was back home. Maybe they would see the van and do something about it.

******

The truck rumbled west again, steered toward Cooper's home. Jake broke the silence.

"Why did they kill Mr. Nevins?"

Cooper glanced at his son, who returned a mixed expression of curiosity and apprehension at what he might hear. "There are some people that are bad people, son."

"Evil?"

"Not evil. Careless, I think."

"Careless?"

"Yeah, careless. They aren't thinking about what they're doing.

They didn't go there to kill anyone. But, they did kill because they were careless with a gun."

"What is an evil person, then?"

Cooper thought for a moment before responding, "Evil is something bad done on purpose and is something that hurts people."

"So stealing isn't evil?"

"Stealing is bad, but it isn't evil. Things can always be replaced, but people can't be." Cooper's throat tightened on the last two words as he thought of Elena.

Jake had the same thought and his eyes filled with tears.

"Well, lookey here!" Mark shouted out. Cooper's grip tightened on the steering wheel with his left hand and his right immediately went to his holster.

About twenty yards up, two people were approaching each other. The first was an ill-kept man, dressed in a motley collection of ragged clothes, including a red down jacket with several puffs of white feathers sticking out through the torn fabric. He looked to be in his sixties, white bedraggled hair sticking out haphazardly from a green, well-worn, woolen cap. Like the jacket, several wisps of hair stuck out of holes in the hat. The old man pushed a shopping cart full of supplies, but mostly the cart was full of several cases of bottled water. The man struggled pushing the weight.

Opposite him and coming toward him at a fast walk was a man wearing a matching Columbia jogging suit and windproof jacket, all black. He was middle-aged, with gray staining the sides of his head. He wore an athletic build, but beset by his age; flab beginning to show on his sides and in his face. He had neatly trimmed black eyebrows, framing deep-set blue eyes. He was gesticulating wildly as he shouted to get the man's attention. Cooper couldn't help but notice his manicured hands as he did so.

Cooper pulled the truck to the curb and reflexively pushed Jake's head below the dashboard.

"Stay here," he muttered as he slid out of the pickup, and stood behind the opened door. They were only about fifteen yards away, so Cooper pulled the pistol out of its holster, but kept it out of view.

"Old man! Old man!" The well-dressed man shouted from ten feet away.

"I ain't deaf, son! Whatchya want?" the white-haired man replied gruffly.

"Water. Just water, my friend. The stores are all out. I'll pay you. Whatever you want."

The old man began laughing. "Money? Now?" He paused, scratching his head, "Let me ask you a question, son. Did you ever give me anything when I was standing at the freeway entrance with my cardboard sign?"

The black-suited man looked confused, "I...I don't know. I don't remember ever seeing you there."

Cooper couldn't see the old man's face from this angle, but he heard a wry smile in his voice, "I'm not talking about just me. It's all of us. We're all the same. Did you ever give anything to *anybody* at the freeway exit?"

He dipped his head, "No...no I didn't....but I have lots of money now." He pulled out a handful of twenty and hundred dollar bills from his pocket.

Cooper heard the old man laughing again, "I thought not. I don't need your money *now*. Just tell me, why I should *give* you any of *my* water."

The other man was flummoxed and shifted his feet restlessly. Finally, he turned his head back up toward the old man, outstretched his hands, and whined, "Because I need it?"

The old man rocked back onto his heels and nodded, "Exactly. That's a good enough reason to give someone something isn't it? They *need* it. Take a case and I hope you remember that, son."

The other man hesitated for a moment, surprised at the man's answer. His eyes flashed in a moment of recognition at the other man's point. Then, he grabbed a case from the man's cart, leaving three remaining, muttered a 'thank you' and rushed off towards a BMW parked across the street.

Cooper turned to look across the cab in amused surprise at Mark. He saw Jake, eyes perched just over the dashboard. He wagged his finger at him in reproach, but couldn't help smiling.

He briskly walked toward the old man, re-holstering his pistol, "Old timer, hold up a minute."

The old man turned toward him. Mark and Jake came up behind Cooper.

"That was a nice thing you just did."

"Nice? No. Necessary, but not nice."

"Why'd you do it," Jake piped up.

The old man bent slightly and looked at Jake, "Just like I done said. He needed the water, so I gave it to him."

"But, you needed lots of things and no one gave them to you? People just don't give things to those who need them, that's just the way things work in this world," Mark blurted out in surprise.

The old man turned towards Mark, "And, look around, son," he waved his left hand in a wide circle. "That way doesn't work very well, does it?"

Everyone thought in silence for a few moments. Then, Cooper cut in, "But what about you? Do you have enough water now? Do you need anymore?"

The old man laughed again, sparking a brief wet cough. "I've got plenty. This water isn't for me. It's for *them*." Again, he gestured in a wide arc, with both hands this time. He then turned back towards his cart, grabbed it with both hands and began lumbering back up the boulevard, whistling faintly as he did so.

The three of them looked at each with bemused smiles and wagging of heads.

"Dad, was that a good man?"

"Yes, son. It certainly was. One of the best, I'd say."

They turned back towards the pickup.

Chapter 11

The lightheartedness induced by the old man and the lessons he taught amidst the chaos and death was wrenched away from them on their journey home. When they passed the wreck that they had skirted on the way to the hardware store, the body of the woman who had begged them to take her to the waterfront lay in the street. Her body lay twisted in a gruesome mockery of a rag doll; torn and bloody. Her legs were outstretched in opposite directions. They looked like they had been squashed by a vehicle driving over them. Her arms lay directly above her head, as if reaching for something. Her chest was a mash of red and gore. She had been hit multiple times with a large caliber rifle of some kind. Mercifully, her face was a picture of peace and perfection, a tight-lipped smile concealing her misshapen teeth and her eyes gazed skyward as if beholding the gates of Heaven itself. Cooper tried to shield Jake's eyes from the horrific scene, but it was too late.

A few hundred yards further up the road, a blue Corolla was listless, with its right wheels stuck over the curb and blocking the sidewalk. It was another bloody mess. All the windows had been shot out and the car's body was riddled with bullet holes. Inside, it was a morbid jumble of blood and flesh torn asunder.

Mark whistled, "What the hell?" He shot up a hand to block Jake's view, beating Cooper's own flashing hand. Jake's eyes squinted and his mouth fell open in shock. His left hand shot instinctively to cover his mouth as he gagged.

"Keep an eye out, have your pistol at the ready!" Cooper barked. He drew his own pistol and gunned his motor, in hope of throwing any would-be ambushers off their plan. "Jake, get down!" Jake slithered down below the dashboard and curled up between the legs of the two men.

Cooper's eyes scanned the surrounding buildings and shrubs. He saw nothing as the pickup pulled alongside the car. He could not help but looking inside. The scene that met his eyes made everything pass in slow motion.

A family lay slaughtered. The father was slumped over the steering wheel. A shotgun blast had taken off the top half of his head, which lay flopped over, like a Pez dispenser. In the passenger seat, a woman sat upright, eyes open looking blankly ahead. She looked oddly peaceful, save two softball sized bloody wounds in her torso. One was right over her heart and the other in her stomach. In the rear seat were three children, with a toddler in the middle strapped into her car seat. The close stitching of bullet holes and wounds told him that all three had been cut almost in half by a submachine gun blast from close range. The boy closest to them, with a shock of blonde hair standing out amidst all the blood, had powder burns on his face. He couldn't have been older than twelve.

Mark frantically lowered his window and gulped fresh air. Cooper clamped down his jaw and gritted his teeth. Anger flushed blood to his face and he tightened his grip on the pistol until his fingers hurt.

Mark brought his head back inside the cab, "What was this? Did they shoot them up close?"

"It was point blank. See those dark marks around the boy? Those are powder burns. This was up close, execution style."

Mark's jaw dropped, "Sick bastards."

"The wheels have come off."

Mark looked puzzled, "What'd you say?"

Cooper returned a grim look, his lips tight, "The wheels have come off the cart. The protective veneer of civilization is coming off in large swaths, as fast as a buzz saw would make its way through pressboard furniture. We've descended to the law of the jungle. Use whatever favorite expression you want. But, we're in a different world now. The rules and laws are gone. When that happens, those who have been kept in check by those very same rules and laws will now cross over," he paused surveying the mess in the car once more and then turned back towards Mark. "With devastating results."

"The psychos you mean?"

"Not just the psychos. This here was the work of at least two people. Cooperating. One firing a shotgun and the other wielding a damned submachine gun! So, not just the crazy. We also have to worry about the near crazy, those with fantasies, those who celebrate violence, those with a grudge against society, etcetera, and etcetera. They will all now be equally dangerous to you and me."

Mark slumped in his seat, "My God."

Cooper caught Jake's wide-eyed expression. "Mark…and Jake…we will be alright. We just have to keep our eyes open and our wits about us. We need to stay armed, at all times now. And, we will need to get our neighbors organized."

"Organized? What good will that do against *this*?"

"Plenty. This will sound cold, but we don't have to outrun the bear, just outrun the others that the bear is chasing."

"What the hell does that mean?" Mark shot back.

"It is simple really. The lone psychos won't stand a chance against a group that is armed, however ragtag they are. And, the organized predators will go where it is easiest. They always have and always will. Simply by getting our act together, we can keep ourselves safe. Trust me, there will be plenty of places where they won't get themselves organized. That's where the bad boys will go."

Mark sighed, "Wow that *is* calculated. But, it sounds true."

As they rounded the last corner to Cooper's house, Mark continued, "So, what do we do now?"

Mark's question sparked something deep inside Cooper. He felt alive again. Not since he had received the urgent phone call from Elena a few days ago had he felt such a jolt. He felt a strong sense of purpose well up inside of him from down deep. He knew what he had to do. He needed to plan for not only his welfare and Jake's, he had to keep as many people safe as he could during this troubled time. His father's words came back to him. *Do the greatest good for the greatest number.* His father had been trying to help people get a little *more* out of jobs. A slightly larger paycheck. More time with their families. A more secure pension. Cooper knew he'd be simply helping people survive. Cooper couldn't help but gaze skyward and deliver a deliberate wink.

Mark watched Cooper with a quizzical expression before Cooper turned back toward him, his eyes blazing with intensity, "We need to get organized."

Mark looked blankly at him, "Can you speak English please?"

Cooper chuckled before continuing, "First, we need to survey the block. Figure out who is sick and who has died. We need to seal them into their rooms to limit the smell."

Mark interrupted, "Don't we need to bury them?"

Cooper shook his head firmly, "No, the risk of disease from dead bodies is grossly exaggerated and misunderstood. The truth is, as long as you keep corpses away from your water supply, there isn't a risk of any disease spreading"

Mark remained unconvinced. Cooper continued, "But, I tell you what. We *should* bury them because it will help with people's spirits. Give closure." *And eliminate everyone worrying about disease spreading just as you're doing.*

Mark nodded.

"Second, we need to round up every able bodied adult who has ever handled a firearm before *or* is willing to learn. Third, we need to inventory all of our available means of defense. We'll start with firearms, but we should include knives, baseball bats, and other hand to hand weapons. I suspect we will be noticeably short of guns. Finally, we pull everyone together, say first thing in the morning, and go over our plan."

Mark nodded as Cooper talked. A light returned to his eyes and a wide smile graced his lips. "Right on. I like it. We can't just wait around like sitting ducks wondering what will happen." Mark's reaction proved the old axiom that getting people into motion during a crisis always elevated spirits.

As the pickup pulled up curbside, Cooper finished his thoughts, "While Jake and I unload the truck, why don't you go find us enough people to put a few pairs together to survey the block?"

"Got it," Mark responded, a twinge of excitement in his voice.

"I'll put together some sheets of paper and clipboards for people to use."

Mark nodded and trotted off. He was confident that Dranko would be one of the people Mark would ask to help out. He wondered if his friend had calmed down enough to join them.

An hour later, the pickup was unloaded, the clipboards were ready, and three pairs were ready to go. Mark and Peter, Lisa and Lily, John and Freddie Jones. Freddie was in his mid-twenties and rented a room out in the neighborhood. His blonde hair would bob uncontrollably whenever he was laughing, which was often. He enjoyed laughing at his own jokes, most of which were, thankfully, funny. He was short but muscular. Today, he had a grim expression on his face and his normally alert blue eyes were downcast and placid.

The others naturally gathered around Cooper when he moved toward them.

"What we're going to do is very simple. I know Mark has probably explained it, but let's review it real quick. We need to knock on every door in our block, including the houses that face our block. We want to know three things: any deaths experienced in the household, any unburied deceased in the household, and what weapons they have available for the common defense. This last one is important: be clear you are asking if they have weapons they can lend to the neighborhood during this emergency. We aren't *taking* anyone's guns."

"*That's* not a misunderstanding we want," Freddie piped in. Everyone laughed nervously.

"Right. We also want to invite everyone to a meeting, this evening at five o'clock. Right here, on my lawn. Ask each household to send one person. Tell them we're going to make a plan to protect our neighborhood and we're starting with a plan to defend our block. Questions?"

"Won't people be too afraid of getting sick to come to a meeting?" asked Peter.

Cooper paused for a moment, the corners of his mouth turning downward, "That's a good question. Some will be. But, you all weren't too afraid. Why?"

"I figured I've already been exposed to whatever this thing was and I just didn't want to hunker down and wait to see if I was gonna get sick," John chimed in without hesitation.

"For me, I just didn't want to be alone anymore. I knew it was probably dumb to come out, but I couldn't stand it!" Freddie remarked.

Cooper nodded, "Right. Some people will be too afraid to come out, but many won't be for a variety of reasons. So, let's ask people and see what we get." The group nodded in agreement.

"Shouldn't we also track how many are sick in the household?" Lisa asked.

Cooper didn't hesitate, "No. We shouldn't." The faces around him went slack in surprise. He let what he'd said sink in before continuing. "One, we can't do anything for those who are sick and all it will do is raise expectations that we will help them somehow. Second, people are still afraid so the data we collect wouldn't be reliable. And, third, it could sound people's alarm bells just by... "

Peter interjected, "Yeah, someone might think we're going to round up all the sick people or something."

"Exactly. Since there is nothing we can do for them, it just isn't worth it. We can do two things: dispose of the dead properly and respectfully, and keep those alive from getting hurt or worse by the bad guys."

"Any other questions?" Cooper paused for several seconds before continuing, "OK, let's head out and meet back here when we're done. Remember, don't get caught into long conversations and try to be back here in two hours."

The groups nodded in response, gathered up their belongings and headed out.

******

Later, a loud rapping of knuckles on the wooden door roused Cooper from the table where he had been cleaning his pistol. He moved quickly to the window and, peering out, saw Calvin furiously readying himself for another barrage on the door. He pivoted, moved a few steps to the door, and swung it open.

Calvin pushed his way in, his face inches from Cooper's, "What the hell is going on here," he yelled.

Cooper took a step back and waved his hands in front of himself, open-palmed, "Whoa, wait a second. What are you *talking* about?"

"What are you *doing* is the real question, Cooper. *I'm* the President of our Neighborhood Association. Where do you get off sending out Gestapo teams to invade people's privacy?"

Cooper's face flushed crimson, "Are you joking? *That's* what has your panties in a bunch?" He immediately realized his mistake in saying that.

Calvin stepped forward and poked Cooper hard in the chest with his middle fingers, "Don't you *dare* patronize me like that! I ain't takin' that from you!" He had never seen Calvin get physical in anger or use anything less than proper English. *Damn, he's angry!* His mind whirred, seeking a way to defuse him.

Cooper disengaged his eyes and looked downward for a moment, "Look, I didn't send out any Gestapo teams for Chrissakes. I just thought we needed to gather some information to organize the defense of our neighborhood."

"Defense? From what?" Calvin asked this as he took a step backward.

"Haven't you been watching the news? Have you gone outside the neighborhood? There's chaos. People being shot."

Calvin shook his head in disbelief, "Well, of course, I have seen the news. But that has been in other cities and certainly nowhere near *our* neighborhood." Cooper heard his pride shine through as he pronounced "our."

Cooper brokered a smile, "Calvin, there was a family massacred in their car less than a mile from here. Including three children." He paused to let the words sink in and watched some of the color drain from Calvin's face. "Look, our middle-class neighborhood doesn't give us the security it used to. Before, most criminals would stay away, knowing we had good police patrols around here. It's different now."

Calvin recovered, "OK. Maybe you're right. Maybe we need to get ready. But, we have a structure here. We have an Association. We have meetings to decide things. I am the President of it. I, and the other officers, have worked hard for years to keep this neighborhood in order. I…I mean we can handle the job now."

Cooper kicked himself, *I should have thought about this. The Association is Calvin's life. He has always taken it too seriously. It is a large part of his identity. I hate politics and I hate ego more than that, but I need to be smart and deal with it.* He swallowed hard and tasted the dryness of compromise, "You're right. I should have called you and talked to you about this."

Calvin's body loosened, "It's more than that. We could have helped. *I* could have helped. I have already received several phone calls from people who were freaked out when the teams knocked on their door. *If* I had known what was going on, I could have calmed them down."

Cooper bobbed his head up and down, "I got it. It won't happen again. Can we sit down so I can fill you in on what's been happening and what I've seen so far?"

Calvin let loose a palpable exhale of relief and smiled, "That would be great."

******

When the teams reunited a few hours later and finished their debriefing, the news was sobering. Most of the homes had someone who had died from the plague or someone who was seriously ill. This was especially true of the homes with three or more people living there. They had encountered a few homes where no one answered and, upon entering, found the sole resident dead. In some cases, they found a couple both having died. Cooper's rough estimate was that approximately one in six people had died, with that number likely to grow. He was staggered by the figures staring back at him and the pencil slipped from his fingers. He closed his eyes to steady himself.

Their survey also revealed that several dozen bodies needed to be buried. Cooper knew that would take a lot of manpower. He was tempted to suggest the much simpler method of wrapping the bodies in blankets and putting them in a closed-up room, but he recalled from his talk with Mark how that could erode people's spirits too much.

When he turned to look toward the future, the worst news was the lack of weapons available for defense. Between all the homes, they had scarcely a dozen hunting rifles and shotguns and that number again in handguns. Worse, there was very little ammunition available and a few of the firearms had none available at all. Several of the rifles and handguns were small caliber .22s, which had limited value from a defensive standpoint. The one bright spot in the weapons report was that Mr. Hutchison unearthed a World War Two era Browning Automatic Rifle, also known as a BAR, which he had brought back from the war. This was a portable, light machine gun. He had a dozen magazines for it and a few hundred rounds of ammunition. Lisa had mentioned this at the end of the report and this news lifted Cooper's spirits.

Thinking to himself he muttered out loud without realizing it, "That can be our force multiplier."

Freddie asked the question on everyone else's mind, "A what?"

Cooper shook his head, "Sorry. Just thinking to myself. A force multiplier is a weapon that increases the strength of your force in excess of the weapon itself."

Lisa wagged her finger at him, "In English, please."

"It means that the BAR will be extremely effective. Any bad guys hearing a fully automatic weapon shooting bursts of high-powered bullets will think twice before continuing their attack. Just the sound of machine gun fire is psychologically intimidating, especially to people who have never been around it before. It sounds like the air is just full of bullets. Machine guns are also very effective at controlling lines of fire...in our case...the streets. In short, we'll need to keep the BAR at an intersection to control as much street territory as possible *and* keep it mobile in the event of an attack so it can move quickly to the point of engagement."

"Got it," Calvin responded for the group.

"Alright, this is great work, everyone. Why doesn't everyone go home, get some rest before tonight's meeting, and come back a little before five to help me set up?"

As everyone started to leave, Cooper remembered the lesson from earlier.

"Calvin, can you stay behind a minute? You and I need to make a game plan for the meeting tonight."

"Of course."

After the others had left, Cooper motioned Calvin to the table and grabbed two cups of coffee from the kitchen.

"I wanted to run by you some ideas I had for tonight's meeting."

"Go ahead," Calvin said measuredly.

"Well, the first thing is to make plans to bury the dead over the next few days. Digging graves is hard work, but I figure that each two man crew could finish two to three a day without overexertion. They'll have to be shallow. How many crews do you think we could pull together?"

"It depends on who shows up. But, I would estimate that we could have four or five crews out of tonight's meeting."

"That would be good. This would take three or so days then."

"Except more will keep dying," Calvin said glumly.

"True, but at least we'll have started. That should lift spirits." Calvin nodded in agreement. Cooper continued, "The next thing, the big topic, is organizing a neighborhood defense."

"Yes, tell me what you had in mind for that," Calvin asked, stroking his chin.

"It's fairly simple. We need to organize a group of volunteers and then arm them with whatever we have. We'll first take anyone who has military, police, or simply firearms training. After that, we'll just take any able-bodied adult who's willing. Then, we'll establish a checkpoint and patrol schedule."

"Checkpoints?" Calvin's eyebrows arched upward and his distaste for the word was apparent.

"Yes, checkpoints. We put checkpoints on the four corners of our neighborhood and then have two roving patrols. It will be the easiest way to send a message to anyone looking for trouble that our neighborhood is organized and not easy pickings. My guess is that this will prevent ninety percent of any potential problems because they will see this and just drive on further down the road. The last thing we do is set up an easy protocol—if you hear gunfire or such, you grab your weapon and head towards it."

Calvin leaned back in his chair, "I don't know Cooper. Checkpoints? It sounds kind of drastic to me. I like the idea of arming a team and even having patrols. But checkpoints that restrict people's freedom to move around seems a bit extreme to me."

Cooper felt irritation flush his face, "Calvin, if you saw what I did today, you would understand that things have become extreme. In the last forty-eight hours, I've been involved in two shootings and seen over a half-dozen people killed by violence."

Calvin nodded his head for a moment, "OK. I understand your viewpoint. Let me think about it. I want to make sure we take all prudent measures without overreacting."

Cooper breathed deeply, barely hiding his frustration, "Alright, good enough. We can talk it over more tonight, but it would work a lot better if it had your support given how respected you are." Calvin smiled at the compliment.

"Tonight then," he said as he rose to leave.

Cooper couldn't help but get the feeling that tonight's meeting had just turned into a debating society. He grimaced at the thought. *He's still thinking things are roughly 'normal', unable to see that everything is coming completely unhinged around him.* Cooper knew that Calvin wouldn't be the only one caught in that outmoded way of thinking. In times of extreme crisis, one of the most difficult things for people to do was to acknowledge the crisis and then deal with it. The human predilection to deny unpleasant news—especially *extremely* unpleasant news—was very strong.

He decided to prepare some shock treatment for the meeting tonight.

Chapter 12

A few streaks of sunlight cut through the overcast sky as they gathered in Cooper's front yard. A chill enveloped them as afternoon turned to evening. The steps leading up to Cooper's front door formed an impromptu speakers' platform, on which Cooper, Calvin, and Jake stood. Off to their right, an eighty foot tall Deodar Cedar tree flanked the house. To the left, a clutch of white birch trees separated his home from the sidewalk. In between, close to fifty of his neighbors were assembled.

The previous fifteen minutes had been marked by a growing murmur of a dozen conversations as they came together. The murmurs were often punctuated sharply by exclamations as they told one another of their losses. Very few exchanged a comforting hug, however. It was as if the physical restraint expressed itself in exaggerated verbal demonstrations of sympathy and support. *Those who are here overcame any paranoia of the plague, but at some subconscious level they are still afraid and are keeping some distance.*

While standing outside waiting for the past half hour, Cooper noticed only a few cars had passed and even less pedestrian traffic. Cooper noticed that only two other people had a handgun holstered to their side and Harry Ledger, a middle-aged insurance salesman who lived at the far end of the block, had a shotgun cradled in his arms. Cooper had been careful to keep his handgun on him, but had left his shotgun just inside the front door. Cooper knew that the task before him would be daunting. *Too many don't grasp that everything has fundamentally changed. Safety can no longer be assumed.*

He took a step forward and raised his hands. Within a few moments, the crowd had quieted. Taking a deep breath, Cooper was thankful he had seen his father address many a group when he was a young boy. He had learned many important lessons.

"Good evening, neighbors," he said and waited for the response back from the crowd. *Create the group's identity at the outset.*

"I want to thank you all for being here today. We live in fearful times and I know it took courage to come here." *Compliment the people, but be sincere.*

"Next time, we'll all even shake hands." *Make a joke to put everyone at ease.* People laughed, but Cooper heard the anxiety that hid behind it.

"For those who know me well, you know I get straight to the point. I've asked you to be here because we must talk about the security of our neighborhood. The police are no longer on the streets. I've left this neighborhood three times in the last few days, been involved in two shootings, and seen the results of two other shootings. I believe most people are good, but it's the few bad ones we all need to be worried about now. We need to make a plan for our neighborhood." He paused, awaiting a response.

Amidst people exchanging side glances and shuffling their feet, a voice rang out, "So, what's the plan?"

"First, we form a volunteer group of people willing to provide security to the neighborhood. Second, we put up checkpoints at the four road entrances to our neighborhood. Third, we have patrols that work the inside of our neighborhood. Finally, everyone here adopt a simple rule: if you hear conflict and you are armed, you move toward the fight to help our side win."

As Cooper stopped talking, the expected commotion of numerous individual conversations broke out. Cooper let it proceed for almost a minute until the crescendo started to fall.

"Let's do one question at a time. That way, everyone can hear each other."

Gus Valesta, a lawyer who lived around the corner from Cooper, spoke first, "Cooper, I want to thank you for thinking of everyone's safety at a time like this. But, is all this really necessary? We haven't had any problems in our neighborhood besides those high schoolers who were goofing off."

Cooper breathed deeply to contain himself. "Gus, those high-schoolers had guns. If I hadn't been armed and had Dranko at my side, I don't know what would have happened. So, I do think we've already had a problem in our neighborhood."

"But, you're describing a lot of work when most of us are just trying to keep everyone healthy and cared for in our homes right now," added Michelle Jamison, a homemaker whose husband was absent from the meeting.

"I agree. It's a lot of work. But, I believe if we all agree to this plan then we'll have enough volunteers who are willing and able to take this on."

Gus, a good friend of Calvin's, spoke up again, "My other question is whether checkpoints are really necessary. I mean, having to check in and out with our neighbors every time we go somewhere. I don't want our neighborhood to feel like Russia!"

Cooper shot a hard glance at Calvin who offered a tepid, close-lipped, smile in response. "I want to show everyone something," Cooper said as he grabbed a handful of photos from a folder he had left at his feet. "These are off of my home computer, so the quality is not great. But these are of a family that was gunned down in their car less than a half mile from where we stand tonight." He passed out the pictures that he had gone back and shot earlier of the gruesomely murdered family and allowed them to circulate in the crowd. The gasps of shock grew louder as they were handed from person to person. "These people were not robbed or raped. They were just killed. Killed for no reason except that someone else saw a chance to do it," he paused for effect. "So, they did it."

Cooper waited until Gus held one of the pictures in his hand before continuing, "Trust me, I don't want my neighborhood to feel like Russia. But, this isn't Russia. These would be checkpoints and patrols made up of our neighbors and friends. We are deciding this democratically. It's very different. And, at its worst it is better to be inconvenienced or feel uncomfortable than it is to not feel anything anymore, like the family in those pictures."

Heads began to nod as the crowd came around. Inside, he smiled. He knew he had them.

Then, a familiar voice rang out from the back of the group, "The real question is whether this plan will do any good at all." Dranko stepped into the circle that had formed in front of him when he began speaking. He was looking straight at Cooper, emotionless. Cooper glared back at him as he continued, "I agree with Cooper that things are unsafe now. But, it's worse than that. To be blunt, there isn't a way to keep ourselves safe here in the city. There are more bad guys out there. I've been on my ham radio since this all started and riots and waves of crime are overrunning cities across America. It's simply not safe in *any* city." The crowd rippled with the dull roar of fear as people exclaimed in nervous reaction to his words.

A terrified voice called out, "What do we do, then?"

"My advice is if you have somewhere else to go in the country or to a small town, go. That's what I'm doing first thing in the morning."

"What if we don't have anywhere else to go?"

"Then bunker down as best you can and may God help you," Dranko replied coldly.

The murmurs rose again as the group was thrown into confusion. Cooper's face flushed red and the muscles around his neck tightened, as strong as a vice.

"Dranko is wrong. He is only hearing the worst news out of the other cities. In every natural disaster, some groups and neighborhoods stick together and they come out alright. It happened in Haiti, in Chile, even in Manila! We can do that right here too!"

"Cooper, your pictures showed the work of one, maybe two, psychos who didn't think twice before pulling the trigger. What will happen in this city when the gangs decide they want to take advantage of the situation? Not to mention the *newly* formed gangs of common criminals who now see a new opportunity? In a week's time, those pictures will be multiplied by hundreds or possibly, thousands."

Cooper felt the sting of betrayal in his back, "You're wrong, Dranko. We can protect ourselves. United We Stand. Don't you remember that? You want us to pull up stakes and run. These are our homes. We can't abandon them now." Cooper choked on the last sentence as emotion welled up from deep inside.

"Brother, she's dead. You're not abandoning her by leaving."

Cooper took a step forward, ready to charge at him. But, he controlled himself. The two men stood facing one another, fifteen yards apart. But now, a world separated them. Cooper felt the momentum drain from the crowd as it devolved into whispers, some shouts, and most simply standing in confused silence.

Calvin stepped forward, ever the diplomat, "As President of the Neighborhood Association I move that we adjourn for the evening. Many useful comments and ideas have been presented tonight, but I do not see any consensus for action to move forward at this time."

Cooper stood in silence, looking hard at Dranko, as the seconds ticked by. Finally, he just shook his head and turned to go back inside. Calvin tried to put his hand on Cooper's shoulder, but Cooper stopped his arm in mid-air with a glare. He looked upward, but the sky had returned to a depressing gray. He went into his home, dejected, Jake following him. His heart was pounding, his fists were clenched, and he wanted to punch the walls.

Jake spoke up, "Dad, can I tell you something?"

"Sure. Shoot."

"You were right and they were all wrong. I never knew Uncle Dranko was such a scaredy cat!"

Cooper burst out laughing.

Cooper had meant what he'd said about the need for safety in their neighborhood. That night, they slept on a worn mattress and blankets in the basement. That decision saved their lives.

Chapter 13

Cooper's eyes popped open like they did at boot camp when the Drill Instructor shouted at them to wake up. This time though, it was the quiet creak of a loose floorboard on the first floor that awakened him. His right hand immediately went to his pistol at his side and he moved silently into a crouching position. His left hand instinctively felt for Jake's peaceful, slumbering body next to his in the down sleeping bag. Jake's chest rose and fell in steady rhythm.

Cooper looked intently up at the doorway that led from the basement into their home. Just beyond the doorway, he heard hushed voices in frantic whispering. *Amateurs. Professional thieves wouldn't be talking inside the home.* He distinctly heard two voices, male, but could not make out what they were saying. After a brief discussion, the footsteps moved in opposite directions and away from the doorway.

Cooper clasped one hand over Jake's mouth and used the other to jostle him awake. Jake awoke with terrified eyes and immediately attempted to make a noise. Cooper clamped down harder to prevent him from making any noise at all, and ordered him to silence with a single finger to his mouth and intense, squinted eyes. Jake relaxed and Cooper released the hold on his mouth.

Cooper put his mouth next to his son's ear and whispered, "Stay calm. We have intruders in our house above. At least two."

Fear clouded Jake's eyes and they turned into narrow slits. "Don't worry son, I will deal with them."

Jake nodded, then whispered with an unsteady voice, "Wh...What are you going to do?"

Jake was unnerved by what he saw in his father's eyes and the icy tone in his voice, "They will leave or I will kill them." Cooper moved a few feet away and grabbed the .22 rifle that they had put next to where they'd slept.

He thrust the rifle into his son's hands. For the first, but not the last time, he inwardly cursed the way this plague was forcing his son to lose his childhood. He knew his son was losing it in large, hacked out, slices instead of the slow erosion of innocence lost.

"I need you to take this. If anyone comes down these stairs that isn't me, aim this at the center of their chest. Keep squeezing the trigger until the gun is empty," he racked the bolt to chamber a round. "This magazine holds twenty-five rounds. You can protect yourself. Kill the first man who comes down. Anyone behind him will run. Got it?"

Jake gripped the rifle tightly, the way he used to crush his teddy bear when he had been scared by a bad dream. Cooper was surprised by the steady gaze on Jake's face. Eleven-year-olds shouldn't have such a hard stare. Cooper was torn between feelings of pride and remorse seeing it on his own son.

"Don't worry. I remember how to shoot," Jake whispered with exaggerated confidence; referring to the two or three times that Cooper had taken him target shooting.

Cooper gave him a squeeze on his shoulder, grabbed the shotgun from where it leaned against the concrete foundation wall, and turned to head upstairs to deal with the danger that waited above.

In normal times, he would have stayed put and simply defended the basement if they had decided to come down here. Now, however, he knew they could not afford to lose anything that they had upstairs that the burglars had come to steal. Going to the store for replacements was no longer an option. Worse, his gun safe was in the guest bedroom closet and he was certain they would find that, as well.

He began the silent ascent on the stairway, taking time to avoid any sound coming from the old, creaky, steps. He was like an old man, bent over and taking each step in due time. He had the shotgun firmly in grasp, while his pistol was holstered with a round in the chamber. Cooper steadied his breath to keep his reflexes alert and adrenaline flowing, while still keeping himself under control. This discipline had saved his life during firefights in Iraq.

Finally, he reached the top stair and slowly turned the doorknob. Once he had enough room to squeeze through, he stepped onto the main level of their home, did a scan in all directions and closed the door behind him. He listened intently and heard footsteps from upstairs, moving rapidly from room to room. He smelled a sour whiff of fear-laced sweat and he wrinkled his nose. He took a step to his left to begin circling the staircase that rose to the second floor. The house was darkened; the only light was from the streetlamp cascading through the windows on the south side of the house. He now wished that he had set up his shotgun to accommodate a tactical flashlight. Dranko had urged him several times to do so, but he'd never gotten around to it. *Hopefully, my strong night vision will be good enough.*

He continued creeping down the hallway, stopping to listen for several seconds between steps. He heard one of the thieves upstairs rummaging opening and closing drawers. What worried Cooper was that he couldn't tell if the second person was upstairs or not based upon what he was hearing. However, he heard nothing on the main level other than the faint sound of his own breath, measured and steady.

Jake's room was now on his right and he peered in. From what he could see, everything looked to still be in its place. With the barrel of the shotgun, he pushed the door open further and it emitted what sounded like a thunderous creak from its hinges. Cooper stopped immediately and cocked his head to point his ears upward. The noise from upstairs continued unabated. The burglars were apparently intent on their search and not paying attention to security. He scanned the room from side to side and saw nothing out of the ordinary.

He turned back towards the staircase and started moving a little faster, taking only a second to pause between steps instead of several. A few paces later, he approached the office, also on the right. He heard it a split second before it happened.

A loud, animal-like grunt preceded a heavy-set man crashing into him from the office. Cooper smashed into the opposite wall, breaking one of the picture frames that hung in the hallway. The glass splintered and a shard tore into his shoulder. As glass pierced flesh, he felt the burning pain shoot across his body. His head was pushed into the wall with a thud and he was stunned. He smelled the foul breath of his attacker, the rank smell of whiskey mixed with Frito Lay corn chips. The other man ripped furiously on the shotgun, trying to wrench it from Cooper's hands.

Cooper held on. He gritted his teeth and shook his head to rid himself of the loud ringing he now heard. With his left hand, he clamped down with a vice-like grip on the shotgun. With his right, he delivered a hard, straight punch to his attacker's face. He felt bone and cartilage crunching and realized that he had delivered a direct blow to his nose. The man fell backwards, releasing his grip on the gun. He fell to his knees and gathered himself to leap at Cooper once more.

Cooper pivoted the shotgun, pointed it directly at the middle of his body. Time slowed and Cooper saw everything happening frame by frame. He saw the man's face clearly, blood covering his shattered nose and flowing down to cover his lips and teeth. Bloody spittle sprayed as he breathed heavily. Some of his dark hair had escaped the black knit cap that lay crooked on his head. He was young, probably just a teenager. In the dim light, Cooper couldn't tell the color of his eyes, but they were wide open in terror. Cooper had stared down the barrel of a shotgun once before and he knew when you were on the receiving end, it looked as large as a howitzer. The boy began raising his hands in the universal sign of surrender. Cooper began to lower the shotgun just a hair and readied himself to call out to the intruder's partner upstairs to give himself up, as well.

Then, to his shock, someone else tackled Cooper from behind. The blow vaulted Cooper forward. The shotgun was pushed against his trigger finger and exploded. The boy in front of Cooper was shredded with a point blank blast of 00 Buckshot. This close, Cooper was sprayed in blood and bits of ruined flesh. The boy pitched forward, his knees scraping the wooden floor. The other attacker landed on the back of Cooper's legs and hip. Cooper knew enough to slide one leg to a bent position as he went down. This allowed him some leverage to swing his body over and to the left, lifting his opponent off of him and slamming into the right side of the hallway. Cooper was surprised how easy it was to swing this guy off him, he was so light. Now, on his back, Cooper got a good view of his second attacker as he ricocheted into the wall and bounced off.

He saw another teenager. This one was skinny, almost frail. He had blonde hair, which hung in ragged clumps, covering his eyes. He had not taken the blow well and had collapsed in a heap onto the floor. Cooper couldn't see his face. The lower half had impacted on his dead friend, but his torso had slammed into the wall hard. He lay on the floor, gasping and moaning from pain and fear.

Without thinking, Cooper racked the slide of the shotgun, with the distinctive *cha-chuk* sound, and braced it against his shoulder. He aimed it straight at the new attacker over his body from where he lay.

"I wouldn't do that if I were you!" a voice shouted at him from the landing of the stairwell.

Cooper turned his head slightly to the right and was staring straight into the face of the teenagers' leader from the other day. Dark long hair reached his shoulders; he had deep-set, intense eyes. Now it hit him. *The other two guys are Rick and Smartie. Dumbasses decided to come back.* Cooper was also staring down the barrel of a .45 pistol, 1911-style, the gaping bore looming large. He kept his breath steady and lowered the shotgun.

"That's a good boy. Rick," he said motioning to the blonde that Cooper had just catapulted into the wall, "grab his gun."

Rick rose unsteadily onto his feet. He cradled his head with both hands and was slowly regaining his bearings.

"Hurry up, will you? We don't have all night. Can't you handle a little toss into a wall, you fucking pansy?"

Rick looked back at the leader, stung by the rebuke. He kicked

Cooper in the leg for good measure and then leaned over to retrieve the shotgun. Cooper had landed at an angle, so his pistol was digging into his hip, but it was concealed from their view.

The long-haired man spoke again, "I'm going to make you a deal. You tell me the combination to your gun safe upstairs and we'll let you live. No muss, no fuss."

Cooper paused, buying time, before speaking. "How do I know you won't just kill me after I give you the combination?"

The other man laughed, "Well, you don't." He cackled at his own joke and Rick joined in, but nervously. "But, I'll make you another deal. You give me the combination, and I won't go through your whole house looking for that little boy of yours. If I can get your guns, then tonight's work will be well worth it. Even with losing Smartie, who was the dumbest bastard I've ever known. God rest his soul," he leered sarcastically. "This way, you have two deals with me and even a snake slick punk like me will keep at least half of my word. Isn't that right, Rick?"

Rick nodded rapidly, "That's right Woody!" Rick was visibly nervous, standing next to Smartie's corpse. *Probably first time he's ever smelled the blood and mess of a dead man.* Cooper could see the shotgun shaking in his hands.

Cooper waited, breathing steadily.

Woody grew impatient and took a half-step towards Cooper and pointed the pistol at him, "Well, what's it gonna be, old man? You gonna give us the combination to your safe or not?"

Cooper grunted, "Sure. I'll do it. But, I have to go up there with you. I don't remember the numbers without actually working the dial. Muscle memory, you know."

Woody thought for a moment, weighing the truth of his words, "OK, OK. You can get up, but do it real slow."

Cooper feigned an old man, rising ever-so-slowly onto his knees.

"Hurry up! I don't have all night. I know the cops aren't doing much these days, but I have no doubt one of your neighbors heard you give the buckshot greeting to Smartie and have dialed 911 by now. If you're lucky, it might have been answered."

As Cooper straightened up, he kept his right hip pointed away from Rick and Woody.

"It's not the cops you have to worry about in our neighborhood. Drop it!" Dranko's voice rang out strong and clear as he buried the barrel of his rifle into Woody's head, just behind the ear.

Cooper knew Woody couldn't see the barrel, but it must have *felt* like a cannon notched against his head. Woody's .45 clattered as it hit the floor.

In a quick, fluid motion, Cooper had his pistol trained on Rick. Rick lowered the shotgun and held it out for Cooper, holding it by the stock, barrel pointed at the ground.

"So, just what are we going to do with you two boys?" Cooper asked. "I think we warned you last time we'd give you a bullet if you came back into our neighborhood. This time you came *into* my home. Doesn't that mean I should give you two a bullet as promised?"

Rick whimpered and began to cry. Woody looked at him with disgust and then turned back toward Cooper, defiant, "Do whatever you want. You got us fair and square. I ain't scared of you."

"Oh, this guy's a tough one, a real hard case," Dranko mocked, pushing the barrel harder against his skull. Woody winced in pain.

"My, my, he is. Tough as nails. I would put you down like the cur that you are. But, see, that would be illegal as you don't pose a threat to me right now. While the law isn't very operative right now, it would still be wrong. Besides, I have a better idea than that," Cooper said smiling confidently.

"What're you gonna do, call the cops?"

"Hmmm, we can try that, but I'm guessing 911 is busy right now. No, my idea is much simpler than that. First, you two are going to strip naked. Then, you are going to hoist what's left of your friend Smartie onto your back. We're then going to escort you out of our neighborhood and down the road a bit, maybe a mile or two."

"What the hell you doing all this for?" Woody interrupted.

"It's simple. Carrying a half-torn apart dead man, especially one that was your friend, will take the piss and vinegar out of any man. You included. I'm betting that fifteen minutes of feeling his blood drip down your body, having to smell all that *death* right up close and personal will make you rethink your current line of work. I think when you return to your gang, most of whom are just along for the joy ride, naked, covered in blood, and humiliated, that your days of leading that ragtag band will be over. You see, they're going to ask what happened to Smartie and you'll have to tell them how he died. I think they'll then see following you around is bad for their health. You really should just go back to playing video games and kicking the occasional dog."

"My boys won't abandon me," Woody shot back.

"Oh yeah? I think once they realize that a night out with you can bring them home dead, they will drop you like a hot potato. Young men don't like to think about dying and Smartie here will ensure that your boys will have no choice. They will know their leader can't even pull off a simple home burglary—in this neighborhood anyway—without getting one of his boys killed. You see, your *gang* is nothing more than a bunch of scared and misguided teenagers who've watched one too many Tarantino movies. You all thought this would be fun and games. Now, they're gonna see that what you're doing is serious business. So serious, they could end up *dead*."

Woody stared back at him, fuming. Woody knew his leadership was being eviscerated in front of Rick which meant it would spread to the others once they got back.

Cooper broke the silence quickly, "I'm done with you. Let's get going."

A half hour later, Woody and Rick were gone. Dranko had escorted them, naked and carrying Smartie's limp body, a mile or so down Division Street, headed east. No police crossed their path, which showed just how far law enforcement had fallen. Dranko had used their assailant's pickup and returned with it to the neighborhood. They also kept Woody's .45 pistol which turned out to be a well-maintained original Colt. Cooper had spent the time cleaning up the mess that Smartie had left behind. He kept Jake in the basement until everything had been returned to normal, save the broken picture frame that now hung on their wall without any glass in it. He had also bandaged his shoulder wound, which fortunately had not cut into any muscle.

When Dranko returned, Cooper reached out a hand to his friend, "Thank you. You saved my ass back there."

Dranko smiled, "You're lucky I'm a night owl. I was already up when I heard that 12 gauge blast, I just came running." His smile grew wider as he continued, "Despite me being pissed off at you, I couldn't let you get killed by some no good teenagers."

Cooper returned the smile, "Good that keeps us square because I'm still pissed off at you. But, I'm too damn tired to talk about it right now."

"Me too. Let's talk later, over some breakfast, brother."

"Sounds good."

Dranko left as quickly as he had come.

Cooper decided to watch the latest news on the television, but when he turned it on, he discovered his cable was out. Not a single station came on. He shook his head, and turned on his radio instead. Every station was carrying news. He quickly settled on his favorite station.

"...in Des Moines, there are at least fifteen confirmed dead and seventy-six wounded after a riot at a Wal-Mart distribution center. Hundreds had gathered there as the shelves in retail grocery stories emptied. That concludes our latest round-up of news related to the Brushfire Plague.

In direct news, the Center for Disease Control has announced that it is working around the clock to identify the source and structure of this virus so that work on a vaccine can begin in earnest. They announced significant progress on identifying and mapping its structure.

Dr. Leonard Luciani from John Hopkins University has caused a firestorm of controversy with his recent claim that he believes that the Brushfire Plague was not an accidental mutation. He said yesterday, during an interview on CNN, "...the rapidity at which this virus spread indicates it was not accidental. I've read the explanations that this virus appearing across the globe, almost simultaneously, is due to the commonality of international travel is complete hogwash." He has been roundly condemned across the scientific community for his comments and has been called "irresponsible", "dangerous", and even "criminal."

Casualty figures continue to be difficult to ascertain accurately, but most estimates are that between thirty and fifty million are either dead or infected across America..."

Cooper turned off the radio. He'd heard enough.

******

A few hours later, they reassembled at Cooper's house. Cooper had decided to begin emptying out his freezer first and so he had fried a dozen frozen sausages, cooked a mess of hash browns, and mixed up some orange juice from concentrate. A pot of hot coffee rounded off the repast. Cooper and Dranko gathered at the table. Jake was still asleep in the basement. After the night's events, Cooper wanted him to sleep as much as he could. He would warm the breakfast for him later.

Uncharacteristically, Dranko spoke first. "I owe you an apology, brother. I shouldn't have come at you the other night like that. Not publicly, anyway."

"Well, I owe..." Cooper began, but Dranko waved him off with a sausage link skewered firmly by his fork. He was chomping on it as he talked.

"Let me finish. You *are* wrong, Cooper. It would be safer where I want to go. Hell, last night proved that beyond a doubt. But, I understand you aren't going to leave. This means I have an important decision to make: to go where I know it'd be safer or stick around here with a stubborn old friend who isn't thinking sensibly."

Cooper interjected this time, impossible to restrain, "I just *can't* leave. I know you think it's silly, but *she's* still here. There's something in every room. I don't want to leave it all behind and I sure don't want to take Jake away from it all either."

"I get it, brother. Your stubborn stance on this — and the reason why — got me thinking. What do I want to survive *for*? I know my carcass isn't worth keeping safe and sound based upon any *intrinsic* value!" He paused to laugh at his own joke and almost choked on a piece of sausage. "I thought about this a good long time. I decided that you were right. You survive so you can help keep some other good people alive with you. It's no secret that I'm a guy who keeps to himself mostly. But, your bond with Elena and Jake has me thinking about all that too."

Cooper smiled impishly at his friend, "Does that mean you'll stay around here, then?"

Without looking up, Dranko stuffed a dollop of hash browns into his mouth and waved the empty fork in the air, "For now. For now, brother."

Cooper thumped the table with an open-palmed hand, spilling coffee as the table bounced in response, "Nice! Very nice! I can't tell you how much it means to me. As the last few days have shown, I need you around to make it through. Last night being Exhibit A," he paused and took a swig of coffee.

His tone turned serious, "But let me apologize to you. I shouldn't have been so stubborn about all this, I know part of it is crazy and doesn't make sense to anyone else. But it makes sense to *me*. And, I could have done a better job of explaining it to you instead of just getting angry. I owed you that."

The two men looked at each other in the eye, catching the deep gaze that only longtime friends can exchange.

"So, we're good?" Cooper asked.

"We're better than good, brother."

They ate the rest of their breakfast in companionable silence, only the sounds of slurping coffee and chomping of sausage links to punctuate it.

******

Dranko helped Cooper clean the dishes from the table, rinse them, and put them in the dishwasher. As they turned to clear the remaining items from the table, Dranko stopped in mid-stride.

"We need a redo."

"A what?" Cooper asked.

"We need to reassemble everyone. Since I screwed up the meeting yesterday, I'm going to help make it right. I'll make the rounds, tell everyone what happened last night, and get 'em all here at noon today."

Cooper thought for a moment, "That's right. After last night, it's more serious than even I thought. Go get it done." Dranko launched the towel he'd been holding toward Cooper and rose to leave.

As he reached the door, Cooper called out, "Oh, wait. Can you visit Calvin and make sure he's on board with pulling another meeting together?"

"Yeah, got it," he said and scampered out of the house at full speed.

Chapter 14

The scene at Cooper's house looked almost the same as the meeting yesterday, except the sun was shining brightly and there were a dozen more people clustered around his front yard. A brisk breeze brought the faintest hint of spring to his nose and goose pimples on his bare arms.

He was ready to begin addressing the crowd when Dranko leapt onto the steps and nudged him out of the way. He looked at the small crowd, grew nervous, and began awkwardly.

"Ah, this isn't easy for me. But, I need to apologize to everyone. I was wrong yesterday. We *can* defend our homes and neighborhood and keep ourselves safe. Most of you have heard this by now, but we stopped three attackers last night. Three. In a surprise attack. So, we all should listen to Cooper today. I should have yesterday. We *all* should have listened."

A smattering of unsteady applause broke out as Dranko jumped down to the ground like a man fleeing the porch after a bad first date. He hated having attention focused on him. Cooper smiled and stepped to the front again. He motioned for Calvin to join him on the steps and he did so.

"Last night was my worst nightmare. Waking up to the sound of intruders in your own home is terrifying. I was armed and I've had some experience. Dranko's right, we can defend ourselves. But, last night I got lucky. It could have been much worse. If Dranko hadn't been awake, heard the gunshot, and come over, I would be dead and Jake would be an orphan, or worse." Remembering his father's advice, Cooper paused to let the words sink in. Whispers broke out and several people clutched their hand to their mouth in fear.

"Some checkpoints and patrols could have stopped that from happening. At a minimum, we'll have some warning before anyone is inside our home."

Heads began nodding furiously throughout the group. Cooper interjected before it rose to a crescendo, "I know Calvin, the President of our Neighborhood Association, was wise in recognizing our divisions yesterday. For any plan to work, we must *all* be behind it. I'm sure he has good insight to share as well today." Calvin recognized political graciousness when he saw it and winked at Cooper as he stepped forward. Cooper's gleam in his eye was the only response that

Calvin needed. *What little political chops I have, I owe to my father.* Cooper smiled to himself at the thought.

Calvin turned toward the audience, "First, I want to thank Cooper and Dranko for their heroism last night. Because of them, one punk was dealt with and the other two were run out of our neighborhood on a rail!" Everyone began clapping at once and pumping their fists in the air at Cooper. Dranko, in the audience, was thumped on the back by several men and hugged by a few women. His face turned bright red and he looked intently at the ground.

Calvin adroitly waited for the noise to subside, "Second, what happened last night gave us all new information. We have *never* had a home invasion situation in this neighborhood before last night. Third, after due consideration of this new evidence, I now fully support yesterday's plan to defend our neighborhood."

More applause greeted this announcement and he continued without pause by raising his voice, "Any discussion?" People looked at each other and shook their heads.

A moment later, Gus Varela called out, "I like the plan, but let's include nominating Calvin as our Defense Captain, too!" Cooper couldn't tell if he'd imagined a sly glance between the two men just before Gus blurted out the suggestion.

Calvin bellowed, "All in favor say 'Aye'." A thunderous chorus of "Ayes" rang out.

"All opposed say 'Nay'." Dead silence.

Pandemonium broke out. A few hats were thrown into the air. Some started to applaud. Others embraced in tight hugs. There was lots of backslapping. Hands reached up and pulled Calvin and Cooper off the steps to shake their hands. Cooper found himself being hugged and palms thudding against his back. It was a sea of smiling faces and a chorus of "thanks" and "I should have listened to you yesterday."

The overwhelming reaction made Cooper pause in confusion. Then, it hit him. *Catharsis. All the pent up stress and emotion from the last several days is being released. The community has come back together. People are planning for tomorrow again.* He knew this was what was eliciting such emotion. He stood watching it all unfold. His body ached to join in and get lost in the emotion and enthusiasm, but he knew the possible bloodshed, terror, and horror that awaited them; that awaited anyone who had to pick up weapons to defend themselves. *Here I go again, worrying about tomorrow,* he mused to himself. He recalled his father's words,

"Men like us lose a bit of today, because we are always

thinking of the needs of tomorrow." His father had accepted this trait, even embraced it. Cooper had never been able to do so. So, he stood apart, watching wistfully at the joy erupting around him, which he could not lose himself in.

As if on cue, Dranko was at his side with a clipboard. He thrust it into Cooper's hand, and he looked down at it.

It was a sign-up sheet for the checkpoints and patrols, broken down by shift. *Thanks dad, the needs of tomorrow indeed.*

Dranko whispered into his ear, "No time like the present to get volunteers."

Just like that Cooper was back at work.

******

The crowd outside his home lingered. Pairs and small groups stayed put and continued in conversations. Periodically, the groups would dissolve and then reassemble with others, like at a party where everyone is having such a good time they look for excuses, and new people to talk to, in order to stay. They would first talk of matters relevant to the crisis of the plague, but then would move on to mundane matters: the weather, hobbies, or sports. Their faces started off grave and serious, but then would morph into smiles, laughter, and loud voices of exclamation. Cooper watched, wondering at the display. Slowly, it dawned on him. Having overcome their fear of disease and embracing the welcome emotion of community, everyone was loath to leave and return to their isolated homes. Their homes were now a place where most faced the presence of a loved one ill and dying or a fresh memory of one who had died. Death awaited them at home, in one way or another. Here, they could live. This meeting had transformed from a necessary evil, into a welcome escape from the plague and the isolation it had wrought.

Cooper breathed in a deep sigh of satisfaction. They had not had a problem assembling a schedule for the checkpoints and patrols. In addition, they had three burial teams sign up and they would begin the first of their grisly work in the morning. *This* felt right. He had always been a person of action and now that a plan was in motion, he could relax a little. The sun was still shining and the chill had disappeared from the air. Fluffy white clouds moved lazily across the sky, driving east to points unknown. As they had done throughout, the birds flittered on the wind, oblivious to the troubles of man below.

Dranko grunted, bringing Cooper's attention back down to

earth. Cooper turned to face him and noticed an impish smile on his face. *Something must be up, I've never seen him smile like that!* Cooper, Mark, Calvin, Freddie, and Jake gathered around him. Dranko had carefully whispered to each of them and asked them to remain behind after the meeting.

"If you would please, follow me, gentlemen," Dranko intoned, mimicking an eighteenth century butler.

The other men exchanged humored looks and fell in line behind Dranko as he walked toward his home. Jake gripped his father's hand with his left and with his right motioned the universal sign for "he's crazy" toward Dranko, smiling broadly the entire time. Cooper couldn't repress a laugh in return.

Dranko led them through his back door into his kitchen and stopped there to face the group. His face had grown serious and the excitement had faded. *OK, this is the Dranko I know, serious as a heart attack.*

"I have something to show you. Some tools that can help us in our current predicament. But, before I can show any of them to you, I need your word you won't tell another soul what it is that I reveal to you."

"C'mon Dranko, what's with the drama?" Mark asked first.

Dranko looked straight back at him, "Mark, not drama. Security. I need your word."

"Well, how can I promise something when I do not even know what you are going to reveal? I'm the President of the Association; I couldn't keep it quiet if you had 500 doses of something that would cure this illness, for example. Give us a hint at least," Dranko shifted his gaze to Calvin as he spoke.

Dranko shook his head in frustration, "Calvin, my request for silence will enhance the welfare of this neighborhood, I assure you of that. Like I said, I have some tools that will help us through this current crisis, but I can't show them to you unless I have your word.

Cooper knew that Dranko was talking about guns or weapons of some kind, so he decided to assist his friend, "I'm in. You have my word. I trust you. Jake you'll keep it silent as well, right?" Jake nodded quickly and seriously. A forced grave look scarcely concealed a lurking smile. You could tell he was immensely pleased to be in the room during this grown-up conversation.

"Alright, with your assurance that my silence benefits our neighborhood, you have my word," Calvin added.

Mark nodded his head with an ironic corner of his mouth

upturned, "Sure. You have my word as well." Everyone had agreed in quick order.

Dranko clapped his hands, the excitement returning, "OK then, follow me."

He grabbed a set of keys off of the wall and moved to the door that led to his basement. He unlocked the door, flicked on a light, and led them downstairs. The old stairs creaked in rapid succession as they descended.

At the bottom, a large room off to the right was blocked by a heavy steel door. To the left was a washer, a dryer and assorted detritus of camping gear, cleaning supplies, and tools. Cooper realized now that as long as he had known Dranko, he had never been down in the basement.

"My Lord, what the hell do you have down here, Fort Knox?" Mark asked incredulously as he noticed the steel door had a large lock combination dial and a handle with five spokes coming to open it. In fact, it did look like a smaller version of a bank vault door.

Dranko didn't miss a beat as he fiddled with the dial, "Not Fort Knox; it's what I call Depot Prudence. You'll see why I have this security in a moment."

Calvin looked at Cooper with an upturned eyebrow and Cooper could only shrug his shoulders, "I know no more than you. Dranko's never shown me down here."

Dranko stepped back from the dial, turned the spoked handle, and opened the heavy door, "Please step in."

They ambled into the darkened room slowly. Dranko followed them in and then turned on a few light switches. Their eyes recoiled from the sudden brightness of the multiple banks of fluorescent lighting overhead. Apparently, Mark's vision recovered quickest.

"Wow, Dranko what the hell have you got here?

Now, Cooper could see it too. He involuntarily let out a low whistle.

Jake shouted excitedly, "There must be a hundred in here!"

Dranko laughed out loud, "No, no, only a few dozen."

Calvin stood gaping, slack-jawed, "Are those legal?" He pointed at a couple military-style rifles that were displayed, mounted on a peg board; the way most men organized their hammers or screwdrivers.

"Of course," Dranko responded, with a sly wink that only Cooper noticed.

They were standing a few feet inside the door. Immediately in front of them, opposite the entrance was a rack that held over a dozen shotguns and hunting rifles, evenly split between them. The hunting rifles seemed nothing out of the ordinary, a mixture of synthetic and wooden stocks, most with scopes.

To their right were the pegboard-mounted assault rifles.

"Do any of these go full-auto?" Cooper asked.

"Only one. The M16. The other two are a semi-automatic AK-47 and a FAL." Dranko noticed the apprehensive furrowed eyebrows that popped onto Calvin's face and so he quickly added, "Don't worry Calvin, the M16 is legal too. Bought and processed through the good ole' Bureau of Alcohol, Tobacco, and Firearms. Machine guns, with the right paperwork, are legal here in Oregon."

"...and God Bless America!" Freddie sang. At that, everyone laughed.

Calvin laughed loudest and longest, a deep baritone, and grabbed his sides.

"C'mon, my joke wasn't *that* funny," Freddie said.

Calvin gathered himself and shook his head back and forth, "I was a liberal my entire life. I *hated* guns. Always fought against them. And, now, standing here, I'm as happy as a lark that Dranko has a damned *machine gun* that we can use! That, my friends, is ironic!" Everyone chuckled once more.

"Well, the times have changed," Mark said.

"Yes. Yes, they have," Calvin finished with a wide grin.

Dranko turned his attention to the wall behind them, next to the door. Mounted on hooks on the wall were over a dozen pistols and revolvers of different makes and calibers. He recognized Glocks, Smith and Wessons, Colts, and a few Berettas.

"Depot Prudence, you say? Damn, Dranko, this is Fort Disneyland!" Mark exclaimed when he had finished scanning the room.

Dranko tried to remain serious, but couldn't contain a wide grin from breaking out on his face. He coughed to clear his throat, "Let's just say I've always had an interest in firearms and in being ready for anything that might happen. I tried building this collection up, but always lacked the time or money."

Cooper clapped him on the back, knocking him off balance, "How about we just say you've always been a pessimistic son of a bitch and we're all a damn sight thankful for it right about now!"

Everyone burst out laughing. After it subsided, Dranko spoke up, "Alright, it's time to gear up, but first some basics."

"Let me guess, the first rule of Gun Club is we don't talk about Gun Club," Freddie's quip elicited another round of laughter.

Dranko let it subside before proceeding. The others gathered around him, in a small semi-circle. Cooper had never seen him like this before, confident and in command around others. Here, Cooper knew they were on his terrain. Firearms and weapons was a subject that Dranko was an expert in; at least relative to everyone else in this room. Dranko spread his feet shoulder width apart, folded his hands together, and began.

"As a matter of fact, Freddie, the first rule *is* not to talk about what I have. To anyone. Wives too."

"Why not?" Calvin queried.

Cooper answered so Dranko didn't have to, "One word: security. You tell someone and then they tell someone. Before we know it, some bad guys find out there are some weapons here and they'll come looking for them. And, they won't be coming to politely ask for them. Weapons are in short supply right now — *everyone* will be looking to get their hands on them."

Cooper could tell that Dranko was about to move on, so he stopped him. "Everyone understand this? Silence is the rule. When we leave here today, our story is we each had this weapon put aside or you tell them you got it from me. Everyone agree?"

Cooper looked around the room, making each man nod his head. When the circle had been completed, he allowed Dranko to continue.

"The rest is pretty simple. You will all leave here with a rifle and a pistol of your choosing. We'll do this organized. I'll explain each of the firearms as best I can and then you'll choose which ones you want. Got it?"

A series of grunts and nods was his response. "These weapons are now your responsibility. Don't lose them. You keep 'em on you or locked up at all times. You sleep with it next to you. You shower with it. You lose one, I will be very unhappy and you will not receive a replacement. Understand?" Everyone did.

"Let me add one thing," Cooper cut in. "If there's a fight, and I think there will be, *we* are going to be the difference. Those with the military-style weapons will be bringing firepower the bad dudes won't be counting on. Remember that. Surprise is key. If you're joining a fight, come in from a different direction and lay down as much fire as you can. They will think they're being hit from their flank by a much larger group. For everyone else, you're the steadiest hands we have in our neighborhood, so be smart and use your rifle or shotgun to best effect in the fight."

The smiles and giddiness left the men's faces as he talked. Straight lips, furrowed eyebrows, and clenched jaws replaced them. Cooper knew they felt the same tightness in their bellies that he did in his. Contemplating a firefight in your own neighborhood, where you had played ball in the street with your kids and had bar-b-q's in your backyards, was a terrifying thought.

Dranko moved to the wall holding the pistols and began explaining the main differences in function between revolvers and automatics. Cooper knew most of the basics and his mind drifted to other needs.

Two hours later, the group was finished kitting itself out. Cooper hoisted Dranko's prized possession—a FAL with a folding stock. The FAL was a Belgian-made assault rifle that fired the .308 round that was popular in a lot of hunting rifles. At the right distance, it was powerful enough to drop an elk. Against man, it was a devastating round. When he took it from Dranko's hands, he could feel the resistance when it came time to let go. Cooper took it because he knew his marksmanship would make better use of the harder-hitting round the FAL fired, rather than the lighter-weight M16 round. It had a twenty-round magazine, so he didn't feel as if he'd lack for ammunition supply. He kept his own pistol. His was chambered in the .357SIG caliber, which was a good pistol round for penetrating car doors and windshields. He suspected that could come in handy.

Dranko kept the M16 assault rifle for himself. Freddie had a Dirty Harry-looking .44 magnum revolver on his hip, while Mark had chosen a .45 auto. Remembering the grocery store, Cooper decided not to mention how that pistol had come into Dranko's armory. Calvin was pleasantly shifting the weight of a wood-stocked, semi-automatic, AK-47 back and forth between his hands.

"Being a black man in politics, I'm always accused of being a revolutionary. I guess I might as well look the part!" He let loose deep, booming, laughter and the others joined in.

"Maybe back in college they called you that, but you have a house and mortgage now!" Freddie laughed. It was true, 'revolutionary' was the last word you would ever associate with Calvin. He was as mainstream as they came.

Calvin had a no-nonsense Glock, in 9mm, holstered to his hip. Jake had been given a tricked out Ruger 10/22 that used the diminutive

.22 round but looked like an M16 with a synthetic stock, pistol grip, and forearm grip added on. Jake was beaming from ear to ear. *He feels like the big boys now.* The other men were leaving with an equal mix of hunting rifles with scopes on them and shotguns.

When they were ready to go, Dranko handed them each a slip of paper with names and a time. "These will be the people you will most likely be doing patrol and guard duty with. Tell them each to be at Cooper's house at their scheduled time. I will give them weapons and ammunition then."

"Why Cooper's?" Freddie asked.

"Like I said before, misdirection. If anyone does find out we have some gear, they go to the wrong house," Cooper answered. When he saw the look of worry on Jake's face, he winced. He knew there was nothing he could do about it now. *My father told me about the burdens of leadership. He never told me they could involve your son shouldering the burden too.* In truth, he hadn't needed to. Cooper had learned that truth first-hand, while growing up. A shiver ran down his spine thinking that his own son might have to learn it the hard way as well.

Dranko received many thanks as they dispersed. As the group made their way upstairs he called after them, "Thank me by using it all well out there, God forbid the need arises," he paused, "and keeping your damn mouths shut about where you got any of it!"

After everyone else had left, Cooper turned to Dranko, "I have to say, you are one cunning bastard. How'd you keep all of this," he said with a wide sweep of his hand, "secret from *me*, your theoretical best friend?"

A sheepish smile swept onto Dranko's face, "Damn, I just had to keep this from everyone. Too many problems with people knowing."

"I wouldn't have told anyone about it."

"True. I trusted you not to tell anyone. Except one person. You would have told Elena. Every man tells his wife everything. He has no secrets from her—except his mistress or his gambling, of course" he laughed at his own joke. Turning serious, "And, I had no idea who she might tell."

Cooper looked at his shoes, "OK. You got me there. Well, it's a damn fine thing, you having all this."

"Exactly." Dranko paused and then the same smile he'd worn before crept back onto his face, "There's just one more thing." Cooper cocked his eyebrow as he watched Dranko move to a corner of the room and open a locked cabinet.

"You've got to be kidding me!" he exclaimed as Dranko turned around, revealing what he had recovered.

Dranko was smiling like a boy who'd stolen a cookie from his mother's jar, "I only had one extra, so I had to wait until everyone else had left." Dranko crossed the room and handed it to him.

Cooper took the vest, heavy with bulletproof armor plates, "Well, thank you, Dranko. I appreciate your trust." Cooper nodded to Dranko and the warmth of friendship lingered between them.

The two men held their gaze for a long pause. Then, Dranko interjected, "Hell, brother, it ain't trust. I just know you're a lousy soldier and you're liable to be shot a dozen times for every one you dish out. You *need* the protection more than anything else!"

Cooper returned the smile, "Duly noted. But, there's no doubt that all of my combat time is going to be pulling *your* sorry ass out of trouble, so it's clear that it's your self-interest in protecting your virtually worthless bag o' bones that has you giving me this."

The two men laughed until they cried. Jake stood silently in the corner, smiling but not fully understanding the men's humor.

After the laughter subsided, Cooper looked back at him, "As you're distributing things at my place, I need to make a circuit of our neighborhood. We need to do some things to restrict access and to create some defensible positions."

Dranko nodded, "I was wondering when you'd get around to that."

******

Two hours later, Cooper met Dranko back at his own house. He and Calvin had sketched out a rudimentary plan for installing barricades and firing positions at each of the entrances to their neighborhood. Cooper had clapped himself on the back for remembering to pull Calvin into the plan early. The main building materials for the barricades would be cars and anything else with enough bulk to stop a bullet. They had come up with a plan to construct a centrally located defensive position as a fallback in case a major attack occurred. Cooper grinned in satisfaction at that.

Dranko had finished disbursing the last of the weapons and reviewed the plans with Cooper intently. He made a few helpful suggestions.

"I need to make the circuit and round up the men again. I'd like to get this set-up before nightfall."

"Why don't you just call them up?"

"I don't have their," Cooper said seeing the sheet of paper bearing names, weapon, and cell phone numbers that Dranko was holding up, "numbers."

Dranko grunted a smile at him.

"You are one damned fine logistics man, Mr. Dranko," he said grabbed the list from him and tore it carefully in half, watching with amusement Dranko's look of horror. "Now, you can help me with the calls."

In no time, the men and women had reassembled. Cooper noticed how most of them now walked with more swagger and confidence, carrying their arms at port or slung over their shoulders, as they entered his home.

He had transferred his sketched diagrams onto a much larger piece of butcher paper, torn off some roll that had supplied Jake with art projects in the past. He wanted everyone to be able to see and understand the plans for the entire neighborhood. He pegged it to the wall so the group of thirty-odd could cluster around it and see it as he talked. As the group was assembling, Dranko sidled next to him and whispered, "Feels like the Sandbox," referring to their shared time in Iraq.

"If we were in a tent, sand was filling my boots, and someone *else* was at the map laying out the mission parameters," Cooper intoned back at him.

Dranko punched him in the shoulder, "You're incorrigible."

Cooper turned to the group, "Alright, soldiers…"

"Soldiers? Hey, Sarge, when we getting' paid?" Freddie joked. The room echoed with nervous laughter.

Cooper remained at the front of the room, stone-faced, ensuring the laughter died prematurely, before it could reach its natural crescendo. He stared right at Freddie, "When you pick up that weapon, you become a soldier. What we're about to go over is deadly serious. It could save someone's life. More importantly, it could save mine. Or, the person sitting next to you." He paused and people looked at each nervously. He had their attention.

Freddie had turned bright red, "Sorry."

"There is no apology needed, Freddie. I know you'll be a good, solid man on the line out there. Let's review the plan."

He turned toward the hand drawn map and began explaining what it all meant: the symbols, what the angles of fire were, basic protocols of guard duty, and the most rudimentary fundamentals of combat. He took questions as he went, but a few remained at the end.

"What vehicles do we use for the roadblocks? They could get destroyed, I can guess some people won't want to put their car in harm's way," asked John.

"The older and more metal, the better," Dranko answered.

"Raise your hand if you'll agree to share in the cost of replacement for anyone's car or truck that is destroyed or damaged during this crisis," Cooper asked the group. Every hand went up. Except one. John's. He gave him a hard look and John slowly, meekly raised his arm halfway up. "Dranko, take down the names of those with their hand up. John, we have your answer — we'll replace them, if need be."

"We can start with any cars that are no longer...er...needed," Freddie added. As he realized what he was saying, his lips curled back in disgust.

"That's a good idea. But, let's get the oldest, most solid cars first. Think old Detroit Rolling Steel! They will stop bullets better than anything else."

Mark piped up, "What do we call this fallback position, in case we need to use it?"

"The Alamo!" Peter shouted excitedly. There were spattering calls of approval.

"Everyone died at the Alamo," Dranko remarked.

The room fell silent.

Calvin shot Dranko a wink, "How about Fort Prudence? We should only retreat if it's prudent to do so and not out of panic. This will help us all remember it."

"I like it," Cooper said, "All in favor, say aye!" The room erupted in easy agreement.

"What is our password and response?" asked Marilyn Chambers, a forty-something lesbian whose partner had died two days ago. She was an electrician with an athletic build, and wore dun colored overalls over a flannel shirt. When out of her work clothes, she would don stylish clothing, expensive jewelry, and painted nails. Her now deceased partner, Sherry Timmons, would joke that her "Mari" was the only woman she'd ever known who could dress any way she liked and look drop-dead gorgeous doing so.

Everyone thought for several seconds.

Suddenly, Lisa leapt to her feet, "I got it! This keeps it easy, but won't be obvious either. The call is 'Mount' and the response is

'Prudence'! None of us will forget this under pressure and outsiders might easily guess 'Tabor' and we can get 'em." Cooper noted the venom that accompanied the words 'get 'em'. *Doesn't take long, does it? Put up a wall and, just like instant coffee, you get 'outsiders' who you naturally hate.*

The room liked her suggestion immediately and shouts of affirmation followed. Cooper held up his hands for silence, "OK. Your call is 'Mount' and the right response is 'Prudence'. Repeat it." They did so.

Lisa sat back down with a self-satisfied look on her face.

"Anything else?"

There was silence. "I have one last thing. Everyone should fortify their homes as best as they can. Board up your first floor windows to prevent anyone from busting them out and climbing in too easily. Add a board to bar your doors. Park your car in your lawn if you can; to create another firing position. Move some furniture up against any walls that face the street."

"What will that do?" someone asked from the back of the room.

"It will stop a bullet that is already tumbling from hitting the wall of your house," Cooper answered.

"Huh? In English, please," Mark said.

"Let me start with the basics. I could walk through the neighborhood with a rifle and shoot *into* everyone's houses. Your walls are too thin to stop a bullet." The looks of surprise on their faces told him he had their attention. "But, when a bullet hits something solid it will become destabilized. A second barrier that is solid and separated from the first by about a foot of air will usually be able to stop the bullet then."

"How thick does the second barrier need to be?"

"Thicker is better, but a bookshelf filled with books should do the trick. A good wood table overturned could work too. Hell, a stack of phonebooks might even work. Don't worry about covering your whole house. Think about creating positions you can fire out of. If all you're doing is taking cover, get to your basement, or flat on the floor, and wait for the shooting to stop."

After the meeting broke up, Dranko gave Cooper a report on the dead, the dying, and the buried. Most of the dead had been buried and the numbers of dead and dying had leveled off. Cooper felt a little sick at being happy no one he knew very well had died today. He didn't like the way desensitization felt.

Chapter 15

The next morning, Cooper was on the barricade facing 60th Avenue. He mused that the term "barricade" may be overblown. What they had were two hulking vehicles, a panel van and a station wagon parked nose to nose blocking the street. A jumble of old furniture tried in vain to fill in the gaps. Cooper's favorite was the matching washer and dryer that had been stood end to end. He doubted they would stop more than a pistol round. Peter and Freddie were both on the line with him. Jake was with Lisa helping her collect and prepare medical supplies. Cooper knew he was in good, capable hands.

Despite the light rain that was falling, he could see fires rising from parts of the city. When the wind shifted to the right direction, he could smell them, too. Subtle shifts in the wind brought dramatic changes in the smell. The sickly sweet of the dead burning turned to the acrid smell of smoldering rubber and plastic which became the nostalgic smell of wood smoke.

Cooper heard squealing tires before he could see anything. He brought his rifle swiftly into his hands, his finger clenching the grips. All three of them instinctively ducked behind the beat-up, but hulking, 1972 Dodge station wagon that made up one-half of their makeshift blockade. Cooper rapped his fist against the side of the Dodge. It gave back a dull, reassuring, thud.

"Thank God for old steel cars that got two miles to the gallon," Freddie joked.

A car came careening around the corner, three blocks away, and crashed into a telephone pole. Thankfully, the pole held. The car, however, was smashed up good. Three figures, most likely all women, darted from the car. The driver was noticeably absent from the bail-out. Cooper focused and saw the windshield awash in red.

The three scrambled in different directions. An open-topped Jeep came to a screeching halt behind the crashed car and four men went chasing after the women. The men were armed with a mixture of pistols and rifles.

Freddie and Peter immediately jumped up and began to scramble over the Dodge's hood. Cooper yanked them both back to the ground by grabbing their belts. They both thudded to the ground and looked at him like they were ready to kill.

"What the hell! We have to help them!" Peter screamed in

Cooper's face, spittle flying from his lips.

Cooper pushed him back onto the ground, wiped his sleeve across his face, and responded in a calm, measured voice, "Listen, charging across open ground will just get you killed. Lay down covering fire. Shoot OVER their heads unless you can get a clean shot. Give them a chance to get away. A fight you *don't* have to fight is the best kind, boy!"

The other two men hesitated, so Cooper yelled, "Do it *now!*"

Cooper raised himself back up and readied his rifle, using his left hand to rack the charging handle to chamber a round. It made a reassuring "sha-schink" as he did so. Already, one of the men had a red haired woman in his grip and was dragging her back to the Jeep. Her legs struggled and her feet scratched the ground to and fro, trying to find purchase on the asphalt and keep herself from the Jeep. Her frantic efforts yielded little success.

Cooper intentionally fired a round a foot to the man's right. Startled, the man dropped the woman abruptly onto the pavement. She hit the ground with a thud that Cooper could only imagine, as far away as he was. The man's head swung side to side looking for the source of the shot, his right hand swinging toward the holstered pistol on his hip. Cooper quickly pivoted the rifle and lined up the sights on the man's midsection. He was wearing a faded yellow t-shirt underneath a black and white checkered thick, cotton flannel shirt. The front post of Cooper's rifle rested on the man's sternum. Cooper took a breath, released half of it, and then slowly squeezed the trigger. The chambered round exploded towards its target.

The flannel-clad man was lifted up onto his tiptoes, clutching fruitlessly at his chest, which had disappeared in a splash of red. At this range, he could not discern the expression on the man's face, but he could guess the look of surprise and shock. He stumbled backward several feet. His arms dropped limp and lifeless to his side. Then, he collapsed to the ground.

Two loud pops from either side of him, in near succession, told him that Freddie and Peter had begun firing.

Cooper took a deep breath and refocused from the pinpoint he needed for effective rifle fire to a broader view, so he could take in the full situation. Another woman had been wrestled to the ground by an attacker, who was now trying to use her as a human shield. She was dark-haired and of average height and build. One of the attackers wore a bright red hoodie, blue jeans, and white sneakers. He had dark hair tied back in a ponytail. The other had tight, close-cropped black hair and a black baseball cap that said "POLICE" across its front. He wore a dark blue windbreaker that was also emblazoned with the word "POLICE," black shirt underneath, black police-style pants, and black service boots. The fourth attacker had been hit in the leg by either Peter or Freddie and was sitting on the ground, clutching his right leg, and bellowing in pain. His intended victim, a woman with black hair, gray pants and blouse, and a long black coat, was running in a zigzag pattern. She was running away from the Jeep but not toward Cooper's position either. Instinctively, she was staying out of the line of fire, moving down Division Street. *Smart.* The red haired woman who Cooper had freed had collapsed to the ground and sat with hands clutched to her face, wailing in panic and fear.

Without warning, the man wearing the bright red hooded sweatshirt raised his pistol, pointed it straight at the red-headed woman and fired two rounds. Both hit her in the head. Cooper could see a red cloud erupt around her head as each round impacted. She slumped over like a rag doll; the kind that has been abused so badly that its head is nearly ripped off and the stuffing is oozing out from all sides.

He then tried burrowing deeper behind the woman he was using as his human shield.

"I've got him," Cooper hissed to the others. He breathed deeply to squelch the anger bubbling up from his stomach. He knew angry men made bad marksmen.

He pivoted his rifle and sighted in on the shoulder that was exposed. The hoodie stood out in stark contrast to the woman's olive-colored Columbia jacket. *Thanks for wearing a bright red shirt, dumbass.* Only a few square inches of red were exposed where the top part of his shoulder could not get low enough behind her. Cooper knew this would be a close shot. The FAL was not a sniper-grade rifle and he lacked a scope. Thankfully, they were only about one hundred and fifty yards away. He knew he had no choice, this guy was already mentally unstable and there was no predicting what he might do next.

Cooper took two more measured breaths, stopped halfway on the second, and squeezed. In the bang, flash, and smoke that followed, he couldn't see what had happened. He shifted his body to the right to get a better view, just as Peter yelled.

"You got him. Jesus Christ, you got him!"

Cooper could see that he had rolled onto his back, his right hand clutching his left shoulder. The woman was already rapidly crawling away from him. Without waiting, Cooper stood halfway up, took precise aim at the man's mid-section and fired two more rounds in quick succession. With each impact, the man's body bounced up a few inches off the ground before settling back to the asphalt. Then, he lay motionless.

The other man, dressed in police-style gear, tossed his pistol several yards in front of where he lay and raised his hands in surrender. The one with the wounded leg mimicked him.

Peter raised his rifle to draw a bead on him. Cooper lowered the rifle barrel with his left hand.

"No, we don't kill in cold blood."

"We can't just let these animals go. They'll do it again."

"Maybe. We'll have to take that chance. But, we can't become them. Besides, they're going home with two dead and the third wounded. Hopefully, they'll learn a lesson. Besides, we aren't done with them yet." A sly grin spread across his face.

"Whatdya mean?" Freddie asked.

Just then, Mark came running up, bolt-action hunting rifle in hand. He was panting, out of breath. Sweat covered his face, which was red from exertion.

Cooper nodded to him, "You're just in time. You two go down there. First, make sure they are disarmed. Do a full pat down as the other covers. Then, make the guy with the police clothes strip down. We'll take that tactic away from them. Take their shoes and make them march until they are out of your sight. Then, bring the Jeep back to Fort Prudence. By then, others will have come and you put them on the barricade. Help the two women if they want it, but don't force it. They've just been through a major trauma. Mark can cover you from here with the scoped rifle."

"What are you gonna do?" Peter asked.

"Try to round up the woman who ran away and make sure she's OK. You guys got it?"

They both nodded. The trio moved out in two different directions. Cooper wanted to catch up with the woman who had moved down Division Street. He didn't want her wandering through the city after such a violent attack.

Cooper sprinted down the side street that led to Division. He chose the speed that was just below sprinting, a pace he could keep up for a while. He carried his rifle in his arms, swinging it slightly to each side for balance, as he ran. His lungs churned like bellows as sweat began beading down his face.

When he reached Division, he turned toward his right. Without much trouble, he saw her thirty yards up the road, walking with a stumbling gait. From this vantage point, she looked as if she were drunk, pitching from one edge of the sidewalk to the other. Cooper silently and quickly walked until he was within about ten yards and then stopped. He knew if he approached too closely, she might take off in a blind run.

"Ma'am, you forgot something," he called. He'd read somewhere that when dealing with those in panic, a familiar, habitual phrase could often work in breaking them out of it.

She stopped, unsteady on her feet. Then, she turned back around to face him, "What did you say?"

Despite the dirt streaks on her face, her disheveled hair, and her wrinkled business attire, she was a strikingly beautiful woman. He noticed her eyes first. They were large, dark, deep pools of brown. Her lips were full and she had a round, friendly, open face. Her hair was shoulder length and as black as night. It almost glowed, the sheen was so high. She was short, a few inches over five feet. Underneath her clothing, he could see her thin, athletic build. In various places, her toned muscles tone pushed up against her clothing. Her breasts were medium in size. A long black coat was unbuttoned and flapped lazily behind her in the stiff breeze. For a moment, he was sure he had met her before, but couldn't place where.

"I said you forgot something back there," Cooper responded.

Her eyes were alert now, sizing him up. The daze had faded. "What's that?"

"You forgot to say thank you," he said, hoping she would get the joke.

A smile spread across her face, revealing ivory, gleaming white teeth. "Oh, did I? Well, thank you, Mr. Sheriff, and hats off to your fine deputies."

He shouldered his rifle, took a few steps closer, and extended his hand, "Name's Cooper. Cooper Adams. I just wanted to make sure you were OK."

She took several steps to meet him halfway and extended her hand, "Julianne Wheeler."

He took it and shook her hand lightly, a quizzical look on her face, "Do we know each other?" He was sure he recognized her name, but couldn't place it.

She smiled coyly, "I don't think so. I live in the Northeast part of town. But, I'm certainly glad I met you today!" Cooper smiled at that. Her voice turned serious, "Thank you for your help back there. I don't want to think what might have happened."

"What *did* happen?"

Her eyes misted over and her voice choked with emotion, "It was crazy. I was at the grocery store, which was completely chaotic, but I made it through. I was on my way back to my car when that Jeep pulled into the parking lot. I was the first one they tried to grab. It was like a damned rodeo. They just drove through going after a group of us until they had us cornered. No one did a damned thing to help us, including some worthless armed security guard at the store's entrance." She spat the last words, bitterness dripping from them. "Finally, a woman saved us," she said, crying. Cooper waited for her to go on.

"She pulled up next to us and yelled at us to jump in. We did and barely got away. Then, they kept chasing us, halfway across town, until she crashed back there."

Cooper put his hand on her shoulder, "I'm sorry. Some people are going crazy with the rule of law breaking down. Why don't you come back into our neighborhood? As you can see, we have organized security. It's getting late for you to try to walk home, unless you're nearby."

Her eyes met his once again. Up this close, they were stunning. He could *feel* her sizing him up, as her eyes bored into him. "OK. Yes, thank you. No, I'm not close. Neither is my car."

"Great. It's just a block up. You're safe now."

His last words had a dramatic effect on her. Her eyes filled with tears and she clutched her hand to cover her mouth. Sobbing quickly wracked her body and she began shaking. She grew unsteady on her feet and Cooper quickly stepped in to support her, throwing an arm around her waist. He guessed it was post-traumatic release. She pulled him in close to her and buried her face into his chest. Her grip was fierce, causing him to wince as she squeezed hard on his ribs. *Yes, she's athletic alright.* Cooper had comforted other soldiers in Iraq after firefights or ambushes, but this was very, very different.

He put his arms around her and softly stroked her back in circles. "It's OK. It's OK," he constantly repeated, whispering softly into her ear. She eased her grip to a firm, but no longer painful, hug. He could feel her breath, panting hot on his chest.

"Take a deep breath, breathe in."

He was relieved when she followed his instruction. Slowly, her breath slowed down and her grip eased. She pulled away from him to speak, her eyes looking at his chest.

"I'm sorry for that. I'm not used to breaking down like that. I don't know what happened," she said, her voice breaking up, and quickly wiping tears away from her cheeks.

"It's OK. It's very common. You just went through a traumatic ordeal. You *survived* it by *not* letting your emotions in. Now, they'll come up when it's safe to do so. Don't feel bad about it."

She looked up at him, and patted him on the chest, "Thank you. Thank you."

Her eyes glistened with her tears. Her face was soft with emotion. Her lips, a deep red, were pressed hard against each other. The setting sun made her hair glow. Suddenly, he could feel every part of his body where hers touched him. He didn't like what he felt. It wasn't arousal; it was something deeper than that. It was just like when he'd first met Elena. He swallowed hard, a chill of apprehension running down his spine.

No. I won't let myself feel that. He put his hands on her shoulders, moved back a step, and broke eye contact with her. His action was abrupt enough that Julianne knew he'd suddenly become uncomfortable, but she didn't say anything. He stepped around her and grunted, "This way." She gave him a curious look, but fell in a step behind him, bustling to keep up with his urgent, and longer, strides.

******

When they arrived at the main intersection, the place was buzzing. About twenty people were clustered in small groups, discussing recent events with animated conversation. Neither Peter nor Freddie had arrived yet, so when the crowd saw Cooper approaching, they streamed toward him. Jake ran to his side at a dead run. He slammed into Cooper and hugged him tightly. Cooper laughed and hugged him back, "I'm OK, son. Everything is fine."

When he loosened his grip, he directed his attention to Julianne, "Jake, this is Julianne Wheeler."

"Pleased to meet you, young man," she offered him her hand. Jake shook it warily and buried his face against his father's side.

Arthur Stamm, a twenty-two year old with bright red hair who stood a shade under seven feet, came up, "What happened, Cooper? We heard we repulsed an attack by a dozen men!" He was panting from excitement.

Cooper shook his head and chuckled, "No. No, nothing like that. We just saw some people in trouble down the road a bit and we helped them out."

Julianne stepped from behind Cooper, pushing him aside, "Cooper is being too humble. This man helped us, saved us. No one else dared raise a finger when we were *attacked* by a group of violent bastards, in public, at a grocery store. But, this man," she grabbed his arm and squeezed it, "he stepped up and saved us."

"What'd you do to them?" Arthur asked.

"Two are dead. Two wounded. The last we stripped down to his underwear. We sent the two that were still alive back home without their shoes. I think we showed that this neighborhood is well defended."

Unexpectedly, the group erupted into a round of cheers. He spent the next ten minutes answering questions and recounting further details. When Peter and Freddie arrived, the excitement picked up again and he was forced to endure another round of questions, most of which he'd already answered. Julianne was interrogated, as well. Finally, he was able to break away from the group and head into his house. He motioned for Julianne to follow him and she did so.

He leaned the rifle up against the wall, next to the front door. He kept the automatic pistol on his hip. *Funny how quickly guns have become normal to have around all the time.*

He turned toward Julianne, "I think it'd be best for you to stay here." The flash of an impetuous smile from Julianne's face made him quickly add, "I mean in our neighborhood, tonight. It's almost dark and I don't think it's worth the risk to run you back home in it. You can either stay here with us or I can find you some space at Lisa's across the street if you'd prefer that."

"If it's OK with you, I'd prefer to just stay here. I know you already and I trust you, a little bit at least. Both of you," she added, indicating Jake. He looked back at her like a cat defending his turf, with squinted eyes and tight lips.

"Alright. We'll make something to eat and then turn in. We'll sleep upstairs. Jake and I in the bedroom and you in the loft, just outside."

"We're not sleeping in the basement?" Jake asked.

"Not after what happened the other night. If those idiots come back, we need to be in a different place to catch them off guard."

Julianne left eyebrow cocked. Cooper responded, "We had some unwelcome guests the other night. We dealt with them and I'm 99% sure we won't see them again. But, I like to be safe." She nodded in agreement.

Chapter 16

Cooper cooked dinner, with some help from Jake and Julianne. Jake circled her, avoiding contact. *Must be what a bear looks like guarding her brood,* Cooper chuckled to himself. He cooked some steaks from the freezer, rice pilaf from a box, and some broccoli with butter and garlic. Uncharacteristically, he downed two whiskeys on the rocks while cooking. *After today, I deserve it.* He was thankful his body performed well in combat, reflexes sharp and without hesitation. However, he always felt like crap afterwards. A doctor in the army had once told him that there were two kinds of people: those who performed well under extreme stress but felt lousy later and those who didn't and ended up lousy *during* combat. Cooper was happy to be the former, but he still hated how badly his body felt afterwards. Julianne joined him, but drank red wine instead.

They made small talk at dinner. Cooper learned that Julianne worked for a medical firm doing who knows what. She had a PhD in medical biology and did research where she worked. Cooper became animated and sought her opinion on the plague sweeping the country. She adroitly evaded his questions and only responded in generalities. As he pressed her a few different times, she became emotional, teared up, and changed the conversation. Cooper assumed she had lost someone, or some *people*, who were very close to her. She didn't wear a wedding ring, but perhaps it was a long-term lover, parents, or a sibling. She wouldn't talk about her family either, so he had no way to know. In fact, as the night wore on, he noticed that she deliberately kept away from any serious or personal topics. Cooper chomped on a bite of steak, *and I thought it was supposed to be men who were closed off!* She asked him what he was smiling about, but he demurred by shaking his head. Cooper couldn't remember if he'd had two or three whiskeys with dinner. There was no ignoring the empty bottle of red wine next to Julianne and the second one started. *I guess we both had a rough day, didn't we?*

After dinner, he put Jake to bed upstairs. Cooper tried to read a story to Jake, but he fell asleep before he finished. *I guess these events are taking their toll on him too.* Looking down at his peaceful, slumbering face, he couldn't help but believe that it had grown more mature looking in the last few days. His jaw line appeared more square, the eyes a bit deeper set, and his mouth more firm.

Cooper returned to find Julianne in the kitchen, holding a drink out towards him. His head was already swimming a little. The whiskey had warmed his belly and now it was working up past his chest, toward his head. Julianne's constant smile and slow gait revealed she was feeling it too. They moved to the living room and sat down on the couch. It was a deep, chocolate brown, with a high back; Victorian-style.

They sat down, each at either end of the couch. She brushed her hair back over her ear and looked deeply into his eyes, "I just wanted to thank you again for what you did today. I owe you a lot for it."

Her eyes had an electric effect on him. They pulled him in. *Closer,* they cooed. This close, he could not deny how stunningly beautiful she was.

"No thanks needed. Anyone would have done the same."

She shook her head emphatically and waved her hand side to side, spilling a drop of wine onto her blouse without noticing, "No. No! Not anyone, Cooper. I saw a dozen men watch us all get rounded up in that parking lot today. Like *cattle,*" she spat the word. "Not a one lifted a finger."

"Maybe they weren't armed," he defended.

"You are too damned kind. Since two days ago, every other man on the street has a gun with him. *Some* of them had to be armed. But, they just stood aside. A damned women *round up!* Yippee-kai-yay!" She mimicked a lasso.

"OK, I give in! You're welcome."

"Thank you. Was that so hard? That's all I wanted from you," she said, tilting her head to the side and looking up at him. The top few buttons on her shiny gray blouse were undone and a hint of cleavage drew his eyes. Her firm breasts pressed against the blouse as if they wanted to push the next button open, as well. He felt the cushions move as she edged closer to him.

Hovering at the edge of touching hip to hip, she bit her lower lip. Her lips were red, full, and moist, "Well, it's not the *only* thing I wanted from you." Her hand was on his thigh and she leaned in to whisper into his ear. "I hope you won't think this is too forward. I need something else from you. Will you hold me tonight? I can't bear to be alone. Not tonight." He felt the wetness of a tear fall onto his neck as she nuzzled her nose against his ear and recalled the intense connection he had felt when they'd met earlier. Her hand squeezed his thigh, moving to the inside. Her right arm snaked around his waist and pulled her closer to him.

Cooper's head whirled. He couldn't believe this was happening. He had had other women come on to him, some very strongly, but never in his living room. *And never one so beautiful.* There was no denying what feeling stirred now. This was pure lust. The mix of adrenaline from what had happened earlier in the day, the whiskey, and her attraction was overpowering. He was drawn to her, powerfully so. He wanted her, right now, on the couch, and yearned to bury himself inside of her. He wanted that connection with her. He felt as if he *needed* it.

He felt her moist, full lips on his neck, delivering a gentle soft kiss, with a seductive hint of suction. "Just hold me. Please." Her hand slid further up his thigh.

He pulled her head away from him. His eyes furiously swept over her. He couldn't help but imagine how it would feel to run his hands over her, feeling every part of her firm body. Her eyes tantalized him again. Wet from her tears, they beckoned him. They beseeched him to come in and become lost inside of her; lost inside the moment. He ached to pull her in close and give in to what he desired.

But I won't. He moved away from her, breaking the spell. "I'm sorry. I can't do this. My boy is upstairs and my wife, who I still love, is not a few days gone."

She pulled back, her arm uncurling from his waist and withdrawing from his thigh. He couldn't help noticing how she squeezed his waist as she did so. She averted her eyes towards the floor.

"It goes without saying that I *want* to. But, I just can't."

Her face looked crestfallen, "You're a rare man, Cooper Adams. Will you at least give me a hug before we turn in? I could really use that."

"Of course. And, you can tease me twenty years from now about how I missed the opportunity of my life to spend the night with such a stunning woman," he smiled at her.

They stood up, drained the last of their drinks, and embraced. She pressed herself fully into him. Her grip was strong, one arm around his lower back and the other going over his back with the hand gripping his shoulder. He squeezed back. Her left leg slid in between his and she pressed it along the inner side of his right leg. For just a moment, her thigh pressed against his groin, arousing him again. *She never gives up.* Before he could pull away, she withdrew her leg and resumed a wider stance.

They stood in this embrace for a long time. Their breath synchronized. The intense physical attraction faded and it felt like earlier today. He couldn't help the connection he felt towards her. She must have felt it too. She caressed his back, moving her hands from time to time. He didn't grow impatient in her arms. It just felt right to him.

When she pulled away, he felt a twinge of regret. "Thank you. I needed that," she breathed.

"It was my pleasure. You give good hug, Ms. Julianne Wheeler."

She smiled impishly at him, "It's not all I'm good at, Mr. Cooper Adams." With that, she turned and sashayed her way to the bathroom. She exaggerated the swing of her hips as she did so.

He looked after her, admiringly, and shook his head in silent, amused, appreciation.

******

A voice startled him awake well past midnight. Cat-like, he slid out of the bed and with shotgun already in hand, crouched at the ready. There it was again. Female. From the next room. *It must be Julianne.* He crept forward on his toes silently and quickly. He pushed the door fully open and took several steps into the loft area that adjoined his bedroom.

Julianne lay on the air mattress that they kept on hand for guests. He lay the shotgun against the wall. She was restless, moaning unintelligible words and phrases. The blanket had been pushed off of her. She was wearing an oversized red flannel shirt that he had loaned her. It came to just above her knees. Now, it clustered just below her waist, failing to conceal her sapphire blue lace panties. Her well-muscled legs moved in slow tandem, rubbing against each other.

He stepped next to her, grabbed the blanket, and draped it over her. As the blanket dropped onto her, her voice startled him.

"It's been worse than you thought," she said wearily, deep sadness clouding her voice.

Cooper looked at her quizzically. Her eyes were half open. He almost started to ask her, "What was worse?" before he realized she was still asleep.

She moved again, rolling over so he could no longer see her face.

144

"So much worse than you said it would be," each word catching in her throat.

Cooper pivoted and resumed his position at the foot of the air mattress. Minutes crept past and all he heard was her breathing rhythmically. She had fallen back into deep slumber. Cooper's mind buzzed with questions. *What was she talking about? What was worse? Who was she talking to in her sleep?*

The mystery tantalized him. After five minutes of relative silence, he knelt down and lightly tickled her foot.

She stirred again and rolled onto her back. Her half-open eyes stared right at him. For a moment, he was terrified that she had awoken and would ask what the hell he was doing. But, the eyes were unmoving. He let out a silent sigh of relief.

She hissed angrily, "We shouldn't have done it, don't you see? It's cost too much."

Surprised by her angry outburst, he stood up and backed away. She shifted again, onto her right side and resumed breathing steadily. He watched for several more minutes, but she did not speak again. He decided not to risk disturbing her again, despite how his mind was alive with questions about what she'd said. A ray of light from the streetlamp caressed her face. A full minute later, Cooper realized he'd been staring at her. He shook his head to clear his mind and went back to bed. His alarm clock told him it was just after three in the morning. He couldn't sleep, as questions about what she'd said, and the powerful emotions she had stirred pestered him.

Around five o'clock he gave up and went downstairs to begin preparing breakfast.

******

Cooper had almost finished making a breakfast of French toast, sausage links, and hash browns when he heard the creak of the stairs as someone descended. *Louder than Jake. It must be Julianne.* He was setting a pitcher of orange juice onto the table when she rounded the landing and stepped into the dining room.

The long flannel shirt he had let her borrow hung just below her knees. Her deep black hair was only finger-combed. She brushed the left side behind her ear and looked up at him. Her eyes were alight. Powerful as black holes, they pulled him in, and seemed to go on forever.

145

"Good morning," she said.

"Good morning. How'd you sleep?" He knew he was going to ask her about what she'd said in her sleep, but he'd wait before doing so.

"Oh, I slept well. As good as could be expected after yesterday, I guess."

"Good. I'm sorry I didn't have something better to offer you than that air mattress. We were never set up well for guests."

"Oh, it was fine," she leaned in, setting her hand on the small of his back. She whispered into his ear, "I'm sorry about last night. I know I came on strong last night. I can be unbearable when I want something. I'm sorry for that."

He craned his neck back, so he could look at her, "Don't worry about it. I was flattered, really. You are an...incredible woman. But, I'm still in love...I know it sounds crazy...but I'm still in love with my wife."

She patted him on his shoulder, "It's not crazy at all. It's normal. I was the one who was off base. It's sweet. It's why I said you're such a rare man." She stopped and laughed to herself.

Cooper looked puzzled, "What?"

"Oh, I can't. It will make me sound like an arrogant slut."

He looked plaintively at her, "Oh, you have to tell me now. You can't bring something like that up and not say anything."

She dropped her shoulders, "Oh, alright. I guess I owe you that. It's just that you're the first man, ever, to reject my advances. Single. Married. It hasn't mattered. I do believe once even a gay man said yes to me."

He looked back at her, straight faced.

"What?" she pleaded.

"You're right. You are an arrogant slut," a wide smile betrayed the levity.

She punched him in the shoulder. "Oh, c'mon. I didn't say it's been *that* many. I just said you were the first to say no."

"Well, if it makes you feel better, I didn't really say no."

Her eyes turned coy, she cocked her head, and her voice lilted, flirting again, "Really?"

"I just didn't say yes," and he turned and walked back into the kitchen to grab the coffee pot.

He deliberately rocked his hips on his way out, imitating her departure from last night. She burst out laughing.

She was sitting at the table when he came back in, steaming coffee pot in hand. Lighter footsteps were heard on the stairs, and Jake soon bounced into the dining room.

"What's everyone laughing about?" he asked.

"Your father is just one funny guy," Julianne responded.

"Funny looking, you mean?"

Cooper pointed the pot at his son, "Watch it, young man." Jake grinned widely, while Cooper snarled at him, playfully.

Cooper poured Julianne and himself a cup of coffee and sat down to eat. They ate and had amiable conversation. It was painfully obvious now how Julianne avoided talking about her work or the plague. On other topics, however, she was an able conversationalist. Cooper enjoyed talking with her. She was witty, humorous, and intelligent. *She's awfully pleasant to look at, too.* Jake watched the banter warily. Cooper noted his growing foul mood. *I better be careful, he's taking this the wrong way.* He slowly fell silent. Julianne picked up the cue and did likewise.

When they had finished the meal, Cooper sent Jake upstairs to shower. He departed reluctantly, afraid of what might happen while he was gone. Cooper swatted him on the rear to get him moving.

Julianne started to clear the dishes and Cooper pitched in.

"Can I ask you something?"

"Sure."

"I'm sorry, but last night I overheard you talking in your sleep."

It was barely perceptible, but her motions hiccuped as he finished the sentence, "Really? I hope I wasn't talking about you in some *inappropriate* manner." Her joke fell flat. He heard the discomfort in her voice.

He wanted to keep her comfortable, loose. "Despite my fervent hopes when I first woke up, no, it wasn't that." He laughed. She joined in, but it sounded forced. "You said some curious things."

"Like what?" She turned to face him. He paused, dirty dishes in hand.

"You said 'you were wrong' and 'it's cost too much.'"

She dropped her eyes quickly to the floor. "I'm sorry you heard that."

"What were you talking about?"

She cradled a spoon in her hands, stroking it, and delaying her response. After a few moments passed, she set the spoon onto the table, "I made a mistake. A big one," she stopped. He waited for her to

147

continue. She knotted her fingers together, clenching and unclenching. "I had an affair. A married man. He told me it wouldn't hurt anyone. He told me his wife would never know. But, she did find out and it wrecked their home. I never wanted that." She looked back up at him with glistening eyes.

He offered a curt, biting, smile in return. Her deep eyes were suddenly shallow. "I don't know what you're hiding. But, I'm disappointed you aren't telling me the truth."

Her eyebrows knotted up, becoming indignant, "I don't know…"

He interrupted her, an angry edge to his voice, "I don't like being lied to. You've barely told me what you do for a living. Someone like you wouldn't lay down such a painful secret so easily. It just doesn't add…"

His words were cut short by a cavalcade of gunfire in the distance; from up the street. He started at the sound, dropping a plate that shattered when it hit the ground.

Chapter 17

"Get Jake into the basement. Keep him there until I get back. He knows where his .22 is."

Cooper ran to the front door. He clambered into the bulletproof vest, slung a bandoleer of magazines across his chest, and grabbed his rifle. His pistol was already on his hip, as it was now anytime he was awake. He gave a look back at Julianne. She stood motionless in the kitchen where he'd left her.

"*Please!*" he shouted, desperate. She turned towards him, nodded, and ran towards the stairs.

Cooper bolted out the front door and slammed it behind on his way out. He began sprinting up the street, toward the sound of constant gunfire. Fifty yards ahead of him, he could see Dranko running towards it, as well. He shouted to him to wait.

Dranko turned and waited as Cooper ran at a breakneck speed towards him. Cooper stopped when he'd reached him, sucking air deep into his lungs. *A quick dash didn't used to wind me.*

As he came alongside, they moved as a pair in a fast jog toward the growing battle. "Let's work as a fire team. Shoot and scoot," Cooper said as they ran. Dranko carried his M16. A chest rig, full of magazines, was on over his body armor.

The roar of a motorcycle engine racing towards them cut short the banter. Cooper took cover behind a thick oak tree and Dranko darted across the street to hunker down behind a Toyota Prius and create a crossfire ambush. *Piss poor cover, that plastic car will be.*

Cooper switched off the safety and chambered a round into the FAL. A split second later the motorcycle came into view. It was something straight out of *Mad Max*. The high whine of the motor told him it was an imported bike. There were two men on the bike. The driver wore black boots, cut-up denim jeans, and an open leather vest with no shirt underneath. His ears were festooned with numerous piercings and his nose bore a large metal ring. A bright red Mohawk adorned his otherwise shiny bald head. A large bore pistol was holstered to his hip, but both hands clung to the handlebars. The passenger was clad in black leather from head to toe, including a black full head mask that looked like it came from cheap horror movie. He brandished two pistols, an auto in the left and a revolver in the right. The outrageous dress told him they were dealing with amateurs.

Nothing more than costumes meant to frighten those they attacked.

He almost felt bad as he sighted his rifle onto on the rear passenger. *Easy pickings. This might work against some defenseless people, but you guys chose the wrong neighborhood.* The man's chest quickly filled his sights, racing closer. At about twenty-five yards, Cooper squeezed the trigger. The deep 'boom' of his rifle was followed quickly by the sharp 'pop-pop-pop' of a three-round burst from Dranko's M16.

The strong recoil of the hard-hitting .308 cartridge punched Cooper in the shoulder. He remained focused on his target. The leather clad man's chest exploded as he was lifted off the back of the bike. The pistols dropped from his hands as he grasped at his chest. For a split second, he hung in mid-air as the motorcycle thundered onward without him. His body slammed into the ground. He remained frozen in this awkward sitting position for a long moment. Then, his torso fell lazily to one side.

The driver fared no better. Dranko's three round burst hit home, crisscrossing the man's chest in making the upward stroke of half of an "X." He slid off the motorbike, which raced onward for ten yards or so, without a rider. Then it crashed, flipping end over end, spurting gravel and then dirt, before coming to rest in Mrs. Patterson's rose garden. The driver attempted to crawl away, spraying a fine shower of blood with each tortured breath. He had landed just a few feet away from where Cooper was crouched behind the tree and was futilely trying to get away.

Cooper took a few steps until he stood over the crippled driver. The Mohawk-haired biker who was so fearsome a few moments ago now begged for his mother in a voice that belonged to a child, gurgling blood as he did so.

"You don't deserve the mercy of a bullet, but you'll get it." Cooper pointed the barrel at the man's head and fired. His head exploded in a mass of bone, blood, and skin, dirtying Cooper's boot. Scowling, he wiped it clean on the man's pant leg.

Dranko was at his side. Cooper re-focused on the still raging firefight further up their street. Sporadic fusillades were punctuated by long seconds of silence. The gunfire told them both sides had settled in behind cover and were at a rough stalemate. *Best we could hope for, with untrained guards on the line.*

They resumed their fast, but steady run towards the battle.

"Damn stalemate," panted Dranko.

"Yeah, isn't it great?"

"Whatd'ya mean?"

"We get to be the SWAT team and break the bastards down!"

Dranko shook his head in wonderment at his friend's cavalier attitude. Cooper responded with a reproachful smirk at his friend's negativity.

When they came into view of the gunfight, they both instinctively took cover behind a Toyota Tundra pickup parked in someone's driveway. At the top of the street, they could see Mark and Leroy Johnson to their left, crouched behind a battered old pickup truck that made up one-half of their hasty barricade. Miguel Aguilar was lying on the ground, shooting at their enemies from underneath a Buick sedan. His eldest son who was in his twenties, Antonio, lay in the street, sprawled out, riddled with several bullet wounds. *Damn it, not his son!* He pushed any thought of Jake from his mind.

A fury of gunfire erupted from the white house that lay opposite their barricaded position. The attackers must have retreated to it after the first shots were fired. A man lay face down in the yard, two red circles in the back of the white t-shirt he wore. Cooper saw a pistol-grip shotgun lying next to him.

Mark and Leroy ducked further behind the pickup and Miguel hastily scrabbled back, away from the front of the Buick. Both Mark and Leroy were armed with shotguns, while Miguel was shooting a bolt-action hunting rifle. Taking note, Cooper yelled to Dranko, "Cover me!"

Without hesitation, he began laying down deliberate fire intended to keep their opponents' heads down; rather than trying to hit them. Dranko smiled to himself as he fired short, three-round bursts at the house. The sound was distinctive. The enemy would know they were facing at least one machine gun now. Mark, Leroy, and Miguel all glanced back at Dranko as soon as he began firing. Panicked fear quickly transformed into bravado and rapid hand waving and hooting once they saw Dranko's face behind the M16.

Cooper ran forward and to his far right. He landed with a *humph* behind a cement stoop, scraping a knee raw. Now, he had the angle he wanted. He took cover and used the stoop as a rifle rest. He caught Dranko's eye with rapid hand movements and signaled to him to stop firing with rapid brushes of his hand across his throat.

After several seconds of silence, activity resumed in the house. Cooper saw a flutter of a curtain and the glint of a rifle barrel. Cooper carefully sighted his rifle on where he thought the man was hiding behind the window. He fired two shots in rapid succession, pulling the trigger twice as fast as he could. The bullets made two neat holes in the side of the house. Cooper was rewarded by seeing the rifle barrel swing violently to the right and away from the window. He knew he'd hit the man on the other side.

"Welcome to the .308 boys, turning cover into concealment for fifty years," he muttered to himself, a mischievous grin on his face. "Wood and drywall ain't no match for it!"

A sharp report from a large caliber handgun in a window on the second floor drew Cooper's attention. Mark fired back at the window with his 12 gauge. He was a split-second too late. The shooter had already sought cover behind the wall. Cooper guessed he had crouched behind the left side of the window, as most right hand shooters would naturally do. He fired three shots in a neat triangle pattern against the wall just to the left of the window and then waited. Seconds ticked past, but they seemed like hours.

Cooper flinched as a shotgun blast shredded the last remaining window in the Buick. A billow of smoke drifting outward from behind a green Subaru revealed another foe in the driveway that led to the house the others had taken refuge in.

The second story window came to life as the shooter fired again. Leroy screamed in pain, dropped his shotgun, and grabbed his right shoulder. Mark pulled him closer to the pickup and began applying direct pressure to the wound.

Must be left-handed. This time, Cooper repeated the triangle pattern on the *right* side of the window. He was rewarded by the strained cry of a man who has just realized he's been shot. The man's cry of pain quickly shifted to a plaintive whine, "God! Help me please! I promise I'll do good!"

Cooper turned toward the shot gunner behind the Subaru. *Someone beat me to it.* He saw upturned black boots to the right of the front tire. Euphoric, Leroy jumped up, pumping his one good arm up and down.

"Yeah, we got them bastards!"

Cooper was shouting, "No" as movement from the house drew his eye. He saw a barrel emerge from a window and he frantically swung his own rifle towards it.

Too late. In slow motion, he watched a shiny stainless steel pistol barrel aim at Leroy. He could see the hammer draw back as the trigger was pulled. The revolver spat flame and thunder. He didn't have to look to know the worst. A second later, with his rifle on target, he fired two shots quickly and watched the man's body thrown backward into the room, disappearing from view.

Reluctantly, he looked back towards the barricade. Leroy lay splayed out on the ground, arms and legs outstretched at awkward angles. A neat bullet hole was in the middle of his chest. His eyes stared blankly at the sky filled with gathering clouds.

Miguel ran from his cover to Antonio's side, yelling "Noooo!" in a gut-wrenching wail.

Two dead. That is all that he could think about as they cleaned up the mess of this attack. With, the gunfire gone, neighbors cautiously emerged from their homes and filed into the street. Miguel knelt at his dead son's head, clutching it in his arms and crying out for God's mercy. Miguel's wife, Isabella, had died a few days ago from the illness. His daughter, Irina, had joined her father in mourning.

Leroy had no immediate family and a cloister of people simply gathered around him, standing and looking down at him in bizarre curiosity. Cooper realized this was the first violent death most people in the neighborhood had ever seen.

Mark called out, "Eleanor, can you get a sheet or blanket to cover him with?" The demure elderly woman, who lived next to Leroy, sauntered off.

A shrill, crotchety voice made Cooper turn around, "Anyone like what they see? Dead men lying in our streets? If not, then thank the men, and their families, who have fallen. 'Fore if they hadn't been on their posts, we'd have many more dead to mourn. Or worse." Lily Stott stood, waving her black cane as she spoke. Her face was flushed and damp from coming all the way up the block in short order.

"And let us thank the men who told us we should set up these barricades in the first place," she continued. She pointed her cane directly at Cooper in closing. Heads turned towards him and a few hands set to clapping.

Cooper waved it off, "We have lost friends today. There is no place for applause. Ms. Stott is right; all thanks are due to the men who protected us today. Please join their family in mourning and offer your help to them."

A line quickly formed around the Aguilars to offer support and pay their respects. Eleanor returned, and Cooper helped cover Leroy's body with a brown blanket.

Dranko and Mark came jogging up to Cooper's side. He hadn't noticed that they'd left.

"We've policed the attackers' bodies. All dead," Dranko reported. Cooper caught Mark's expression and determined that they hadn't all been dead when they'd found them. "They looked like freelancers out for fun. I didn't see any coordinated gang markings on their tattoos or their clothing."

"That's good. It would have been worse if they'd been experienced," Cooper commented.

Dranko continued, "We have eight pistols we can hand out and one pistol-gripped twelve gauge. We're also the proud owners of one slightly damaged, but usable, motorbike and a van in good shape."

"OK, here's what I want. Tomorrow, offer Miguel any of what we've found today. It's the least respect we can show. Whatever is left, we put in the armory for duty use. The bike may be useful transport. Add the van to strengthen our weakest barrier. Gather the bodies and pitch them onto the other side of the barricade here. Finally, spread the word that we'll meet tonight at five, here. Everyone, except those on duty."

Mark looked at Cooper with an eyebrow cocked, "What are we going to do with the bodies of these vermin?"

"Heads on pikes, brother," Dranko intoned with a devilish grin.

"Almost. That's too nineteenth century," Cooper said smirking in Dranko's direction. "We'll burn them instead and leave the bones. But the principle remains; nothing says 'stay out' like the remains of those who tried to cross you."

Cooper left Mark and Dranko to finish returning things to normal at the barricade and ensuring it was staffed by fresh faces. He jogged at a quick clip back to his home. His determined look warded off the questions of those headed to the north barricade.

When he arrived at his home, the front door was slightly ajar. His heart leapt into his throat. Forcing calm, he took a deep breath, shouldered his rifle and brought the pistol into his hands. He knew a round from the FAL would likely go through every wall in the house, if he had to fire it. He couldn't risk that with Jake likely inside.

Without warning, he pushed the door wide open with the toe of his boot and swept the room from right to left with the pistol barrel. His house looked like it did when he'd left with no sign of disturbance. Keeping the gun at the ready, he moved quickly from room to room on the first level. Finally, he came to the basement door.

He called down through the closed door, "Jake, you down there?"

"Yes."

"What's the password?"

"Rutabaga," his son called up.

Cooper relaxed, holstered the pistol and opened the door. 'Rutabaga' was the all clear sign. If the response had been 'chili' it would have meant there was trouble.

Before he could take a step down, Jake came bounding up the steps, his rifle in his hands.

"Where's Julianne?"

"Dunno. She put me down here, said she had to check on something, and then I heard her leave the house." The relief in his voice was unmistakable.

Cooper's fist thundered against the thin wood on the door, "She rabbited, eh?"

"She what?" Jake asked, confused.

Cooper patted his head, "Sorry, it means she panicked and ran off. I don't think she liked the questions I was asking her." *Now I know she had something to hide.*

Jake shrugged his shoulders, nonplussed. *He's happy she is gone.* "What happened up the street? I heard a lot of shooting."

Cooper led him to the kitchen and poured them both a glass of water. As he drank his down in one long pull, it felt like cold nirvana to his parched, dry throat. *A fight always does that to me. Instant dehydration.*

He poured himself another full glass and then sat down with Jake at the kitchen table. "Well, the good news is that we got rid of some bad guys trying to come here and do us all harm."

"What's the bad news?" Jake's wide eyes revealed deep concern.

"Antonio Aguilar and Leroy Johnson were both killed, son."

Jake's eyes glazed over in deep consideration, and soon glistened. He didn't know Leroy very well, but he had shot hoops and played touch football a few times with Antonio. *He's having to learn about death way too fast and much too often.* Cooper could see it.

Cooper put his hand firmly on his son's shoulder. "You alright?"

"Yeah. It just sucks, dad. Leroy seemed like a good guy and Antonio was a friend of mine. Why do these guys have to add to the death already happening all around us? It doesn't make sense."

"You're right son, it doesn't make sense. Some people and some things just don't make sense. This was one of those things." Cooper knew his words were inadequate, but it was the best that could be said.

"Look, I'm bushed. You wanna lie down with me to take a

nap?"

"Sure."

He took his son's hand as they made their way upstairs. *Almost the picture of Norman Rockwell, except for the hardware I'm carrying.* Less than five minutes later, he was in deep slumber. Jake lay awake watching his father's chest rise and fall. After a while, he laid his head on it, savoring the reassurance of its steady breath. He was thinking about the last time he and Antonio had shot baskets. He fell asleep remembering how Antonio had shown him, many times over, how to properly hold the ball while shooting. His eyes were wet when he fell asleep.

*****

Cooper awoke a few hours later. He left Jake sleeping and quietly crept from the room. He cleaned the rifle and when Jake woke up, made them both a hearty lunch of grilled cheese sandwiches, fruit, and tall glasses of cold milk. He clenched his jaw tight while frying the sandwiches. The smell of the melted butter and cheese was overpowering. Grilled cheese had been something Elena always made their son to comfort him after a bad day at school or sometimes simply on one of the sad, cold, gray rainy days in mid-winter that were so common in the Northwest. His mind drifted to a memory from several years ago.

******

When Cooper came home, Elena was standing in the kitchen, in front of the stove. Jake sat at the kitchen counter, chin in both hands and sad, droopy eyes. Cooper immediately smelled the reassuring aroma of butter and cheese frying amid toasted bread.

"Uh-oh, what's going on buddy?" he asked his son as he patted his head.

His son grunted in return. His wife turned to him, corners turned down at the mouth, "C'mon darling, tell your daddy why you're sad."

Jake shifted in his seat uncomfortably but remained mute and new tears welled up. Cooper put his arm around his son and gave Elena a beckoning look.

She shrugged her shoulders, "George scraped his knee today and now won't play with Jake," she said with mustered seriousness.

Cooper fell out laughing uncontrollably. Elena looked at him aghast and Jake turned and gave him a glare full of hurt and anger. Cooper pleaded, desperately trying to stop, "I'm sorry. I'm sorry. It's just..." he collapsed again into a fresh round of loud chortling. Elena harrumphed her shoulders and returned to frying the grilled cheese sandwich and Cooper had to leave the room to regain his composure. Jake's sharp eyes and snarled lips escorted him out.

An hour later, Cooper, forgiven for his impoliteness was back with the family playing UNO. Later that night, in her arms, Elena poked him in the ribs and chastised him for not taking George, Jake's imaginary friend, more seriously.

******

Cooper returned from reminiscing. His smile was bittersweet. *Damn, I miss her.*

He spent the afternoon reading to Jake, sitting together on the couch. Cooper was thankful there were no interruptions. The past several days had been a blur of adrenaline, chaos, and fear. These few hours of near normalcy felt like an oasis. Cooper noticed Jake pulling closer and closer to him as he read the last chapters from Rick Riordan's latest tale of childhood adventure.

As he read, contentment grew inside Cooper. He realized he had become completely lost in the sheer joy of connection with his son. His heart was full and his breath deep. His mind drifted and he thought about how he had done this hundreds of times with his son before the plague and only rarely had appreciated it as much. *I took it all for granted. Time with my boy, the touch of my wife, the simple peace. We had so much joy at our fingertips and didn't realize it.* He fought the emotion that threatened to bellow up from deep within. He didn't want to ruin the moment. He tightened his throat and kept reading. Slowly, he returned to the rhythm of the written word, felt his son's chest moving in tandem with his, and bathed in the look of love he saw in Jake's eyes.

Seeing the time on his watch jarred him back to reality. At four thirty, with heavyset shoulders, he gathered their things and left for the meeting. Forlornly, Jake picked up the Ruger rifle to take with him. Cooper looked on in surrender to the necessity of it.

"Go grab an extra magazine or two. If you're going to take it, bring adequate ammunition."

Jake's steps were heavy as he left the room and went into the basement. Cooper waited for him to return and then they left together, heading north to the barricade.

Chapter 18

When Cooper arrived, Dranko and a few others were already there. The bodies had been moved, and an attempt had been made to wash away the blood from where Antonio and Leroy had fallen. However, faint outlines of blood and water were still visible on the pavement. The coppery smell of blood and the pungent odor of raw meat that remained reminded Cooper of the time he'd visited a meat packing house. Cooper wrinkled his nose. Next to him, Jake grimaced and put his free hand to cover his nose and mouth. Cooper tried his best to shield his eyes from the bodies, which had been tossed together, across the street from the car barricade. Cooper's nose told him they were downwind.

Dranko sidled up next to him, handed him a list, and whispered, "I have a can of gasoline and matches, as well."

Cooper looked at the list and realized it had the names of those who had died recently, those recently fallen ill, and those remaining to be buried. Thankfully, the last column was short. The other two were not.

"We did another canvass of the neighborhood today. It was Calvin's idea, and I figured you wouldn't mind."

"No, this is great. We should do this every two days. We need to track what's happening with this thing," Cooper responded, still digesting the names on the list.

Calvin was within earshot, so Cooper called him over, "Calvin, this was a great idea. What do you think about doing this every two days?"

He fondled his chin between his thumb and his index finger for a moment, "I like it. We can recruit a team for this. It would make good work for those who don't want to be on the defense teams."

Cooper nodded, "Right. Why don't you make that happen at this meeting? I have something I need to tackle."

Cooper proceeded to explain his plan, answer Calvin's questions, and secured his agreement.

At five o'clock, approximately seventy people had gathered around. *Nothing like imminent danger of attack to draw the crowds, eh?*

Cooper and Calvin climbed onto the hood of the Buick so that everyone could see them. Calvin started the meeting by thanking the bravery of those involved in the gun battle earlier in the day. When

Cooper's name was called out, Cooper felt uncomfortable amidst the near-worshipful gazes that came his way. *With those unaccustomed to violence, those who can handle it are held in exaggerated esteem,* he thought to himself.

Calvin outlined his idea to do the neighborhood canvasses every other day and easily found a half-dozen volunteers to do the work. When he'd finished, he turned the meeting over to Cooper.

Cooper cleared his throat, "I too want to start by acknowledging the sacrifices made by our neighbors today. Mr. Leroy Johnson and the entire Aguilar family. But for them, some of us would not be standing here right now. We owe them a lot." He let several seconds pass as muted applause rippled through the gathering.

"We now have a serious subject to discuss and I'd like to ask a few volunteers to take the children further down the street, out of earshot."

A murmur of curiosity ran through those assembled, but his instructions were carried out. Jake stood his ground, until Cooper looked at him and waved him off to join the others walking away. Jake stared back at him, harrumphed his shoulders, and stomped off.

"I have a proposal that is going to be shocking to some. All I ask is that you hear me out because my idea is aimed at *preventing* other attacks like today. Can everyone agree to that?" A chorus of nodding heads and calls of "yes" and "sure" resounded.

"Good. The best way to dissuade others from taking on our neighborhood is to show that we're organized, ready, and not defenseless. We've done that with our barricades. However, we can move that to another level by *showing* everyone that we're neither afraid nor incapable of using our weapons." He paused for a moment until he saw a lot of nodding heads in the audience.

"We can show this by incinerating the bodies of those who…"

"Wait! You want to *burn* them?!" Michelle called, incredulous.

Cooper planted his feet firmly on the metal hood, "Let me clear, I don't *want* to do anything except sit at home and read to my boy. But, I think we *should* burn the bodies of those who killed our neighbors and display the remains in front of our barricades. It will make anyone think twice before attacking us again."

"That's barbaric," Michelle shouted with shock.

"Tell me one thing, Michelle: if I had told you two weeks ago that a gang of armed men would drive into our neighborhood and kill Antonio Aguilar and Leroy Johnson, wouldn't you have said *that* was barbaric?" He paused and silence hung in the air. "The fact is, we live

160

in a new world. The same rules, the same conventions, from before don't always apply anymore."

Unconvinced, Michelle crossed her arms, took a step back, and remained wordless. He could hear others murmuring around her.

"Won't this just attract the police's attention?" asked Gus.

Cooper wanted to laugh, but Calvin answered for him, "I don't know. But, I haven't seen a police car in days and the 911 lines just say they are busy all the time. I think we're on our own for the time being and we need to focus on what's the best for us to do, right now."

"What will everyone else think of us? When this is all over, I don't want to be known as the neighborhood that put dead bodies on display," asked a woman from the group whom Cooper didn't recognize.

Cooper's patience was wearing thin. He readied himself to answer. Before he could, Lily Stott rapped her cane on the hood of the Buick. Clanging metal brought rippled silence to the group.

She spoke softly. The crowd grew even quieter and he saw heads lean in, straining to hear her. *Quieter than normal, the sly woman!* "You all know, I'm a Southern lady and it is in my blood to be polite and respect traditions and the law," her voice gathered strength. "But, let's stop all this fussin'. We're livin' in dangerous times. We have to do whatever we need to do to *survive*. I don't care how unsightly it might be," she turned to the person who had asked the last question, her voice rising to crescendo, "I tell you what I will tell any simpering neighbor who comes to ask. I will tell them I did what I thought best to protect my family and neighbors and then ask them if they did the same."

Someone started clapping and soon the whole group was, including Michelle and Gus. Hoots of "You tell 'em!" and "Right on!" filled the night's gathering air.

Mark stepped in, "All in favor of Cooper's plan, say 'Hell yeah!'!" The sound was deafening.

"Any opposed, say 'Nay'."

A lone voice declared an emphatic, "Nay!" In disbelief, Cooper looked down and saw that it was Lily Stott. She realized all eyes were on her.

She gave a dismissive wave to the crowd, "Don't get me wrong, I support this. But, I cast my vote 'Nay' so that none of us forget that we should do this with reluctance and regret of its necessity. We hold onto our morality that way." She gripped her cane fiercely as she finished and jabbed it onto the black asphalt. Without awaiting a response, she began ambling back towards her home.

Cooper, and most of the crowd, shook their heads and grinned at old Lily Stott as she walked home.

Cooper knew he had to personally carry out what they had just decided to do since it was his idea. He and Dranko piled the bodies together. The dead men looked ridiculous. Colored hair, body piercings, and leathers might look tough while you were alive, but they became comical in death.

Cooper grabbed the gas can that Dranko had brought and began dousing the bodies liberally with the acrid smelling liquid. He took a final look down the street to ensure the children had all been moved much further away. About a dozen people remained behind to witness the gruesome act. Their eyes looked at him pensively, unsure how to act. *We're crossing the Rubicon now, a giant step away from how we've all been raised.*

He struck the match and tossed it onto the middle of the pile. The gasoline lit up immediately, the flames licking among and between the bodies. Cooper refused to watch the sizzling flesh; he knew the smell and sound would be enough to haunt him.

Within seconds, the strong sweet-sick smell of burning flesh, and the stink of petroleum as polyester and faux leather went up in flames, assaulted his nose. His hand sprung to cover his mouth and nose, but it offered scant defense. His mouth wrinkled in disgust. *I hope this is worth it and wards off anyone else from trying to mess with us.*

He heard the clatter of wood banging against wood and turned to see Dranko tossing scrap pieces of lumber onto the burning bodies. He kept his arm sleeve over his mouth and nose but shouted over the din of the flames, "What're you doing?"

Dranko had a wet handkerchief plastered over his mouth, "Making the fire burn hotter. It'll be better to have them burnt down to the bone. You don't want to try hauling around bodies only partly burned." Cooper could only imagine the matter-of-fact expression underneath the mask as he detailed such a macabre fact.

Cooper found himself shaking his head in wonder as he moved around the bodies to begin helping Dranko, "You think of everything, you son of a bitch!"

"Someone's got to around here; otherwise your arse wouldn't get wiped!"

Cooper playfully hit him in the back with a length of 2x4 he had just picked up, "I'll grant you're the expert on burning bodies!" He tossed the wood onto the pile of bodies, his lips turning downward as he did so.

By the time they'd finished, they were both covered in sweat from the heat and the exertion. They had built a large bonfire over the bodies with flames leaping eight feet into the air.

Dranko broke the silence first, "You go on home and be with Jake. I'll take care of the rest. I'll keep this fire going long enough."

"Thanks. We can move the bodies into position at first light, after they've cooled."

Dranko nodded. Cooper turned to leave and realized the group that had stayed behind were all still standing there, transfixed, gazing at the gruesome scene of bodies burning in the street near their homes.

"You all go home now. We've had enough unpleasantness today. There's no reason to watch more of it."

His words sparked them into action and they slowly ambled off in different directions.

*****

He made his way to where Jake was playing a game of tag with three other children in the street. They were out of view of the fire and, thankfully, upwind as well.

The quartet of children raced to and fro, lost in the sheer joy of child's play.

Cooper hung back, not wishing to disturb them by his presence. He leaned back against an early budding cherry tree and lowered himself into a squatting position.

The contrast of the scene before him with the grisly work he had just performed shook him to his core. The innocence of watching his son play some invented game that looked like a cross between tag and dodge ball was a joy for Cooper. He hadn't seen Jake smile like this in days. He drank it in like a welcome tonic. It washed away the stench and grisliness of what he'd just done.

The children played on for several more minutes before a parent's call broke the spell. The other three children ran off towards home. Cooper stood up, unfolding his stiffening muscles with a grimace.

His movement caught Jake's eye. The two gazed at each other for a long moment. Jake's face changed right before Cooper's eyes, the innocence fading away. His eyes lost the wrinkles of joy. They became encircled by tight lines of worry. His smile shrank from a wide, unencumbered grin, to a tight-lipped visage. His face fell unto itself. His ears dropped lower. Cooper knew that this grim look of determination didn't belong on an eleven year-old. In submission, he turned to fetch his rifle that he had left leaned up against a car. When he turned back towards Cooper, the transformation was complete. A child-soldier had replaced his young son. Impotent to stop it, Cooper wanted to rage at the sky. Instead, like sour milk after cake, sorrow's foul taste lingered.

Cooper picked up his own rifle from its resting position and began walking towards Jake. The rifle had never been so heavy. His heart was heavier.

Chapter 19

After dinner, he and Jake tried reading together again. They returned to the same position on the couch, but now everything seemed cold, stale. Cooper's mind was filled with the stench and sight of bodies burning. Jake's was still swirling with the thought of Antonio's death. They soldiered on, trying to recapture the magic from earlier in the day. Neither wanted to be the first to admit defeat. So, the charade continued.

A sharp rap on the front door interrupted them. Cooper glided to the second story window that overlooked their door, shotgun in hand. Dranko was looking right at him and waved. He knew Cooper's security procedures. Cooper went downstairs, stretching his muscles out as he did so.

Cooper opened the door and Dranko barreled past Cooper, bumping his shoulder as he rushed in.

"We gotta do something. The news isn't good," he panted.

"Slow down, what's happening?"

"I've spent the last hour catching up on the news, both broadcast and internet. It's coming loose all over."

Cooper sat down on his couch, "Start from the top, please."

"The short version is that what happened here today was no fluke. Attacks are going on everywhere, too many for the news to keep track of. But they know there are a lot. Most end badly because they aren't organized like we are."

"You mean everywhere, Portland? Or, everywhere, USA?"

His eyes were grim, "Both. The worst part is some are random, like ours, and some are definitely with a purpose to steal or even take over."

"Take over?" Cooper's eyebrows came together in surprise.

"Yes, there have been reports of gangs moving into an area and taking it over, getting the residents to hand over money, supplies, or do work for them."

"What kind of work?"

"All kinds. Using them to carry loot back from other raids. Medical people are pressed to treat injured gang members. There are at least two reports of them being used as human shields. Women are being put into sexual service. One group in Detroit is building a monument to their leader from wood and scrap metal. It's crazy."

"Unbelievable," Cooper sighed.

"No, not unbelievable. Lots of people are making the call that it is 'game over' time. They see people dying all around them with no cure or remedy in sight. All levels of government seem to have broken down. When a vacuum this big gets created, strong men always step in to fill the gap. I told you it was a bad idea to try and stay here."

Cooper held up a finger, "Don't go there."

Dranko retreated with a flurry of waving his hands back and forth, "Of course, forget I said it. But, the bottom line is its going to get worse, much worse. What happened today will happen again. It was no fluke."

"Did the news have any estimate of casualties?"

Dranko's face went slack, "Yeah, over tens of millions. Mostly from plague, but a goodly number from violence. So far."

Cooper shook his head in disbelief, "That's almost five percent of America. Gone?"

"Yeah. No end in sight either."

"One in twenty? More sick every day. No wonder the wheels are coming off."

Cooper leaned back into the couch, cocked his head to stare into space, and cradled his head in his hands. He let out a deep sigh and then remained in silence. Dranko counted the seconds, knowing his friend would soon have a response.

Sure enough, a few moments later, Cooper returned to the upright position, his eyes alive again.

"I know just what we should do."

"What's that, brother?"

"Get bigger," Cooper said as a sly smile crept across his face.

"Why don't you fill us little people in on your grand master plan, Obi Wan Kanobi," Dranko mocked.

Cooper ignored the jibe. "We survey all the neighborhoods around us. We can find out if they are organized. If they are, we work out mutual assistance pacts. If they're not, we try to help them become organized. It will be like…"

"…our own gang," Dranko finished for him. "But, we are still talking about untrained people fighting back against hardened gangbangers. I just don't see how…"

"People defending their own homes is a powerful thing. Don't underestimate it. Every occupying power has learned it the hard way throughout history. So, too will anyone coming here," Cooper's jaw was firmly set as he talked. "Besides, we will find some ex-military who *do* have experience. We build the defenses around those people. Don't forget, barricades will buy us time against the real gangs. They will go after easier pickings first. The random crazies, like today, won't be as well trained or organized as you think."

"OK," Dranko reluctantly agreed. "If nothing else, the wider reach out will give us more warning before *our* neighborhood is attacked."

"That's why I love you Dranko, you're the master of low expectations!"

He fished a spent shell casing from his pocket and threw it playfully at Cooper, "I do my best!"

"First thing tomorrow morning, we should send out survey teams to find out what's happening around us."

"How many?"

"Four teams, four people per team. The right number for security without appearing to be a threat."

"Consider it done. I'll convene everyone involved with defense in the morning and send out the teams."

Cooper nodded in approval. Just then, his walkie-talkie buzzed alive.

"Boss, you there? This is western post."

"Eagle's nest here. What's the report?"

"You better get down here. We have refugees."

"Refugees?" Cooper gave a quizzical look at Dranko.

"Yes, refugees. Can you get down here, please?"

"Coming," Cooper stuffed the walkie-talkie back into his pocket.

"Can you stay with Jake while I go check this out?"

"Yes, ring me up if you need anything."

Cooper grabbed his gear and donned his body armor as he left and began trotting towards the western barricade.

As Cooper jogged, the late afternoon sun played wistfully among the leaves. Every so often, he would step into a gap between the trees and catch the full sun, becoming momentarily blinded. When lit up by the bright sun, the myriad shades of green in the leaves fascinated Cooper. It always had. He'd never known why.

Today, it dawned on him. Now, as he made his way west, naked tears of emotion ran down his face. *Life. They show life happening. And, they're beautiful. Just like Elena.*

He stopped just out of view of the barricade and hastily wiped the tears away. He couldn't afford to take the time to think about all of this. He pounded his fist against his chest, taking comfort in the body armor, and ran onward.

He heard the problem before he could see it. Loud voices arguing. Plaintive voices begging to be let past the barricade. Other voices stern in refusal. The pleading turned angry, to no avail, and then back to begging once more.

The normal three guard detachment had swollen to eight as reinforcements had come over. They formed a human wall to close the gap between two large pickup trucks that had been used to set up the checkpoint. Beyond them, a few dozen desperate looking people, most carrying a suitcase or bag of possessions, were taking turns shouting and begging to be let in. For a moment, Cooper thought he was watching news footage of refugees from World War Two, only in color. A woman held a crying child, an elderly couple stood clutching each other as if they'd fall if they let go, and a man in a pressed business suit looked like he was headed to work at a downtown bank. Most in the group were dirty, disheveled, and bewildered. They looked hungry and scared, too. Mark was arguing with the group.

"Mr. Moretti, please report!" Cooper shouted over the din, seeking to establish order.

Mark's head jerked around until he saw Cooper. Then, he smiled, disengaged from the group and quickly stepped towards Cooper.

"What's happening?"

"Near as I can tell, this group was kicked out of their homes over on Division and 28th. They say a group arrived, in pickups and panel vans, and just kicked them all out, forcing them on foot and with no time to collect their things. They said they were looking for someone, but no one knows who or why. They've been walking along aimlessly since. They saw our armed guard post and they think we're a safe place. They want in. I told them no. I wanted to wait until you got here."

Cooper scratched his chin for a moment and then strode over to address the group. He held his hand high until silence overtook the group.

"Good afternoon! My name is Cooper Adams. I am very sorry for what has happened to you. We would…"

"You gonna let us in or not?" A deep, rumbling voice shouted from the group. It belonged to a large man wearing a gray sweatshirt that barely covered his enormous pot belly. A few others joined him in catcalls of affirmation.

Cooper stared at the man for a long moment. Silence regained control of the group. The man dropped his eyes. Finally, deliberately, Cooper turned back towards the group.

"We will do two things for you. We are not the police, nor the government. So, we don't owe you anything. So, we do these things from kindness, not from obligation. If there is a peep," Cooper shot the man who had shouted a stern look, "from anyone, then the offer I am about to make will be withdrawn completely. Is that understood?"

The group nodded and grunted reluctant affirmations.

"We will interview each and every one of you. If we determine you will add a benefit to our community, you will be allowed in; at least temporarily. If we determine you will not, we will give you a small ration of food, taken from our own cupboards, and send you on your way. Any problems with this?"

The reaction was immediate and diverse. A handful glared at him. The man in the gray sweatshirt spat at the ground in disgust, but a neighbor elbowed him in the stomach and he held his tongue. The majority stared blankly at him, without response. He noticed a significant number of eyes light up with a glimmer of hope. Some began to straighten the collars on their shirt or realign the hem of their coat. This group began nodding their heads and saying, "Yes." Slowly, this response spread throughout the entire group. When the nods had reached consensus, Cooper turned to the guards gathered about him.

He pointed at the two that looked to be the fastest, "Go house to house and gather portable food for two dozen people. Be back no later than thirty minutes."

A young woman dressed in a red Columbia jacket and neat black synthetic jogging pants and a young man wearing a red flannel coat with dark blue jeans ran off down the street. *I must remember to put out some guidelines about the best clothing to wear to the guard stations. Red?* He asked three of the guards to maintain the position and had Mark bring each refugee behind the barricade one person at a time for the interviews.

Cooper leaned against a black Volkswagen Jetta that was parked just behind the barricade on the side of the street. He wished he had a chair to sit in, as he knew what he was about to do would be tedious and tiring.

The first person that Mark brought back was in her twenties, blond, and undeniably attractive. Her red wool sweater was unbuttoned halfway down, revealing a black bra that cradled two full breasts. She sauntered over to Cooper, whisking her hips back and forth. She wore a tight fitting pair of ski pants and carried a red parka in her arms. Cooper glared at Mark, who smiled sheepishly back at him as if to say, "I couldn't help it."

"Good afternoon, ma'am."

She deftly tilted her head and looked up at him with full eyes, "Good afternoon to you. But please call me Rachel."

"I just have a few questions for you. Please answer honestly as I don't like BS and if we determine that you've lied to us later, you will be turned out of here...or worse. Understand?"

Her coy smile disappeared for a second as the blunt force of his words hit her, but quickly returned, "Yes, sir."

"Rachel, do you have any experience with firearms?"

"No," a furrow of concern knitted her manicured eyebrows together.

"Do you have any experience fixing things? Mechanical or carpentry, stuff like that?"

"No, but..."

Cooper wouldn't let her continue, "Do you have any military experience or background?"

"No," her smile had disappeared and been replaced by a grim mouth and drooping eyes.

"Do you have any medical experience?"

Her eyes lit up and she blurted out, "Oh, yes. Considerable experience!"

Cooper's eyebrow cocked in surprise, "Great, where was this and what did you do?"

"I worked with Dr. Sanders, one of Portland's best cosmetic dentists. I worked the front desk in reception," she said proudly.

Cooper's eyebrows deflated as he forced the smile from his face and tamped the laughter in his belly. "Great. Are there any other skills you can bring to our neighborhood?"

Her instant transformation startled him. She took a step closer and leaned in so that she whispered softly in his ear, "I know how to keep a man happy." He felt her hand squeeze his hip. "The right man would be *very* happy." Her words dripped with lust. She tilted her head back just enough so that he had full view of her cleavage. He caught a whiff of her perfume, which was sweet and smelled of lavender.

He took his right hand and firmly moved her back a step. "Thank you for your time, Rachel. You're a number 'one', please remember that, OK?"

She smiled and clapped her hands lightly together. "Thank you! You won't regret this."

"I haven't said you're accepted, just that your number is One, OK?"

She smiled at him knowingly, "Yeah, sure. I got it," and winked at him.

She walked back towards the rest of the group, looking back once to catch his eye and winking again. He waved uncomfortably at her. He couldn't deny that she looked as good leaving as she had on the approach.

He shook his head, "Next!"

A nervous man claiming to be an auto mechanic was next. Cooper looked at his fingernails. Clean. Well-kept. Thin fingers. Cooper frowned, dismissed him quickly, and assigned him the number 'three'.

When Cooper looked back up after calling for the next person, another woman was walking towards him. She had an open, friendly face with her dark hair pulled back into a loose ponytail. She wore baggy khaki-colored hiking pants, a brown long-sleeved shirt, and a bright blue jacket. He noticed she was also wearing sturdy hiking boots and she walked confidently in them. *At least she dressed for the exodus.*

He learned that her name was Angela. Angela McIntosh. Cooper then repeated his opening mantra about telling the truth and then dove into the questions.

"Do you have any experience with firearms?"

"I was a good shot when I was a kid, but it's been years since I've fired one."

"Where'd you learn?"

"I grew up on a farm. My father didn't have any boys, so it was my job to deal with the coyotes," Angela answered, pronouncing it as "kay-otes."

"So, you could shoot some distance?"

"Oh, yeah," she said nonchalantly.

"What kind of farm did you grow up on?"

"The drowning kind," a sardonic grin crossed her face.

Cooper cocked an eyebrow, "The drowning kind?"

"Sure. Drowning in debt, drowning in water, or drowning in the foreign markets, that's the fate of any family farm these days. Take your pick. On a good year, it was only one of the three," she laughed heartily at her own joke. Her deep, solid, joyful laugh drew him in and he couldn't resist chuckling with her.

"Can you fix or repair things?"

"I restored my 1903 house that I live in myself, so I'm handy in a general sort of way," her cavalier confidence oozed out.

"Can you work on cars?"

"No, not really."

"What about medical experience, do you have any?"

"I'm an ER nurse. I've seen it all."

He didn't doubt her for a second, "Can you work without your hospital equipment?" Cooper knew enough that modern medicine was heavily reliant upon technology, which they *didn't* have.

"Well, I'm also a trained Wilderness EMT, so I'm used to treating injuries and illness in the field without too much equipment. It's mostly just common sense anyway."

Cooper nodded and didn't try to conceal his satisfied look, "Had some training in that area, too. They never told us someday we might use those same skills in the middle of a city, did they?"

"Back then, no one could imagine you'd be in the middle of a city *and* be without access to modern medical care," her words were laced with lament.

Cooper nodded, then looked back up at her, mustering a weak smile, "I'm giving you the number two, remember that number, alright?"

"Sure. Do you mind if I ask you a question?"

Cooper laughed, "Sure."

"The ones you let in, are we coming in as equals or as something else?"

Cooper tightened his eyes, taking offense to the question, "Equals. People coming in will contribute to our neighborhood, so they'll be equals."

Angela noticed and waved her hand, "I didn't mean to offend you, Cooper. But, you wouldn't believe some of the 'offers' of help we've heard today. The world is turning around very, very quickly."

Cooper sighed, "I hear you. It is changing, but our job is to prevent it from changing too much and in the wrong direction."

As Angela walked away, he watched her in silent respect. This was someone who could handle herself. And, best of all, she *knew* it.

"Next!"

After an hour, Cooper was down to the last person. His head hurt from the wide range of emotion he had encountered. Some cried, some yelled, and most begged him. In addition to Angela, he had decided to let four others in.

Frank Stephens was a former career Marine infantry officer who, although in his early sixties, was still in excellent shape. Cooper felt that if he could put a cigar in his mouth and an M16 in his hand, he would have had a spitting image of Clint Eastwood in *Heartbreak Ridge* standing in front of him. Gus had cursed his late wife for making him get rid of his firearms. "I coulda taken those punks with one good rifle and thirty rounds," he'd grunted when first meeting Cooper. Cooper believed him too.

Michaela Evans worked as a trained botanist by day and hobbied as a competition pistol shooter by night. She wore her hair short, had smooth, ebony skin, and a no-nonsense attitude that Cooper liked immediately. Allowing her in was an easy decision because he needed anyone with weapons experience.

Betty Gray was his charity case. The old woman reminded him too much of his long-dead grandmother. He couldn't turn her away, even though he knew she didn't bring too much. She knew how to can, but that was the only practical skill he could identify.

Miko Martoulis was a recent immigrant who had served in the Greek army for several years. He had been a cook, but had been under fire a few times during their brief, but bloody, civil war that followed their economic collapse a few years ago. He worked as an auto mechanic at a local shop.

But, it was the last interview that changed everything.

*****

After the long session, Cooper shouted, "Last," and grinned at his own joke.

A short man with fidgeting hands ambled towards him. He was young, but prematurely bald. His steps were haphazard and Cooper kept thinking he was going to stumble and fall down. Nervously, he looked in all directions. Cooper thought he might be high.

Cooper stood up, angry, "Don't waste my time if you're on something!"

The man's eyes, suddenly alert, zeroed in on Cooper's, "I'm not on anything. I swear."

As he drew closer, Cooper saw dark stains under his arms, despite the chill air, "Then why are you as nervous as a flea on a skillet?"

He gripped Cooper's jacket collar, his eyes darted back and forth, "Because, *they* are after me." The man's breath reeked with fear.

Cooper pushed him to arm's length, grabbing his collar in turn, "What? Who?"

The man's eyes pleaded, "Look. I know something. That gang that attacked us wasn't random. They were looking for me."

Cooper's eyes buzzed in confusion, "Slow down. What the hell are you talking about?"

"No one will listen to me. They were coming for me, but they must not have had the full address, so they attacked our whole block."

Cooper was growing impatient, "*Why* would anyone be looking for you?"

"Because I know how all of *this*," he waved his hands in a wide arc, "got started."

Cooper relaxed his grip and took an involuntary step back, "You mean..."

"Yes, that's what I mean. I worked at Admonitus for God's sake. I was just a lab rat, low on the food chain. But, I heard things. I *knew* what they were working on. It..."

The man's head exploded in a flash of red. Blood splashed wholesale across Cooper's face, plastering his mouth, and burning his eyes. Cooper was on the ground before the man's body had time to slump to the ground. Everyone was screaming as bursts of weapons fire sprayed the barricade in a wild fusillade. The roar of engines coming to life completed the cacophony.

Cooper had his rifle at the ready position as he rolled to take cover next to the car he had been leaning against most of the day. A gaggle of vans and SUVs were racing from left to right, heading north. He was only able to get off two hasty shots at the last of them. His bullets disappeared into a green van and a black SUV to unknown effect.

They were gone as quickly as they had appeared.

Cooper waited a few seconds, but the engines continued to fade into the distance. The screams and moans of the wounded and dying were the loudest noise now.

As he clambered back onto his feet, Mark came running over to him.

"What the hell was that?"

Cooper looked at the man lying at his feet, "I think it was a hit."

Mark looked at him in confusion, "A what?"

"An assassination. They hit him with a long-range rifle head shot. The vehicles and gunfire were just a diversion. To make it look random. But, he was the target."

"Who would want him dead and why?"

"I don't know. But, I'm going to find out." He'd remembered that Julianne had worked at Admonitus, as well.

Cooper moved to tend to the injured.

Chapter 20

Cooper discovered his charity had been short-lived. Betty Gray had been mowed down by a burst from a submachine gun and lay dead in the street. The old woman appeared markedly smaller in death. Three others had been killed from close-in shotgun blasts or handguns. A half-dozen had been injured, most severely.

Others from the neighborhood were coming up after the gunfire had subsided. Cooper barked orders at them to go and get first aid supplies as quickly as possible. As they ran off, Cooper saw Calvin coming straight at him. He looked like an angry bull, taking long, deliberate strides toward him. As soon as he was within earshot, he yelled at Cooper.

"What the hell is going on here?"

Cooper waved his hands in a wide arc, indicating the dozen bodies strewn about him, "We were just attacked."

Calvin was now within arm's length, "*Who* are these people?" Cooper could see his face flushed a shade darker and his neck muscles as taut as a piano wire.

"Ah, refugees from several blocks over. They were driven from their homes by the same gang that just attacked them here," Cooper, confused, saw the rage in Calvin's eyes. "Look, why are you so *angry?*"

Calvin stood eye to eye with him, "Is it true that you were deciding to let some in?" Specks of spittle flew from his lips.

"Sure I was. I was figuring out who had skills that we could..."

Calvin poked him in the chest with the four fingers of his right hand, "*You* aren't in *charge* Mr. Adams. What gives you the right to do this without consulting anyone else?"

Now, Cooper's patience burst. *This is what he's upset about? His ego being bruised? Christ.* Cooper pushed him back to arm's length with the flat palm of hand, striking Calvin just hard enough to cause some pain, "You mean *you,* don't you?"

Calvin's eyes burned brighter and his fists balled up, "You're damn right! I'm the President of our Association and the Captain of our Guard! Have you forgotten?"

Cooper cut him off, clipping his words to stay just on the shy side of yelling, "I don't have time for this. I was called by those at this barricade to deal with an emerging situation. And, I dealt with it. No decision I made here was irreversible. I was clear that anyone's admittance was temporary."

Calvin's fist relaxed and he took a half-step back, "That's good to hear. But that doesn't change the fact that you over-stepped your authority."

Cooper interrupted, "Exactly. It was a new, unknown, situation. I acted. So, what, are you and Gus going to do, sue me?"

Calvin exploded, "Cooper, I've had enough of you. You constantly undermine me. You made decisions of import with *zero* consultation! I've *worked* hard for every ounce of responsibility I have in my life. I will not stand by while you tear it down." Veins crept across his neck, bulging.

Cooper remained speechless as Calvin continued, "You don't know *where* I've come from or *what* I've overcome. It's time you respected my role here!"

Cooper, taken aback, lowered his head and nodded, "You're right." His voice was scarcely more than a murmur.

Calvin cocked his eyebrows and leaned in to hear him, "What?"

He looked him in the eye, "I said you're right. I'm sorry. I get it now."

Now, it was Calvin's turn to be taken off guard, "Really?"

Cooper cracked a grin, "Yeah, I've been too overbearing. You earned your place here. I need to honor that."

Calvin returned the smile, "Thank you, Cooper. To be fair, I've been on edge. This situation we're dealing is out of my realm of experience."

"It's out of *everyone's* realm of experience," Cooper chuckled.

Calvin turned to the wounded, "Let's get to work and help these folks out. I need *you* to get things done, Cooper." He extended his hand. Cooper took it and the two men clasped hands firmly.

Mark and the other guards had begun tending to the wounded and had already helped the most serious cases. As he helped bandage the victims with torn-up sheets that someone had brought, Cooper noted that most of those wounded wouldn't make it through the night.

He called Calvin over and pulled him away from the group. "You wanted decisions? I got one for you. Most of these wounded won't live until morning. Bleeding in ways we can't stop."

"What's the decision?"

Cooper pulled his face close, "We should think about putting them down."

Calvin recoiled and pulled away, "What? Kill them? Like dogs at the pound?"

Cooper exhaled, whispering, "Calvin, they're already dead. The question is whether we let them suffer through the night in pain. *That's* the decision."

He paced in a tight circle, "I can't believe this. How is this happening?"

Cooper stepped forward and put a hand on his shoulder, "It's happening because the world got turned upside down. You gotta make the call on this. I've got to send the unwounded away before it gets dark."

He turned and walked back to the main group. Cooper reassembled the non-wounded people who had been displaced from their homes earlier that day. He made sure Mark had the small bundles of food gathered nearby, ready to hand out. He grabbed one and held it above his head.

"I want to remind everyone of our agreement from earlier today. Because we are decent people here, we are modifying it. We will take the wounded in until they can travel or we can find alternative care. As I said, we have interviewed everyone. I will announce who we have accepted, but I wish to remind you, if anyone argues about our decision, they will forego this bundle of food that we will give to everyone who we do not accept. We do this from the goodness of our heart."

He let his words sink in to the group. He heard some disgruntled mumbles. He knew the attack had everyone on edge.

"There is one more thing. If anyone gets threatening towards us or tries to sneak into our community later, they will be shot. No questions asked. So, think very hard before you react. I know those who are not accepted will be disappointed and maybe angry. But, we are giving you food to last you a few days. That's more than anyone else has offered you. I hope you'll remember that."

He turned to Mark. "You ready?"

"Yes."

He looked over at Peter Garcia, who held a shotgun at the ready, "You ready?"

"Yes, sir!"

Cooper positioned himself to face the group once more, "If I gave you an odd number, please stand over to my left. If you received an even number, please step to my right."

As the much larger group moved to his left, a few people quickly figured out they were in the wrong group. Two of these tried to move back to his right. Cooper saw them and gave them a firm shake of his head and put his hand on the butt of his pistol. They quickly rejoined the larger group.

"OK, those on my right can step across the barricade. You are welcome to our neighborhood. Mark, please start handing out the supplies to those on my left."

Cooper watched the unaccepted group very closely. He expected an outburst, or worse. He noted several faces that screwed themselves up in anger. However, they *did* nothing. He was shocked at the resignation that overtook the group once he had spoken. They dejectedly queued up behind Mark to accept the meager bundles that they had to offer. He swallowed hard to stiffen his resolve in the face of such heartbreak and despair. *We can't save everyone*, he reminded himself.

A woman with a young child in hand tried to rush past Mark. He stopped her with a firm hand. She yelled to catch Cooper's attention.

"Please, help us. It's almost dark. We cannot sleep on the *streets* for God's sake. Please let us stay, just one night."

Cooper had dealt with desperation worse than this in Iraq. But this was different. In Iraq the victimized had been strangers, oddly dressed, foreign customs and tongue. Here, they were his people. He'd probably seen this woman and her child at the grocery store or the park. Cooper's stomach grew tight. He averted the woman's eyes and didn't respond. Mark shoved a bag of goods into her hands and told her to move on. She did so, after spitting at the ground in contempt.

Cooper grabbed his walkie-talkie, "Dranko, you there?"

After a moment's pause, "Yes, what's up?"

"We need to relieve the west guard, they've been through a rough spell. Also, let's put an additional guard on each post tonight and put another patrol out. I want to be ready if the attackers return or any of these refugees try to come back," Cooper raised his voice so that the second half of what he said could be heard by the departing refugees.

"Got it. We are low on men, but I'll do what I can. You coming back?"

"Yeah, I'll be there in a minute. There are three more I'm bringing with me who we can arm and put on rotation."

Cooper left Mark in charge until he was relieved. He quickly assigned the new residents to be housed for the night with those from the neighborhood who had gathered to help. Out of the corner of his eye, he saw Calvin dealing with the wounded and the dead lying in the street. Calvin saw him and stood up, holding a towel and nodding somberly to him. Cooper nodded heavily in response, then turned to walk back home. Angela, Frank, Michaela, and Miko fell in step several paces behind him.

They had taken only a few steps when he heard the first pistol shot ring out. The others jerked their heads around. Cooper didn't. He knew what it was. *Calvin, I knew you were big enough to make the right call.* Sure enough, another *crack* followed a few seconds later.

Cooper continued walking home. His slow, plodding steps reflected the exhaustion that had overtaken him.. His rifle felt like a suitcase loaded with rocks. He had to make a conscious effort to keep it from banging into the ground. *I didn't sign up for this.* He could hear his father's voice in response, "We don't volunteer for responsibility, son. It finds those who can handle it and then it bites you in the ankle and holds on like a wolverine." His father had lived his life in service to others. The stress, scars, and his eventual death could all be traced to that choice. His father had chosen the cause of the average working stiff. Cooper had tried to choose no cause at all. He was worried that one had finally found him. Absently, he kicked his leg out, as if to shake something from his ankle.

Chapter 21

Cooper found himself awake as the first rays of sunlight came streaming into his bedroom. Jake lay curled up against him, in the fetal position. Cooper carefully got up so that his son could continue sleeping. He made his way downstairs, taking the FAL with him and strapping on the holster.

Within a half-hour, he had a full breakfast made from his nearly-depleted freezer supply of sausages and orange juice. He had cooked up a healthy pile of pancakes with frozen blueberries thrown in. They'd run out of eggs this morning. Cooper had reflexively reached into the fridge to grab a carton, but was surprised when his hand returned empty. He was thankful he had some pancake mix on hand that only required adding water. He wondered how long it'd be before he tasted eggs again. He knew Portland had some people with chickens in their backyards, but that couldn't supply an entire city. He shook the thoughts from his head, *no use worrying about that now.*

He put Jake's portion aside, covered. He ate ravenously, like a prisoner getting his first homemade meal after a long stretch in stir. Within minutes, the food was gone and he leaned back, patting his belly in satisfaction. *Ah, I feel like a new man, now.* He was surprised at his rapacity and it hit him just how much the previous day had taken from him.

He was just starting his second cup of coffee when he heard a light rap on his front door. *Not a moment's peace.* He tread lightly across the floor so as not to cause the floorboards to creak, his hand on the hilt of his pistol. Looking out, he saw the ponytail-bobbed hair that belonged to Angela. The intent look on her face instantly made him smile.

He forced his lips together in a straight line as he opened the door, "Good morning."

Her face lit up as the door came open, "Good Morning, Mr. Adams. I was hoping I could have a word with you. I hope it's not too early, but I saw you moving around, making your breakfast." Her friendly, open face was difficult to resist, even if he'd wanted to try.

"Oh, sure. Come on in," he motioned her in with a sweep of his arm. "Can I get you a cup of coffee?"

"Sure, that would be great."

She sat down at his kitchen table while Cooper poured another cup. He called to her from the kitchen, "Cream? Sugar?"

"Nope, I like it straight up," she responded. He smiled inwardly.

He had barely landed back into his chair when she began, "I'm going to be direct because that's just how I am. I hope you can handle it."

He stared intently back at her, his dark eyes staring at her over the rim of his coffee cup, "Try me."

"It doesn't take a rocket scientist to see things are going to be…ah…*unstable*…for a while. I want in here. *Fully* in, until things go back to normal. I don't want to be a refugee here."

Cooper bristled and leaned forward like a leopard getting ready to pounce. She stopped him with a hand gesture, "Just let me finish. I know what you said about us not being second-class citizens, and I believe you. But, I want more than that. I want people to forget that I didn't live here when this all started. That's how far I want to be 'in'."

"What are your requests?" he said impatiently.

"First, I want to be armed—if you have something—and to become a regular part of your defense team. I'd be at least as good as some of the people you have out there on the line." He knew that was true.

Cooper paused for a moment, but only for effect. He knew he was going to agree, but wanted to make her wait for it. "OK. See Dranko. He's up the street. Tell him I sent you. What's your second request?"

"I want to move in here."

Coffee sprayed across the room as he burst out laughing, "Damn lady, you don't mess around, do you?" He wiped the coffee from his mouth with his shirtsleeve.

Embarrassed and turning red, Angela waved her hands, "No. I didn't mean it like that," she looked at the ground. "Words aren't my best suit."

"I guess not," Cooper chuckled.

"I just want to move in *here*. I'm not trying to get laid. Look, I'm smart enough to see that you're the guy who most knows what he's doing. I want to survive this thing and I figured bunked up here gives me the best chance. And, I won't lie to you. Being here will help me be more quickly accepted with the others."

Cooper nodded his head, "OK, I get it. That makes sense," he looked at her with a wry grin, "why didn't you just say so?"

She threw a napkin at him and chuckled, "I did! It took me a second to get there, that's all."

"Of course you can stay here. We have a spare bedroom. It's yours as long as you want it. You will have to help out around here and I may have you keep an eye on Jake sometimes."

"Not a problem. Thank you."

"And, don't you worry about the other thing." He stood up to leave the room and with his back towards her he added, "You're probably not my type." He missed the flash of disappointment across her face.

From the kitchen, he heard another knock on his door. He repeated his security precautions and gestured for Angela to remain seated and quiet.

It was Dranko.

"C'mon in Dranko. You can have my last cup of coffee."

Dranko saw Angela and stopped, "I'm not interrupting anything am I?" Cooper had known Dranko long enough to notice the imperceptible smile lurking on his face.

Angela didn't miss a beat, "Just me joining your militia."

Dranko looked at Cooper incredulous. "That's right. She's in. Arm her up."

"And, no, I didn't sleep my way in. I can shoot," Angela added impishly.

"OK, boss. I've seen you spot the lone, honest card player from that joint in Baghdad and the one virtuous lawyer in all of Oregon, so I trust your judgment."

"Thank you for your vote of confidence, brother. I don't know how I'd get up every morning without it," Cooper's sarcasm was biting.

"Screw you. You want to hear what brought me over here this morning?"

"One question before that."

"What?" Dranko said in exasperation.

"What was the name of that lawyer again? I don't remember ever finding one like you say."

Dranko burst out laughing and punched him in the shoulder. Angela sat to the side, grinning widely and shaking her head.

After it subsided, Dranko turned serious, "I've got the teams ready to survey the surrounding neighborhoods, like we discussed yesterday."

"Good.

"But there is some news I thought you'd want to know. First, it was announced today that the Chinese are sending a flotilla of relief ships. Also, advance flights of airplanes are to start arriving in the next few days."

"What?" Cooper exclaimed.

"The news is that they've been hit by this thing, but not as bad as everyone else. They quarantined faster than anyone else and there are some rumors that they have a medicine that is working."

"Famous Chinese discipline, eh?"

"Something like that."

"Traditional Chinese medicine most likely too," Angela added.

Dranko and Cooper both looked at her in surprise, as if they'd both forgotten she was sitting there alongside them.

"Sure, every virus or illness is different. Maybe they have something that is working that isn't in the Big Pharma handbook. We don't make anything that doesn't turn a profit. On the other hand, they've kept stuff around for centuries."

"She is an ER Nurse," Cooper quipped to Dranko. He pressed his lips downward in agreement.

"Do we know what they're bringing, exactly?" Cooper continued.

"Just medicine and food. A few doctors. And police."

Cooper jerked his head up from his cup, "Police?"

"Yes, they say to help us keep order during the crisis."

"What's our Big Chief saying about this?"

"So far, welcoming the help."

Cooper shook his head, "I never thought I'd see the day when *we* were the subject of relief. Hell, we are the ones who used to help everyone else."

"Not this time," Dranko intoned.

"Alright, what's the other news?"

"The National Guard is getting deployed, as well. Portland is on the list. Should be here any day now."

"That's good news at least. What's the latest news from across America?" He said, imitating the lilting voice of a newscaster.

"Pretty bad. Complete breakdown in some cities. The bigger ones are doing worse. Panic is a terrible thing. In some places, the violence is killing roughly as many as the illness."

"You're kidding me?" Angela gasped.

"I wish I were. Word is that electricity is starting to falter in lots of places. Too many workers not showing up."

"Any word of any medicine that *is* working?"

"No. You either get it and die within forty-eight hours or you don't."

Light footfalls on the landing brought their eyes in unison to see Jake standing there, clutching a blue blanket up to his face. He let out a cough that was deafening.

"Dad, I don't feel so good."

Chapter 22

Cooper's coffee cup clattered against the table. Coffee spilled, staining the alabaster tablecloth.

Adrenaline shot through Cooper like lightning. His stomach felt like he'd been hit with a sledgehammer. *No, no, no, not this.* He vaulted to Jake's side immediately. He wrapped him up in his blanket, carried him to his room, and laid him on his bed.

"We need to make sure you get rest, son."

Jake's eyes were full, unblinking, "I'm going to die. Just like mom." It was a statement, not a question. Cooper flinched, taken aback.

Cooper cocked his head back to get a better look at him, "Don't say that."

Cooper's insides roiled. He frantically wanted to lie to his son, to tell him he would be OK. He knew the power of hope was all his son had now. He knew something else: because he had never lied to his son, he would *believe* him if he did so now. He also knew belief and faith could sometimes work miracle cures. The thought tortured him; *I might save him if I give up my principles.* His mind crashed back and forth.

Finally, he found an answer.

He laid Jake down in his bed and pulled the covers over him, "Here's what we're going to do. The Chinese are sending us help because they haven't been affected as bad as we have. We think it's because they have some medicine that is working. I'm going to find some of the medicine and you're going to rest as best you can. OK?"

Jake nodded. Cooper kissed him on the forehead and left the room.

Dranko and Angela remained at the table, transfixed where they'd been. Deep lines of concern crossed their faces. Cooper motioned them to follow him into the kitchen, where they huddled.

"How could he get this *now*? He was exposed days ago," Cooper asked in a whisper.

"Maybe it's just a regular cold?" Angela offered hopefully.

Cooper looked at her sharply, "I said 'maybe'," Angela responded, waving her hands, palms towards Cooper.

"Maybe it's mutated. Maybe it takes longer to incubate in kids. And, it *is* possible Angela is right and it's a normal cold. Those do still exist."

Cooper pounded a fist into an open hand and talked through clenched teeth, "Don't *jerk me around*. I don't wish on stars or believe in the tooth fairy anymore. What I'm gonna do is everything I can to keep my boy alive," he said emphatically.

Even Dranko, who had known him a long time, was unsettled by his vehemence. Unnerved, Angela involuntarily took a step from him. She took a deep breath to calm herself. Dranko recovered first.

"What do you want from us, brother?"

"First, I need some kind of bitter tasting root or tea. I've got to convince Jake he has the new medicine." He paused and held up his index finger, "But, don't lie to him. Just tell him it's Chinese tea, which it will be. Then, I've got to pray that mind over matter works."

He failed to see Dranko give Angela a wink when he was talking about the Chinese tea. Dranko didn't have Cooper's compunction about lies, even white ones.

"Second, get Calvin over here. I'm turning the reigns over to him once and for all. I've got to get a few things done."

Dranko looked at him intently, "I've seen that look before and I like it. What do you have in mind?"

"I'm going to find out more about Admonitus. If there *is* something that can cure Jake, I'll find it there."

"What?" Dranko and Angela exclaimed simultaneously.

Cooper explained what the murdered lab technician had said to him and Julianne's cryptic words. They listened in rapt attention, agreeing that it was worth an investigation.

******

Angela returned first, with Lisa from across the street who delivered a packet of crushed birch bark.

"This should do the trick. But, we think you should let us give it to him. Between the two of us nurses, we can convince him it will work. And, it just might."

Cooper thought for a moment and then nodded, "OK. Can you two keep an eye on him today? As much as I want to be with him, I need to go check out this Admonitus company because I think they might know something. I'm hoping there is medicine or a cure there."

Angela looked at Lisa and then responded for them both, "Of course, Cooper. We'll have it covered. Keep your cell phone close and we can call you if anything develops."

He placed a hand on both their shoulders and looked them each, in turn, in the eye, "Thank you." He enjoyed, just for a moment, the deep satisfaction that came with friendship.

A knock at the door broke the spell. Angela set about brewing the tea, while Lisa went to check on Jake. Cooper glided to the door and saw that it was Calvin.

His face wore a jumble of emotions. Cooper stifled a chuckle as he opened the door to let him in.

He clapped him on the shoulder, "Relax, Calvin. You look like a hangman who showed up for work with dental floss in his bag by mistake!"

Calvin chuckled nervously, unsure of what to expect. Cooper motioned him to the living room sofa and they sat down opposite one another. Cooper leaned in toward Calvin.

Calvin spoke first, "I wanted to finish our conversation from earlier. I wanted to discuss some details about how we'd work together going..."

Cooper waved him off, "I'll make this easy. You're in charge. Of everything. I need to be free to attend to some other things anyway."

Calvin sat back in surprise as the faintest smile escaped to his lips, "I'll admit that was easy. But, I don't want you to step *aside*."

Cooper grinned, "Well, I guess this will be another of our disagreements. I don't have a choice."

His eyebrows drew together, "What's going on?"

"Jake's sick."

Calvin's face stiffened and he clenched his hands, "I'm so sorry to hear that. Oh my Lord, Cooper. I am sorry."

Cooper waved both his emotions and Calvin off with a flurry of his left hand, "Don't worry about it. It will be OK, you hear me? It will be OK." He spoke with the fury that only those trying to convince themselves can muster.

"Sure, alright, Cooper," Calvin said nodding in quick agreement. "I'll take things in hand. But, I tell you this — as soon as everything is OK, I want you back. In fact, I've been thinking about it. I want you as Captain of our Guard. I'll handle civilian matters, while you handle security." His sincerity threw Cooper off.

With a confused look on his face, he responded, "Alright, you have yourself a deal."

The two men shook hands and Cooper gave Calvin a few

points of advice regarding their defenses. He promised to be as available as he could in the coming days. He informed him of the neighborhood survey teams that were going out today and they agreed to meet at Calvin's house at five o'clock to debrief those teams together.

Chapter 23

Cooper was in the middle of looking in on Jake, when another knock on the door interrupted him. He kissed him on the forehead, which was already warm, and told his son to rest and do whatever Lisa or Angela told him. Cooper bounded to the door, restless to get moving.

It was Dranko at the door, carrying two shoulder bags. Cooper let him in, asking, "What do you have there?"

"The groceries," he responded with a chuckle. He went to the couch and unzipped the two bags, "You need good food to stay healthy, right?" The bags revealed a few handguns and plenty of extra magazines filled with ammunition.

Cooper grinned, "And sometimes you need more good food to keep you healthy while travelling, eh?"

"Exactly."

"You never cease to surprise me."

Dranko grew a frown, "Well, I wish I'd liked guns even more or had more money. The list of what I *wish* we had is a mile long. An Uzi, for example would be…"

Cooper clapped his shoulder, "There you go again, thinking about what we *don't* have. Think about what you *did* bring to our table."

Dranko laughed, "You're right. You'd be going out there with a spitwad shooter if it wasn't for me!"

"Not quite," Cooper said, tapping his sidearm.

He kept his pistol in the concealed carry holster, but added a few magazine pouches to his belt. He now carried a total of five magazines, one in the gun and four on the belt. After he donned a dun-colored windbreaker, there was no evidence that he was wearing body armor or carrying a pistol.

Cooper patted the body armor reassuringly, "I am glad you had an extra set."

Dranko nodded, "Hell, best couple hundred bucks I ever spent. It's priceless now! I knew some others at the gun range who'd buy gun after gun after gun, but would never think to get armor. I bet they regret that now."

"I know *I* regret not getting some of the things you'd recommended," Cooper responded.

"Don't worry, I still think you're perfect!" Dranko mocked.

Dranko was kitted up with a .45 pistol in a shoulder holster, extra magazines, another pistol holstered on his hip, and body armor. He wore a leather coat that flared out just below the hips. Finally, he had a lightweight .38 revolver strapped to his ankle. "My bail out gun, if everything else fails me," Dranko stated.

"Where are we going first?" he asked Cooper.

"Julianne Wheeler's house. I have to return *this*," he responded, holding up an auto insurance notice.

"You sly devil," Dranko said, feigning astonishment.

"I wish I could claim to have been so forward-thinking. I just got lucky. I found it lying near where she had put her belongings. It must have fallen out when she ran off. Sometimes it's better to be lucky than smart."

"That's a good thing, because you don't ever meet the latter," Dranko retorted.

Cooper didn't miss a beat, "That's why I travel with such *genius* friends. Can you get the door, Mr. Einstein." His mocking tone forced the smile off of Dranko's face.

******

The two men piled into Cooper's pickup. Cooper brought his shotgun and extra shells along. He let Dranko drive, giving him the address. While they drove, Cooper filled him on the little he knew, so far, of Admonitus and the chilling warning from the man just before he was killed.

"So, what're we looking for?" Dranko asked.

"Information. Anything at all that can help Jake, and everyone else."

As they wended their way through several miles of the city's streets, the various neighborhoods were a kaleidoscope of a society grappling with the plague's effect. They passed areas that looked almost normal, except the dramatic reduction in both vehicle and foot traffic. A mile to the north, they encountered a neighborhood with a hastily erected defensive system, similar to their own.

As they drove, startling images burned themselves into Cooper's mind. A charred rocking horse was pitching back and forth in the street without a rider. He wondered where its owner was. The front door to the closest house was smashed open. Curtains from a large picture window that had been broken fluttered forlornly outside the

194

home, wafting against the home's walls. Dolls lay scattered about the lawn. Cooper's heart sank.

Further on, they passed a shot-up blue Dodge minivan. It was littered with hundreds of bullet holes from stem to stern. Every shard of glass had been ripped out of the windows' frames. The ground sparkled around it, disconcertingly beautiful. Peering in, Cooper saw no bodies. Instead, thick bloodstains covered all three rows of seats. The side doors all lay ajar and blood trails moved away from the van before disappearing a few feet further into the street. *Did they transfer the dead into another car?*

Then, they came upon a bizarre spectacle. A stand had been cobbled together from mismatched wood lengths. A sign over it, painted in black, "Lemonade! It's cured hundreds in Australia!" Three heavily armed, dirty, men stood around it. Two clutched shotguns while a third wielded an AK-47. Sitting behind the stand, a blond child, Jake's age, sat ready to serve. She was clean, wearing a pressed white dress, with her hair done up in bows. The contrast struck Cooper as comical. Down below, also in black, "$100 per glass!" They didn't stop to ask.

Just beyond that, they drove past several streets where almost every other house had been burned to the ground. The detritus of ruined households was strewn about the street and lawns: clothing, broken furniture, smashed dishes, and…dead bodies. The dead has been that way for more than a day and the flies flew thick around them. After a few pensive moments of observation, the shotgun clasped firmly, Cooper saw that the men had been killed execution style. There were bullet wounds to the head, from close range. Worse, the women's bodies were in various stages of undress, clothing torn, and usually bloody. He grimaced in disgust when he saw how young some of them were.

"I guess we know why the other neighborhood has their barricades up," Dranko said, shaking his head.

"Yeah. I wonder who did this. I'm guessing amateurs riled up on drugs or drink. A professional gang would be focused on getting money and goods right now; not random stuff like this," Cooper conjectured in response.

"You're probably right. I just wish someone would cover these bodies up."

The wheels of the truck crunched broken glass as they wove their way around obstacles in the road.

As they neared the area where Julianne lived, both men saw

something that made them exhale in shock. Dranko's came out as a low whistle.

A police car, with two officers, was driving towards them.

Neither had seen any police in over a week. Cooper let the shotgun rest on the floorboard so that he could ensure his hands remained in a casual position.

"Must be nice to live in such a high-class part of town?" Dranko quipped.

"You know what they say, the last place you'll still find the police in bad times and the tax collector in good times is where the rich folk live."

Dranko looked at him quizzically, "*Who's* the *they?* I've never heard that before."

"My father," Cooper said as both men laughed.

Their faces turned serious and they looked straight ahead as the police cruiser drove past them. They could feel their eyes dressing them down. Thankfully, the car kept going.

Cooper instructed Dranko to park a half block away from Julianne's house. He stuffed the shotgun under the seat and they locked the doors. The street was deserted, quiet. It looked like it probably had before the plague had struck. Cars were still parked neatly in driveways and along the street. Windows and doors were all intact and closed. Halfway down the street, a neatly stenciled wooden sign beseeching, "God Forgive Us!" was the only evidence that something was amiss in the world.

As they approached the home, he had Dranko remain out of sight. If Julianne was home, he figured it would be smoother that way. She lived in an ornate Victorian home. The outside walls came alive with a deep chocolate trim, silver-painted scallops, and red accents. Leaded glass windows with a chevron motif and a wraparound porch completed the idyllic view.

Cooper climbed the stairs and rang the doorbell. He waited. Then, he rapped on the door and heard the sounds reverberate throughout the home. He did so a second time before whistling for Dranko to come forward.

The two men didn't exchange a word as Cooper backed away from the door and did his best to nonchalantly shield Dranko from any passerby's view. Dranko immediately went to work with his lock pick tools and had the door open in less than a minute. They stepped inside. The wood floors shined, conveying warmth and security. A skinny rug ran the length of the hallway and led away from the door to a large foyer. The hallway and foyer were sparsely furnished. The furniture screamed "eco-friendly" at them; made from recycled and natural materials. Art decorated the walls, depicting the natural world in all of its splendor. Opposite the front door, an impressive painting of a white birch forest with a majestic buck commanding the scene, dominated the wall with its size and grace. Scattered on the other walls were paintings depicting sea turtles, an eagle, wildflower fields, waterfalls, and other animals. Muted light shone in through a phalanx of windows on the south wall.

"Feels like a shrine, don't it," Dranko whispered in awe. Cooper nodded slowly.

As previously agreed, Dranko stayed at the door, just inside, as a lookout. Cooper would do the searching. He found the den on the first floor and headed there first.

******

The den had two stout oak doors that opened inward. Cooper almost bumped into the door when he tried to open it and, unexpectedly, he discovered it was locked. He whistled for Dranko and indicated the locked door. As Dranko came over to work on it, Cooper replaced him at the front door post. Seconds ticked by, without event outside. Cooper saw one vehicle drive by, a large SUV loaded up with a family and what must have been all of their worldly possessions. *Getting out of dodge, eh?* Cooper didn't think they'd make it very far. Their overloaded vehicle was just begging for the attention of every petty criminal out there. *Candy store on wheels.*

Dranko clucked his lips to get Cooper's attention. He turned and saw that the door was open. As they passed each other once again, Dranko whispered, "Complex lock on that bad boy." Cooper nodded, his anticipation growing. He took a deep breath before stepping into the room.

Two of the four walls were lined with nine foot tall bookcases. A quick scan revealed a myriad of books on philosophy, history, politics, environmental sciences, physics, and current events. Curiously, he saw only one shelf that contained works of fiction. With such an extensive library, he would have expected at least a few shelves dedicated to fiction. Of those, they were all of the classical variety, the likes of Shakespeare, Chekhov, and Dickens. An avid reader himself, when he had the time, he was immediately impressed with the size and scope of Julianne's collection.

The wall opposite the door contained a large leaded glass window, half of which was a beautiful stained glass picture depicting Atlas carrying the world on his shoulders. This portion rose so high, it would have prevented easy inspection of this room from the outside. The top of the window allowed bright sunlight into the room which, when combined with the colors from the stained glass, bestowed a sacred aura to the room.

However, it was the wall immediately to his left which proved the most intriguing. Half of the wall was blanketed by a large whiteboard. Writings and diagrams were festooned across it. The other half of the wall was a confused mélange of magazine and newspaper articles. Cooper was stunned by the blizzard of information before him. He blankly ambled over to the solid oak desk that dominated the middle of the room. He leaned against it so that he could digest the wall's contents.

He quickly ascertained that the focus for the display was environmental degradation. Headlines blaring about pollution, toxins, oil spills, and acid rain were scattered about. However, the most common were articles, pictures, and headlines focused on global warming and its effects. One blazoned phrase in the middle of the whiteboard was, "Global Warming = Climate Chaos." Right next to that clarion call, a much smaller phrase in red ink required him to take two steps forward to read it. "Worst marketing failure ever. They needed to call it based upon what it would make *happen*. Stupid scientists!" Cooper cocked his head when he realized that the handwriting looked like it'd been written by a man.

A map of the United States looked familiar to Cooper. *That's right, it's the one from Al Gore's movie that shows sea level rise.* But, this one looked different; a lot different. A moment later he realized it, "Wow, there's a lot *more* land underwater," he whispered to himself in surprise. Some coastal cities had completely disappeared in this edition. And, the flooding extended much further inland than he recalled. Next to the map of America, were maps of Europe and Asia. These showed many cities there underwater, as well.

The magazine and newspaper articles were a contrasting mixture of dire scientific warnings about the coming catastrophe of global warming, news reports of failed efforts by the global community to take action to limit climate change, and analyses by economists on the economic impacts. One report from the UK declared "Global Warming Akin to Great Depression" was written by someone named

Sir Nicholas Stern. Another that stood out proclaimed, "Rate of Warming Greatly Exceeding Most Aggressive Modeling." Julianne had written notes in blue on most of the articles, circling a phrase or posing a question.

Cooper was hypnotized by the information. Ten minutes passed before he realized how long he had been doing so. He shook his head to clear his thoughts. He had no doubt that Dranko must be growing impatient. The hodgepodge of information revealed three broad themes: the environment's ability to sustain life was in deep jeopardy, the threat of climate change as catastrophic, and that people weren't doing much about either. Cooper was deeply interested in the material, but deeply upset that he found nothing that told him about the plague sweeping the country and threatening his son.

He moved rapidly to the desk and rifled the contents of the desk drawers. He found a random collection of papers, bills, clipped articles, and the other items you'd expect to find on a desk. She had an old-fashioned large desk calendar, which was largely unused. However, there was a post-it note written in bold red letters: "Project Reset Meeting." It was stuck on a day just one week prior to the outbreak. The post-it had the company logo of Admonitus written across the bottom. Written in hard to decipher black ink underneath the big red lettering was a room and a location. The meeting had been held at the Admonitus headquarters.

He spent the next five minutes quickly combing the room for anything else of interest and then ten more after that sweeping through the rest of the house, which all proved fruitless.

When he finally made it back to the front door, Dranko was as jumpy as a cat on a hot griddle. "Find anything?"

"Not as much as I wanted. But, we need to find out about something called 'Project Reset'."

"How are we doing that?"

"We need to go to Admonitus' headquarters. I don't have time to waste," Cooper said intently.

Dranko grinned, "I thought we'd end up there before the day was out. That was why I brought these along," he said, tapping his twin .45s affectionately.

What they saw when they turned to leave left both of them breathless.

******

Julianne Wheeler had just rounded the low stone wall that lined her front yard and was stumbling toward the house. A bright red seam had been opened across her forehead and blood dripped down, covering half of her face. Her left arm hung limply at her side, a gash almost half a foot long was outlined in crimson. Bruises had already welled up on her other arm and on her chin. Her ragged gait was matched by her trance-like gaze that was fixed on the ground directly in front of her. She hadn't looked up, as she lumbered toward them.

The two men exchanged a quick look of surprise and then went into action. Cooper ran outside to help her.

His movement broke Julianne's trance. She jerked back, raising her hands in a pitiful defense as the rank look of terror filled her face.

He slowed his movement and held his own hands up, palms forward, "It's OK, Julianne. It's me, Cooper. Remember? I'm here to help you."

She wavered, trying to process what he was saying. He continued, "You *need* help, Julianne. Let me help you." He did his best to offer a comforting smile.

Then, he was upon her and she collapsed into his arms.

******

A half hour later she regained consciousness. They had propped her up on the couch and covered her in warm blankets. Her wounds had been dressed and fortunately, neither of the gashes required stitches.

Cooper was seated next to her on an oaken chair that he had pulled up next to her.

She blinked up at him and whispered weakly, "Wh...what happened?"

Cooper smiled down at her, "We were hoping you could tell us. You just stumbled here."

Her eyebrows scrunched together as memory returned. Her eyes filled with tears. "I was attacked. For a bag of canned goods. A brick or a rock to the head and a knife to my arm." The tears now ran freely down her face.

Cooper touched her arm in sympathy, "I'm sorry." She continued weeping.

"This was supposed to be clean, quick. Not like this. Not like this, at all," she muttered between sobs.

"What wasn't supposed to be like this," Cooper asked.

Abruptly, she sat up. "Oh, never mind. It's too late now. What were you doing here anyway?"

"I wanted to learn more about what happened at Admonitus."

She shocked him by bolting to a standing position, wobbling unsteadily on her feet in doing so, "You have to leave. You have to leave now." She stammered, anger mixed with near panic.

Cooper stood up and offered his hands up in a defensive position, "Calm down, Julianne. I just have a couple of questions."

Her face flushed, red replacing the pale look she had worn just moments before. "You've just *got* to go. Now. It's all too late to *talk* about," she screamed hysterically.

He was stunned and yammered, "My God! Calm down. I just want to *help* you!"

She shook her head back and forth ferociously, her hair swinging in a wide arc despite the grime and blood that had dried in it, "No, no, no! I'm *beyond* help, don't you get it," she pleaded. "With what I've done, we're *all* beyond help now!" With that, she slumped back into the sofa, clasped her face in her hands and sobbed uncontrollably.

Cooper backed away and shot a glance at Dranko who had been standing sentry-like at the front door. He shrugged his shoulders in response.

Cooper remained for a few moments debating what to do next. He was torn between deep sympathy for her, confusion, and raging anger for the mysteries she presented without any solution. Finally, resigned, he spoke to her, "OK. We'll leave. But, here is my number, call me if you need anything." He hastily scribbled his number on a Post-It note that lay on her entry table.

Julianne flapped her hands about her, as if waving off pesky gnats at a mid-summer picnic, "Go. Please go," was all that she said.

Cooper left bewildered, dumbstruck by what he had just witnessed.

Once outside, Dranko offered a one word explanation, "Shock."

Cooper found it lacking. His curiosity about what had been going on at Admonitus was rising rapidly. When he reached the car, he tried home on his cell phone. Thankfully, the call went through. The report, however, was haunting: *fever rising*.

Chapter 24

As Dranko drove west towards the city's high tech corridor, Cooper fiddled with his pistol. As he inserted and removed the magazine, repeatedly, he knew he was burning off nervous energy as much as anything else. His mind kept turning what little he knew over and over in his head. His stomach churned as he considered the notion that these people had *known* about the plague before it had started.

If the people at Admonitus knew about this *before* it started, it was damning. *Why hadn't they warned anyone?* Cooper clenched his fists and gritted his teeth as he considered the deaths that could have been prevented with just a little foreknowledge. *Elena.* He racked the slide on his pistol, chambering a round.

"How much further?"

"Just about five more minutes, brother," Dranko responded. "What's the plan when we get there?"

Cooper returned a twisted grin, "Simple. We're gonna find someone in charge and make them talk. I want to know just what the hell is going on."

******

Cooper had Dranko drive past the Admonitus facility so that he could do a little reconnaissance. It was a nondescript, low-slung cluster of one story buildings that looked similar to any other office park spread out across America, but particularly popular in areas with high-tech companies. Gentle, rolling, lawns created a campus-like setting with benches and picnic tables scattered about. The buildings were made of gray concrete, with large banks of windows covering a good portion of the walls. The windows were darkly tinted so it was impossible to see inside the buildings.

The parking lot was almost completely deserted. Notably, a large black Mercedes sedan occupied a parking spot up front, underneath a large sign that declared "President's Parking, Only."

"You see that? Luck could be on our side," Cooper remarked, gesturing to Dranko.

"Or just his fortune ran out and he's lying dead somewhere else," he responded sardonically.

Cooper just shook his head at his friend's pessimism, "Remind me *not* to let you buy my lottery tickets next time."

Dranko winked, "That assumes there will *be* another lottery, my eternally hopeful friend."

Cooper shrugged dismissively and returned to surveying Admonitus' headquarters. Only a few other cars were scattered about the facility's parking lot. A white security guard pickup drove in a wide arc around the parking lot. It appeared to be circling the campus in a lazy, random pattern.

There was no other traffic on the road, so the guard could not have helped but notice their pickup. Dranko did his best to accelerate imperceptibly and continue past their entrance.

As they stopped, a quarter mile down the road, Dranko leaned onto the steering wheel and turned towards Cooper, "What's the plan, boss?"

"A bum rush. We park where we can watch that security pickup. Once it passes the front entrance and rounds the corner, we go in fast and tight. We try to find someone in charge and demand some answers. I don't see another way. There's no way to blend in and infiltrate because there's *no one* else out here!"

Dranko nodded his head slowly, reasoning to the same conclusion.

They performed one last weapons check and then Dranko drifted the pickup behind a bank of bushes where Cooper could see the front of the Admonitus headquarters. They timed one full circuit of the security truck. It took about ten minutes to make the route around the dispersed cluster of buildings and parking lots.

"Since we have to wait for it to round the far right corner, we should have about eight minutes before it comes back around and he sees our pickup truck. We should plan on him coming in to investigate," Cooper noted.

"Got it," Dranko responded. He set the alarm on his wrist watch to seven minutes, "This will give us a one minute warning."

The security guard's pickup rounded the far corner for the second time and Dranko gunned the motor of Cooper's truck. Dirt kicked up as they surged forward. Dranko expertly guided the pickup through the parking lot, driving at a breakneck speed, but not so fast as to cause a loud squeal of tires on pavement. The truck lurched to a stop in a parking spot near the front door and the two men bounded out, slamming the pickup's doors behind them. *Thirty seconds gone.*

They had decided not to go in with guns drawn, as that might invite trouble that they could avoid, but they moved in a two-man tandem that was unmistakably martial. Both men had a ready hand on a firearm, for any needed quick draw. Dranko's right hand remained snaked underneath the brown leather jacket, with a firm hold on the pistol grip. Cooper kept his right hand halfway back towards his pistol that was holstered at the 3:30 position, just behind his right hip.

Dranko reached the door first and held it open as Cooper raced inside. The lobby that greeted them was empty. The receptionist's desk and waiting area looked as if they might have been occupied yesterday. Magazines were scattered on the low table that was surrounded by office chairs. The lights were only halfway on, in dimmed mode. They paused for a moment and listened.

The silence was tomblike. They could, however, hear the mutterings coming from an office at the end of the hallway. A bright wash of light from that office filled the dimmed hallway outside of it.

Using hand signals, Dranko motioned Cooper to move down the hallway.

Cooper hugged the left-hand wall and moved on the balls of his feet to minimize any noise. Dranko followed about five yards behind him. He kept a lookout to their rear as they moved.

Within seconds, Cooper was at that entrance to the room. He caught a furtive glance into the room. What he saw was overwhelming.

A lone man stood behind a large metal desk. The man looked unimpressive. He stood several shades under an average man's height and was pudgy around the middle. He looked to be in his later fifties. He was bald, with a short-cropped ring of hair circling his head. He had a flat-face, devoid of any single feature standing out. He was, however, dressed impeccably. He wore a navy blue, pinstriped, three-piece suit. An expensive looking black fedora lay resting on the desk.

To the man's right was a large electronic map of the United States with lights of varying colors and intensities. Despite the pell-mell of lighting, it was clear that the largest cities were swathed in bright red circles. The wall opposite from where he was standing was a whiteboard with markings that Cooper could not see from his angle. Finally, to the man's left was a long table with multiple printers. One came to life and spat out a page as Cooper looked in.

Cooper turned to Dranko to give him the "go" sign. With that, he stepped into the room.

"Good afternoon, sir."

The short man looked up at him; a flash of surprise crossed his face. Almost instantly, he returned to a controlled, sober look.

Cooper drew his pistol and barked, "I wouldn't do that if I

were you," as the man's right hand motioned toward a corner of his desk, likely an alarm. "I'll have to blow your brains out if you do that."

"Please, don't insult me. We both know you cannot do that," the short man responded with a steady voice.

"What makes you say that?"

"Because you want *something* from me. You can't get it if I'm dead," the man's self-assuredness grated on Cooper.

Cooper nodded deliberately, "You're right. Thank you for that correction. I won't blow your *brains* out. Instead, I'll put a round into your right leg," Cooper lowered the pistol to point there to reinforce his words.

The other man couldn't help it as his leg reflexively flinched. He cleared his throat a little too deliberately, "Why don't we start over. I'm Ethan Mitchell, President of Admonitus corporation and you fine gentlemen are?" He made a sweeping gesture with his right hand. *Like most men in power, he's used to being in charge and doesn't like it when the tables are turned on him.*

Cooper decided not to play his game. He jerked a thumb at Dranko, who stood at the doorway looking back into the hallway, "He's a man that is a good shot. Best of all, he shoots when and *who* I tell him to." Dranko looked over his shoulder and nodded firmly, a sinister grin revealing a thin line of gleaming white teeth.

Then, he brought the thumb to his own chest, "I'm a man who's lost his wife to this plague. So, I have nothing to live for except getting some answers. You got it?"

Mr. Mitchell's stolid façade was shaken. A dollop of nervousness showed through his nod. He shuffled his feet, as if to gain surer footing, "You do have something to live for though. Your child, perhaps."

Baffled, Cooper blurted, "How'd you?"

"Know? I wouldn't be where I am today if I wasn't an adept reader of people. First, I know you're not the nervous type. You wouldn't be in my office waving a pistol around if you were. So, that leaves only one explanation for the worry lines that cross your face. You're a father."

Cooper laughed, "You're good. I'll give you that. If you can see all that, I'm betting you can see that I've killed men before?"

Mr. Mitchell eyed him again and swallowed hard, "Yes, I can see that."

Cooper maintained a steadfast stare, "Recently?"

Ethan gulped and only nodded in agreement.

"Furthermore, I'm guessing you can see that I'm a serious man. A deliberate man. A man who gets what he needs, when he needs it, yeah?"

"Yes, I see that too."

"Good. So, let's start with what you know about this plague."

A long silence followed as a slow, smug, grin took shape on Mr. Mitchell's face, "Maybe a better question would be: what do I *not* know about it?"

Cooper tried to hide his surprise, and did a poor job of it, "Sure, why don't you start there then?"

Mr. Mitchell responded slowly and deliberately, "First, it was unavoidable. We had too many people, living too close together, for too long. Something like this was bound to happen."

Cooper interrupted him, "I'm not asking about something *like* this, I'm asking about *this* plague."

Mr. Mitchell pursed his lips, irritated at being interrupted, "May I finish answering your question?"

Cooper stared back at him. Eyes locked, Mr. Mitchell continued, "Second, as unfortunate as it is, it was necessary. Despite the high number of deaths occurring now, it would have been much, much worse later."

Agitated, Cooper shook his head and squinted his eyes, "What the hell are you talking about?"

Mr. Mitchell looked like a schoolteacher disappointed in one of his students, "Look around you. Do you not read? Do you pay attention at all? The planet is *dying* out there. It is losing its ability to support life."

Cooper was confused, "Are you saying Mother Nature concocted this thing to save the whales?"

Mr. Mitchell burst out laughing, "No. I'm saying she *should* have done exactly that, but she didn't know how. We just..." He stopped himself and paused. "Or, maybe she did, but she was just taking too long to pull the trigger." He chuckled to himself at a joke that Cooper didn't understand.

Cooper heard the buzz of Dranko's watch. *Already? I've let this guy banter too much.*

"Just tell me if there's a cure for this thing?"

"We're working on it."

"Who's we? This place is empty," Cooper shouted, waving his pistol around to indicate the empty building.

"A small team of specialists is dedicated to it around the clock, but not at this facility."

Cooper didn't believe him. His head hurt from everything he'd heard as he desperately tried to make sense of it all.

"We got company. Multiples," Dranko shouted from the doorway. Cooper turned towards him.

Moments later, he was rocked to the floor by concussion from a blast that came from Mr. Mitchell's direction. Simultaneously, a flash lit up the room. He fell to the floor, dazed. He was dimly aware of Dranko firing down the hallway. He whirled his head around back towards Mr. Mitchell, but the metal desk had been overturned. Through the smoke, he couldn't see him. Finally, it hit him. *He detonated a flash-bang grenade.*

Cooper stumbled towards the desk and looked frantically for Mr. Mitchell. That's when he noticed a panel in the wall was slightly ajar. He pushed it open and looked into another room which had three doors on different walls. Mr. Mitchell wasn't in that room either. "Damn you!" Cooper cursed.

As if through a long tunnel, he heard Dranko shouting for him, "Let's go! Let's go!"

Cooper sprinted back towards the doorway and landed next to Dranko, "What's our situation?" he shouted.

"Three guards, pinned down near the receptionist area. They didn't expect two-fisted .45 firepower!" Dranko yelled gleefully.

Cooper surveyed the hallway. Across from them was a long hallway marked with an "Exit" sign.

"You hold them down. I will circle around their rear flank!"

"Got it," Dranko responded, "but hurry!" He slammed home a fresh magazine into his pistol. He resumed firing to cover Cooper as he raced across the hallway. A random pistol shot rang out in their direction, shattering a window behind them.

Cooper ran down the hallway at full speed. He reached the door and crashed into it. It was locked. Swiftly, he drew his pistol, stepped back, and fired three rounds into the lock. He kicked the push bar once more. This time, the door flew open, and he was out into the dull Oregon sunshine. He turned to his right and sprinted the length of the building, making a final right hand turn that would return him to the front of the building.

He longed for the intimidation provided by fully automatic fire. He remembered his drill Sergeant from boot camp, "I never met EF Hutton, but I know damn well that when Rat-Tat-Tat speaks, people *do* listen!" He had never understood the joke—apparently an obscure reference to a commercial—but he had seen the veracity of the sentiment proven many times over in combat. He clenched the pistol tightly in his hand. *You'll have to do today.*

He rounded the corner and saw three guards sprawled on the floor, desperately seeking cover amidst bullet-riddled furniture.

Cooper wasted no time in peppering the ceiling with gunfire. The *boom-boom-boom* of close-up pistol fire would both shock the guards and, as importantly, let Dranko know he was now firmly in his line of fire. "Hands up," Cooper screamed.

The three guards, after a moment's surprise, rolled onto their backs and saw Cooper standing over them. They looked at each other as Cooper swept over them with the looming muzzle of his pistol. At this close range, they knew he couldn't miss. In turn, they each tossed their pistols to the ground and held their hands up.

Dranko came running in from the opposite direction, pistols at the ready.

Cooper began questioning the guards, "Where does Mitchell's secret passage lead to?"

Dranko scooped up the guard's sidearm and then stood up to face Cooper, "We can't do this now. We gotta go!"

Cooper looked at him blankly, "Why?"

"Don't you hear that?"

"No," Cooper said, indicating his still-deafened ears.

"Sirens. Police. And, if I can hear them after all that shooting, it means they are close," he shouted into Cooper's ear.

They ran to the pickup, jumped in, and sped away.

Chapter 25

They arrived back at Cooper's house safely. Given how close things had come, Cooper was glad he had put grease over several key numbers on the license plates. If the guards had been thinking and had written it down, he was hoping the partial plate would prevent them from finding him.

As soon as the truck rolled to a stop, Cooper leapt from the truck to check on Jake's condition. Covered in sweat and grime from the shoot-out, Cooper only made it halfway to the room before Angela stopped him with the flat of her hand.

"No. You can't go in there like this! Go clean up. I know he's already ill, but there's no good to come from bringing all of *that* in there," she said indicating the grime covering him.

Cooper gritted his teeth and looked at her defiantly. She maintained her gaze and crossed her arms for good measure. Chastened, he cast his eyes down sheepdog-style. He shuffled his way upstairs and took a brief, steaming hot shower. Halfway through, the light went out. The bathroom fan had stopped whirring too. He ventured a dubious hope that it was merely a broken fuse.

He rushed to finish his shower and slapped a white towel across his waist. As he ran downstairs, Angela met him on the landing. He couldn't help notice her quick appraisal of his mostly uncovered body.

"All out?" he asked.

"Yes, afraid so. Lisa's porch light that was left on all day is out too," Angela responded, bringing her eyes to his.

"Damn!" Cooper pounded his fists together. "I thought it might happen, but was hoping not *yet*."

"What do you think caused it?"

"It could be almost anything. A burned out generator. A tree fell across some wires. The point is, with less workers—or *no* workers—showing up, a glitch anywhere in the system can cause the power to go down. Our best hope right now is that it isn't the entire city and it's just in our area."

"I'm going to check on Jake. How is he?"

Her light face grew dark, "He's showing all the symptoms of the illness. His fever is rising. He's listless. There is some small hope that it is just a run of the mill fever, but I doubt it. I'm sorry, Cooper," her hand touched his arm.

Cooper pressed his lips together in frustration, "Alright. I know you're doing everything you can. I'm going to check in on him. Can you do me a favor?"

"Name it."

"I have four rain barrels, fifty-five gallons each. Use our hose to make sure that they are all full. Fill anything else you see that will hold water. With the electricity out, I don't want to risk losing water too. We are gravity-fed here, so we should be OK, but it's better to be safe than sorry."

"Right," she pivoted on her heel and headed towards the back door.

Cooper tightened the towel on his waist and went in to see his son. Now, he got a view of what Elena must have looked like in the early hours of the sickness. Jake still had his color and he wasn't bathed in sweat. But, his face was flushed and he looked very, very tired.

Cooper sat on the edge of the bed and felt his boy's forehead. It was sweaty and very warm. *Probably 102 or 103.* Jake's eyes opened.

"Uh, hello, Dad."

"Hello, son."

"I don't think that medicine is working," Jake said, as if to apologize to his father. His intent expression of regret made Cooper involuntarily choke up. He fought the emotion and won.

He cleared his throat, desperately wanting to say more, "You need to give yourself more time." Cooper knew his son's faith in the placebo medicine was his best hope at survival, but he still couldn't bring himself to lie directly about it. This deft lie of omission was the best he could do.

Throughout his life, each time he had tried to use a lie, even a white one, to make someone feel better or make his own life go easier, he would recall what had happened. Remembering his father's early death, his mother's evisceration, and his own suffering as a child, he would choke on the lie. His devotion to the truth was a distinction that often drove a wedge between those around him. He was often mocked for his steadfast adherence to veracity. Sometimes, he'd ponder bitterly. *It's only half principle. The other half was my damned* impotence *to spit the words out.*

Now, looking into his son's anxious eyes, he suffered that familiar, agonizing, debility once more.

Jake nodded as a smile came back to his lips, "OK."

"How are you feeling? Do you need anything?"

Jake shook his head back and forth, "No."

They sat together in silence for a long while, Cooper rubbing his son's arm or chest for stretches to comfort him. Eventually, Jake fell asleep and Cooper kept watching him. The dread that he was watching his son slowly die, as he had watched Elena, was too much. He wept silently. Bitter, hot tears fell from his cheeks onto his chest and stomach. After a long while, he managed to stop. He dried his tears, and turned to leave.

Angela was standing in the doorway. Her eyes were wet. As he pressed past her, she reached out, grabbed his wrist, stopping him. She squeezed it in comfort. He paused to look at her. She leaned in and pulled him into a gentle hug. He welcomed the embrace and his arms folded across her back. They stood in this gentle clinch as Cooper thought how he appreciated that she wasn't muttering platitudes like, "He'll be OK." He squeezed her a little more tightly, muttered "Thank you," and then walked back upstairs. She watched him go as sympathy and affection washed over her. After he'd disappeared from view, she took a deep breath, clutched her arms across her chest, and returned to maintaining a vigil over Jake.

******

Cooper had planned on getting dressed. Instead, he collapsed into his bed, worn out by the day's shooting and the worries about Jake. His nap was short, but deep. He woke up in the early afternoon, ravenous. With the electricity out, he knew he would need to eat as much of his food as possible, quickly. He dressed in a pair of faded blue jeans, a t-shirt, and an unbuttoned black and white flannel top.

When he reached the stairs' bottom, he found Dranko in his dining room. He was working the slide on his pistol, ensuring the action was smooth and reliable. He looked up from the oiled metal when Cooper arrived.

"There's news," he said dryly.

Cooper was still groggy from the deep sleep, "Yeah?"

"The military has arrived. A company of National Guardsmen has set up operations downtown," Dranko said, the slide smacking forward with a loud metallic snap.

"A company? That's barely enough to police a few city blocks, never mind the entire city," Cooper said skeptically.

Dranko shrugged his shoulders and re-holstered his sidearm, "Hell, I must be getting sloppy. I took it as a good sign, until I bumped into Pessimistic Patty over here."

Cooper laughed and clapped him on the shoulder, "Alright, you got me there. No, you're right. It is good news. I'm just not sure it's good enough for Jake."

Dranko's eyebrows came together and his lips straightened, "Right, brother. How is he?"

"So far? As bad as this thing gets," Cooper's fingers kneaded his temples.

Dranko put his hand on Cooper's shoulder, "I'm sorry, brother. I wish I could do more right now, but that's all I got."

Cooper's looked into his friend's sympathetic eyes and nodded, "That's enough. Thank you," he said as he put his own hand on Dranko's shoulder.

Cooper wrinkled his nose at the pungent smell of meat cooking, "What's that?"

Dranko jerked his thumb towards Cooper's back patio, "That, brother, is that woman doing her best Betty Crocker meets Davey Crockett impersonation. As soon as the electricity went down, she's been out back cooking and smoking all of the meat you had on hand."

Cooper looked incredulous, "Smoking? I don't *own* a smoker!"

"Don't I know it. She's barbequing on one Weber and jerry-rigged another to do some smoking," he folded his arms as if to verify his words.

Cooper shook his head in disbelief. He took one step toward the back patio, but stopped in his tracks when three sharp knocks resounded from his front door. *I wonder who that is.*

He motioned for Dranko to look out the side window that overlooked the door. His visible surprise was confirmed when he blurted out, "It's the mailman!"

******

Cooper stood in disbelief for a moment, but then stepped forward and jerked the door open. Before him stood his regular US Postal Worker, Mr. Joe Vang. Joe's hair was jet black and hung loose, framing a square head. His light blue shirt, darker blue pants, and jacket were complemented by the dull brown leather mailbag over his shoulder. The man wore a wide smile.

"Good afternoon," he said.

"Is that really you, Joe? I can't believe it," Cooper said, his mouth agape.

"I'm getting a lot of that today. Yes, I'm here. The U.S. Postal Service apologizes for the delays in service over the last week, we've..."

"Oh, spare me the speech. It's damn good to see you, Joe. Come on in," Cooper beckoned him.

Joe shook his head, "Sorry, I can't do that. If I accepted all my invitations, I wouldn't finish half of my route. I'm already well behind schedule."

"At least tell us what's happening. What news do you have?"

Joe's cheerful demeanor vanished, "It's mostly bad. Our slogan about 'rain, sleet, and hail' and the rest of it didn't include a plague burning across America the way a lottery winner goes through cash. In the last week, we've only had one truck in, from Washington State. Nothing in from California or through Idaho. In fact, we sent out a truck down south and it came back. It couldn't cross the border. Near Medford, some of our guys were keeping everything out from California and weren't allowing anyone to leave Oregon, either."

"Who's 'some of our guys'?" Dranko asked.

"Our side of the border. Oregonians. Militia-types."

The three sat in silence as Dranko and Cooper digested the news.

Joe broke the quiet, "That's a temporary situation. The National Guard has arrived in Portland and we hear more troops are on the way."

"It looks like you all have had a rough go of things around here? I saw your welcome mat coming in," Cooper remembered that Joe had a very rough childhood. He had been an active gang member in his youth. So, the wry grin that spread across his face wasn't a surprise.

Cooper shrugged, "Yeah, we've had a few scrapes. Is it like that most places or are we just special around here?"

"It's hit or miss. I've been into some areas today that made my skin crawl and others were just like before. And *some*, I avoided altogether. This thing has been so bad, so fast, that no one *knew* how to react. So, you get too many kinds of crazy in too many places. Luckily for me, this uniform is something everyone, and I mean *everyone*, has been happy to see."

"I guess we've just been unlucky," Dranko lamented.

Joe shook his head, "Trust me, there are many places worse off. It looks like you guys got organized and kept the worst stuff from happening," he paused for a moment, considering.

"Something else on your mind?" Cooper queried.

"If you need additional help, my cousin is involved in the Vietnamese Protection Society," he looked at him with squinted, evaluating eyes.

"The what?"

"The VPS. I won't mince words with you guys. It's a gang pure and simple. I'm not proud of what my cousin does. But, I know they're helping a lot of people keep things safe, right now."

Dranko scoffed, "For a price, I'm sure."

Joe straightened his back and stared right at Dranko, "Look, don't get high and mighty with me. Sure, they charge a price, and a hefty one at that. But, they have lots of guys who know their way around guns and how to deal with ugly situations. That's in high demand right now."

"How do we contact him?"

Dranko's head whirled around to gape at Cooper, "What? Are you serious?"

Cooper dismissed him with a wave of his hand and a wrinkle in the corner of his mouth, "Don't get hysterical. We might have a need. I want to be prepared."

Joe scribbled a phone number and address onto the back of an envelope and handed it to Cooper, "You know what the great irony is, don't you?"

"What's that?"

"There are only three groups organized and functioning right now: the churches, organized crime, and some street punks."

"What's ironic about that?" Dranko asked.

"All three of those have been called gangs at one time or another. Yet, the biggest gang of them all—the US Government—is barely functioning with a few scattered mailmen and national Guardsmen. It'd be funny if it didn't want to make you cry," he chuckled hollowly. He turned, began walking away, and called over his shoulder, "I'll see you guys tomorrow. Hopefully!"

"Stay safe, Joe," Cooper called after him.

******

As soon as the door shut behind him, Cooper turned to Dranko, "Can you be kitted up and ready to go in five?"

Dranko clapped his hands together, "Sure, where we going?"

Cooper began donning his bulletproof vest, "We have two people to see before the five o'clock meeting here."

"Who's that?" Dranko asked, reassembling his pistol without letting his gaze drop from Cooper.

"Joe's cousin and whoever is in charge of the National Guard downtown."

At the mention of Joe's cousin, Dranko wrinkled his nose, but he didn't say a word.

Cooper quickly finished assembling his gear. He crossed the kitchen, grabbed a Kaiser roll, and went out back. There he found Angela covered in grease and sweat from the barbeque and the smoker, both belching heat and smoke.

"Thank you," he said as he grabbed two sausage links, stuffing them into the roll.

She saluted him patronizingly, using a large spatula, "You're welcome. Someone had to keep things going while Rip Van Winkle was sleeping." Her smile gave a healthy glint to her eyes.

"Oops! Being a hard-ass just cost you your overtime pay!"

"We'll see about that. You forget. Not only am I a union nurse, I also carry a gun these days. You might say I'm protected seven ways to Sunday," a confident smile spreading across her face.

Cooper's face grimaced in mock pain, "Ouch, you got me there!" His face turned serious once more, "I'm going out with Dranko to see a few people—including the military group downtown. I will be back by five, when Calvin and some others will be coming for a meeting. Can you hold things down while I'm out?"

She nodded as her face turned grave, "Be careful, alright?"

He raised the Kaiser roll in response, took a big bite out of it, nodded, and then retreated back through the house. The sausage tasted wonderful. He figured it was a combination of how hungry he was and the quality of the meat. Crunching the sesame seeds from the roll certainly helped. The sausage bit back with just the right amount of spice and tang. Hot oil dripped down his chin as he ate. He wiped it away, luxuriously, with his left hand.

Chapter 26

Dranko had convinced him that they should visit the National Guard first, reasoning that knowing the extent of coming security would be helpful in any conversation with Vang's cousin. The pickup was headed west on Division Street, toward downtown. They soon passed the car with the dead family inside, the bodies were still there, unmoved, and beginning to bloat.

More damage and violence had happened since their last trip through. Cooper had his rifle with him on this trip and he gripped it, at the ready. Dranko was driving again, his fully automatic M-16 close at hand on the bench seat.

A gas station at Division and 39th was burned to the ground. A building to the immediate west of it had caught fire, as well. It was halfway burned to the ground. Cooper mused at what had stopped the fire. The fire department? Neighbors? A dramatic shift in the wind?

As they drove, it looked like every third or fourth business had been looted. Some made sense: the hardware store, a corner grocery store, a bar. But, when they passed a pet store which had been burned down with most of the animals still inside, Cooper could only shake his head in wonder. Later, an art store's windows had been smashed and the contents of the store trashed, but one large pane remained intact. In blood-red spray paint, someone had written, "Devilish Art Played Its Part!" A large cross of black paint lay directly beneath this graffiti. Dranko and Cooper exchanged confused looks at that.

Cooper shrugged, "I guess you could say this plague is of Biblical proportions?"

"But, it's hard to see how a store selling paint-by-number kits and paint brushes caused this."

"True," Cooper said as they drove onward.

At 32nd Avenue, they encountered a roadblock. It looked similar to theirs. An old pickup and an even older station wagon were parked nose to nose to block the road. Three people, two men and a woman, were in position behind the vehicles. One man trained a bolt-action hunting rifle on them, the other a shotgun, and the woman held a pistol aloft.

"Hold it up. No fast moves," she shouted to them when they were about thirty yards away.

Dranko slowly raised his hand from the steering wheel and

leaned his head out of the driver's side window, "We are from up near Tabor and heading downtown. How can we get through?"

She pointed north with her pistol, "You can go up to Hawthorne. No roadblocks there that I know of. You can squeeze through here and take a right, but don't try anything stupid." They both saw the gap she was referring to, as the vehicles formed a V to block anyone coming further up Division, it did allow enough space for a pickup to pass north up 32nd. He considered their strategy. On the one hand, it allowed a car to pass dangerously close to their barricade. On the other, it could prevent a confrontation by having a safety valve of allowing people to continue moving without having to turn around.

"Pretty clever, eh?" Dranko said, echoing his thoughts.

"It has its pros and cons," Cooper caught the glint of light on a scope and now saw two rifles trained on them from a windows across the street, as they rounded the barricade. He nodded appreciatively in their direction so that Dranko spotted them as well.

"I stand corrected, mostly pros. These guys know what they are doing," Cooper said as it became clear that anyone trying anything untoward as they drove past the barricade would have two high-powered, scoped, rifles to contend with. At the range of less than fifty yards, even a minimally trained shooter would be able to hit whatever he was shooting at.

Cooper leaned over so he could shout out of Dranko's window, "Nicely done. We're up on 58th and Lincoln if you need anything." The woman, who was clearly in charge, held a nickel-plated revolver in her left hand. Her ears were festooned with piercings, and her nose had two. Her black hair was shaved to a coarse stubble. She wore a denim jacket with the sleeves cut off. Her arms were alive with vibrant-colored tattoos of various animals and symbols. The unbuttoned jacket revealed a faded black t-shirt announcing a long-ago Joan Jett concert. Her black leather pants and motorcycle boots completed the garb of hard-knocks. Dranko appraised her as well as they passed. Something on his face must have given away his thoughts.

"Yeah, some of *us* carry guns too, my boys!" she called after them, laughing at her own humor. "We might call on you yet. Name's Lucy if you need anything from us."

Cooper gave her a broad smile, admiring her aplomb, "Mine's Cooper. Likewise and good luck."

"You too," she shouted as Dranko completed the right hand turn and drove up 32nd. That short drive was without event and all looked normal, save for the noticeable absence of anyone on the street and a few windows that had been boarded up by their occupants. *I wish people knew that a two-by-four won't stop most bullets.*

Dranko took the left onto Hawthorne and they immediately began passing wrecked cars, some burned, and a series of looted storefronts. They both wrinkled their noses as they smelled before they saw dead bodies in various places.

A bevy of motorcycles parked out front of a still functioning bar immediately caught their attention. A score of leather-clad bikers were scattered in front of it, some sitting and some standing, but all drinking.

"Take it slow, but be ready. Let's see what they do," Cooper whispered to Dranko, as if they could hear him.

A few bikers stood up and others turned toward the pickup truck as they approached. Cooper's grip grew tighter on his rifle. He counted it fortunate that the bar was on the right-hand side, giving him a good line of sight.

Suddenly, like ants on a threatened hill, the bikers swung into frenzied action. Tables were lifted onto their sides, hands went for guns, and one biker stepped into the street and yelled at them to stop.

"Gun it!" Cooper shouted as he trained his rifle on the biker spokesman.

A loud report thundered inside the truck's cab and the lead biker's chest exploded as he was knocked backward from taking the .308 round from only twenty yards away. Cooper marveled that he could hear the spent shell casing making a loud metallic ring as it bounced off the rifle's ejection port and landed inside the truck.

Cooper quickly moved to lay down shots intended to keep their opponents' heads down, as opposed to aimed fire. His finger squeezed as fast as he could as he stitched fire from one end of the clustered bikers to the other. Dranko swerved the truck to their left, putting as much distance between them as possible. Cooper had only fired a few more rounds before they started receiving return fire from the bikers.

The loud crack of pistol fire shouted back at them. Half of their windshield spider-cracked as a round hit just in front of Cooper. He *felt* a round impact the passenger-side door and pass into the cab. Thankfully, he felt no burning sensation of being hit. Dranko didn't cry out, as the round passed harmlessly through. Near simultaneous *ting – ting-tings* told him the pickup's bed was being pockmarked by shells.

Cooper emptied the FAL's magazine in this random-fire mode, hitting at least two bikers. When the last round had been shot, the bolt locked back open, telling him the weapon was empty. He dropped the rifle between his legs and grabbed the M-16. A shotgun blast destroyed the passenger-side mirror, and Cooper winced as shards of metal and glass impacted the right side of his face and head.

He cursed loudly as he switched the selector to full-auto and brought the M-16 to bear. He yanked the trigger back, firing controlled bursts, in rapid succession. He prayed the buzz of automatic fire would force the bikers to seek further cover. Having been on the receiving end a few times, he knew first-hand the terror that automatic weapons fire could instill even on those trained to withstand it. The sheer volume of bullets flying nearby instinctively made anyone believe the next one was *guaranteed* to hit them. He hoped its effect on untrained civilians would be even greater.

It worked. The volume of fire lessened dramatically as bikers scrambled for cover behind the tables or back into the building, desperately trying to avoid the buzzing rounds, the splintering wood, and the cratered pavement as the M16's rounds struck home. Adding to the effect, one of his rounds struck a biker in the leg and he tumbled over, shrieking in a frenzy of pain.

Dranko's hand jabbed him in the side, holding a fresh magazine, just as the M16 ran dry. *Damn, he knows his stuff.* Cooper hit the magazine ejector button, keeping his eyes on the bikers. The truck was now past them, as Dranko expertly drove around a burned out car using only one hand. Cooper's eyes flew wide open as he spotted a biker, hovering just inside the bar's doorway, covered in shadow. Enough light made its way inside that Cooper could see he held a scoped rifle and he was carefully sizing up his target on the moving truck; gauging speed and trajectory.

Cooper slammed home the fresh magazine and shouted at Dranko, "Evade!" Cooper racked the bolt to chamber a round as Dranko jerked the wheel hard, and to the right.

The biker's rifle spat red-orange flame and the round passed just behind Cooper, shattering the rear window. He felt the sting of more glass burying itself in the back of his head and his shoulders. The bullet continued on its angle, passing just in front of Dranko's face and smashing through the driver's side window.

Cooper ignored his painful wounds and pulled the trigger to send a hail of fire toward the biker marksman. He burned half the magazine stitching the doorway frame. He couldn't tell if he hit the rifleman, but the long, slender, black rifle disappeared back into the bar. For good measure, he emptied the rest of the magazine by spraying a long burst across the front of the bar.

As the pickup raced away, a few dispirited pistol shots rang back at them, but none came close to the truck. Cooper kept an eye on the bar as it receded in the distance. Thankfully, there was no pursuit.

"Must have thought we were easy pickings; the M-16 showed them otherwise," he mused.

Dranko gave him a frantic look, the first time he had time to avert his eyes from the road, "You need medical."

"Do I?" Cooper asked in disbelief. He brought his hand to the side of his head and flinched in pain as he found a glass shard and pulled it out. The hand returned, covered in blood. "I guess you're right." He suddenly became woozy and forced himself to breathe deeply.

"I *hate* the sight of my own blood!" Cooper complained.

Dranko gained the distance of several city blocks and then turned into a parking lot and rounded his way behind a burned out mechanic's shop. He looked furtively around to ensure its relative safety and then grabbed a first aid kit from underneath the seat. He made Cooper turn around, facing rearward, so he could get a better look at his wounds.

"OK, luckily, it's all superficial wounds. Lots of blood, but it won't kill you. Here, take these," Dranko said handing him several painkillers. Cooper gulped them down with the water bottle that Dranko provided. Instantly, he was *very* thirsty and he drained the bottle in seconds.

"Keep an eye out. This is gonna hurt, brother," Dranko reported as he fetched metal tweezers from the first-aid kit. Dranko quickly, and expertly, went to work. He removed shards of glass that covered Cooper's head on the right side and rear. His shoulder had, luckily, only been grazed. He knew he had to work quickly, because the blood flow increased as he removed each piece. Cooper's ear had been sliced nearly in half and the lobe clung loosely to the ear, hanging by a scant piece of skin.

"Your ear will need stitches later," Dranko told him as he pulled out the last shard. He doused the wound in antiseptic and Cooper cursed Dranko's mother for birthing such a bastard of a son. Dranko ignored him and applied direct pressure with a bandage. Then, he began wrapping his head in layer after layer of gauze to fasten the bandage. When he finished with that, he employed two large bandages to cover the shallower shoulder wounds. These had bled only slightly and already stopped.

Dranko's brow was bathed in sweat as he finished, "You're all set now. As good as new."

Cooper pivoted his head back and forth, "I guess so. Still works. Let's go." He turned his body slowly back to facing the front and reloaded both weapons with fresh magazines.

"You don't miss a beat do you?" Dranko said as he put the truck in drive and began rolling forward, back toward Hawthorne.

"I'm on a clock because Jake is. I don't have time for something as small as pain," Cooper said firmly, his eyes already scanning their path forward. His grip was tight on the FAL with his right hand as he worked the bolt and chambered a round with his left.

Chapter 27

The rest of their drive was uneventful until they neared the Hawthorne bridge, which crossed the Willamette River into downtown. A half mile away, they ran headlong into a gaggle of cars, bicycles, and people that formed a chaotic mishmash of a traffic jam. The air was filled with the blaring of horns, the cries of children in distress, and shouts of anger as people jostled for position leading to the bridge.

"Looks like some scene from an overseas disaster," Dranko muttered.

"Overseas? Have you forgotten Katrina?" Cooper countered.

Dranko blew out harshly and his lips fluttered in disdain, "Either way, it's a damn shame. Look at them. Desperate. Some already hungry. Clamoring for someone *else* to save them."

A wry grin crept onto Cooper's face, "Look Dranko, not everyone can be as smart and well prepared as you." He elbowed his friend in the side as he talked.

Dranko crossed his arms, unimpressed, "Look, we're not even two weeks into this crisis. I can understand looking for medical help, but look at the number of damned people in line clearly looking for food. Damn sheeple is all they are, unprepared for even a *short-term* disruption in their lives."

Cooper merely nodded to placate Dranko's temper, "You're right. People ought to have had a few weeks of supplies on hand. That hardly matters now."

Dranko jumped the GMC partially onto the sidewalk and killed the engine. From a distance they could see an Army armored personnel carrier barricading the bridge. A soldier in camouflage fatigues stood vigil, lazily sweeping a .30 caliber machine gun from left to right, the barrel trained just over the heads of the swirling mash of people. The soldier's Kevlar helmet and darkened goggles gave him a sinister look. Next to the armored vehicle, a half dozen other soldiers formed a semi-circle, M16s at the ready, behind shiny coils of barbed wire. A dozen yards behind it, a tent was set up as the apparent command post.

They watched for a few minutes, appraising the situation. They saw the occasional civilian brought into the tent as others left. More frequently, soldiers moved in and out with rapid speed.

"What now, boss?" asked Dranko.

"I'm not waiting in that line," Cooper said, gesturing to a line that ran a hundred yards long. "We're going to see someone on the double-quick, just follow my lead."

He jumped from the pickup, shouldered the FAL, and began briskly walking toward the line. Dranko grabbed the M16, slung it onto his back, and fell in a half step behind, "This should be fun, brother," he grumbled.

Cooper turned back towards him, whispering as they walked, "Here's the plan, I'm the leader of the Mt. Tabor Militia and we have important news for the Major. Your job is to announce me as we get to the line."

A wry grin crept onto Dranko's face, "I like it. What's your job?"

"Act like an important SOB," Cooper winked at him before straightening his shoulders and picking up his pace as they neared the end of the line.

Dranko took up the siren song of authority, "Make room, Captain of the Mount Tabor Militia coming through. Make room, he has an urgent report for the Major!"

Cooper intentionally bumped a few people here and there to lend a greater sense of urgency. Dranko continued the mantra over and over. A few people cried out in protest, but they ignored them and kept hustling forward, to the front of the line. Halfway to the front, a young man with a clump of oily red hair and outfitted in camouflage stepped out of the line to bar their way.

"Wait in line like the rest of us!"

Cooper didn't hesitate, but closed the distance, shot his leg out and swept the man's legs out from underneath him. He collapsed with an "Umph." As Dranko stepped over him, he grabbed the butt of his holstered pistol so he could see it and whispered to the man, "I'd stay down if I were you."

A minute later, they were at the front of the line.

A young-faced soldier who barely looked old enough to shave barred their way.

"Just a minute, you gotta wait in line like the rest of these good people," the soldier said. Those within earshot shouted their approval and some clapped their hands.

"The hell I do, soldier. You tell the Major that the Captain of the Mount Tabor Militia is here to report to him. I have important news," Cooper leaned in to whisper the last part into the soldier's ear, "about the origin of the plague." The soldier gulped.

The Guardsman stammered, "I...ah"

Cooper pressed the opening, "Christ to Hell, son, where's your Sergeant?"

The soldier's look of relief was as if someone had thrown a safety line to a drowning man, "Sarge!" he yelled.

A middle-aged, bald-headed man, more round in the middle than he should have been for military service came striding up, "What is it Private? Can't you handle this line? I'm getting damn tired of babysitting you all day long!"

The Private merely nodded to indicate Cooper. *He won't be as easy to buffalo.*

"Good afternoon Sergeant. I'm former military, served in Iraq," Cooper said. The way the Sergeant cocked his head told him he had served as well in combat so Cooper quickly added his rank and where he had served, "May I have a word in private with you, Sergeant?"

The Sergeant motioned him and Dranko past the barricade, to hoots and howls of protest from those nearest the front of the line. Once they had walked about ten yards inside the barricade, the Sergeant turned to Cooper, "What do you have? Make it quick, you might have noticed we have a *lot* of chaos to tidy up."

"I need to see the Major. We have information about the conditions from here up to Mount Tabor. We are both former military so our reconnaissance is quality. In addition, I have some potentially urgent news about the plague's origins."

The Sergeant scoffed, "What kind of information?"

"I have a lead about a person, here in Portland, who might have information about how it *started*," Cooper's face was intent and he pressed it to within a few inches of the Sergeant's.

The Sergeant shook his head, "I'm not buying that part, but I will bring you to the Major. We need intelligence of what's happening in the next arc out from the downtown core. We've heard some crazy stories and we *need* to know what's real and what's bullshit."

"Good enough. Thank you," Cooper said as the Sergeant motioned them to a Humvee parked a dozen yards further to the rear.

"We're encamped in the Waterfront Park, just across the bridge," the Sergeant said, pointing to a series of military tents dotting the Willamette on the opposite side. "Of course, I don't know why we aren't in the Hyatt sleeping on some nice beds," he groused.

"When's the last time Uncle Sam ever spent money for a grunt's *comfort*?" Cooper quipped.

"Valley Forge," the Sergeant deadpanned and the three of them laughed together.

"Corporal Michelson can take you over, under my orders. You will have to leave your firearms here though." As he saw their look of unease, he quickly added, "Don't worry, they will be waiting for you when you return. My word on that."

It took them a few minutes to fill out some paperwork documenting the firearms they were entrusting to the Oregon National Guard. After that, they piled into the Humvee and the Corporal drove them the short distance to the cluster of tents on the other side.

******

They waited twenty minutes before being ushered in to see the Major. Cooper ducked inside the tent, with Dranko following close on his heels.

Inside, a large table was festooned with a myriad of maps. In turn, each map was adorned with colored push pins, a variety of colors highlighting various sections of the map, and indiscernible writing in multiple colors. To their left, a mobile bulletin board had, presumably, been turned over because what faced them was a blank corkboard. On the other side, they could see bits of paper sprawling over the edges of the board.

A large, powerful man dressed in olive drab fatigues moved quickly so that he could stand in front of the table with the maps and prevent them from getting a close view of them. He stood at least six feet tall and it was easy to discern his muscular tone underneath the baggy uniform. His gray hair was close-cropped as was a thin mustache. A prominent scar was seared across his forehead. Cooper guessed it was from a bullet or shrapnel.

"Good afternoon, gentlemen. I am Major Cummings. You must have something good for me to get past the Sergeant. I hope I won't be disappointed," his commanding presence was unmistakable.

Cooper didn't blink, "I'm Cooper Adams and this is Paul Dranko. We live up near Mount Tabor. It looks like you still carry a calling card from the war," he said touching a finger to his own forehead.

The Major laughed, recognizing the deft play at small talk. "Yes I do. I was coming down a stairway after we had cleared a building. Someone missed a hidey hole and I caught an AK round from down below. Doc told me my ramrod back kept my head up and the bullet from punching through my gullet and out the top of my head."

"Iraq or 'Ghanistan?"

The Major smiled proudly, "I did both of those. The bullet was from Iraq One."

Cooper nodded, "We both served there as well, although not as distinguished as you. I was a diesel mechanic who only saw a little action. Dranko here," he said jerking his thumb backward, "was a Marine good for nothing, but bragging." The Major laughed as Dranko used the tip of his foot to hit Cooper's knee from behind. Cooper caught himself before he stumbled.

The Major's forced his face straight again as he realized that Cooper was pulling him into a casual conversation, "Look, I could shoot the breeze with you two all day. It would sure beat the work I have to do. But, my time is limited. I've got more holes in the dike than we have fingers *and* toes to plug 'em. So, what do you have for me?"

"Right. First, let me give you our report from the Mt. Tabor area. The Sergeant said that would be useful to you."

"It would."

Cooper and Dranko took turns recounting the events since the plague had broken out. They focused on the incidents of violence and what they had done to set up security in their area. They left out the part about their firefight at Admonitus. Their reports were short and concise, using their shared military knowledge to hasten it. Major Cummings paused to scribble a few times, but a Staff Sergeant sitting in the corner made copious notes of what they said.

"Thank you, that is all very helpful," the Major said as they finished. "The Corporal said you had additional information about the plague?"

"Nothing definitive, sir. But, I have a few scraps of information that need to be investigated further. I'm hoping you can help us?"

"Well, what do you have?" the Major said impatiently as he waved off an orderly trying to enter the tent. It was already the second time he had done so since they had arrived.

In short order, Cooper recounted his encounters with Julianne Wheeler, the lab technician and the attack that killed him and the words exchanged with Mitchell at Admonitus, deftly avoiding any mention of the gunplay. Cooper whispered a silent prayer that any news of it hadn't reached the Major yet.

Cooper was taken aback as he saw the Major's face flush crimson as he finished recounting the facts. The Major's fists were clenched as well.

"Is that all? You come in here with *that*? A woman's whispers in a dream and an unfortunate victim of a gang attack who is spouting craziness? With that, you waste my time with innuendos? Slander against one of the pillars in Oregon's business community, I might add?"

Cooper's own fists clenched, "My son just came down sick yesterday. If Mitchell knows something...anything, it's worth finding out! All I'm saying is that you should question him!"

The Major shook his head emphatically, "No. It isn't going to happen. We are ass over teakettle with *real* problems..."

Cooper interrupted him, "Problems caused by the plague! If there is a way to get to the root of it..."

Cooper quickly realized his mistake as the Major cut *him* off, "We're done. The Sergeant will escort you out."

Cooper took a step forward, to reach out and grab the Major's shoulder, "Please, Major! So much depends on this!"

He was stopped cold by a hard thrust from the Major's hand to his chest, "Don't think about it, son. This interview is over."

The Major turned on his heels, his back looming as an unassailable wall. The Sergeant was at their side and gesturing them out with his left hand. His right hand lay resting on the butt of a holstered Beretta pistol. Cooper gave one last look at the Major and then hung his head before turning to leave. He throttled the fury of curses that he wanted to scream. *Some damned bureaucrat who's too afraid to ruffle the feathers of someone prominent.*

The short ride back across the bridge seemed like it took hours. They retrieved their weapons from the tent. The Sergeant took one look at their tense body language and guessed their interview with the Major hadn't gone well. He decided against any small talk.

After crossing the river, they retrieved their weapons as promised. As soon as Cooper and Dranko were out of earshot of the soldiers, Cooper let loose, "Can you believe that? He didn't pause to even *think* about what we had told him."

Dranko stopped his friend and put his hand on his shoulder, "Look Cooper. Here's what we have. There's *not* a lot to connect the dots."

Cooper interrupted, "But..."

"Just *let* me finish. On the face of it, there's not a lot here. But, what's filling it in is your *instincts*. Now, I trust those as good as any facts. The Major, however, doesn't know you from Adam. So, the connections we have just don't pencil out for a career military officer. You *know* that, brother."

Cooper took a deep breath, "Alright, you're right. You're right." He paused for a long moment. "Then, it's time for Plan B," he declared.

"What's Plan B?"

A dark gleam came to his eyes and his words were sinister, "Tonight, we visit Mr. Mitchell at his home. Unannounced and uninvited." Then, he relaxed before continuing, "Now, let's talk to Joe's cousin and hope it goes better than it did with the Major." He pivoted sharply and resumed walking back to the GMC pickup truck.

Dranko called after him, "Brother, you might have a short fuse, but at least you recover quick!" He hastened an extra few steps to catch up.

Chapter 28

Dranko rumbled the old pickup truck eastward, taking a route to avoid the bar where the bikers were congregated. They passed more of the same: burned out buildings, wrecked and burned cars, scattered dead bodies, followed by stretches of normalcy where everything looked the same as before. Usually, these stretches were guarded by people behind barricades or on top of roofs. They experienced a few tense moments, but Cooper would raise the military-style FAL above the cab level so others could see they were well armed. On this trip, the display worked.

Along the way, one burned out shell of a building made Cooper's heart leap into his throat. As they approached, everything moved in slow motion.

"Wow, that's the Pinehouse Arcade?"

"It used to be," Dranko intoned.

The building had burned almost to the ground. The neon sign that had for many years proclaimed "Pinehouse Arcade, Fun for All!" lay half-splintered on the ground. Shattered glass and a few piles of debris lay strewn about where the front entrance had previously resided. The buildings to either side lay singed, but mostly intact. It was clear the fire had started inside the arcade.

"Why the hell would anyone do that?" Cooper bellowed.

"Who knows? What's the big deal? It's just a bunch of old coin-operated video games from the 1980s," Dranko asked, surprised at his friend's outburst.

Cooper's face grew long, "It was more than that." He inhaled deeply, "Jake and I used to come here all the time. It was his favorite place."

Dranko responded with awkward silence, but reached across the cab to put his hand on Cooper's shoulder, "You'll come here again someday, just like before." Dranko's forced optimism sounded like an instrument played off-note. Cooper managed a quick grin for his friend's effort.

They drove onward in silence through the decaying city.

******

As they rounded a corner, Cooper exhaled, "Well, look at that!"

A blazing neon sign above a low-slung, nondescript building, called out, "Hungry Hoang's, Chinese-American Cuisine."

"They still got juice," Dranko said, stating the obvious.

"Lit up like this, they want everyone else to know that they do," Cooper added.

As they approached, the parking lot was full of vehicles: lowered Hondas, Toyota pick-up trucks, a few Cadillacs. Cooper did a double-take when he saw a World War Two-era halftrack with a machine gun mounted on top.

"Well, I'll be…" he exclaimed.

Two of the Toyotas were configured as "Tacticals": pickups with an improvised machine gun mounted in the bed. "Those are straight off of CNN when they report on an uprising in Africa," Dranko called to Cooper out of the side of his mouth. The welding work on the machine gun mounts were shiny and appeared hastily done.

A half-dozen guards were scattered throughout the lot, as well. One was resting on the halftrack's machine gun. Two stood by the main entrance with matching Uzi submachine guns. The others were armed with an assortment of M16's and AK-47's. While their weapons were different, they wore a common uniform made up of dark sunglasses, black slicked back hair, black dress pants and white-button shirts that had the first few buttons undone. The crew wore identical black leather jackets and similarly wore them unzipped.

"These guys out front are going for the look of TV gangsters meant to intimidate the general public. I wonder if they have more men either hidden or inside that are the real deal—dressed for, trained for, and ready for combat?" Cooper asked himself as much as Dranko. Dranko simply grunted in agreement.

All the guards moved from their various positions of relaxation to alertness as Dranko navigated the pickup into the lot. The guard nearest to them spat his cigarette out and gestured with an AK-47.

"Come out. Real slow. Hands where I can see them."

Cooper and Dranko complied. As soon as they had disembarked from the pickup, the guard asked, "What's your business here?"

Cooper responded, "We are here to see Michael Huynh. We are here at Mr. Joe Vang's recommendation."

The guard nodded and barked orders in Vietnamese to one of his men near the door. Everyone waited in silence as several minutes ticked by. Cooper noted how quickly the guards lowered their alertness and slowly drifted back to relaxed positions, although no one resumed sitting. The guard closest to them wore a deep scar across his right cheek, most likely the result of a knife wound.

The other guard returned and waved Dranko and Cooper on to approach the door.

"You'll need to leave your weapons...all of them...in your pickup. We'll keep a good eye on them," the first guard grunted with a mischievous grin.

They both removed the pistols from their holsters and laid them on the seat in the pickup. Cooper gave the guard a stern look as he did so, telling him not to disturb their weapons with the cock of his left eyebrow. They turned to the entrance and briskly walked towards it. When they arrived, the guard frisked them and then told them to follow him inside.

As they entered the restaurant, another half dozen men in black fatigues and carrying M16s were lounging in the lobby. Three were shooting dice in the corner, one dozed in a chair, and the remaining two were playing a card game that Cooper couldn't decipher. They barely gave Cooper and Dranko a glance as they passed through.

The guard talked as they walked, "It is well you were recommended by Mr. Vang. He is respected here. The boss is comfortable with those he recommends to us. What part of town are you in?"

"Near Mount Tabor," Cooper replied curtly, hoping his gruff tone would curtail the conversation. It didn't.

"That is a nice part of town. Very close to here. How are things there?"

"We're doing OK. Better than most."

"Yes, it's been very bad in parts of town. Did you hear what happened over in Sellwood?" he asked.

"No, I haven't," Cooper replied.

"Burned to the ground, all of it. Last night," the guard said nonchalantly.

"All of it?" Dranko asked in surprise.

"Nearly so."

"Why?" Cooper asked.

"We heard it was a very large group of teenagers from over in South Portland. Some clown down there claiming the plague is here to end the old world and that the youth must rise to build a new one."

"Why Sellwood?"

"Not sure. Because it was close by? They just rioted after a speech given by this guy. Hundreds of them. Lots and lots of dead. They killed and burned without discretion," emotion did not cloud his voice. It was if he was reporting the weather. "OK, we are here. It was nice talking to you gentlemen."

They stood before a large door that looked to be made of solid oak. It was in the far back of the restaurant. Two more guards stood on either side of the door, armed with shotguns in their arms and pistols on their hips.

An elderly man and an attractive young woman, both Asian, were leaving. The man was bowing to everyone and grasping a tattered black hat in his gnarled hands. The woman was holding him by his shoulders, supporting him, as they shuffled by.

"Your turn, good luck," their escort said to them as he pushed open the large door. It groaned on its hinges.

They stepped into the room that lay beyond. Michael Huynh sat at a massive desk of solid mahogany. The dark wood shined and they could smell the fresh oil that had been rubbed into it. The legs were carved in the shape of dragons and the feet were large claws. Huynh had his jet black hair pulled back into a ponytail and he wore a finely-tailored black suit, with a white silk shirt, and a blood red tie, also made of silk. He fingered an unlit cigar in his left hand and twirled a thin, gleaming knife with his right. The desk was clear of any objects, save a nickel-plated 1911-style pistol that lay within easy reach.

"Good afternoon, gentlemen. You come to me on the word of my cousin Joseph Vang?"

Two large-framed guards stood on either side of the desk. They were attired in suits, with submachine guns resting on a sling across their chests.

Cooper took a step forward and chose his words carefully, "Yes, sir. He said you have trained staff to provide protection."

"Why, yes. Yes, I do. For a small fee of course," a wide grin spread across his face, revealing a small scar that dipped from the left corner of his mouth towards the side of his jaw line.

Cooper clenched his jaw, "And what would the fee be?"

A knife was laid upon the table and Huynh slowly, methodically retrieved a butane lighter from a breast pocket. *This guy knows his theatrics.* A bright blue flame spat from the lighter and a puff of smoke drifted from the red circle on the end of the cigar as he lit it.

"Mmmm, that is good. You like Cuban?"

"Of course," Cooper responded.

"The complexity of the tobacco is like none other." Cooper endured the staged silence. He refused to shift on his feet, despite the inclination. He knew something of negotiation tactics from his father's days of standing up for the rights of the common man.

A few puffs later, Huynh spoke again, "Where were we? Oh yes, the bothersome business of the costs for services rendered. As I said, it would depend on how many men you want and in what currency you will be paying."

Cooper cocked an eyebrow, "Currency?"

"Why yes. In times like these, Mr. Adams, the forms of currency multiply. Unlike some, I still accept the US dollar. Unlike others, I think we will bounce back from the current challenges facing us as a nation. But, I accept other forms of payment as well."

"Such as?"

"Some are paying me in gold, some in jewelry, and a few are paying me in commodities I can use in my other lines of business," he said in between blowing smoke rings toward the ceiling. *Drugs and women*, Cooper guessed.

"We would be paying in dollars."

"How many men?"

"Do they come armed with automatic weapons?"

"They could."

Cooper thought for a moment, "We would need four."

Huynh took a long pause, "Four men. Automatic weapons. That would be $20,000 per week."

Cooper let loose a false cough and then paused a long moment, "With all due respect, that would be very challenging for us to come up with."

Recognizing the negotiation, Huynh's smile returned, "Come now, Mr. Adams. Do not take me for some simpleton. I know the neighborhood you live in. You will have the money if you value your safety and are willing to pay for it."

"The challenge is gathering the *cash*. My neighbors use banks to keep their money and do not have large sums of cash on hand."

"I like you, Mr. Adams. I will tell you what I will do for you. I'll accept $10,000 in cash and a promise from those in your neighborhood for another $15,000 when the crisis abates and the banks reopen."

Cooper retained a straight face, but smiled inside, "That should be more doable. My other difficulty will be convincing my neighbors that this sum is legitimate for only four men. While I can see the value of your men, my neighbors who do not understand security will be more challenging to convince."

Huynh's smile faded and he deliberately clipped his words, "Alright, I can add two men."

"Thank you. That will make my task of convincing easier."

"Surely. We are here to help one another, after all. The extra two men will carry shotguns only."

Taking care to be overly polite, Cooper smiled and nodded, "Of course. I would not expect more than that." *Translation: he will send two untrained expendables with shotguns.*

"I will take your generous offer before our neighborhood tonight. I can let you know soon whether we will move forward with your protection."

"Good enough. But do not delay in making your decision. I have many requests for protection and a limited number of men I can deploy."

"Of course. Thank you for your time, Mr. Huynh."

Huynh responded by turning the large leather chair he sat in to face outwards towards the windows.

Cooper and Dranko retreated from the room. Their escort led them back to the parking lot. This time he was silent. *I wonder if the Sellwood story is even true? Maybe it was all to heighten our fear of random violence before we met with Mr. Huynh?*

As promised, their pickup and weapons were undisturbed. Cooper and Dranko piled back into it and steered towards home.

Chapter 29

They arrived back at Cooper's home with a half-hour to spare before the meeting would begin. Dranko collapsed on his living room sofa and was snoring before Cooper had removed his body armor and stowed the rifle.

Cooper went immediately to Jake's room. Angela was seated on a chair next to his bed, dozing. Jake was sleeping soundly on his bed, his chest rising and falling with regularity. *Thank God.* He turned his view back towards Angela. He had been impressed with how she had stepped in and done what was needed to be done. Cooper admired that trait in people. He took a moment and smiled as he watched her peaceful face bob up and down as she slept in the chair.

He tip-toed over to the edge of the bed and then knelt down beside it. Jake lay just a few inches from the edge. Cooper buried his face into his hands and pressed them deeply into the softness of the bed. Exhaustion, worry, and grief overtook him. Tears came readily, washing down his face. He struggled to remain quiet, so that Jake's sleep would remain undisturbed.

His thoughts pleaded: *Please God, let him live. Let me find a way to save him. I cannot, I will not, survive if I lose him, too.* His fists tightened into balls of frustration as he pressed them hard against his ribs. He turned his head from side to side, welcoming the almost painful friction from the mattress' edge.

After a few moments, his tears stopped and his thoughts turned. *I've given too much already. Elena is gone. I've been forced to kill again. I have no more to give.*

He raised his eyes and looked at Jake again. The only telltale signs that he was ill were his flushed face and the tiny beads of sweat across his face. *Damn you God, you cannot have him too. I will not let you have him. Damn you if you try.*

His own face, flushed with anger as he stood up resolutely, and walked from the room. He failed to notice Angela watching him from the corner of her eye. She had watched him transition from grief to rage by witnessing the shifting lines in his face. It had been like a violent summer storm rolling across the Plains. At first, distant and seemingly calm. Then building to a sudden, and growing, fury that seems like it will never end. Suddenly, it passes as swiftly as it had arrived.

******

He had scarcely stepped into the hallway and closed the door quietly behind him, when he heard someone rapping on the door. Looking out a window, he saw Calvin waiting on the doorstep.

He opened the door, "How ya doin', Calvin?"

"Good, considering the circumstances," he chuckled briefly. "We have the reports in from the survey teams."

Cooper invited him to sit down in his living room with a wave of his hand. Cooper still couldn't get used to the sight of people visiting him with a handgun on their hip and a long arm in their hands. Calvin sat down heavily into the soft welcoming arms of Cooper's sofa. *Everyone must be dead tired by now.*

Calvin looked up with worry-worn eyes, "Do you want the good news or the bad news first?"

A wry smile crossed Cooper's lips, "Today, I will take the good first."

"The two-block area immediately to our north is pretty well organized. They have defensives positions and patrols up, much like we do. However, they are not very well armed. "

"Thank God for Dranko's paranoia, eh?"

Calvin's head bobbed up and down, "Absolutely. I guess he turned out to be not so paranoid, did he?"

Cooper nodded in reply before Calvin continued, "They have also taken over the Second Lots grocery store and are disbursing the food in an organized fashion."

"Lucky for them to have a store selling odd lots of canned goods and jars of peanuts in their backyard." Inside, Cooper was kicking himself for not having thought of that store as a resource point, since it was so close to them.

"I'll say. However, we might be able to trade a few weapons for some food. Our survey team told me that they were salivating as they saw the weapons our guys were carrying. All they have are a handful of old hunting rifles and a couple handguns."

Cooper scratched his chin, "That's a good idea. The better defended they are, the better it is for us. For example, we can reduce the barricades on our northern side and use the few extra people elsewhere. We will have more warning if a serious threat develops there."

Calvin nodded; chin in hand, "Good. I will talk to Dranko about it and see what we can do."

"Right. OK. So what's the bad news?"

"Just to our south, some bad elements are developing. Apparently, there were about a dozen families who all belonged to the same church in that neighborhood. The church has become a focal point of organization."

"Isn't that a good thing?" Cooper interrupted.

"You're right, it *should* be. However, the churchgoers are using their access to food and other supplies as a heavy-handed recruitment tool. Our team talked to some in the neighborhood who are getting pretty upset about being forced to attend daily services at the church if they want food. It's very possible it could turn violent," Calvin concluded gravely.

"That's too bad. From what Dranko has told me, churches have become a rallying point in lots of different places. All kinds of religions too—from Christian, to Buddhist, to Muslim, to Jewish. Why would these guys take this route?"

"They are short-sighted. Or, maybe their God told them to do it this way. It *is* small church, so who knows what their religious grounding is."

Cooper shook his head, "Alright, we should make a point to keep in contact with those we met there and keep an eye on that situation. Anything else of interest?"

"Not really. To our east and west are mostly just disorganized. There is one last tidbit," Calvin finished and a wide grin spread across his face, despite his best efforts to control it.

Cooper's brow wrinkled, "What is it, man? Spit it out!"

Calvin chuckled, "This is why I never could play poker." He leaned in and whispered, "As our teams asked about the illness, they all found out something incredible."

Cooper raised his eyebrows, "And?"

"All the neighborhoods had the same report: no one new has come down with the illness within the last twenty-four hours," his words came rapidly now. "I couldn't believe it. So, I had our internal team do another round-up through the neighborhood. We haven't had anyone come down with it since..."

Cooper leaned back heavily, "Since Jake. It's been about twenty-four hours since he came down with it." A roil of emotions washed over him. "So, what does this mean?"

Calvin's face was aglow with excitement, "It could mean this thing is *over*, Cooper. Think about it. We've been dropping like flies since the outbreak. Just in our neighborhood, we've had several people coming down with the symptoms every single day. I think it *has* to mean something that no one in a *wider* area has got it for a full day!"

Cooper knocked his head with his hands, trying to make sense of it, "OK. Let's get Lisa and Angela in here. They are our best medical minds available to us."

"I've already talked with Lisa. She's cautiously optimistic like me. She said it is possible it is an anomaly. Since the outbreak, the radio and internet have been rife with rumors of 'it's ending' every day. So, I wouldn't trust much of that kind of news, anyway."

"What does she recommend?"

"She said we should watch it closely. If we get another twenty-four hours without any more with symptoms, she said that would mean something else entirely."

"I can't believe it. I don't know what to say," Cooper said as he sank back again into the sofa, his hands clapping his forehead.

"I couldn't either. It took me an hour of pacing about my living room to finally, remotely, start believing it."

Cooper sat up with a start, "Oh, no! If this thing really is ending, Jake could be one of the *last* ones to have got it."

Calvin's smile disappeared instantly and he let out a loud exhale, "I'm sorry."

Cooper waved his hand, "It's not your fault. Don't get me wrong, I will be happy if this thing is over. It just means I *really* have to get to Admonitus and do what needs to be done to save my boy." Cooper paused for a moment and his face brightened, "It's *also* possible that Jake may have a weaker strain in him. Usually, viruses become weaker as they go from person to person. So, if it is fading out, maybe he has a weaker variety!"

Calvin hesitated and then nodded emphatically, "Yes! That sounds like a possibility to me, too. Let's hope for that."

Cooper stood up and shuffled his feet as he collected his thoughts. Calvin stood as well, readying himself to leave.

"I have some information for you as well."

Calvin's face grew puzzled, "What's that?"

"You know Joe Vang, the mailman, right?"

"Of course."

"We visited his cousin, who leads the Vietnamese Protection Society."

Calvin's face grew hard, muscles bulging on his jawline, "You mean, he's a gangster?"

"Sure, whatever it's called, they have trained men with good weapons. They've offered us six men for a week to help protect our neighborhood."

Calvin took a step back, "At what cost, Cooper?"

"Ten-thousand now. Fifteen thousand later, when the banks reopen."

"I wasn't asking about the cost in money," he paused gathering himself. He began shaking his head, "No, no, no. We *cannot* do this. I lost a brother because he joined a *Protection Society,*" Calvin's words dripped with scorn.

Cooper held up his hands, palms outward, "Look. We can't get emotional about this. We need to be objective about how we protect our neighborhood."

Calvin looked back at him steely-eyed, "It's true Cooper. I'm *emotional* on this," he said defiantly. "When I found my brother's body lying face down in the street in a pool of blood when I was twelve-years old—it did make me *emotional* about steering clear of anything to do with gangs. But, there's more to it than that. Once you let these guys in—you won't *ever* get them out. Trust me."

"*I* can handle that part. It won't become permanent. Having that extra firepower could be a difference maker if we face a more serious threat. *Everything* is unstable right now."

Calvin shook his head, "I'm not going to argue this. There is no way I'm going to agree to do this."

"At least, let's present it at tonight's meeting. The neighborhood can decide," Cooper offered.

"That's fine with me, but you know which side I'll be arguing."

The two men stared at each other, "And you, mine."

Calvin maintained the steady gaze for several more seconds before turning and walking out the front door. As he opened it, Cooper saw that people had already begun gathering on the sidewalk adjoining his yard." *Is it time already?*

Cooper rubbed his temples, took a deep breath, and then stepped outside.

******

The group that gathered in the front yard was larger than it had ever been before. Almost a hundred people stood clustered tightly together to stay within earshot. The mood was better as well, with more people smiling. *More people have overcome their fear of getting the illness and are now coming out.*

Cooper began the meeting, but then turned it over to Calvin to give the report of the survey teams that had gone out. The group came alive with animation and side conversations when he talked of the neighborhood to the north and their grocery store.

"My kitchen's almost empty; can we get some Spam from them?" Freddie shouted, but his joke fell flat. Cooper wondered if it struck too close to home for many.

"We know they need guns, so we are going to see if we can make a trade with them," Calvin reported.

More smiles appeared in the crowd and murmurs of approval rippled through it.

Calvin continued, "We'd also like to supplement our daily survey about the illness. Please raise your hand if a member of your household has come down with it within the last twenty-four hours?"

Cooper watched as people shuffled their feet and looked around, but no one raised their hands.

"Raise your hand if you have heard of anyone else, a neighbor, a friend, who has come down with it in the last twenty-four hours."

Again, no hands were raised. Smiles grew wider and several people clapped their hands together in joyous surprise.

"Does this mean it's over?" Someone shouted.

Calvin waved his hands from side to side, "No, no, no. While its good news, we need to keep an eye on things. It could be a just a temporary blip, or it could mean something better than that."

Calvin paused for other questions, but there were none. He then turned the meeting over to Cooper.

"What I want to talk about is very simple, really. The city is still very chaotic. The only order is what people are making for themselves. I've met with the Vietnamese Protection Society and they've offered to send six men, four with automatic weapons, to help us defend our neighborhood for the next week."

The group erupted in whispers to one another and shouts directed at Cooper. The cacophony was impossible to discern.

Cooper outstretched his hands and yelled to gain everyone's attention, "Please, one at a time!"

"Let me get this straight, you want to invite a gang into our neighborhood?" John asked.

"I don't want anything. It is an option that I'm bringing to you for your consideration and decision. That's all. Do I think it's a good idea? Yes, I do. Money is a small price to pay for increasing my son's safety."

"Money? How much are they asking for?" Gus asked.

"I negotiated them down to $10,000 for the week up front. Fifteen thousand more after the banks reopen." A barrage of whistles and exclamations rang out.

"Might as well be a million," Freddie joked to a smattering of laughter. "Who has that kind of money?"

"We would have to take up a collection to raise the funds," Cooper responded, tamping the frustration rising in his belly.

"I think we should do it!" yelled Mark Moretti, who was standing at the back of the crowd, leaning against a white birch tree. Silence fell on the crowd and all eyes turned towards him. Cooper waved him on to continue. Mark brushed back his black hair and stood up straight.

"It's simple to me. We can take something that has very little value to all of us *right now*—money—and transform it into something that is *very* valuable at the current time—more security. Sure, when things get back to normal we might all complain about the money we spent, but we'll have a better chance of *being around* to complain about it by spending the money now."

Cooper watched a wave of nodding heads and whispered words wash over the crowd. Calvin stirred next to him.

"Wait a second, Mark. I'd agree with you if we were talking about spending money on a security company or some other group we could *trust*. We're talking about gangbangers. Hardened criminals. We've fought to keep those kinds of people *out* of our neighborhood. Why would we not only *invite* them in now, but *pay* them for the privilege?"

Mark shouted back, "But, they'd be working for us, *that's* the difference."

Calvin's words burned with contempt, "But what will happen on the third week when we can't pay them anymore? And now they know everything about us—how many armed people we have, what our defenses look like, and on and on. What then?"

Mark fired back, "It will increase our odds of all *making it* to the third week. Haven't you been following the news? Other cities are much worse off than we are, but we're headed in that direction. The coming weeks are going to still being very chaotic and dangerous, maybe even more so."

The crowd was clearly moving over to Mark's position when Lily Stott stepped forward, her voice graveled by age, "You lie down with the dogs, you'll come up with fleas." Her eyes scanned back and forth across the crowd, intently looking at anyone she could make eye contact with. She said nothing more and then sat down once more on the lone bench in Cooper's yard.

A terse silence passed as her words brought everyone to a dead stop.

Calvin broke the spell, "I couldn't agree more, Miss Stott. We get involved with these guys, we won't *ever* be free of them."

"Lily, Calvin, you're right. There *are* no easy discussions anymore. But, I'd prefer my boy gets bit by some fleas than watch his father catch a bullet, like the one that *almost* got me *today*." Cooper turned his head so the crowd could see the bandages swathing his ear. He let it sink in before continuing, "Furthermore, I'll be damned if I'll watch my son get killed, or worse, by some attack that we could have stopped with a few more guns on our side. Five hundred bucks in my pocket would be cold comfort on *that* day."

Cooper's words had a dramatic effect on the crowd. More were murmuring support for the idea. However, the opposition continued. He listened as the debate dragged on. With each passing minute, Cooper grew anxious about the upcoming visit to Mitchell's home. He wanted to end the meeting so he could rest again and then make a plan of attack with Dranko.

Like a balloon that wouldn't inflate, the meeting meandered without resolution. An hour later the meeting ended with the group deciding to table any decision until tomorrow so everyone could "sleep on it."

Chapter 30

Twenty minutes later, Cooper was fast asleep, after asking Dranko to wake him in an hour. His exhaustion was complete, and he slept more soundly than he had in weeks. He dreamt of Jake. They were living in normal times, except for Elena's absence. Cooper was dropping him off at school on his way to work. He watched his son walk into the school and immediately fall in line with friends. The children's smiles were wide and the sound of laughter reached his ears. The sun shone brightly as Jake turned from his friends to wave to his father. Cooper's heart overflowed with the dull warmth of tranquility. As that feeling took hold, his heart began to ache, like a muscle that hadn't been used for a while, but feels good the next day from the exertion.

When Dranko woke him up, his eyes were moist and the pillow was damp where his head lay. *I hope that's the vision of his future,* he thought as he dried his eyes, got up, and stretched. His alarm clock sat blank, the numbers dark. *Electricity is still out, so it wasn't a temporary problem.* He looked at his watch; he'd been asleep for almost exactly one hour.

Five minutes later, he was dressed and downstairs. Dranko had a steaming cup of coffee ready for him. The table was spread with maps and photographs of Mitchell's estate.

"How'd you do all this?" Cooper asked incredulously.

"The coffee is instant. I boiled the water on my camp stove. The maps and the rest are from the miracles of the Internet," he paused as Cooper gave him a quizzical look. "Oh, I've got a generator so I can still run my computer. And, I have a network card so I'm not limited to the local net being up and running to get onto the Web."

"You really did think of everything, didn't you?"

Dranko only grinned in return.

"Where's Angela?"

"Right here," the voice came from behind Cooper and he swung his head to see her, "I was just checking in on Jake."

"How is he?"

Her full face was alight with optimism, "Lisa was just here a half hour ago. She was surprised that he hasn't degenerated like most everyone else. He still has a fever, but it hasn't worsened. As you know, it usually does. She said to tell you to not get your hopes up, but that this was an *unusual* sign."

Cooper closed his eyes and breathed a deep sigh, "Well, that makes our visit with Mitchell more urgent. Jake may have just a little more time. If we can find some kind of cure," he stumbled trying to find the right words, then gave up. "There's more time, that's all."

Dranko nodded sympathetically, "What's the plan?"

Cooper reviewed the photographs, which were top-shot satellite images from Google Maps of Mitchell's home. He showed Dranko their likely line of approach and two backup approaches if those were compromised. They each pointed out potential concealment points for any guards that might be there. They discussed how they would operate once inside the home.

"I think we'll be OK once we get to his home. I'm confident that we can handle any rent-a-cops that he has employed there," Cooper concluded.

"We don't know the quality of who he has. I wouldn't be surprised that a guy like him has top-notch security," Dranko said.

"What you need is a distraction. You should let me help. I can snipe from here," Angela said, indicating a hill that overlooked Mitchell's estate. "Given how rusty I am, even if I don't hit anything, they will be forced to send someone, or more, to investigate."

Cooper's hand went to his chin as he contemplated her suggestion, "But, what will they do if they catch you?"

"They won't. I'll be gone long before they get close enough. They will be coming up that steep hill if they come on foot. And, it's across the road, so I'll hear any vehicle and can cut back on the reverse slope well before they reach me. It's really low risk."

Cooper looked intently at her, "Are you sure you want to do this?"

"Dranko filled me in. I'm not going to lie to you, I'm going to shoot to wound, not kill. But, *that* I can do to help you. And, I want to do that for Jake. The only real question is, does Dranko have a good sniping rifle for me to use?"

Cooper and Dranko laughed for a moment before Dranko responded, "My larder has been depleted for sure, but there are still a couple of choices left. I have a nice Remington, scoped, medium caliber. It has more than enough range, is accurate, with low recoil. The smaller cartridge will increase your odds of wounding versus killing too."

Angela nodded, "Sounds perfect. What time are we leaving? I should go find Lisa and make sure she can be here with Jake."

"We should leave soon, by nine. I don't want to be driving into the West Hills too late. We might get stopped. So, we'll go out there early. Stay out of sight and then hit Mitchell's estate at three fifteen in the dark and early," Cooper suggested.

Angela and Dranko nodded. Angela left to find Lisa while Dranko went to retrieve the rifle for Angela and other needed supplies. Cooper gathered up a shotgun and pistol, and soon was methodically cleaning and oiling them.

Dranko was back first, after only being gone for ten minutes. "You rolling with the shotgun?" he asked.

"Yes. I figured you'd have the full-auto M16 so you can deal with anything on our way in. I'll take point once we're close-in and inside. The shotgun will be ideal for that. The old maxim of war is that the *louder* side wins. This will give us that advantage on the inside, without question."

"I never understood the absurdity of bagpipes going into battle until I read about that very fact. So, I'm guessing you'd like one of these?" Dranko said as he held up a pair of fragmentation grenades.

Cooper sat halfway up in astonishment, "Where'd you get *those* for Chrissakes?"

"It pays to be forward thinking, and have friends in the right places. You want one? I only have two."

"Damn straight," Cooper answered. Dranko tossed him one and Cooper caught it, giving him a reproachful look. "A pessimist should never toss a live grenade to a friend in a living room."

"Maybe I don't think you're such a great friend. Have you seen all the trouble you're getting me into lately?"

"Trouble? Hell, you used to worry about falling over and breaking your leg when you'd put your pants on in the morning. At least now I'm giving you something *real* to worry about."

Dranko chuckled and then Angela's voice caught them both by surprise, "Are you old women ready to stop flirting with each other?"

Cooper and Dranko looked at her, then each other, and shrugged their shoulders in exaggerated fashion. Dranko handed Angela the rifle, solid and made for hunting deer. "I only have one box of shells for it, which is why we hadn't already distributed this one. But, for tonight's work, it will be plenty. I brought this for you too, just in case. He held up a small pistol with an extra magazine.

Angela took both weapons from him. She checked the actions and practiced racking the bolt on the rifle a dozen times. Keeping the muzzle pointed at the floor, she dry-fired at least as many times, to get a feel for the trigger pull, "Very nice. Balanced. The bolt throws fast and smooth. The trigger is light, consistent, and it breaks clean. The glass on it looks sharp and clear."

"It holds four rounds in that box magazine. Don't forget, with the bolt open, you can top off the magazine."

Angela nodded, "Got it." She moved her attention to the .380 pistol, practicing racking the slide, dry-firing, and checking the sights.

Dranko had his M16 strapped across his back. "And, I also have these," he clanked a set of rifle plates together. "When added to our soft body armor, these can stop most rifle rounds, too. They are heavy, but for a short run like this, it won't be a problem."

Angela shook her head, "I don't need a set. My game tonight will be speed. Those will just slow me down too much. You wear them."

Cooper started to protest, but stopped himself. *What she says makes sense. I'm not going to play out something from a movie and be the over-protective male.*

Finally, Dranko handed her a camouflage smock, "I didn't have a full set of pants and shirt, but this should work to cover most of you."

"Thanks. With a pair of dark pants, they'll be fine."

Cooper spoke up, "We wear regular clothes getting there, weapons stowed. We'll change in the field. There may be more police up in the West Hills, I don't want to risk a stop."

The corners of Angela's lips turned down in thought, "True. True. I'll work up a nurse's bag from Lisa. Our cover story can be that I'm a private nurse going to see a patient."

"And who are we?" Dranko asked, skeptically.

"My gallant bodyguards, of course!" she winked.

Cooper smiled, "That's believable enough these days. I like it. Good idea."

Chapter 31

A few minutes later, Cooper was outside. The cold air nipped at his exposed ears and fingers. He knelt beside Elena's grave, propping himself up with the butt of his rifle. The earth that had consumed his wife was still fresh enough that he could smell its dampened odor. He thrust a hand into the dirt and grabbed a fistful of it. He brought it to his nose and inhaled. He imagined he could smell a whiff of her perfume. The clumps of dirt slowly fell through his fingers back onto her grave.

"I need your help tonight. I'm going to save our son, I hope." He worked hard to keep his voice steady amidst the emotion.

He listened in silence, hoping for an answer of some kind. But, the night was deathly quiet, save the bark of a dog in the distance. Suddenly, he heard the flutter of wings and looked up. A black crow had alighted on the wire above. A part of Cooper wanted to believe it was the same bird from days before, but he couldn't be sure.

His eyes fell again to the freshly tilled earth and what lay beneath. "I miss you, love. I miss you every minute. I don't know how I can raise our boy without..." His voice cracked and fresh tears plied their way down his face and fell onto the earth, darkening it. He stared, thinking in the silence at the ground where his wife's body lay.

Then, from the east, the deep roar of an engine disturbed his thoughts. He'd heard that sound before. A second later, it clicked. It was the whine of a military Humvee. A chill ran down his spine and the pit of his stomach turned over.

*****

Cooper turned, ripped open the door, and shouted inside, "Angela, watch Jake. Dranko, on me! Now!"

Seconds later, Dranko had gathered his gear and appeared at Cooper's side. Already, the first barks and pops of gunfire from the eastern barricade were echoing off his home's walls. The telltale rapid popping, *tat-tat-tat*, of automatic weapons fire greeted their ears.

"Military," Cooper breathed to Dranko as they set out on a full sprint towards the gunfire. Dranko nodded as they ran.

Within seconds, the gunfire had grown deathly silent. The roar of the engine revving up again, drawing closer, confirmed his worst fears: *the barricade had been quickly overrun.*

Cooper and Dranko had run barely fifty yards when the Humvee came into view. They flung themselves to the ground and behind two small trees that were scattered about six feet apart. The Humvee raced towards them, straight towards Cooper's house. They saw the driver, a passenger, and the gunner who stood behind the machine gun that was mounted on top of the vehicle's roof.

"Got gunner," Cooper whispered to his friend as he sighted his rifle on the man's torso that lay exposed.

When the vehicle was within thirty yards, they opened fire. Caught by surprise, their volley was devastating. Cooper fired three shots in rapid succession. The first caught the man square in the chest and rocked him back against the opening. The second ripped the man's neck wide open and a red geyser erupted. The third shot missed entirely as the machine gunner's body slumped and banged against the vehicle.

Dranko had let loose a controlled burst of gunfire from his M16, stitching a pattern from the driver to the passenger-side. Both men were cut down in seconds. The vehicle, driverless, swerved and then flipped over. It skidded, on its side, to a stop just twenty feet from Cooper's front lawn.

Cooper and Dranko turned toward each and exchanged smiles. A second later, Cooper saw Dranko's face look aghast just as he heard another engine roaring up the street and the first burst of gunfire.

He felt something set his left arm on fire. He rapidly pushed himself backward, trying to find more cover behind a low retainer wall. His left arm burned where the bullet had hit him. He clenched his fingers and moved his arm to confirm it hadn't broken any bones or destroyed any key muscles.

He popped up and shot blindly in the direction of the sound of the second Humvee. Dranko lay absurdly exposed and he hoped to give him some cover. Two of his rounds impacted on the Humvee's body, one close to the machine gunner up top.

Within a second, Cooper was staring down the barrel of the heavy barrel machine gun. He dropped to the flat of his belly as a burst of gunfire hit the low wall he was hiding behind. Dirt showered him and rock chips bit into his arms and face. With his arm, he shielded his eyes from the stinging debris and looked up.

Dranko had swung his body around the tree to gain as much cover as it could afford—which wasn't much. The machine gun fire was stitching across the ground, arcing in slow motion from where

Cooper lay towards Dranko's position. Dranko was firing back blindly at the Humvee as he tried to shrivel his body up enough to hide behind the all-too-skinny tree. Fear throttled Cooper's throat as he saw his friend's impending fate. He rose back to his knees, but rifle fire that came from behind the Humvee forced him back down. *More men, dismounted.*

Then, he heard the deep-throated *boom, boom, boom* of what could only be a heavy caliber machine gun firing from his left *toward* the Humvee.

Across the street, he saw the ancient BAR spitting fire! The face behind the light machine gun startled him. It belonged to Hank Hutchison. As startling was the crazed, but ecstatic, smile plastered across his face.

His fire was surprisingly accurate for someone who hadn't fired the gun in decades. The .30-06 rounds first shattering the windshield and then tracing their way up to the machine gunner. In turn, he was swinging the machine gun toward Hank in a desperate race.

Hank won.

The machine gunner's body was ripped apart as a half-dozen rounds shred his torso—despite the body armor and pulped the man's head like a watermelon smashed by a sledgehammer. Hank pivoted his body to replace the magazine in the BAR, which had run dry. The passenger in the Humvee bailed out and rolled across the pavement as the Humvee careened out of control before crashing into the first Humvee that had flipped earlier.

Cooper rose once more onto his knees to get a better view of the rest of the area. He could see at least a half dozen men moving leap-frog fashion up the street toward them.

In the seconds-long lull, the passenger from the Humvee called out, "We come for Cooper Adams! No one else needs to get hurt! Send us Cooper Adams!"

Cooper's mind reeled. *Me? Damn, the Major! Defending Mitchell?*

Before Cooper could finish processing what he'd just heard, Hank yelled back, "To hell with you! You come for Cooper, you come for *all* of us!" He punctuated his sentence by letting loose another burst of fire from the BAR, which forced the soldier lying next to the Humvee to scurry up against it for more cover. Unfortunately for him, doing so exposed him to Dranko's line of fire. In turn, he fired a controlled three-round burst that battered the man and left him slumped over.

From further down the street, more gunfire rang out. First, Cooper saw soldiers firing in their direction. Dranko was forced once more to take cover behind the tree. Suddenly, he jumped to a half crouch and sprinted towards the crashed Humvees, bullets chasing him and tearing up chunks of asphalt. As he raised his own rifle to return fire, he also saw a few muzzle flashes farther to the east as some of the neighborhood defenders had begun shooting at the soldiers from behind. A sharp cry of pain told him one of their rounds had hit home.

He directed his fire toward a soldier who was flattened behind a mailbox, hugging the ground and shooting at Hank. He breathed deeply, steadying his breath. His target was almost a hundred yards away and only a small patch of green camouflage presented itself. He let out half of his breath and slowly squeezed the trigger back. His rifle barked and a split second later, the soldier rolled over, yelling in pain.

Just then, movement to his left caught his eye. Hank had leapt to his feet and was running towards the soldiers' position, firing the BAR wildly from his hip. Cooper's mind screamed *"No!"*, as he desperately fired at the other soldiers. Dranko's M16 erupted in a furious long burst of gunfire as he tried vainly to give Hank covering fire. From the east, the pace of fire from the other defenders, who must have also seen Hank charging, also picked up.

Seconds later, the bolt on the BAR slammed home empty. He kept charging forward, screaming madly. Then, a single shot rang out, stopping his forward momentum and knocking him backward. He stood for a moment, wobbling on his feet, the BAR falling from his grasp towards the ground. As he stood motionless, teetering, three more shots hit him in the chest. Cooper could vividly see each round's impact, slamming Hank's body this way and that in slow motion. Cooper could only look on in helpless agony. Finally, mercilessly, Hank's body fell to the ground and found escape from the deadly fire.

Rage consumed Cooper. He found the source of the fire that had killed Hank; a soldier who lay propped against a white birch tree. The tree gave him cover from Cooper. A wry smile crept across Cooper's face as he aimed directly at the tree and fired several rounds. The bullets tore through the tree and punched into the soldier behind it. From the range of fifty yards and in the moonlight, Cooper imagined more than saw the man's stunned look as he fell to the ground. He tapped the FAL affectionately.

Cooper scanned for more targets, but could find none. No one was firing back against them. He took the risk and raced towards

Hank's side, some thirty yards distant.

He found him a mess. His breath came in raspy gasps. Blood smothered his torso. Cooper cradled his head in his arms, "Why'd you do that? Why?"

Hank mustered a smile, "Dunno. Just came over me. Worked at Normandy against some lousy Krauts," blood dribbled out of the side of his mouth.

Cooper peered into his eyes, "I think you saved us all. Everyone found their courage and fired when they saw you charging."

Hank nodded slightly, "Yeah. I felt *useful* again." A gleam returned to his eyes.

"You're a damned useful man, Hank Hutchison."

He smiled dryly, "Not anymore." Hank let loose a long gurgle before coughing up a mouthful of blood onto his shirt. A few rapid, seizing breathes later and then he was gone. Cooper rocked his body back and forth in anguish.

Moments later, Lisa came up, put her hand on his shoulder and kneeled down to examine Hank. Quickly, she closed his eyes. "I'll take care of him."

Cooper wandered off, dazed for a moment. Dranko came up, "Dead?"

"Yeah, dead," he muttered.

"Surprising isn't it?"

"What?"

"Hank barely could walk. To see him running across the street, guns blazing, it was just surprising."

"It was amazing." Cooper said, shaking his head in disbelief. Then, he turned to the matters at hand, "What's our situation?"

"Well, Hank's charge inspired a flurry of gunfire from our side. There's about eight soldiers not in the Humvees. They're all dead or might as well be. Our guys...and gals," he said, correcting himself, "went a little crazy and just kept firing at them, even when they were down."

"Cooper! You alright?" A female voice called from afar.

Cooper turned and saw Angela on his doorstep. She had come out after the gunfire ended. He waved at her. Seeing her galvanized him and he looked back at Dranko, "We gotta get going. Appoint someone to police up the bodies and restore our defenses. You and me, we need to move. We leave in five."

"Yup, got it," Dranko said and moved down the street.

Cooper strode over to Angela, "How's Jake?"

"Same, but scared. I got him onto the ground. What was this all about? Soldiers? Attacking us?"

Cooper looked stolidly at the ground, "Yeah. Soldiers. Coming for *me*."

"What?" she gasped.

Cooper's tone grew harsh, "Yes. For me. That Major downtown, who Dranko and I went to see, must have talked to Mitchell. Must have decided they wanted me dead." He spat the last few words.

"Oh, my! I can't believe it."

"I wouldn't have either a half hour ago. It's obvious now."

"What's obvious?"

"Whatever happened at Admonitus, they were up to something big. We need to move quickly. Hopefully, we can get to Mitchell before the Major realizes his attack failed. We leave in four," he said, brushing past her to go into his house to gather the last of his supplies. He bandaged his arm as well, which thankfully, turned out to be a nothing more than a graze.

Chapter 32

At nine o'clock, they left Cooper's house. Cooper took the wheel of his sedan, with Angela in the passenger seat and her nurse's bag in her lap. Dranko was in the rear seat, passenger side. The M16 was stowed in the trunk, as was Angela's rifle. Cooper's shotgun was on the seat next to him, under a blanket. All three of them had their pistols holstered and concealed on their hips. They kept the shotgun on the seat, believing it would bolster the bodyguard story. Driving Cooper's unassuming sedan was similarly chosen to be less threatening than his pickup or Dranko's Jeep.

Slowly and precisely, they picked their way across the city. None of them had driven this far at night since the plague had struck, and the nervous tension clouded the air inside the car. The barricade that Cooper and Dranko had encountered earlier on Division lay deserted. One of the vehicles comprising the obstacle lay aflame, sending soot into the air, black against the dark night sky. There were no signs of bodies, only stains of crimson in a few places on the asphalt that were made visible by the burning car. Inside their moving car, the trio's alertness heightened, grips tightened on weapons, and their breathing became shallower. They drove onward.

The streets were largely deserted. Whenever they encountered another vehicle or pedestrians, they would circle each other like predators on the Serengeti, giving one another wide, wary berths as they passed. The city's blocks were as before, a hodgepodge of untouched areas, with others showing the effects of fire, bullet holes, or the dead. Only this time, there was more of the latter. They also encountered a few more roadblocks and barricades, but were able to skirt around those without incident.

Nearing the Morrison Street bridge on the corner of Grand Avenue, they encountered a solitary figure. The man was tall, pushing seven feet. He wore a dirty basketball tank top and matching shorts. The shirt was smeared with blood. They could not tell if it was his own or not. Dranko deftly maneuvered the car to give themselves separation from him. His eyes locked onto Dranko's and a thin, accusing finger pointed at him. Suddenly, his head fell backward and he laughed hysterically, "Off on an errand? What errands are there to do now? But the dying, the dying is all there is. No need to leave home for that!" As he rambled, his eyes fell back inside his head, so that only the whites were visible. Angela shivered.

"I hope that's not some kind of omen for our attack," Dranko complained. Cooper ignored him.

"I wish we could help the poor soul," Angela said sympathetically.

"Psychosis," Dranko mumbled. "It must be overtaking a good number of people as the situation overwhelms them."

"And medications run out," Cooper added.

As they crossed the bridge, they scanned in all directions. The elevation the bridge provided helped them see further around the city. To the south, fires burned.

"Sellwood," observed Cooper.

"Looks like it's spread beyond that area," Dranko said.

"Those hills to the west, there's fire there too. West Linn and Lake Oswego," Angela whispered, her voice weakened by disbelief.

In fact, scattered fires burned in all directions. Most looked limited to a house or two, but others appeared to cover entire blocks. They saw the eerie, blood-orange glow that signified fires in the distance as far north as Vancouver and as far south as Wilsonville. To their east, Mount Tabor and Powell Buttes limited their view. To the west, the hills there did the same. As they witnessed the city burning, Dranko couldn't help but shudder.

"Roll up the windows," Angela called. Dranko had them all cracked a bit to allow the night air in and prevent fogging of the windows. As if conjured by her mention, Dranko and Cooper both could now smell what Angela had already. The mixture of odors that assaulted them was a contradiction of allurement and repugnance. The nostalgic wood smoke, reminiscent of fireplaces and campfires, abutted sharply against the acrid smell of tires and other plastics burning. Most disturbing was that the sickly sweet smell of flesh burning mixed with the cavalcade of aromas.

"Maybe it's just animals," Dranko offered weakly as he pushed buttons to close the windows up tightly.

******

The road that led to Mitchell's home was lonely, with homes spread out amidst the forest. Cooper pulled the car off into a pullout and they quickly gathered their gear from the car. They disappeared into the woods. They made their way slowly and carefully in the near total darkness. The moon was at half-strength and her light battled mightily to peak through the towering trees above. Mostly, she failed.

Cooper picked his way carefully through the woods, taking each step in time. He carried a small flashlight with a red filter on it, but he used this with great caution. He was thankful that after only a few hundred yards, he was able to find a small clearing that was completely hidden from the road.

"Let's post up here. Change your clothing and we'll begin moving towards Mitchell's from here. He felt their heads nod.

The soft swishing noise of clothing moving was all that was heard as the three of them changed into the darker clothes they would wear in the assault on Mitchell's home.

"It's not a hot cup of joe, but it'll do," he heard Dranko say, pressing his hands toward theirs. Cooper felt something fall into his palms and he popped them into his mouth, tasting the delicious chocolate-covered espresso beans. He gobbled down a dozen or more, grateful for the caffeine rush. Angela murmured softly, "Mmm...."

Within seconds, they were moving again, leaving their unneeded clothing behind. The dark woods seemed to close in and swallow them up. *Perfect cover for an approach though.* About halfway there, they came to a stream that ran bubbling across their path.

Cooper pulled Angela close and breathed into her ear, "You follow this up to the road, cross it, get on the reverse slope and then move the last quarter-mile to take up position across from Mitchell's home. Take your first shot in fifteen minutes. Exactly, OK? Be careful."

Her hair brushed his cheek in a rapid up and down motion as she nodded. She found his ear, "You too." She gave him a kiss on his cheek and then disappeared into the dark. Cooper pushed aside the warmth that flushed across his face. He stared after her into the dark, until her shadow disappeared.

He and Dranko resumed moving, climbing slowly up a hillside that would bring them to the west side of Mitchell's estate. Their breathing was rhythmic as they fell into a deliberate climb. Cooper didn't risk using the penlight at all now, and so they picked their way carefully amidst the underbrush. Here, a loud crash to the ground on a tangled root could prove catastrophic.

Soon, between the trees, they could see the lights from Mitchell's home. It was a well-lit area, covered by floodlights. Cooper recounted the layout from the photographs: a large central mansion that must have covered five thousand square feet, a guest home about one-quarter of that, a garage as big as Cooper's home, and two other small outbuildings would dot the grounds. Twin tennis courts were to the south of the main home. An enormous swimming pool was to its west. As they moved closer, they could see the buildings come in and out of view as they moved between trees and up and down small rises in the ground.

They were probably a hundred yards from the edge of the woods when a shot rang out from where Angela would have been positioned. A loud yell of pain responded from in front of them. Cooper glared down at his watch. The illuminated dial screamed back at him. She was three minutes early!

"Damn!" he let out a whispered curse.

They began double-timing it through the woods. Cooper decided that speed mattered more than stealth, and flicked on his red-filtered flashlight so they could see the ground in front of them.

A second shot thundered from their left and this time they heard shattering glass, but no shrieks of pain. Dranko grunted next to him as a shin smashed into an unseen rock. They were both breathing hard. Covering wooded, uneven ground at breakneck speed, while carrying weapons, ammunition, and body armor was taking its toll.

An alarm sounded from the Mitchell home, just as Cooper and Dranko made it to the tree line.

A third shot from Angela found home as another painful shout came from near the garage to their left. About twenty yards in front of them was the first outbuilding they planned to leapfrog to. Dranko already had the M16 unslung from his back, aimed at a guard he saw on the balcony, and waited expectantly for Cooper.

Cooper deployed the shotgun, welcoming the heavy weight of steel in his hands. He pushed the safety to "off", scanned the ground in front of him, and sprinted to the building. He heard Dranko's M16 crack from behind him a moment after he began running. A loud yell, followed two seconds later by a loud thud told him Dranko's shot had found its mark. His boots kicked up forest duff as he ran, his heart pounding in his chest, and lungs sucking in the cold, stinging, air.

As he approached the outbuilding, the lone door swung open. A guard wearing black military-style clothing and carrying a pistol on his hip emerged. He bore a grim look of determination on his face; ready to do his duty and defend the Mitchell estate. He saw Cooper and the looming shotgun barrel. A look of shock rocketed across his face. He grabbed at the pistol and yanked it from his holster. In the long silence that precipitated death, the Velcro fastener that held the weapon sounded like angry lightning tearing across the sky.

Cooper fired from his hip, never breaking stride. At this range, there was no way to miss. If he'd had time, he would have felt pity. The guard only had a scant second to open his mouth wide in shock, before all nine pellets of 00 Buck blasted him squarely in the chest. His body was thrown back a few feet, where he slammed into the building. His body slowly slumped to the ground, leaving a dark streak along the wall. Instinctively, Cooper racked the shotgun's slide to chamber another shell.

He crashed into the wall. Without wasting a moment, he used the barrel of the shotgun to open the door all the way, flicked on the powerful flashlight attached to the barrel, and swept the small room inside. A bank of monitors adjoined a small desk, but no one else was inside. Cooper took a moment to scan the monitors. He found what he was looking for quickly: a bedraggled and silk pajama-clad Mitchell being ushered into a vault-like office by two armed guards, who looked nervously about them as they moved. Cooper studied the other monitors and was able to determine that the room they were in led off from the library which, in turn, was off the main hallway.

Cooper withdrew his head from the guardroom and slithered to the corner of the building. He looked up and around. Something slammed him in the shoulder, spinning him back and around behind the building. It took Cooper a second to realize that he'd just been shot. He plunged a hand underneath the body armor and thanked God when it came back dry. The pain was already beginning to throb in his shoulder, but he ignored it. He rotated his shoulder quickly to verify that no bones had been broken.

He heard Dranko heave his body into the shelter of the building just as he pushed the barrel of the shotgun past the wall and fired two shots in rapid succession. He fired into the area where he believed whoever shot him had done so. Hearing no shots in return, he snapped his head out and back to take in a quick view. The fleeting image of a guard slumped over a railing that ringed a large open porch told him what he needed to know. He quickly fished three shells from his pocket and reloaded the shotgun as Dranko inched his way toward him.

"No surprise here, eh brother?"

"None. It's bum rush time. It's twenty yards to the house, cover me!"

Cooper didn't wait for a response, but simply gathered his legs up underneath him and ran full speed at the body of the man that had just shot him. His shoulder cried out in protest as it rocked back and forth cradling the weight of the shotgun. Halfway there, a bullet made a loud "zing" noise as it zoomed past, just inches from his head. From behind him, Dranko let loose a three-round burst. Someone above him emitted a dull "oof." Cooper didn't bother looking up, thankful he'd made it to the porch without injury. He jumped over the low fence rail that circled the porch and slid up against the wall. Coming to a stop, he scanned the surrounding area, shotgun at the ready. Fifty yards away, he saw three guards racing in the direction of Angela's position. He heard another loud report and saw the muzzle flash out of the corner of his eye. One of the guards toppled to the ground, smashing his face into the dirt. He came up clutching his leg. The other two pressed onward. *I hope she retreats to safety soon.*

To his left, he saw Dranko sprint from the outbuilding. He didn't have a view of the second story, but assumed Dranko had looked it over good before running. No one else was in their vicinity paying attention to them. No sooner had Dranko thudded home next to him, than Cooper began a rapid duck-walk along the wall. He wanted to make sure his head didn't rise above the wall and be silhouetted against the window. His quadriceps began protesting loudly at such unusual exertion and Cooper cursed Mitchell for owning such an enormous home.

This side of the home was over fifty yards long. It felt like an eternity to Cooper before he reached the wall's end. He stretched himself flat on the ground and used his feet to push half his body past the wall, facing to his right. His instincts proved correct.

A pair of guards stood on either side of the massive door that led into Mitchell's home. The one closest to him held an M16 at the ready, looking to his left. Stupidly, his gaze was transfixed at head height. When Cooper came out at ground level, it took him a long second to see the movement and begin to react. By then it was too late.

Cooper's shotgun blast hit him just below the hip and angled upward. From only fifty feet away, the shell devastated him. He fell to the ground immediately, spewing blood in a wide arc. Cooper racked another shell into the chamber and pointed the barrel at the other guard who stood just a few feet further from his recently dispatched co-worker.

From behind the barrel, Cooper saw the guard's eyes fly wide open in shock and fear. His M16 clattered to the ground as he raised his hands above his head in surrender.

From the ground, Cooper used the shotgun to indicate the pistol strapped to his side, "Drop it!" he screamed.

The guard's hands were shaking as he slowly removed the

pistol and dropped it to the ground.

"Now, run home and don't you dare turn around!" The guard nodded quickly, turned on his heels and fled.

He heard another spray of gunfire from behind him and swung his head around. A guard, partially concealed behind the mammoth garage, pitched forward and fell to the ground. A lazy trail of smoke drifted upward from Dranko's muzzle.

The two men quickly assembled on either side of the door that led into Mitchell's home. Cooper told him what he'd learned on Mitchell's whereabouts inside from the guardhouse monitors. Cooper took the grenade from his chest pocket and showed it to Dranko, who nodded in the affirmative.

Cooper pulled the pin while Dranko pulled back on the door to open it just wide enough for Cooper to roll the grenade inside. The door's movement caused angry bursts of gunfire from within, which splintered the wood. Cooper released the trigger on the grenade, and rolled it as deeply as he could into the room. Then, they pulled the doors tightly closed once more.

A deafening explosion soon followed. The concussion forced the massive oak doors to push outward, rocking Cooper's and Dranko's shoulders. The pair wasted no time in pulling the doors wide open and, from a prone position, sprayed the room with several shotgun blasts and a full magazine from the M16.

The two men surveyed the room as they reloaded. It was thick with smoke from the gunfire and the grenade. Much of the room was obscured. An enormous chandelier had been half-wrecked from the grenade, but the remaining half still showered light into the room. They saw two bodies on the ground, about fifteen feet part, but neither moved. Dranko methodically fired two rounds into each one. The bodies twitched under the impact, but no more. *That guy is thorough,* Cooper mused.

An ornate, marble staircase led up to their left, while a long hallway beckoned to them just past the foyer. As they moved forward, Cooper couldn't resist chuckling at the sight of a statue of Venus with bullet holes stitched across her chest. *I guess losing your arms to the ravages of antiquity was not enough,* he thought sardonically.

******

From the monitors, Cooper was unsure which doorway off the hallway led to the room where Mitchell was huddled with his guards.

However, he knew that it wouldn't be the first couple of doors and that it was past the midpoint of the long corridor. He motioned for Dranko to follow him. As he did, he heard a flurry of gunfire from a distance, in the direction where Angela had posted up. *I hope you have already run off, Angela.*

Cooper moved like a cat, slouched, fast, and silent, as he slinked down the hall. Valuable paintings lined the walls. Various portraits of kings, queens, famous artists, and faeries looked down upon the two black-clad men skulking past. Cooper would have sworn he saw their expressions turn to disgust as they did so.

When he reached the first door on the left that could have possibly led to Mitchell's room he paused and readied himself for the entry. Dranko let out a low whistle. Cooper paused without looking back.

"Camera, end of hallway. Assume we are under observation, brother," he whispered, just loud enough for Cooper to hear.

Damn! They're watching us. No surprise here. Any entry they made now would be known and predictable by their opponents. It made getting through the door alive virtually impossible. He knew what had been decent odds for success had just turned much, much worse.

Suddenly, he had an idea. He hoped the artwork were originals, as he suspected.

His voice rang out loud, echoing down the hallway, "Mitchell, come out! I'm not here to hurt you! I just want to talk! If you don't, you'll be very upset in ten seconds...nine...."

Cooper kept glancing from one door to the next, unsure which of the half dozen that Mitchell—or his armed guards—might emerge.

He reached "one" without any movement from in front of him. Cooper raised his shotgun, leveled it at the nearest work of art and wrecked it with a blast of 00 Buck. Expensive art made Rorschach by pellet holes. Slowly, deliberately, he inserted a fresh shell into the Remington. He thought he'd heard a shriek of terror just after firing, but was unsure if it had been his ears playing tricks on him.

He called out again, "You've got a lot of great art out here, Mitchell. I'm sure you are fond of it. Come on out!"

Seconds ticked by with no response. So, Cooper began counting again, "Ten...nine...eight..."

Mitchell's voice was made tinny by the intercom, "You will guarantee my safety Mr. Adams?"

Cooper responded to the ether, "Yes, I will. I'm not here to kill you, just to talk."

More seconds passed and then the suction sound of a vacuum-sealed door opening came from the second door on the right. Mitchell stepped out, resplendent in a custom-tailored black suit.

"And your guards?" Cooper called out.

"You didn't include them in our negotiations, Mr. Adams. They will not be coming out. They are my insurance policy, if you will. If you kill me, at least you know you will have others to deal with."

The man's arrogance grated on Cooper again, "Sure enough. You tell me what I want to know and there will be no more problems tonight."

"Tell you? Christ, man. Why do you set your sights so low? Why do you not want more for yourself? I'll *show* you everything you want to know. It's too late now for you to do anything at all, anyway."

Cooper was momentarily taken by surprise and his mouth fell open by a scant degree. He chastised himself for it.

"Please do not be surprised, Mr. Adams. I am quite proud of what we have accomplished. I *want* to show you. Why don't you and your, ah, associate just step inside and I'll show you it all."

Cooper was leery of going inside, but he desperately wanted the information that Mitchell appeared to have. "Have your guards step outside. I'm not going to walk into a trap."

Mitchell waved his hands nonchalantly, "Fine, fine. Men, come outside, if you will."

Moments later, two burly men who looked almost identical in their gray uniforms, appeared at the door and joined them in the hallway. Their brown hair was cut short as were their matching mustaches. Each carried an M16 with side arms on their hips. The men eyed each other warily.

Mitchell spoke first, "Let's avoid one of those disagreeable Mexican standoffs that have become cliché," He flagged his arms at his men, "Gentlemen, you can shoulder your arms. I am quite confident that Mr. Adams is not some crazed man bent on revenge. He would have shot me already if that was the case. He is here for information, which I'm going to provide." The two guards complied immediately. Mitchell began leading them back into the room. Cooper and Dranko followed.

Chapter 33

Once inside, a dizzying array of monitors, the buzz of printers, and maps of the United States and the world were lit up with a multitude of colored lights and scrolling numbers and graphs. Two guards stood across the room, behind Mitchell on either side.

"Welcome to what we affectionately call Plague Central!" Mitchell declared, waving his arms in a wide arc held high as he spun around in a full circle.

"So this is where you watch the world dying?" Cooper asked, his words drenched in acid.

Mitchell laughed, "Watch? Again, my good man. You underestimate. This is where I *started* everything. But, I didn't start the world dying. *That* was already happening. What I have done is *begin to save* the world!"

From an unseen corner, flame spat with a deafening roar. Cooper felt like he'd been hit in the gut with a sledgehammer, but the body armor held up. Blood rushed to his head and the room began to swim. Absently and from a distance, he heard Dranko's words yell "Get down!" and then the muffled sound of more gunfire.

The sensation of something burning his arm, the sight of blood splattering across his face, and the acrid smell of cordite brought everything back into laser-like focus.

The two guards opposite him, flanking Mitchell, sprang into action. The one on the left grabbed at his holster to draw the pistol, while the one to the right rushed to remove the M16 from his shoulder. Cooper pointed the shotgun at the one on his left, guessing he'd have his gun ready first. He had the advantage of never having slung the shotgun onto his shoulder. He merely had to raise it to waist height and fire.

The guard bounced off the desk. Cooper was dimly aware of how shooting hurt his right arm like hell. He was further confused when the shotgun fell from his hands.

The guard had both hands on his M16 and was bringing it to bear. Cooper dove to his left and, finding his right arm useless, grabbed his pistol out of its holster with his left. The guard's M16 let loose a frantic burst of bullets where Cooper had been standing just a moment before. The bullets began chasing Cooper as they spit marble and dust from the floor. Cooper point shot at the guard, losing three rounds in rapid succession. Two of the three found their mark. One hit the man in the left leg and the second hit him squarely in the stomach. He slumped to the ground, dropping the rifle. Cooper finished him with a shot to the head. He scanned the room and saw a body lying in the corner, from where the original shot had come. Dranko must have got him.

Mitchell looked like a child caught with his hands in the cookie jar. The difference was he knew there could be deadly consequences for his duplicity. Cooper trained his pistol on him, remembering the flash bang grenade from the factory, "Keep your hands up!"

Dranko was swiftly at his side, "Keep your eye on him, brother. You got winged in the right arm. This bastard had a guard hidden. I spotted him right before he fired." Already, Dranko was digging in his backpack and wrapping a pressure bandage on Cooper's arm.

Cooper felt sick to his stomach, but he knew this was not solely from his wound. Mitchell's words had turned his world upside down and his head and stomach were swirling.

"Get me on my feet," he hissed at Dranko. Dranko looked at him in surprise, but lifted him onto his unsteady feet. He continued bandaging his arm.

Cooper stumbled across the few feet that separated him from Mitchell, "I hope you realize that little stunt of yours frees me from my word not to hurt you." He jabbed the muzzle of his pistol into Mitchell's temple. Mitchell tried unsuccessfully to cover a gulping sound with a cough.

"If you want to have any chance of saving your skin, you'll keep talking. Just what the hell did you mean when you said you *started* it all here?"

The fear left Mitchell's eyes and the fire returned. Only the cold steel of Cooper's pistol restrained him from parading about the room as he talked, "Just what I said. I *started* this illness."

Dranko looked up from dressing Cooper's wounds, "Why the hell would you do *that*?"

Mitchell's voice was so calm it sent chills down both men's spines, "Because we *had* to."

Cooper pressed the pistol further into Mitchell's head causing him to grimace in pain. Cooper's words spat out from between grinding teeth, "Stop speaking in riddles. Tell it plainly."

"Can you remove the pistol from digging into my head? I can think more clearly that way. There's so much to explain."

Dranko had finished bandaging the wound and Cooper

directed him to bar the door so they could avoid any more surprises. Cooper relaxed the grip slightly. A sliver of light shone between his pistol and Mitchell's head.

"Thank you," Mitchell said. "You want to know what we did? I'll tell you. We released this virus—codenamed Reset—about two weeks ago. It was designed to spread rapidly across the world, kill quickly with as much mercy as possible, and then mutate out of its lethality."

Both Cooper and Dranko looked at him in shock for several seconds. "What?" was all that Cooper could finally manage.

Mitchell looked like a schoolteacher teaching the slow class, "You wanted to know *what* we did here. So, I've told you. I'll tell you the *why* and then maybe you'll understand. We *had* to do this. Mankind was killing this planet with his extreme wastefulness and lack of care. You've heard of global warming, haven't you?"

Cooper responded first, "Of course." But, Dranko was quick to follow, "Yes, I've heard of it. The threat has been a little exaggerated hasn't it?"

Mitchell's long arm reached out, pointing a slender finger aimed right at Dranko, "You see! This is *exactly* why we needed to act. The threat has, if anything, been under-exaggerated. The scientists, using skepticism and caution as their religion, only released the most *conservative* estimates, the most proven, of the coming damage."

Dranko fought on, "But there were a bunch of scientists who disagreed and said there was nothing we could do about it."

Mitchell shook his head back and forth and looked truly morose, "You see? No, there were a *handful* of scientists who disagreed with the scientific consensus. But, of course you *heard from them* quite a bit, seeing as they were funded quite well by the likes of ExxonMobil. There are a handful of scientists who deny the existence of nearly *every* scientific theory. It doesn't mean those theories aren't accurate."

Cooper had grown impatient, "Yes, I get it. It's a threat. I knew some said it could have catastrophic consequences. But, do you mean to tell us that you started this plague to stop it?"

"That is *exactly* what we did. The world needed a Reset. A breather from the bustling economic activity that was belching carbon dioxide into the atmosphere at rates that would lead to runaway global warming, and a catastrophe for civilization as we know it. So, we designed this plague to do just that."

Cooper exploded, "What are you mad! You killed millions of people...including my wife!"

Mitchell replied coldly, "Actually, we expect the plague and the short-term civil disorder that will follow to kill between 500 and 750 million people. Gross Domestic Product will decline 20-30% for the next two to five years and it will take a decade or more for it to reach current levels. This respite will slow rising carbon dioxide levels dramatically, as well as give the world more time to *see* the effects of global warming and — finally — adopt the medium and long-term measures we need to avert worldwide catastrophe. Do you see now why we *had* to do this? I am sorry for your wife's death. But, her death will give your *son* a future he can actually *survive* in. Name one mother who wouldn't make that trade?"

Cooper looked on in exasperation at him, "Have you no faith in democracy? Yes, progress was slow, but we would have figured it out and done the right thing."

Mitchell scoffed and his words dripped with scorn, "Progress was slow? Progress was non-existent. Figure it out? Not in time. The democratic peoples of the world traded calamitous scientific warnings for SUVs and tons of plastic crap made in China. Worse yet, they did it without even *thinking* for two seconds about the choice." As he continued, his voice rose toward crescendo, "Think about it! Ninety-nine percent of the world's best scientists told us that if we did not lower our greenhouse gas emissions we would leave our children, and certainly our grandchildren, a planet with vastly diminished ability to support *civilization*. What was the answer of the most educated and free population the world has *ever* known? In short they said, 'Good luck with that, I'm going shopping.' *That* was what your precious democracy gave us."

Cooper gathered himself, "Yes, democracy *is* slow. But, it works. You took the easy way, the shortcut, and you took the lives of hundreds of millions of people to satisfy your cynical view of the world. The democracies — while slow — took on the great challenge of fascism and defeated it. We solved the crisis of the hole in the ozone layer and acid rain through *democratic* action. What *right* do you have to do what you did?"

Mitchell's eyes were like steel, "When you see a fire, you act. You put it out. You don't wait for a committee to decide what to do. That is what I did. You should be thanking me."

Something clicked in Cooper's mind, "Then show me. Prove to me why this would work and why it was the only way."

Mitchell's eyes brightened with optimism again. He took the next ten minutes showing Cooper graphs, charts, memos, and numbers all showing just what he had told Cooper. Midway through, Cooper stopped him.

"Hold on, pull that memo up again. Who was that one to?"

Mitchell didn't hesitate, "A Mr. Thomas Wilkins."

"Who is that?"

"He is a strategic advisor to the President."

Cooper scratched his chin, "I thought I recognized his name. He was a big fundraiser during the campaign, wasn't he?"

"Yes. Yes, he was."

"So, the President knew about this?" Cooper could not contain his shock.

"Well, there is plausible deniability and all that rubbish," he said waving his hand dismissively. "But, yes he knew. As did the major leaders in Congress and strategically placed corporate leaders. I assure you, the *right* people knew." Mitchell's pomposity irked Cooper.

Now, it was Cooper's turn to let out a low whistle, "Continue, please."

As Mitchell brought the presentation to a conclusion, Cooper handed him a flash drive that he had found lying on the desk, "Now, I want you to save all these documents and files onto this drive."

Mitchell's face clouded in fear, "Whatever for?"

Cooper smiled, "I'm going to give you a chance to be a hero, since that is what you think you are. I'm going to tell the world what you have done and you can answer directly to them."

He involuntarily staggered a step backward, "Don't be silly. The world is far too *emotional* right now. History will judge me a hero, but not now."

"Well, I cannot abide lies or those who tell them. And, I have a greater faith in the American people than you do. After all, I lost my wife and I haven't put a bullet through your brain, despite the opportunity. Maybe you'll be as lucky with the remaining six billion people left on the planet. Now *do* it," he gestured towards the flash drive with the pistol.

Mitchell grimaced at him, but he set to work saving the files. Cooper kept a close eye on him to make sure they were, indeed, being saved. After several minutes, Mitchell tossed the flash drive to Cooper.

"You know you will be making a huge mistake if you release those documents. You will be making a huge mistake for your *son*."

"What do you mean?" Cooper shot back.

"You know what I mean. Right now, the plague is petering out. You've probably seen it for yourself. No new infections for the past 24-

36, hours, right?"

"Right. What does that have to do with anything?"

"Already, for some the plague is now no more lethal than the common flu. In a few days, it will be like that for everyone as it mutates to its less lethal stage. Yet, society around the world teeters on the edge. If you release the information you have, you will send it over the brink, at least here in America. Think about it, all of society's major institutions colluding in this great scourge? The rioting you've seen so far will look like child's play. Not to mention what the rest of the world might *do* to America for unleashing a Weapon of Mass Destruction that has hit *every* country around the world," Mitchell finished with a satisfied smile on his face.

The truth of his words burned in Cooper's gut. He knew he was right. Mitchell saw the look on his face and seized the opening, "You don't want your boy, to grow up in *that* America, do you? I've given him a chance at a decent life…and his children's children…don't steal that away from him for some hollow sense of revenge."

"It's not revenge, it's justice. The truth must come out because lies do nothing but destroy everything they touch." He paused for a moment, contemplating. "You said America, eh?"

Mitchell waited before responding, warily, "Yeah, America."

"You invoke a powerful word, Mr. Mitchell. You remind me of something. You, sir, *gave up* on America. You gave up on our democracy and decided to take matters into your own hands."

"I had to," Mitchell pleaded.

"Well, then. If you gave up on America, then you gave up on juries and the right to trial as well, didn't you?"

Mitchell's face recoiled in horror. He raised his hands in front of his face, "No! Let me explain!" His voice screeched as thin as a razor.

Cooper calmly raised his pistol and pointed it directly at Mitchell's head, "I've had enough of your explaining." He fired once, the bullet piercing Mitchell's forehead and exploding blood and gore out the back of his head. His body dropped to the floor. Cooper stepped over him and fired twice more, once into the heart and another into his head. Looking down at the prostrate body of the once powerful man, he felt nothing but pity.

Then, Cooper strode out of the room, shotgun at the ready, and Dranko following close behind.

They made it to the car without incident and were grateful to find Angela there, waiting for them, hiding in nearby bushes, pistol in hand.

They drove toward home in silence, but Cooper could not help noticing that several more sections of the city had gone dark from lack of electricity.

Minutes later he stirred, "We have one more stop tonight." Dranko could guess.

Angela couldn't. "Where?"

"Julianne Wheeler's," Cooper said.

Chapter 34

When they arrived near her home, Cooper insisted that Dranko and Angela remain behind. Their protests were stifled by the fire in his eyes. He departed, wide strides bringing him to her home.

A candle burned inside, its faint light reaching the front door. Cooper covered the porch stairs in two giant leaps. He hammered on the door. In the night's silence, the violence echoed down the street.

He peered into the home through the door's glass, just as Julianne came into view from the hallway. He immediately saw the glint of a stainless steel revolver in her hand. Her eyes flew wide open when she saw him. She stopped for a moment, looking at him. He glared right through her.

Then, her weary, red eyes fell. Resigned, shoulders slumped, she shuffled towards the door. She set the revolver down on the entry table and opened the door.

As soon as the lock fell open, Cooper pushed his way in. She winced as he grabbed her shoulders, shaking her, "Why?"

Tears darkened her flannel shirt. She remained mute.

"Why," Cooper pleaded again. He rocked her back a half-step, forcing her head up. She collapsed to the ground. He knelt with her, grasping her chin between his fingers. She inhaled deeply. Her vulnerability sapped his anger.

"Mitchell's dead," he rasped.

She nodded slowly, "I guessed as much." Her words were unfeeling.

He waited. Her breathing steadied.

"I'm sorry," she whispered.

Cooper remained motionless. But, his eyes revealed his desperate plea for an explanation.

"I thought it was the best thing. The right thing. He was *so* damned convincing. The science was...*is*...compelling. We *were* running out of time. You've got to believe that!" Her eyes flashed back and forth, scanning for his reaction.

He said nothing. He looked blankly at her. His emotion drained away.

He despised the rising urge inside that beckoned him to reach out and comfort her.

She lowered her head, "We were wrong. We should have let it

happen. We should have let mankind live through the consequences," she paused, her fingers tracing an outline around one of her bruises, "of its *own* making. Not ours." When she finished, she looked back up at him.

When their eyes met, he was drawn towards her, despite himself. He clapped his hands on his knees and stood up abruptly.

"You must hate me," she lamented.

He paused, contemplating her words. "No. I don't. I saw the best man I've ever known, my father, be misled by someone he trusted. So, I don't blame you for that. But, its worse than that," he looked down again at her.

"What's worse?"

"I *cannot* hate you."

"Even though you want to?" She asked, her eyes pleading for understanding.

His face betrayed nothing. He turned and walked away.

She watched him go. A hint of a smile alighted onto her face as she pondered his last words. Then, anguish overtook her once more. She collapsed into herself, weeping.

When he returned to the car, Dranko and Angela looked up at him expectantly. Cooper lurched into the car wordlessly. Neither asked. Dranko did not smell fresh cordite coming from Cooper's pistol. He was surprised, but did not ask his friend any questions about it.

Silence consumed the car as they drove towards home.

******

A few blocks from their home, Dranko broke the silence. "You think the military will be waiting for us?"

Cooper roused from his stupor, "I'd be surprised. They sent a squad at us earlier and that didn't work. He's low on manpower. The city's in chaos. He's got a lot of problems. If he had extra men, I think we would have seen them at Mitchell's. He doesn't have a platoon to send our way."

Dranko nodded, "True. But, next week may be a different story. He may get more men. He may..."

Cooper raised his hand dismissively, "Not now."

Dranko stopped and smiled to himself, "Sure, brother. Not now."

******

When he returned home, Lisa met him at the door with open arms and excitedly told him that Jake's fever had broken. She was confident he would soon recover. Cooper collapsed onto his knees from sheer joy. Tears streamed down his face unabashedly. Minutes later, he looked in on Jake, but he was fast asleep. He watched him for a while, kissed him on the forehead, and quietly left the room. He knew had one more thing to do this night.

******

He found Dranko at home and asked to use his computer, since he had a functioning generator.

"What are you gonna do, brother?"

"I don't know yet."

He sat down in front of the computer with a heavy heart and a jumbled mind. As he thought about what to do, the past and the future collided furiously. His thoughts swirled back and forth between what lies had done to his father and what future might await his son.

Finally, he shook his head to clear his thoughts and began to write a message to the world. He wrote about truth. His words recalled the value of democracy. He railed about the need for accountability to one's actions. But, he also pleaded for the world's forgiveness. Mostly, he wrote about forgiveness for a sin he had not himself committed.

In the background, the radio was frantic with unconfirmed reports that the planes carrying Chinese policemen and medical personnel carried soldiers instead. Rumors swirled that such planes had landed at several airports across the western United States. He bolted upright when the announcer said, "Portland...Oregon" while reciting the list of cities.

He continued writing as the first rays of morning sunlight streaked through Dranko's basement windows.

He looked at what he had written, satisfied.

He had included every major newspaper, radio, television, and online news outlets he could think of across America and from around the world in the email message.

He hit send and walked upstairs.

Dranko looked at him and saw how his friend had seemed to age a decade in the past few hours, "So, what'd you do?"

"I did what any father would do. I did my best to make sure my boy grows up in a world that values the truth and believes in democracy. If it's a harsher world, so be it. I watched lies destroy my father's life. I won't watch them soil my life, my son's, or my country's."

He walked out of Dranko's home and returned to his own. Angela was seated at the table, cleaning the rifle. She looked up with uncertain eyes when he came in. He nodded once at her. She understood. She rose and took several steps toward him. He saw a deep reservoir of comfort in her eyes. He waited, thinking. Then, he walked towards Jake's room.

As he stepped past her, he clasped her fingers for a moment. They gazed at each other, smiles creeping onto their faces. The electricity of the unknown passed between them. He let her fingers go and continued onward.

His thoughts drifted to Julianne, trying to understand why he couldn't hate her for what she had done. The answers that came troubled him, so he deliberately pushed them aside.

He collapsed into bed next to Jake, despite the unmistakable sounds of small arms fire coming from the direction of the airport. Within minutes, he was fast asleep, breathing in rhythm with his son.

End

Turn the page to read the first chapter in the sequel:

Brushfire Plague: Reckoning

Chapter One from *Brushfire Plague: Reckoning*

Startled, Cooper Adams shuddered awake and bolted upright in bed. His rifle was in his hand without a thought. His heart thundered in his chest, revving up for action as adrenaline raced into his veins. Alert eyes darted about, scanning for danger. His ears fixated on any noises coming from outside or inside his home. They told him nothing was amiss and he emitted a long exhale. He relaxed his nearly six-foot frame, put the rifle against the wall, and laid back into the bed. He stared at the ceiling for a long moment, deliberately slowing his breath and collecting his thoughts. He couldn't tell if some random noise had woken him or if it had been another fitful dream.

Next to him, his eleven-year old son, Jake, lay sound asleep. His chest rose and fell in a steady rhythm, while his eyes moved rapidly about, underneath closed eyelids. *Dreaming. I can only hope for sweet ones.* A chill ran down his spine as he thought about his son's encounter with the Brushfire Plague. The fever had broken just last night. Without thinking, Cooper put the back of his hand to his son's forehead for reassurance and smiled in relief.

His gaze drifted back to the white, monotonous ceiling. For a moment, Cooper wistfully thought the last twenty-four hours could have been a dream, but the distant crackle of gunfire belied the thought. The fact that his son, instead of his wife, slept next to him burned it out of him. The plague had merely scared his son, but it had taken his wife, Elena. It had only been two weeks since she breathed her last breath, but the world was already so different that his life with her was steadily turning into a dream-like memory. Now, he realized what had jolted him awake. He *had* been dreaming of Elena and was terrified that he could not recall her eye color. If the world had somersaulted in just two weeks, it had added a barrel roll in the last twenty-four hours when Cooper learned that the calamitous Brushfire Plague was a deliberate act of men and not some dreadful accident of nature. *A deliberate act that will end up slaying one billion people.* Ethan Mitchell, a zealous CEO of a biotech company, had argued that his actions served the greater good by saving mankind from the civilization-destroying effects of climate change and a ravaged planet. Cooper's mind still whirled at the facts and arguments made by the man who had released the Brushfire Plague across the planet. Luckily, Mitchell's brain thought about these things no more. Cooper had made

1

sure of that. He gritted his teeth at the thought. A pained, wry smile crept onto his face, as he thought of Mitchell's body, cold now, lying in the man's mansion.

A billion dead. The thought staggered Cooper and his breath caught in his throat. Unlike anyone else, Cooper had had the satisfaction of putting a bullet into the brain of the main progenitor of this horrendous act. He did not doubt that Mitchell deserved death for what he had done, but revenge had not lightened his heart nor dulled his pain. He also uniquely carried the burden of having told the world the truth of what he'd learned, with consequences still unknown. The magnitude of those possibilities gnawed at him like a lazy rat nibbling rope.

Cooper was also perplexed by his feelings toward the woman, Julianne Wheeler, who had assisted Mitchell in all that he had done. He wanted to hate her and failed to understand why he didn't. He desperately hoped it was simply the lingering effects of the deep, primal, connection he'd felt toward her when they had met. He could not deny the instant connection. He remembered an oft-quoted line; *the heart wants what it wants.* However, this instant connection happened before he knew anything about her role in the conspiracy to unleash mass death on humanity. So far, this knowledge had done little to sever the bond. While his brain warred with his heart to make it so; the heart kept winning.

Next to him, Jake stirred. His eyes fluttered and opened. He saw his father and smiled. Cooper curled his arm underneath his son's head and pulled him closer.

"Mornin', boy."

"Good morning, dad."

"How are you feeling?"

"Tirrrr-ed," he yawned with a gaping maw. "I feel really tired, dad. But, I *do* feel better. For a while, I thought I was gonna catch on fire!"

"Yeah, you had the fever bad. But, it's passed now. Lisa says you're going to recover," Cooper said, sharing the report he'd received last night from the woman who was their friend, neighbor, and nurse.

Jake smiled incredulously, eyes twinkling and moistening, "I'm not going to die...like mom." His words were caught between question and statement by the force of wonder.

Cooper pulled his son into an embrace, "No, you're not going to die like your sweet, sweet mother." His own heart swelled with a torrent of love for his son and his dead wife; sorrow for the latter and unbridled newfound hope for the former. They held each other for a long time. Finally, curiosity grabbed ahold of Jake.

"So, what happened last night?"

Cooper burst out laughing so loudly it echoed off the walls of Jake's bedroom. When he finally caught his breath, he blurted out, "What *didn't* happen would be a better question, son!"

Jake grimaced in annoyance and returned with mockery in his voice, "Alright then…what *didn't* happen last night!"

Cooper tussled his son's hair. As he did so, levity fled the room like animals fleeing a wildfire. Cooper breathed deeply and looked his son squarely in the eye. "I learned last night that this Plague wasn't an accident, son. It was started by some stupid, stupid…and misguided men."

Jake's eyebrows furrowed in confusion. Tears welled up in his eyes. His breath came in fitful gasps. His lips quivered. "You mean…they…someone *killed* mama on purpose," he wailed between pain-wracked sobs.

Cooper pulled his son in close once more, allowing him to bury his head into his chest. He rocked him back and forth in a vain attempt to comfort him. He breathed more and then said, "Yes, son, they did." His stark words of confirmation sent Jake into another round of deep sobs. Like any father, his son's pain cut him to the core. His fists clenched and his jaw grinded his teeth as rage against Ethan Mitchell surged once more. Then, listening to his son's sobbing, it hit him.

With one billion dead, almost every single person on earth is going to feel this newfound confusion, pain, and fury when they learn this wasn't some malevolent act of Nature…but a calculated act of Man. A man who lived in America. In Portland, Oregon. It slowly dawned on him that a grief-fed rage would consume the world just as the Brushfire Plague was receding.

The realization stunned him. His stomach turned and saliva filled his mouth. He fought back against the presage to vomit. *How did I miss that?* Cooper knew the answer before the question had finished flashing through his mind. *The truth blinded me to everything else.* His fists became tight balls and his nails dug into his palms. He grimaced, trying to steel himself to the decision he'd made just hours before. His heart and mind roiled in a tug of war over right and wrong and what he had done.

"Damn the consequences, the world deserves to know the truth," he shouted defiantly, his voice thundering across the walls.

"What?" Jake asked and only then did Cooper realize he had

3

yelled what he'd been thinking.

"Nothing, son. Nothing," Cooper responded laconically, his eyes downcast.

Jake continued, "Why? Why'd they do it?"

Cooper's unwavering penchant to the truth led him to do his best to relay the thinking that had driven Ethan Mitchell to his deadly act of destruction, "You've heard of global warming, right, son?"

Jake's eyebrows raised in confusion, "Yeah. What has that got to do with anything?"

"Well, this guy, Ethan Mitchell, believed that we weren't going to deal with it and that it would have eventually wiped out civilization."

"What?" Jake mouthed in disbelief.

"I can't fully explain it. But, he believed that, left unchecked, global warming would have heated the planet so much that agriculture would have become near impossible, weather would have become extreme, sea levels would have risen so much that it would have put many major cities underwater. In short, civilization would have ended. So, he thought it was a better idea to *intentionally* kill hundreds of millions *now* to prevent this."

Jake shook his head in disbelief, "But...but, that's wrong." Cooper watched as his son struggled to understand. "How could he decide something like that all on his own?"

"That's exactly what I told him." Cooper weighed his next words carefully. Then, he decided to go forward. "That's exactly what I told him, right before I killed him." His words trailed off.

Jake looked up at Cooper, his eyes wide open in shock, and "You killed him?"

"Yes, I killed him. What he did was wrong. So wrong, that he deserved to die," Cooper's words rolled off his tongue, slowly, deliberately.

Jake absorbed the words even more slowly and a long silence hung in the air. His eyes searched his father's face for understanding or meaning. "How do you feel now?"

"Empty," he said flatly. He paused, drawing a deep breath. He continued with tired words. "It had to be done. He deserved it. It wasn't his *right* to decide the fate of so many. But, it isn't bringing your mother — or anyone else — back."

Jake simply nodded, with vague understanding. "Well, I'm glad he's dead." His son spat on the ground, acting the grown-up. Cooper did not like the snarl that latched onto his face when he did so.

4

"There's something else you need to know. It's more important than any of this." Jake nodded once more, sitting up straighter, readying himself for what was to come.

"Last night, I told the world what I learned, too. I told the world everything. And, I very much fear the consequences. "

Jake interrupted him, "What consequences? The truth is always the right thing. You've taught me that." His last words were laced with the certain truth of childhood.

Cooper nodded slowly, "That's right. The truth is always right. But, I've also taught you that the truth isn't always easy. And, this truth is probably the most difficult of all."

"What do you mean?"

"Think about it, Jake. Think of how sad and angry it made you to realize that your mother didn't just die — but that she was *killed* by this terrible act. The *whole world* is going to get very, very angry. Our country already teeters on the edge. There's *already* been so much chaos and violence. I fear there will be much more."

Jake's eyes slowly morphed from being clouded with confusion to the clarity of understanding. His voice trammeled, "Then, why'd you do it?"

Cooper's eyes wrinkled and his lips curled into a skeptical smile, "Son, I'm not sure I had much choice." Cooper paused and rubbed the stubble on his chin, "But, I guess I did have some choice. At the end, I have faith that we will get through all of this...even knowing the truth. It might be painful and likely worse in the short-term, but the world must...it *must* know the truth. What we do with it is *our* choice. *I* couldn't deny the world that choice. Otherwise, I'd be just as bad as Ethan Mitchell. You understand?"

Jake's mind sorted through his father's words, "I think so. I think so, dad. I just hope it doesn't get too much worse. It's already been very, very bad."

Cooper began to nod in agreement, but a furious pounding on his front door caused his heart to race once again and his mind to doubt his son's hope would be proven true.

****

As Cooper neared the door, there was no mistaking the familiar timbre of his friend, Paul Dranko's, voice yelling from the other side, "Cooper, it's me, Dranko. Open up, brother, open up!"

Cooper yanked the door open and burst out laughing as he

5

caught Dranko in mid-yell, his mouth twisted half-open, "With an adorable face like that, I can see why you've always had trouble with the ladies, my friend."

Dranko scowled and brushed past him, "Screw you. I had problems with the ladies because no one wanted to believe our precious civilization would ever hit a bump in the road...until now, of course." Cooper knew this was true. Since he had known Dranko, the man had been consumed with all manners of theorizing and preparing for the myriad ways that civilization might collapse. For Cooper, it had been an endearing idiosyncrasy. He could only imagine the problems it had caused Dranko in the pre-Brushfire Plague dating world, however. Now? Well, now Cooper understood very well that Dranko's preparations had saved his life and those of many around him.

Cooper turned to follow his friend inside, closing the door behind him, "Just look on the bright side..." Dranko's cocked eyebrow interrupted him, but Cooper bludgeoned onward, waving his hand, "Yes, I know! For a dyed in the wool pessimist like you, looking on the bright side is damn near impossible. But! Try it out. Just imagine how all of the beautiful women whom you dated over the years are, right now, wishing they had stayed with that crazy bastard who was preparing for the end of the world!"

Dranko returned Cooper's beaming smile with a deepening grimace, "Like I said, screw you. You're an ass. Are you ready to get down to what I came to talk about or do you want to discuss my romantic life's prospects in the post-Plague world?"

"Fine, fine," Cooper said, turning serious. "What have you got for me?"

"First, how's Jake doing?"

"Fantastic. Still a little weak, but he's looking good."

Dranko clasped his hands together in excitement, "That's great news. Great news, brother!"

"Don't I know it? We got lucky. Very lucky he caught it as the strain was deliberately mutating itself to a weaker form," Cooper answered.

Dranko nodded. "That's good. I'm afraid I have some bad news for you. You ready?"

Cooper nodded in return, "Yeah. Shoot. I figured you had something bad from how you were banging on my door."

"Well, the world has been on fire with the news you dropped on them. Half the world seems to be calling what you've said the biggest hoax since H.G. Wells' *War of the Worlds*."

Anger at being called untruthful, even by strangers, flashed across Cooper's face, "And, what are the other half saying?"

"The good news is that they believe what you've put out there."

"What's the bad news?"

"They are really pissed off about it." He paused, his eyes squinting, "And, I mean pissed off on a Biblical scale."

Cooper's eyes dropped to the floor, "Yeah, I was thinking about that very thing as I told Jake about what I'd learned and what I had done."

Dranko nodded in agreement, "Losing a loved one is bad enough. When it's been done on purpose, revenge is the first...and often last...thing people feel."

Cooper moved past his friend, striding toward the kitchen, "I had to do it. The world deserves to know the truth, dammit!"

Dranko turned to follow him, "Look, brother, I ain't arguing with you. I am just here to tell you the reaction to that truth, mainly so we can be prepared for it."

Cooper drew his pistol from its holster, laid it on the counter, and leaned back against it, facing Dranko, "Yeah, I know. Keep going."

Dranko settled in, legs in a wide stance and arms folded, "Like I was saying. The other half is pretty damn upset. On the foreign front, recriminations and demands for justice have already started pouring in to our government." Dranko paused and averted his eyes from his friend's.

Cooper looked exasperated, "C'mon. What's the worse news? I can handle it."

"So far, that's been the official reactions. You have opposition parties in many countries screaming for retribution. Some of the most radical have already started calling for nuclear strikes on us. It's already being called an unprecedented 'worldwide genocide' that an American thrust upon the world."

Cooper exhaled loudly; his left hand ran raggedly through his black hair, while his left grasped the countertop until his knuckles turned white, "Jesus. I didn't see that coming." He shook his head once, as if to clear it.

"Yeah, me neither. On the domestic front, it's similarly bad. There are renewed outbreaks of violence and rioting. However, they've shifted from happening near medical and food facilities to anything that is government related. Hell, the funniest has been a report of a firebombing at the U.S. Patent office!"

7

"I wish I was in the mood to laugh, because that *is* ridiculous," Cooper intoned. "How's *our* government responding?"

"As you might expect. They are denying any knowledge of the events in question, promising a swift investigation and severe and unprecedented punishment if they discover a shred of truth about the allegations against Admonitus and the Mr. Ethan Mitchell."

Cooper's eyes grew quizzical, "They haven't announced that he's dead?"

"Nope. But, you'd better be happy about that!"

"Why?" Cooper asked.

"Haven't you thought about it? They'd tie it to you and add murder to the list of charges against you."

Cooper's face went slack in surprise, "I hadn't thought about that. I guess I didn't think of a lot of things that might happen by telling the world the truth." Inwardly, he cursed himself for not having thought it all through. A wave of dizziness hit him and his arm cast about until it found a wall to steady himself with.

Dranko watched him and waited until he was all right before going on, "Well, friend, you can be impulsive sometimes. But, that's why you have me around, to worry about all the angles for you!"

Cooper's smile returned to his face, "Thanks, brother. But, you are the ugliest nursemaid I've ever seen."

"Funny." Dranko quickly held up his hand. "Oh, I almost forgot. The President is holding a full press conference in about a half hour about all of this, too."

"Really? Well, we'll have to tune in," Cooper said, as a wry grin spread across his face. *I wonder how they will try to spin themselves out of this one.*

****

The sharp rap of a cane against his door interrupted Dranko's response. Cooper walked to the door and before he could call out, a raspy voice shrilled from outside, "Let me in Cooper, or I'll have to blow your door down!"

Cooper and Dranko exchanged bemused smiles. Lily Stott's voice was unmistakable and the old woman's wit and wisdom were legendary in the neighborhood. Her reputation had only grown since the outbreak of the plague.

"Coming ol' darlin'," Cooper said, doing his best to mimic Lily's accent from her native Kentucky.

He opened the door and her diminutive frame greeted him, as did her expansive personality, "Ya know, if I was a few decades younger…or you a few decades older, that accent just might get me into a friendly way with ya, Coop." Her piercing blue eyes lit up as she lilted the last few words.

Cooper couldn't stop the blush that ran into his cheeks and he flashed a smile at his embarrassment, "Lily, I know you didn't come over to charm me, so what can I do for you?"

"I came here for this," she said as she rapidly closed the space between them and wrapped Cooper into a tight embrace. It was far tighter than he would imagine an eighty-something woman could pull off. He burst out laughing in surprise.

"What's gotten into you, Lily?"

She held him in the bear hug for several seconds longer. Cooper cast a "help me" gaze at Dranko, who only smiled in return, arms crossed.

"You're on your own, brother. I ain't crossing swords with Ms. Stott," he exclaimed.

At that, Lily released him, "Oh, fool's feathers, you young boys can't handle something you ain't planned or predicted, can you?" She stepped back from Cooper so she could look him directly in the eyes before continuing, "*That* was to thank you for what you done. Paul told me this morning it was you who sent the world the truth about this terrible thing. Plain and simple. What you done was right. And, I know it didn't come easy to go on and tell that truth."

Cooper shrugged nonchalantly, "You know me, Lily. After what happened to my dad, I can't do anything *but* tell the truth." He choked on the last word, as he did every time he was reminded of how deceit had destroyed his father's life. As a boy, he had watched his father wither away in prison, put there by the lies of other men. That wrenching experience had led Cooper to a life of absolute honesty; even in the most difficult of situations.

"Pig doodles! Don't hand me that. You coulda *kept quiet*. I seen you do that, Cooper, because that ain't the same as lying. At least to you it ain't. I believe the good Lord would take a different view. No offense," she said waving her hand dismissively.

"None taken. That's true, I thought about just keeping quiet. I thought about it quite a bit."

"I bet you done. So, don't try to shirk off your hero name tag. I'm planting it on you. And, you know what?"

"What?"

"You know me. Once I aim to do something, it sticks like a dried up bug's wing to flypaper!"

Cooper and Dranko both laughed at that, "I won't even try to deny the truth of that, Lily."

"Alright, so thank you for telling us what really happened. It was mighty difficult to swallow, with so many dying and it being done *on purpose*. That is a bitter pill to choke down," her voice rising to mimic that of a Southern preacher on Sunday. "But, it says so in the Bible, 'the truth shall set you free', so what you did was the *only* thing a righteous man could have done. Yes indeed, Amen!" She clapped her hands in exultation as she finished.

"Well, you're welcome," Cooper said awkwardly. "I don't feel heroic or righteous. I just did what I knew I *had* to do to wake up feeling right about myself and my boy." His eyes gazed into the distance as he talked, "People deserve the truth, even when it's tough to hear. In fact, when you think about it, that was a problem in the country before the plague...no one wanting to tell unpleasant truths."

"You're right about most regular people. But, people like me were always telling you all the truth about what might happen. You just didn't want to hear it," Dranko contravened.

Cooper pushed him with an open palm in the chest, "Can you give it a rest? How many more times do I have to hear some version of 'I told you so' from the great Paul Dranko? Sometimes, I think you helped Mitchell out just so you could be right about *one* of the versions of the end-of-the-world you were always spouting off about." He turned to Lily, "Can you help me put a stop to this and give *my medal* to Dranko instead? I think it might shut him up!"

Dranko pushed him back, "Alright already, I made my point and you made yours. How about we leave it there?"

"Good enough for me," Cooper returned.

Lily wagged her head deliberately back and forth and moved to the door, "You two remind me of my boys, always bickering like they say old women do. But, take this as the truth, when it comes to fussin', you boys are far worse than the worst of any withered up old women I ever did see!" She exited the house and took deliberate care descending his front steps. When she reached the bottom, she looked back, "You all have a good night now, hear?"

Cooper gave her a warm smile, "Sure thing, Lily and thank you for stopping by. You are very kind."

Lily just nodded her head and ambled off back towards her home. Cooper closed the door and turned to Dranko, "So, we can fire up my radio in a little bit and listen to the President?"

Dranko stepped towards the door, "Better yet, come over to my place. I can get it up on the computer most likely."

"Your internet is still working?"

"It is. I don't know how much longer, but my satellite link up is still working its magic."

"Okay, I'll be over on the hour."

Dranko opened the door, left, and then shut it.

Cooper decided to spend the remaining time with Jake before listening in to the President's message.

****

Later, they'd gathered at Dranko's place. Cooper, Dranko, and Jake huddled in his basement room where Dranko had stockpiled all manner of communications equipment over the years. When they'd arrived, Dranko had surveyed the spectrum for their benefit. He had old vacuum-tubed radios that could survive the Electro-Magnetic Pulse he feared would eventually happen from a nuclear device detonated above America. He had several solar and hand-cranked radios that could operate without batteries. However, his most elaborate set-up was reserved for the myriad of ways he could stay connected to the Internet: satellite, cable modem, and satellite phone topped the list. Dranko's small battery of stockpiled weapons had enabled the neighborhood to defend itself during the chaos thus far. Now, Cooper was thankful for his friend's communications equipment that had allowed him to spread his message to the world about the Brushfire Plague and, now, listen to the President's response.

The familiar podium and Seal of the President greeted them as Dranko secured a live streaming telecast of the speech over the Internet. Cooper tuned out the familiar greetings and the platitudes of sorrow the President offered his fellow Americans. His ears literally perked up when he got to the meat of the speech:

"In this trying time for our nation, a time of horrendous loss for so many, a time of unfathomable grief, a time when the strength of our country is being tested like never before, I first want to share that the hopeful rays of God's mercy are shining once again. That's right, my fellow Americans, the first signs that the scourge of the Brushfire Plague is finally abating."

"I receive briefings from the Centers for Disease control three times daily. It pleases me beyond measure that over the last forty-eight

11

hours, those briefings have told the same story: both the infection rate *and* the morbidity rate from this terrible plague have been falling steadily. In short, this means that the number of those becoming infected is falling. More importantly, the rate of those who do contract this disease and then die from it is declining rapidly. At the conclusion of my remarks, Dr. Charles Holmes, the Director of the CDC will speak to the specifics. But, the layman's version is that the virus is mutating to a less lethal form. These developments mean great hope to those who are now sick, and even greater hope that our nation has passed through the darkest hour of this devilish calamity. Rest assured, we will be monitoring this situation carefully, but the best medical minds are confident that this trend will continue."

The President paused as his face turned from one filled with hopeful and sympathetic lines to ones far grimmer. The transformation was slow, subtle, but complete. Despite himself, a riot of goose pimples erupted across Cooper's body.

"However, amidst this moment of enormous hope and guarded relief, I must also respond to a new threat to our great nation. Most of you have probably seen the scandalous and unfounded reports spread across the Internet and some irresponsible media outlets that the Brushfire Plague was no accident. That it was *intentionally started* by a company called Admonitus, based in Portland, Oregon. Yes, I know, my fellow Americans, it is a shocking allegation that is beyond the pale." Cooper felt the others' eyes on him as the President recalled Cooper's email to the world's media detailing the devastating truth that he had learned about the genesis of the Brushfire Plague. The email sharing Mitchell's darkest confessions.

"I want to assure you all that once this administration learned of that frightful rumor, we launched a full scale investigation to determine its veracity. In the reports, you may have also heard that my administration was *aware* of this diabolical plan *and* possibly assisted its implementation."

His face grew angry, dark lines outlining his eyes and his jaw firmly set with muscles twitching, "You may only guess how outraged I was when I first heard of this nonsensical drivel. But, let me state plainly, and for the record, *no one* in my administration knew of such a plan, if it even existed. It is an affront to the honor of my family that such a thing has even been uttered. My family has suffered losses, as well. We were not spared from the death that has spread across our nation. It is incomprehensible to me that any madman *would* have done this on purpose. But, I swear on the word of God, that my administration had no warning of it nor did we enable or abet any such crazy plan."

"We have found no evidence, thus far, that this plague was intentional. But, our investigation will continue, and we will transparently share with the American people any, and all, results that we learn. As I talk to you, officials are on the ground in Portland and we are moving to secure the offices and facilities of Admonitus and the home of its CEO, Ethan Mitchell."

"I wish to say to my fellow Americans, and our neighbors around the world, *America* did *not* start this terrible plague of biblical proportion. *We*, as a nation, did not do…or even conceive…of any such thing. And, I promise you, if we learn that a crazed man or a company led by a madman *did* this, the punishment will be swift and unprecedented. You can know *this* as truth!" He pounded his fist against his desk with a loud thud.

"Now, let me turn to our efforts to track down the origin of these dreadful rumors. The potential harm of these unfounded reports is already evident. Sadly, they have already sparked attacks against innocent government officials and the wanton destruction of property. For that reason, our efforts to track down who started these vicious rumors are being conducted under the auspices of the Patriot Act and this is being treated as an act of terrorism against America."

Once more, he paused for effect. "This decision was not taken lightly, as we deeply value the right of Freedom of Speech within my administration. However, the spreading of these unconfirmed reports at a time of great trial for America *is* a dangerous act. Already, this rumor has resulted in violence upon the innocent. I'm sure that the decent and God-fearing people of America will agree with me that the threat to our shared national security posed by these lies trumps any right to free speech."

The camera now zoomed in further, almost imperceptibly, but the effect was dramatic. Cooper felt the hair on his neck rise. "I wish to announce that we have a person of interest in this investigation. Our evidence indicates that this person may know about, or have been directly involved in, a series of dreadful acts including the killing of Mr. Ethan Mitchell, the CEO of Admonitus. Most importantly, we believe this person is responsible for spreading panic and violence by proclaiming these irresponsible—and unfounded—allegations. This person of interest is Mr. Cooper Adams, of Portland, Oregon."

The President's words sucked all the air out of the room where Cooper, Dranko, and Jake sat. Silence engulfed the room. Both Jake and

Dranko looked at Cooper in shock.

"As you might imagine, prior to this crisis, we would have this person in custody before I would make such an announcement. However, our resources are already taxed beyond heroic measure and I refuse to allow the apprehension of this person to take precedence over tending to the greater, and more immediate, needs of our nation. I am coordinating efforts with the Governor of Oregon to apprehend Cooper Adams and to bring him in for questioning. In the meantime, I urge anyone with information on his whereabouts to contact their local authorities. I also wish to remind my fellow Americans of their power to make a citizen's arrest in the event they encounter Cooper Adams and can secure him until the authorities arrive."

Dranko let out a low whistle, "Christ, Cooper. He just declared open season on you!"

Cooper's face gave Dranko a sharp rebuke as he inclined his head slightly to remind his friend that Jake was in the room with them. Dranko continued undeterred, "I know you don't want to hear this, but we need to get out of here. As soon as they can get themselves organized, they will be coming for you."

"Dranko, we've been through this before. I won't leave my home. It's all I have left of Elena."

Dranko sprung to his feet, "Cooper, don't be ridiculous! *This* changes everything. Hell, yes, we've survived against some teenage hoodlums, some disorganized thugs, and even that squad of National Guarders. We've been far beyond lucky! Tell me you think we can survive the full weight of the U.S. Government, even if they are disorganized and weak right now!"

Cooper stood in turn. His own head was swirling in shock at hearing the President call for his arrest to a national audience, "Damn it, Dranko. Just give me a minute before you start telling me what I *have* to do!"

Dranko knew his friend's lack of outright rejection was his best chance, "I'm sorry, brother, but I have to tell you because you need to think straight right now. You know what I'm talking about! They are figuring out how to land a couple Blackhawk helicopters on your front lawn and send a couple teams of Navy Seals to round your ass up! If the world wasn't a stinking pig pile of shit, it would've *already* happened."

His words deflated Cooper and he sank back into his seat, "Damn you Dranko! How can I leave her?" Cooper's head came to rest in his hands.

Now, Jake jumped up, "We can't leave mama! We can't!" His shrill words, laced with grief as his eyes filled with tears, cut both men to the bone.

Dranko took a step back and his voice calmed, "I know it's hard, for both of you. But, Elena would want you to both live. *She wouldn't want you to sit around waiting to be taken by the government and put into a prison...or worse."* His eyes pleaded back and forth between Cooper and Jake for understanding.

Before either could respond, loud banging on Dranko's front door caused both men to look upward to the basement stairs and reflexively reach for the pistols on their hips.

Cooper welcomed the interruption, "Stay here," he directed Jake. Dranko nodded to Cooper, drawing his .45 caliber pistol to show he understood what he wanted. Dranko barred Cooper with his left arm to prevent him from going first. Cooper drew his own pistol and they began ascending the stairs. Cooper's body tensed, as his mind raced trying to figure out who was at his door. *Could someone already be coming for me after the President's speech? Had some new threat emerged against their neighborhood?*

When they reached the main floor, the pounding had not let up. Dranko moved silently to a side window and looked out. He caught Cooper's gaze and mouthed, "Gus." Cooper breathed a sigh of relief learning that it was Gus Varela, a lawyer who lived in the neighborhood, and not someone more dangerous.

They both put their guns back in their holsters as Dranko opened the door.

Gus' face was red and contorted in rage, "Damn you," he shouted at Cooper as soon as he saw him. Gus tried to bull rush towards Cooper. Dranko quickly overcame his surprise and threw an arm out to bar him.

Cooper welcomed his own anger to push back the confusion Dranko had aroused in him earlier and he moved forward, to put his own face inches from Gus', "What the hell do you mean, Gus?" Cooper deliberately let scorn drip off his name.

Dranko strained under Gus' weight to keep the two men apart. "What the hell do I mean? Why the hell did you put all those lies on the Internet?"

Cooper's rage flushed higher at being called a liar. His arm shot up and caught Gus by the throat, "They *aren't* lies you dumb bastard. It's the truth. Every last word of it!"

Gus choked as he gasped for air. Cooper's firm grasp prevented

15

him from speaking, but he rasped out, "Le...t...me...g...go!"

Cooper waited until Gus' face went from crimson to the first shades of purple and then he abruptly released his grip.

Gus gasped for air and would have collapsed to the ground, but for Dranko's arm catching him, "Breathe in. Take a deep breath, you'll be fine," Dranko said.

Cooper stood in front of him, defiantly, and offered no such words of comfort. A minute later, Gus recovered and stood up straight again. He glared at Cooper, but made no effort to close the scant gap between them. "I don't care if it's true or not. It's either lies or its truth we'd all be better off *not* knowing."

Cooper stared straight back at him, unyielding, "People deserve the truth!"

Gus shook his head, "Not, this. Don't be such a damned naïve Boy Scout! You've caused a lot of damage with what you've done. *More* people are already dying because of what you said!"

Cooper glared at him.

Gus strained once more against Dranko's arm, "Well, we can stop debating this. But, one thing isn't open for debate. You better get the hell out of our neighborhood!"

Cooper exploded, "What the hell are you talking about?"

Gus assumed a self-assured tone, "What I mean is plain. You are now a clear and present danger to our neighborhood. You are going to have to find a new place to inhabit."

"Inhabit?" Cooper said, digesting what Gus had just said.

Then, Cooper lunged at him. Dranko shifted his body to keep the two men separate as Gus backpedaled in surprise, "How dare you! You pompous fat bastard! *I'm* the one who kept you all safe the last few weeks! I ain't going nowhere!"

Gus shook his head and his lips curled up in derision, "We'll see about that!" He retreated down the steps, being careful to keep facing Cooper as he did so. Finally, he turned and walked quickly back towards his own home.

Dranko turned to his friend, "See?"

Cooper just shook his head, "Aw, shut up, will you?" Despite his words, a chill ran down his spine as he realized that anyone might turn on him now. He knew the truth would be hard for the world to hear, but it was dawning on him that even those who knew him well might now become an erstwhile ally...or worse. He turned and made his way back toward the basement where Jake was waiting for him. Dranko paused, shaking his head, and then followed his friend downstairs.

The trio spent the next hour making small talk and listening to Dranko's Ham radio. Dranko pensively wrung his hands. Cooper knew he wanted to talk about the dangers facing him now, but that discussion led to only one conclusion: leaving his home. He reflexively dismissed the idea, so he avoided the topic.

Then, the radio caught his attention.

"...reports, reliable ones, have filtered in about the dangerous rise in gang activity. In Detroit, Cleveland, Los Angeles, New York, Boston, and several other cities, gangs are engaging in outright control of entire sections of the cities in question. With the loss of central authority, organized criminal enterprises are filling the gap..."

"I'm glad we haven't seen that here," Cooper intoned.

The corner of Dranko's mouth curled upward, "Not yet, anyway."

Cooper smiled, "That's right Mr. Sunnyside, not yet indeed!"

"I'm just sayin'...it can still happen here. When you think about it, it has already started."

Cooper's eyebrows drew together, "What?"

"Look at the craziness in Sellwood. Hell, they nearly burned the whole city down! Then there's the Vietnamese Protection Society that we talked to. He's getting organized. And, I worry about that church around the corner."

Cooper nodded, "OK. You have a point with the Sellwood and the Vietnamese group. But, they haven't started taking over and running parts of the..."

"But, they damn well could if they wanted," Dranko interjected. "You've seen their firepower. They're organized when so many are not. What's stopping them?"

"No, you're probably right. What's stopping them is Michael Huynh is more interested in profit than power."

"That's true, too," Dranko returned.

"Now, what do you mean about that church?"

"I just mean that any organized group is going to have power now. Gangs are criminals organized with guns. Churches are people organized and bonded together tightly by faith. They may or may not have guns. Most, from the reports I've heard, are doing good with it. Keeping people fed, helping with security, organizing self-help between people. But, right here, we have that one around the corner is using their access to food to win converts, right?"

"Yeah. Despicable," Cooper spat the word.

"I agree. But, those kinds of things are happening, too. All I'm saying is that, throughout history, some churches have used access to resources, like food, to expand. And, sometimes, conversion has come at the end of the blade of a sword…"

"Or, the barrel of a gun," Cooper finished the thought. "Yeah, I see what you're saying. I agree, we will need to keep close tabs on the other organized groups around. Let's hope that Mr. Huynh stays focused on making money in a semi-legitimate way. And, let's hope our churchgoers next door keep their proselytizing based on the reward system."

Dranko nodded gravely.

"What's that?" Jake asked, cocking his head to the side.

"What's what?" Cooper responded.

"Don't you hear that?"

Dranko moved quickly and turned off the Ham radio. Then, they heard it.

Muffled shouts coming from outside. Seconds lingered as they struggled to make out what they people were shouting. Then, one word hit Cooper as clearly as if it was being shouted out from inside the room.

"Fire!"

Cooper was to the stairs and rocketing up before Dranko had reacted. Then, he and Jake bounded up the stairs in his wake.

****

Dranko's door banged on its hinges as Cooper flung it open and leapt over the front steps. He landed harshly, letting his knees buckle to absorb the shock. He swiveled his head toward where the crowd was shouting from.

His throat tightened when he saw the group gathered around his house. In slow motion, his head kept turning until he saw the black smoke billowing angrily skyward.

"No!" Cooper yelled in fury as he raced towards his burning home.

He quickly rounded the corner. Several neighbors were racing toward his home, buckets and containers of various origins in hand. Mark Moretti, one of his friends, was using his home's garden hose to spray the flames.

18

As he ran headlong toward him, Mark saw the determined look on Cooper's face and handed him the hose as soon as he came up.

"I'll go and get the neighbor's hose going," Mark shouted.

Cooper nodded and concentrated on dousing the flames before him. He breathed a sigh of relief as he realized the fire was, so far, confined to his small detached garage.

Seconds later, Mark brought a second hose to bear and Cooper realized they would get the fire under control before it spread to his house.

Out of the corner of his eye, he spotted Dranko and Jake running across the street to join the makeshift bucket brigade that was coming together.

Within ten minutes, the fire had been put out. As Cooper relaxed, he surveyed the scene. A messy mixture of steam and smoke curled lazily upward from his wrecked garage. The structure was a mishmash of undamaged wood alternating with boards scorched black by the flames. From the heat, most of the paint had blistered or peeled. Then, his gaze fell to the base of the garage. Like a diamond amidst a coal miners' convention, a glistening object jumped out and grabbed his attention.

A mostly melted glass bottle lay broken in half at the foot of the garage.

His heart raced and rage filled his veins as he clenched his fists. "Molotov cocktail," Cooper muttered vehemently to himself before realizing that Dranko and Jake had come to his side.

"What's that?" Jake asked.

"It's a bottle filled with gasoline," Dranko answered.

"You mean someone *wanted* to burn our house down?" Jake asked incredulously.

"Yes, son."

"But, why?"

"Because some men are too weak to handle the truth," Cooper fumed.

He turned to the group of neighbors still clustered about. "First, thanks everyone for helping me get this thing out. This sure looks intentional," he said pointing at the glass bottle. "Did anyone see anything?"

"I saw a white pickup full of teenagers racing down the street just before I saw the flames," Mark offered.

"You've got to be kidding me," Cooper said, remembering the trouble he'd had with Woody and his ragtag band of teenage

19

troublemakers in the first days of the outbreak. After they had broken into his home in the dead of night, two had left humiliated and forced, by Cooper, to carry their dead friend home. Apparently, they had not been chastened enough. *Or, maybe just emboldened with the President calling me out by name.*

At the edge of the crowd, having just walked up, Gus weighed in, "Yeah. Those teenagers coming back is a pretty dangerous thing for our neighborhood. And, it looks like they came for you."

Cooper glared at him, but Mark responded, "Does it matter? We defend each other here. That was our agreement when all this started."

Unrepentant, Gus continued, "It matters if things have changed so much that one man endangers us all."

"What do you mean?" shouted an anonymous voice from the group.

"Didn't you hear the President? Cooper here has told the world a tall tale that the plague was deliberately started by a man hell bent on crashing the world's economy as a way to stop global warming. He's also said the government knew about it and did nothing to stop it. Just an hour ago, the President declared Cooper a liar and asked for the nation's help in bringing him in for questioning."

Gasps and exclamations emanated from half the crowd who had not heard the news yet. Mark was one of them. "Is this true, Cooper?"

Cooper nodded gravely, "It is true, except it isn't a tall tale. Everything I've said is true. You all know me. Tell me you've ever heard me say anything but."

His challenge was greeted with silence.

"Nonetheless, others will be coming for you Cooper. You've put us all in grave danger!" Gus barreled onward in his attack.

Mark turned on him, "Maybe. But Cooper's also the one that's kept us alive so far!"

"Old news," Gus' words dripped with scorn. "This is a new reality now."

"You know, maybe Gus is right." Michelle's voice was soft, but her words sounded to Cooper like they'd been shouted through a bullhorn.

"What?" Dranko's response was flustered.

Michelle spread her feet, standing firmly, "It's not just that Cooper has become a danger to us."

"What do you mean," Mark asked.

"Well, if the government knew Cooper was here in our neighborhood, I bet we'd all get attention and protection from them," Michelle kept her tone flat, but her eyes betrayed a dark and sinister look that shook Cooper to his core.

Mark's reaction shocked him in the other direction. He pulled his pistol and pointed it directly at Michelle, "And, if anyone turns Cooper and Jake in, it will be the last thing they do."

Gus gasped. Michelle took a jagged step backward and fell to her knees.

A dark hand took Mark's into his own and slowly lowered the pistol; the President of the Neighborhood Association and recently elected neighborhood's Captain of Defense, spoke up, "Look. That *is* enough from both of you. I am the chief of security, so let me worry about that. Let us all either help Cooper clean up or go on home. And, *no one*, is turning anyone in. We clear?"

Gus and Michelle slowly nodded.

Cooper gave Calvin a look of appreciation and then turned toward the larger group. When Cooper surveyed the crowd, what he saw disturbed him. Up until that point, the group had looked at him; eyes laden with respect. Now, in at least half of those eyes, he saw fear. Gus and Michelle had poisoned the well and it was spreading outward. *I'm a threat now. Worse, I've become an opportunity.* It was glaring how few people stayed behind to help clean up. Cooper shook his head in disappointment as he went to find a shovel.

****

A few hours later, as they were almost done cleaning up the debris and salvaging what they could from the fire, Dranko put his hand on Cooper's arm and motioned him away from the group. Cooper looked up in surprise, but followed.

"How bad is it?" he asked his friend.

"Well, I'm glad no one was hurt, but I lost most of my tools. Our bicycles and fishing gear, too. Stuff that will be hard to replace now," Cooper responded, as he absentmindedly cleaned his soot-blackened hands with a rag.

Dranko shook his head, "Sorry, brother. This shouldn't have happened."

Cooper chuckled, "I couldn't agree with you more."

"I want to bring up a sore subject," Dranko said, his eyes pleading with Cooper.

21

Cooper stared right back at him, "Yeah, I know. And, the answer is still no."

Dranko's eyes flashed, "Are you kidding me, Cooper? Your name has been on the wire for less than an hour and you've already been attacked! What do you think tomorrow is gonna bring? Or, the next day?"

Cooper spread his feet and straightened up defiantly, "I can handle some teenage punks. I did last time."

Dranko's eyes rolled, "Really? What about when the military finally has enough resources to come and *get* you? Yeah, we got lucky and took out those two HUMVEEs. What about when they send in a Bradley or a *tank* for God's sakes!"

"I'll figure it out," Cooper glared.

"Haven't you noticed that, already, half of the neighbors are now *scared* of you, too?"

Now, it was Cooper's turn to roll his eyes, "Sure. But, the ones that count, their eyes haven't changed."

Dranko paused for a moment, thinking. Then, he grabbed Cooper harshly by both shoulders and only inches separated their faces, "What about him?"

"Who?" Cooper asked him, confused.

"Jake. You know, in your foolish, stubborn, quest to keep him in this house, you are going to get him killed. Just as sure as it rains all year round in Oregon, you're going to get him dead!" Dranko shouted the last words and spittle flew onto Cooper's face.

Cooper pushed Dranko back so hard that he stumbled backward and slammed into the fencepost behind him. "Now, you listen to me! I *can* handle it!" Cooper's voice strained with desperate emotion and Dranko knew he was trying to convince himself as much as Dranko.

He pursed his lips, "You're wrong, Cooper. I know you. You're not thinking straight. You had to *know* the world was gonna come down all around you the moment you hit 'send' on that email! I just assumed you knew that you and Jake would have to go on the run!"

He gave him a blank look.

Dranko pounced, "You've got to be the silliest optimist in the…"

Cooper punched him in the shoulder, "Look, damn it! Yeah, I thought about it. I know it will be rough. But, I think those who can handle…or want…the truth can help me stay safe. Hell, I expect a CNN truck to roll up here any minute. You think the military can just come

22

and get me with that kind of scrutiny?"

Dranko cocked his eyebrows, unimpressed, "Yeah. I do."

"What?"

"Brother, don't you remember Waco, Texas? The feds rolled in on those guys with the whole world watching."

Cooper shrugged his shoulders, "Ah, hell. This is different. I ain't holed up in some compound with a bunch of kids. I told the world about the biggest crime in the history of mankind."

Dranko looked back, unconvinced, "We'll see if your vaunted CNN truck shows up before the next attack does."

"Yeah, we'll see."

"At least stay over at my house tonight. Just to be safe."

Cooper eyed him for a moment, "Sure. That makes sense. Thanks."

"And, one more thing," Dranko said, his eyes twinkling mischievously.

"What now?"

"After it's dark, drive your truck around the block and leave it at the far side, in between here and the barricade. If anyone does come looking for you, maybe they will think you've flown the coop."

Cooper scratched his chin, "Not a bad idea. My car is already on the south barricade, so moving the truck makes sense."

Trying to lighten the tension, Dranko made a display of making a deep bow, "Glad you recognize my genius, kind sir!"

Cooper welcomed the overture and chortled, "Brother, there's a long way from an idea that isn't moronic to genius status. Just be happy that today you're a couple steps above idiot."

Dranko smirked, "See?"

"See what?" Cooper asked, confused.

"Once in my life, I try to be optimistic and see things just a tad better than they are and you just go and shoot those dreams all to hell." As Dranko finished, he mocked a wounded tone.

Cooper didn't miss a beat, "Hey, I'll encourage you to be optimistic every day of the week. But, when it comes to your mental prowess, it's a wide gap between optimism and just plain losing touch with reality!"

Dranko's hands clutched to his chest and his face pantomimed pain, "You wound me!"

"Well, I'll see you tonight if you do not succumb to your grievous wounds!" Cooper turned on his heels and left, chuckling to himself.

"Wake up!" Dranko's breath was hot and urgent as he whispered into his ear.

Cooper, instantly alert, sat up in bed and began reaching for his boots, his eyes pleading for an explanation.

"Your house. It has company. I saw four men, maybe more. In civilian clothes, but they move like they are military."

"Damn!" Cooper cursed.

His boots laced, Cooper rousted Jake who lay sleeping next to him in Dranko's guest room. Jake's eyes fluttered open as Cooper motioned for him to remain quiet. "I need you to get dressed quickly and then wait here for me." Jake nodded and went into motion.

Cooper followed Dranko to his living room where they could get a good view of the front of Cooper's house. He saw multiple figures moving around his home, securing the perimeter. Like Dranko, he counted eight men, likely an equal number deployed around the back, where he could not see. Movement caught his eye from the shadows across the street.

As it registered, his hands balled into fists and a fierce scowl slashed onto his face. Venom dripped, "Gus."

In the shadows, he could see the unmistakable portly figure of Gus Varela standing next to another man, dressed in dark clothing, pointing towards Cooper's home. Moments later, Cooper almost ducked when Gus' finger shifted and pointed towards Dranko's house.

Next to him, Dranko exhaled, "Bastard."

Cooper's vision returned to the activity in front of his house. "They are planning to breach," he whispered to Dranko.

"Yup," his friend agreed.

Cooper wasted no time and returned to where Jake was waiting.

"Son, gather your stuff. From Dranko's back yard, I want you to make your way to the third backyard up the street, away from our house. Then, go over that fence to the backyard behind that one. There are no dogs between here and there, so you shouldn't be noticed. Then, huddle in your sleeping bag and wait for me or Dranko. Got it?"

Jake stared at him with wide eyes and nodded. Only his father noticed they weren't nearly as wide as they were just a few weeks back. *He's getting used to this chaos.* Cooper's insides protested against the necessity of it.

"Don't come out 'til morning if I or Dranko don't come for you. And, you *will* hear gunfire. But, you wait. You hear me?"

Jake nodded, more firmly this time, "Just one thing."

Cooper eyes grew quizzical, "What?"

"Don't die. Please," The innocent sincerity in Jake's eyes stunned Cooper and his knees nearly buckled. He grasped his son's shoulders as Jake's eyes filled with tears.

"I'm not planning on it, son." It was the best he could offer his son in the way of comfort and still tell the truth. "I don't want to, but I gotta go. And, you need to get moving!" Cooper swatted his son to spur him into action. He threw his bulletproof vest on, grabbed his rifle and a bandoleer full of ammunition and ran out. He felt as if he'd left his heart on the floor for abandoning his son.

Angela and Dranko met him at front door, Dranko apparently having awoken her. When they abandoned Cooper's home for the night, Angela had joined them. They were kitted up and ready to follow him into battle.

Cooper saw them and emphatically shook his head, "You wait here."

Both Dranko and Angela shot him furious looks.

"After they find out I'm not home, one of three things happens. They leave. We get into a firefight. Or, they come here looking for me. If it's a fight, join in. If they come here looking for me, you can tell them I hightailed it out of town after the attack today. Got it?"

Angela and Dranko nodded.

"What are you going to do?"

"Watch. But, if it's a fight, there are two people that won't survive it."

"Who?" Angela asked.

"Their commander and that traitor lawyer, Gus Varela." He spat the man's name as his lips curled into a baneful snarl.

****

Cooper closed Dranko's back door quietly just as a furious banging came from his home a few doors down. *They'll make a racket up front, but breech from the back.* He'd learned enough of breeching tactics to guess that.

He circled behind Dranko's house, so that he could exit from the far side and minimize his chances of being seen by the commander or Gus. From the backyard, he saw Jake's backside slipping over the fence into the neighbor's yard and then out of view. When he reached the opposite side of Dranko's house, he heard the battering ram smashing his back door. He imagined the team moving into his deserted home, clearing each room. It would only be a minute before they had swept the house and learned he was not there.

Cooper went prone and crawled forward, until he was at the front of Dranko's porch. He inched his rifle out, sighting in on the commander, still standing out in the open next to Gus. He was relieved to see the man did not appear to have any night vision equipment with him. He silently chambered a round.

Moments later, the commander put a finger to his ear and listened intently. Cooper expected he was getting word that the house was empty and his men were asking for instructions. The commander conferred with Gus, who quickly pointed toward Dranko's house. Although his cover was good, Cooper couldn't help sliding even lower behind the porch and plants.

The commander was mid-sentence when the first shots rang out from behind Cooper's house. The shotgun blast followed by a single rifle shot told him it was the people from their neighborhood patrol who were firing first.

He quickly eased out half a breath and fired at the commander's groin; hoping to avoid his body armor. When he crumpled to the ground, he knew he'd hit him somewhere good.

Cooper shifted his aim and rushed a shot where Gus had been standing. To his surprise, Gus had reacted quickly and disappeared from view. *Moved fast for a big man.*

The cavalcade of gunfire from the rear of Cooper's house told him all he needed to know. He only heard the sharp pops of 5.56mm rounds being fired. The absence of a booming retort of a shotgun or the deep roar of a hunting rifle's round made it likely the pair on patrol lay dead or, at best, wounded. Then, silence, filled the night.

Cooper kept scanning for any sign of movement from the commander or of Gus Varela. To his left, he heard Dranko's back door open and close. Seconds later, he saw Angela and Dranko take positions on opposite sides of the driveway and then crouch down. The seconds drifting past felt like an eternity. Cooper practiced breathing deeply and scanning the street in front of him from left to right. He saw Dranko make some hand motions to Angela and then she moved toward the back of his house once more. *Dranko must be guarding against them coming across the backyards towards us.*

Just then, two figures scurried across the road, running toward the commander. Without thinking, Cooper fired and dropped one of them as his .308 round found purchase. The man was sent sprawling onto the pavement and his rifle clattered across the asphalt. His partner took two more steps and then dove for cover near where the commander lay.

The men covering this pair opened fire in Cooper's direction. Bullets stitched across Dranko's lawn, clods of dirt and grass were flung into the air as angry rounds landed around him. Cooper knew they were laying down suppressing fire because they didn't know exactly where the shot had come from. Thankfully, Dranko was outside their line of fire. On the other side of the street, the man who made it across joined the fray. The front of Dranko's house took his abuse. Wood splinters rocketed out as the man methodically pockmarked the doorway with gunfire.

Just as methodically, Cooper sighted in on him. The man was obviously well trained because he presented very little in the way of a silhouette to target. Cooper took what he could and fired. The man disappeared from view, but Cooper didn't know if he'd hit him or if he'd just scampered back behind the half wall that shielded most of his body from view.

This shot brought a renewed fury of gunfire at him. Now, the men had a better idea of where he was. Bullets impacted very close to him and he heard the whine of several just over his head. Cooper scooted himself behind Dranko's porch to take cover.

He heard Dranko fire a controlled burst, but couldn't tell who he was shooting at. A flurry of gunfire responded and Cooper hoped his friend had found cover. Then, silence descended once more upon the night. He waited a while before pushing himself forward, past Dranko's porch, to survey the scene. He could see Dranko crouching to his left. The street was empty; the man he'd shot previously had either moved off or had been carried away. Likewise, the commander's body was gone. There was no sign of the men.

Dranko motioned for Cooper to come to him. Cooper switched to a crouched position and moved quickly towards him. Angela arrived just as he did.

"What's the situation?" Cooper asked.

"I think they've moved out. After they lit my position up, as I came back up from cover, I saw the tail end of them disappear down the road."

"Makes sense that they would try to be surgical."

"I hope," Angela began but Cooper cut her off with is hand. He

27

cupped his other hand to his ear, to tell the others to listen. From down the block, the deep-throated roar of an engine came to life, revved, and then faded as it moved away from where they were.

"Must have parked outside our barricades and infiltrated through the yards," Angela observed.

"Right," Cooper agreed.

"Good thing you stayed at my place, eh?"

"Sure thing. But our excitement isn't over yet."

"What?" Dranko asked.

"I need to pay a visit to Mr. Varela."

Dranko nodded but looked chagrined, "You won't find him home, I bet. No one is that stupid."

"I know he ain't stupid, but I'm hoping fear will overwhelm him and have him panicked. He did just see someone shot right next to him. That can take the stuffing out of a lot of people. Scared people make dumb decisions all the time."

"I won't argue that," Dranko intoned. "Let's go, then."

The trio moved out. They searched his house from top to bottom, but found it empty. Coming back outside, there was no sign of him, either. The oddest thing that struck Cooper was that no neighbors had come outside of their homes after the gunfire had ended. *Did they know? Or, did they see that it was focused on me so they don't care?*

Cooper retrieved Jake, who he found curled up shivering in his sleeping bag in the neighbor's backyard. His eyes were wet, but they alighted with relief when he saw his father's face.

Taking precaution, the group joined the northern barricade until dawn.

They called out to the guards as they approached the barricade while giving the coded sign that the neighborhood used and that changed every few days. Mark and Freddie were there and they answered their rapid questions about what had happened.

"We wanted to go see what the hell was going down, but we know our job is to stay on the barricade, no matter what," Freddie said excitedly. Cooper could tell Freddie was stressed because typically, the young man in his twenties could barely breathe without telling a joke or performing some antic to make others laugh.

"Your discipline was spot on," Cooper said, still thinking about the many that had *not* come out to help, but weren't constrained by duty like Mark and Freddie had been. Cooper stroked his chin and his stomach felt empty realizing that the world was shifting under his feet yet again.

****

When the sun rose and fought in vain to pierce the gray clouds that were so common in Portland, Cooper and his group gathered away from the barricade.

"Let's survey the damage at my house and then we need to pay Gus another visit," Cooper commanded more than said.

They moved down the street, weapons at the ready. As they neared his home, he saw spent shell casings scattered about. He picked up several and noted they were all the same caliber, the size used by the military.

The front door had been battered off its hinges and the frame splintered. His house struck him as a man missing his two front teeth. Jake let out a gasp when he saw it. Cooper clenched his jaw.

He steeled his voice, "Let's clear the house to make sure it's empty." He chambered a round and Angela and Dranko did the same. He motioned for Angela to stay with Jake on the front lawn as he and Dranko entered the home.

They stepped over the front door that was lying on the ground and noted muddy footprints scuffed across the floor. They moved from room to room, being careful around corners. Dranko had once explained to him how to 'pie' the corners to minimize your exposure while you searched a building. He let Dranko take the lead in doing so. The two quickly fell into rhythm moving through the house. They moved through the front living room, then the dining room, before coming to the kitchen. The back door, which led into the kitchen, was also knocked off its hinges and lay sprawled on the floor. A burn mark in the middle of the room was evidence that a flash-bang grenade had been thrown inside. Fury surged within him, seeing his home violated like this. He grunted and tried to push it aside. Within minutes, the rest of the house was cleared and they moved back to the front lawn.

"Worse than being burglarized," Cooper said, as they gathered once again with Jake and Angela.

"A burglar just comes to steal something. These guys game to steal you," Angela said. Cooper just stared at her, nodding slowly.

"We were lucky they tried the stealth mode first. That gave us the fighting chance. Next they will come in with a tank or an armored vehicle of some kind. Or, maybe a damned Blackhawk!," Dranko added.

Jake's face flashed in alarm and Cooper gave Dranko a stern

look. "But, your dad is too smart and too good for these bums," Dranko offered quickly.

"And, we were lucky they sent in some second-rate crew. These guys didn't have night vision, for example," Cooper added.

Dranko nodded slowly, "That might also explain why they *didn't* roll in with tanks. Not sure they have them on hand. I think they are stretched beyond belief with what Brushfire's wrought."

"I'll make some breakfast while you guys clean up. Jake, do you want to help me?" Jake nodded to Angela in response.

A half hour later, Cooper and Dranko had managed to reattach the front door and enable the door to close, albeit awkwardly. Angela and Jake offered up an equally awkward breakfast of beans, canned fruit cocktail, and crackers. A pot of weak coffee completed the repast. They had barely begun eating when Gus' voice assaulted them.

"Coo-oo-per! Come out!"

Angela fumbled her coffee cup, spilling some of it. Cooper's fork crashed against his plate as he threw it down in rage and disgust, "That bastard!" He leapt to his feet, grabbing his rifle and made a beeline to the door. Dranko and Angela were quickly on his heels.

Cooper nearly tore the hastily rebuilt door from its hinges as he flung his door open, weapon at the ready. What he saw shocked him.

In front of him, stood Gus. A smug look lashed to his face. Behind him stood about twenty of his neighbors, armed, with hostile eyes glaring at Cooper. The shock at seeing such a crowd arrayed gave him a momentary pause. The contrast with the prior times he'd stood on his stoop and addressed his neighbors, guiding them through their fear or instilling hope, struck him to the core. He stopped in his tracks.

Gus saw the muzzle of Cooper's rifle pointed at his stomach and he waved his hands, "Calm down, Cooper, we just came to talk!" Cooper heard the fear in voice in marked contrast to his earlier shouted orders.

Cooper grimaced and barreled into Gus, pushing him backward and off his front steps. Gus backpedaled and barely kept his balance.

"What's this about," Cooper called to the crowd, ignoring Gus.

No one spoke, but instead, heads turned to Gus.

He recovered more than his footing, "Don't play dumb, Cooper. You know what this is about. After last night, you are a clear and present danger to this neighborhood. So..." Cooper's glare made Gus choke in fear.

"So...what," Cooper dared.

Gus coughed once, "So, you need to leave."

Cooper's wry grin unnerved Gus, "Oh, yeah?" His grip tightened on his rifle as a fulsome rage burned inside. "And, what are you gonna do when I say no?"

Gus steadied his feet, "Well, the good people gathered here are hoping you will be reasonable."

Cooper laughed aloud, "Reasonable? Do you mean reasonable like when I've risked my life over and over again to save this neighborhood?" Cooper noticed how half the group looked ashamedly at their feet while the other half tightened their hold on their weapons.

Gus was unfazed now, "Cooper, I know I speak for everyone when I say how much we appreciate what you've done for all of us. But, even you must admit that what has bound us together in this time of crisis has been our mutual desire for safety. It's not any of the prudent people here's fault that you are *now* a danger to that very security." Many in the crowd nodded enthusiastically at that.

Cooper shook his head, "Damn, you're good, Gus. I'll give you that. You know how to tell the people just what they want to hear." He directed his attention back to the group, "So, these cheap words from a lawyer are going to absolve your consciences of putting me and my boy out of our home? Is that all it takes?" Not a single pair of eyes would meet his gaze as he scanned the crowd while talking. "Well, guess what? I have a better way of keeping your consciences clear. I ain't leaving."

"Damn you, Cooper! This isn't our fault. You brought this on yourself! We have to protect our children—those that are still alive!" The voice from the back of the crowd belonged to Michelle Jamison, a homemaker who had lost one of her three children in the plague. Her voice cracked as she finished and tears ran down her face.

"So, you want to throw me out because I told the truth to the world? Told the truth to *you*?"

"Whether your words were truth or not, only time will tell. But, what is clear right now is that you've brought untold danger to us all," Gus fired back. A brief silence hung in the air.

Then, Cooper heard it. A sharp metallic click, followed by another, as someone chambered a round on a bolt-action rifle. Instantly, his rifle was to his shoulder and flashed across the group. Behind him, he heard Angela and Dranko doing the same. In front of him, half the group fumbled with their weapons because of fear while the other half shouldered theirs without hesitation.

Gus moved frantically to the side, to get out of the line of fire.

He flashed his palms up, open, "Calm down, calm down, everyone."

Cooper shouted, "Lower your weapons, now!" Very few in the crowd complied. Seeing their neighbors still keeping their weapons trained on Cooper, they quickly raised them once more.

"Cooper, please. Be reasonable," Gus pleaded.

He pointed his rifle directly at Gus, "You say that word 'reasonable' one more time, Gus, and I will blow you to hell, so help me God!"

From the corner of his eye, he spotted Calvin Little rushing down the street. The President of the Neighborhood Association was unarmed, save the pistol he wore on his hip.

"What is this? What is going on here," he shouted as he came up.

"Gus here and this…ah…lynch mob are telling me I need to move out of my home," Cooper answered first.

"What?" Calvin asked, in surprise.

Gus turned to face him, "We're doing this for everyone's safety, Calvin. Surely you understand that, as the neighborhood's Defense Captain?"

Calvin continued to move through the crowd until he stood in front of Cooper, "Yes, Gus, you are correct. I take security seriously. But, if anyone wants to drive Cooper from his home at gunpoint, they will have to shoot me first. This is not how we do things in *our* neighborhood."

Cooper tried to conceal his shock at Calvin putting himself in harm's way to protect him. Calvin's words had many in the group looking at one another in confusion. The seconds ticked by.

"Goddammit! Lower your fucking weapons!" Calvin exploded. It was less the vehemence of his words, but more the shock of the normally well-spoken man using profanity that commanded compliance. *I'm not sure I've ever heard him swear, Cooper marveled to himself.* He lowered his weapon first, and slowly, everyone else did, too.

"Good, that is more like it," he said and turned to Gus. "Look, you want to discuss Cooper's residence here, we will do it properly. Let us have a meeting here at five o'clock today. *That is* how we make decisions here. Not like *this*," his infused the last word with scorn.

Cooper took a long look at his neighbors, including a few who he would have called friends. At best, he saw fear in their eyes directed towards him. Among the worst, he saw fear and hatred. He took a deep breath and shook his head in disgust, "I'll save you the damned

trouble. Jake and I will be leaving. And you, Gus, can go rot in hell."
Gus reacted to Cooper's pointed finger as if he'd been shot.

Cooper turned sharply on his heels and brushed past Angela and Dranko. Dranko's mouth was agape in shock.

Made in the USA
Lexington, KY
01 November 2015